FROM THE ERA OF MAN
TO THE AGE OF ROBOTS . . .

"The Warm Space" by David Brin—The robots had staked their claim to the stars, but wasn't there any place for those organic units called humans in the greater universe?

"How-2" by Clifford D. Simak—All he'd wanted to build was a pet robot rover, but what he got was a being that was never meant to leave the factory, a metal creature that might be the mother of all robot kind!

"Sally" by Isaac Asimov—They were the automatobiles, cars which understood humans' every request and had obeyed their masters faithfully. But now they'd been retired from service and no one was going to get them on the road again!

These are but a few glimpses of our possible futures, those distant—or not so distant—times, when not only men but machines will have minds of their own.

ROBOTS
ISAAC ASIMOV'S WONDERFUL
WORLDS OF SCIENCE FICTION #9

ROBOTS

Isaac Asimov's Wonderful Worlds of Science Fiction #9

Edited by
Isaac Asimov, Martin H. Greenberg, and Charles G. Waugh

A SIGNET BOOK

NEW AMERICAN LIBRARY

A DIVISION OF PENGUIN BOOKS USA INC., NEW YORK

PUBLISHED IN CANADA BY
PENGUIN BOOKS CANADA LIMITED, MARKHAM, ONTARIO

Acknowledgments

"The Tunnel Under the World" by Frederik Pohl. Copyright © 1955 by Galaxy Publishing Corporation; renewed © 1983 Frederik Pohl. Reprinted by permission of the author.

"Brother Robot" by Henry Slesar. Copyright © 1958 by Ziff-Davis Publishing Corporation. Reprinted by permission of the author.

"The Lifeboat Mutiny" by Robert Sheckley. Copyright © 1955 by Galaxy Publishing Corporation; renewed © 1983 by Robert Sheckley. Reprinted by permission of Kirby McCauley, Ltd.

"The Warm Space" by David Brin. Copyright © 1985 by David Brin. Reprinted by permission of the author.

"How-2" by Clifford D. Simak. Copyright © 1954 by Galaxy Publishing Corporation; renewed © 1982 by Clifford D. Simak. Reprinted by permission of Kirby McCauley, Ltd.

"Too Robot to Marry" by George H. Smith. Copyright © 1959 by Columbia Publications, Inc. Reprinted by permission of the author.

"The Education of Tigress McCardle" by C. M. Kornbluth. Copyright © 1957 by Mercury Press, Inc. Reprinted by permission of Richard Curtis Associates, Inc.

"Sally" by Isaac Asimov. Copyright © 1953 by Ziff-Davis Publishing Company; renewed © 1981 by Isaac Asimov. Reprinted by permission of the author.

"Breakfast of Champions" by Thomas Easton. Copyright © 1980 *Cavalier* magazine. Reprinted by permission of the author.

"Sun Up" by A. A. Jackson & Howard Waldrop. Copyright © 1976 by Howard Waldrop and A. A. Jackson IV. From *Faster Than Light*, edited by Jack Dann and George Zebrowski, Harper & Row, 1976. Reprinted by permission of the authors.

"Second Variety" by Philip K. Dick. Copyright © 1953; renewed © 1981 by Philip K. Dick. Reprinted by permission of the agents for the author's estate, the Scott Meredith Literary Agency, Inc, 845 Third Avenue, New York, NY 10022.

(The following page constitutes an extension of the copyright page.)

SIGNET TRADEMARK REG. U.S. PAT. OFF. AND FOREIGN COUNTRIES
REGISTERED TRADEMARK—MARCA REGISTRADA
HECHO EN DRESDEN, TN.

SIGNET, SIGNET CLASSIC, MENTOR, ONYX, PLUME, MERIDIAN and NAL BOOKS are published by NAL PENGUIN INC., 1633 Broadway, New York, New York 10019

First Printing, April, 1989

1 2 3 4 5 6 7 8 9

PRINTED IN THE UNITED STATES OF AMERICA

CONTENTS

INTRODUCTION: ROBOTS

Robots are not a modern concept. They are as old as pottery at the very least.

Once human beings learned to fashion objects out of clay and bake them hard—especially objects that looked like human beings—it was an easy conceptual leap to suppose that human beings themselves had been fashioned out of clay. Whereas ordinary lifeless statues and figurines needed nothing more than a human potter, the more miraculous human body, living and thinking, required a divine potter.

Thus, in the Bible, God is described as forming the first man, potter-wise, out of clay. "And the Lord God formed man of the dust of the ground, and breathed into his nostrils the breath of life; and man became a living soul." (*Genesis* 2:7)

In the Greek myths, it was Prometheus who fashioned the first human beings out of clay and water and Athena breathed life into them. No doubt one could go through the myths of many nations and find gods busily making little statues that became human beings.

What's more, the gods continued making living things or quasi-living things later on. With time, of course, human beings learned that clay was not the only building material, but that metals were superior, so that the divinely created beings came to be thought of as metallic in nature, and no longer as pottery.

In the eighteenth book of the *Iliad*, for instance, Hephaistos, the divine smith, is forging new armor for Achilles, and he is described as having "a couple of maids to support him. These are made of gold exactly like living girls; they have sense in their heads, they can speak and use their muscles,

9

they can spin and weave and do their work." Hephaistos
was also described as having formed a bronze giant, Talos,
that served to guard the shores of Crete by walking around
the island three times a day and repelling anyone trying to
land.

Folk tales and legends of all nations tell of objects, usually considered inanimate, that through magic of one kind
or another, achieve human or even superhuman intelligence.
These can vary from the "golem," a giant made of clay,
supposedly given magical life by a rabbi in sixteenth-century
Bohemia, down to the magic mirror in "Snow White" who
could tell "who is the fairest of them all." Various medieval
scholars, such as Albertus Magnus, Roger Bacon, and Pope
Sylvester II were supposed to have fashioned talking heads
that gave them needed information.

Human beings, of course, tried to devise "automata"
(singular "automaton"—from Greek words meaning "self-
moving") that would work through springs, levers, and compressed air rather than through magic, and give the illusion
of possessing purpose and intelligence. Even among the
ancients were those who possessed sufficient ingenuity who
could make use of the primitive technologies of those days
to construct such devices.

The breakthrough came, however, with the development
of mechanical clocks in the thirteenth century. Clever tech-
nologists learned how to use "clockwork"—gears, wheels,
springs, and so on—to produce not merely the regular motion of clock hands, but more complex motions that gave
the illusion of life.

The golden age of automata came in the eighteenth century, when automata in the shape of soldiers, or tigers, or
small figures on a stage could mimic various life-related
behavior. Thus, Jacques de Vaucanson built a mechanical duck
in 1738. It quacked, bathed, drank water, ate grain, seemed
to digest it, and then eliminated it. It was all perfectly
automatic, of course, and without volition or consciousness,
but it amazed spectators. In 1774 Pierre Jacquet-Droz devised an automatic scribe, a mechanical boy whose clockwork mechanism caused it to dip a pen in ink and write a
letter (always the same letter, to be sure.)

These were only toys, of course, but important ones. The
principles of automata were applied to automatic machinery
intended for useful purposes, which led to the invention of

punched cards in 1801, which in turn set the feet of humanity on the path toward computers.

The Industrial Revolution, which had its beginnings as the golden age of automata came to an end, was therefore a continuation of the notion of the mechanical production of apparently purposive behavior. As machines grew more and more elaborate, the notion that human beings could eventually construct devices that had some modicum of human intelligence grew stronger.

In 1818 a book by Mary Shelley was published that was entitled *Frankenstein* and that dealt with the construction of a human body that was given life by its inventor. It was subtitled "The New Prometheus" and has been popular ever since its appearance. In the book, the created life-form (called "the Monster") took vengeance on being neglected by killing Frankenstein and his family.

That is considered by some to have initiated modern "science fiction," in which the possibility of manufacturing "mechanical men" remained a frequently recurring subject.

In 1920 Karel Capek, a Czeck playwright, wrote *R.U.R.*, a play in which automata were mass-produced by an Englishman named Rossum. The automata were meant to do the world's work and to make a better life for human beings. In the end, though, the automata rebelled, wiped out humanity, and started a new race of intelligent beings themselves. It was Frankenstein again on a much more grandiose scale.

R.U.R. stood for Rossum's Universal Robots. Rossum seems to be from a Czech word meaning "reason," while "robot" is from a Czech word meaning "slave." The popularity of the play threw the old term, "automaton," out of use. The expression "robot" replaced it in every language, so that now a robot is any artificial device (often metallic and often pictured in vaguely human form, though neither is absolutely necessary) that will perform functions ordinarily thought to be appropriate only for human beings.

In 1939 Isaac Asimov (that's me), who was only nineteen at the time, grew tired of science-fictional robots that were either unrealistically wicked or unrealistically noble, and began to write science-fiction tales in which robots were viewed merely as machines, built, as all machines are, with an attempt at adequate safeguards. In 1942 he formulated these safeguards into the "Three Laws of Robotics." Other

writers adopted the laws, which introduced a useful rational-
ization into the concept of robots. They did not, however,
unduly hamper those writers.

In this collection of modern stories about robots, you will
find robots of all shapes and purposes, some of them, despite the Three Laws, being dedicated to war and destruction. Even a robot story of mine that is included involves
robots built in the shape of automobiles, rather than men,
and allows them to act with (deservedly) hostile intent.

In any case, enjoy.

—Isaac Asimov

THE TUNNEL UNDER THE WORLD

BY FREDERIK POHL

On the morning of June 15th, Guy Burckhardt woke up screaming out of a dream.

It was more real than any dream he had ever had in his life. He could still hear and feel the sharp, ripping-metal explosion, the violent heave that had tossed him furiously out of bed, the searing wave of heat.

He sat up convulsively and stared, not believing what he saw, at the quiet room and the bright sunlight coming in the window.

He croaked, "Mary?"

His wife was not in the bed next to him. The covers were tumbled and awry, as though she had just left it, and the memory of the dream was so strong that instinctively he found himself searching the floor to see if the dream explosion had thrown her down.

But she wasn't there. Of course she wasn't, he told himself, looking at the familiar vanity and slipper chair, the uncracked window, the unbuckled wall. It had only been a dream.

"Guy?" His wife was calling him querulously from the foot of the stairs. "Guy, dear, are you all right?"

He called weakly, "Sure."

There was a pause. Then Mary said doubtfully, "Breakfast is ready. Are you sure you're all right? I thought I heard you yelling."

Burckhardt said more confidently, "I had a bad dream, honey. Be right down."

In the shower, punching the lukewarm-and-cologne he favored, he told himself that it had been a beaut of a dream.

13

Still bad dreams weren't unusual, especially bad dreams about explosions. In the past thirty years of H-bomb jitters, who had not dreamed of explosions?

Even Mary had dreamed of them, it turned out, for he started to tell her about the dream, but she cut him off. "You *did*?" Her voice was astonished. "Why, dear, I dreamed the same thing! Well, almost the same thing. I didn't actually *hear* anything. I dreamed that something woke me up, and then there was a sort of quick bang, and then something hit me on the head. And that was all. Was yours like that?"

Burckhardt coughed. "Well, no," he said. Mary was not one of the strong-as-a-man, brave-as-a-tiger women. It was not necessary, he thought, to tell her all the little details of the dream that made it seem so real. No need to mention the splintered ribs, and the salt bubble in his throat, and the agonized knowledge that this was death. He said, "Maybe there really was some kind of explosion downtown. Maybe we heard it and it started us dreaming."

Mary reached over and patted his hand absently. "Maybe," she agreed. "It's almost half-past eight, dear. Shouldn't you hurry? You don't want to be late to the office."

He gulped his food, kissed her and rushed out—not so much to be on time as to see if his guess had been right.

But downtown Tylerton looked as it always had. Coming in on the bus, Burckhardt watched critically out the window, seeking evidence of an explosion. There wasn't any. If anything, Tylerton looked better than it ever had before. It was a beautiful crisp day, the sky was cloudless, the buildings were clean and inviting. They had, he observed, steam-blasted the Power & Light Building, the town's only skyscraper—that was the penalty of having Contro Chemicals' main plant on the outskirts of town; the fumes from the cascade stills left their mark on stone buildings.

None of the usual crowd were on the bus, so there wasn't anyone Burckhardt could ask about the explosion. And by the time he got out at the corner of Fifth and Lehigh and the bus rolled away with a muted diesel moan, he had pretty well convinced himself that it was all imagination.

He stopped at the cigar stand in the lobby of his office building, but Ralph wasn't behind the counter. The man who sold him his pack of cigarettes was a stranger.

"Where's Mr. Stebbins?" Burckhardt asked.

The man said politely, "Sick, sir. He'll be in tomorrow. A pack of Marlins today?"

"Chesterfields," Burckhardt corrected.

"Certainly, sir," the man said. But what he took from the rack and slid across the counter was an unfamiliar green-and-yellow pack.

"Do try these, sir," he suggested. "They contain an anti-cough factor. Ever notice how ordinary cigarettes make you choke every once in a while?"

Burckhardt said suspiciously, "I never heard of this brand."

"Of course not. They're something new." Burckhardt hesitated, and the man said persuasively, "Look, try them out at my risk. If you don't like them, bring back the empty pack and I'll refund your money. Fair enough?"

Burckhardt shrugged. "How can I lose? But give me a pack of Chesterfields, too, will you?"

He opened the pack and lit one while he waited for the elevator. They weren't bad, he decided, though he was suspicious of cigarettes that had the tobacco chemically treated in any way. But he didn't think much of Ralph's stand-in; it would raise hell with the trade at the cigar stand if the man tried to give every customer the same high-pressure sales talk.

The elevator door opened with a low-pitched sound of music. Burckhardt and two or three others got in and he nodded to them as the door closed. The thread of music switched off and the speaker in the ceiling of the cab began its usual commercials.

No, not the *usual* commercials, Burckhardt realized. He had been exposed to the captive-audience commericals so long that they hardly registered on the outer ear any more, but what was coming from the recorded program in the basement of the building caught his attention. It wasn't merely that the brands were mostly unfamiliar; it was a difference in pattern.

There were jingles with an insistent, bouncy rhythm, about soft drinks he had never tasted. There was a rapid patter dialogue between what sounded like two ten-year-old boys about a candy bar, followed by an authoritative bass rumble: "Go right out and get a DELICIOUS Choco-Bite and eat your TANGY Choco-Bite *all up*. That's *Choco-Bite*!" There was a sobbing female whine: "I *wish* I had a Feckle Freezer! I'd do *anything* for a Feckle Freezer!" Burckhardt reached his floor and left the elevator in the middle of the last one. It left him a little uneasy. The commercials were not for familiar brands; there was no feeling of use and custom to them.

But the office was happily normal—except that Mr. Barth wasn't in. Miss Mitkin, yawning at the reception desk, didn't know exactly why. "His home phoned, that's all. He'll be in tomorrow."

"Maybe he went to the plant. It's right near his house."

She looked indifferent. "Yeah."

A thought struck Burkhardt. "But today is June 15th! It's quarterly tax return day—he has to sign the return!"

Miss Mitkin shrugged to indicate that that was Burckhardt's problem, not hers. She returned to her nails.

Thoroughly exasperated, Burckhardt went to his desk. It wasn't that he couldn't sign the tax returns as well as Barth, he thought resentfully. It simply wasn't his job, that was all; it was a responsibility that Barth, as office manager for Contro Chemicals' downtown office, should have taken.

He thought briefly of calling Barth at his home or trying to reach him at the factory, but he gave up the idea quickly enough. He didn't really care much for the people at the factory and the less contact he had with them, the better. He had been to the factory once, with Barth; it had been a confusing and, in a way, a frightening experience. Barring a handful of executives and engineers, there wasn't a soul in the factory—that is, Burckhardt corrected himself, remembering what Barth had told him, not a *living* soul—just the machines.

According to Barth, each machine was controlled by a sort of computer which reproduced, in its electronic snarl, the actual memory and mind of a human being. It was an unpleasant thought. Barth, laughing, had assured him that there was no Frankenstein business of robbing graveyards and implanting brains in machines. It was only a matter, he said, of transferring a man's habit patterns from brain cells to vacuum-tube cells. It didn't hurt the man and it didn't make the machine into a monster.

But they made Burckhardt uncomfortable all the same.

He put Barth and the factory and all his other irritations out of his mind and tackled the tax returns. It took him until noon to verify the figures—which Barth could have done out of his memory and his private ledger in ten minutes, Burckhardt resentfully reminded himself.

He sealed them in an envelope and walked out to Miss Mitkin. "Since Mr. Barth isn't here, we'd better go to lunch in shifts," he said. "You can go first."

"Thanks." Miss Mitkin languidly took her bag out of the desk drawer and began to apply makeup.

Burckhardt offered her the envelope. "Drop this in the mail for me, will you? Uh—wait a minute. I wonder if I ought to phone Mr. Barth to make sure. Did his wife say whether he was able to take phone calls?"

"Didn't say," Miss Mitkin blotted her lips carefully with a Kleenex. "Wasn't his wife, anyway. It was his daughter who called and left the message."

"The kid?" Burckhardt frowned. "I thought she was away at school."

"She called, that's all I know."

Burckhardt went back to his own office and stared distastefully at the unopened mail on his desk. He didn't like nightmares; they spoiled his whole day. He should have stayed in bed, like Barth.

A funny thing happened on his way home. There was a disturbance at the corner where he usually caught his bus— someone was screaming something about a new kind of deep-freeze—so he walked an extra block. He saw the bus coming and started to trot. But behind him, someone was calling his name. He looked over his shoulder; a small harried-looking man was hurrying toward him.

Burckhardt hesitated, and then recognized him. It was a casual acquaintance named Swanson. Burckhardt sourly observed that he had already missed the bus.

He said, "Hello."

Swanson's face was desperately eager. "Burckhardt?" he asked inquiringly, with an odd intensity. And then he just stood there silently, watching Burckhardt's face, with a burning eagerness that dwindled to a faint hope and died to a regret. He was searching for something, waiting for something, Burckhardt thought. But whatever it was he wanted, Burckhardt didn't know how to supply it.

Burckhardt coughed and said again, "Hello, Swanson."

Swanson didn't even acknowledge the greeting. He merely sighed a very deep sigh.

"Nothing doing," he mumbled, apparently to himself. He nodded abstractedly to Burckhardt and turned away.

Burckhardt watched the slumped shoulders disappear in the crowd. It was an *odd* sort of day, he thought, and one he didn't much like. Things weren't going right.

Riding home on the next bus, he brooded about it. It wasn't anything terrible or disastrous; it was something out of his experience entirely. You live your life, like any man, and you form a network of impressions and reactions. You *expect* things. When you open your medicine chest, your razor is expected to be on the second shelf; when you lock your front door, you expect to have to give it a slight extra tug to make it latch.

It isn't the things that are right and perfect in your life that make it familiar. It is the things that are just a little bit wrong—the sticking latch, the light switch at the head of the stairs that needs an extra push because the spring is old and weak, the rug that unfailingly skids underfoot.

It wasn't just that things were wrong with the pattern of Burckhardt's life; it was that the *wrong* things were wrong. For instance, Barth hadn't come into the office, yet Barth *always* came in.

Burckhardt brooded about it through dinner. He brooded about it, despite his wife's attempt to interest him in a game of bridge with the neighbors, all through the evening. The neighbors were people he liked—Anne and Farley Dennerman. He had known them all their lives. But they were odd and brooding, too, this night and he barely listened to Dennerman's complaints about not being able to get good phone service or his wife's comments on the disgusting variety of television commercials they had these days.

Burckhardt was well on the way to setting an all-time record for continuous abstraction when, around midnight, with a suddenness that surprised him—he was strangely *aware* of it happening—he turned over in his bed and, quickly and completely, fell asleep.

On the morning of June 15th, Burckhardt woke up screaming.

It was more real than any dream he had ever had in his life. He could still hear the explosion, feel the blast that crushed him against a wall. It did not seem right that he should be sitting bolt upright in bed in an undisturbed room.

His wife came pattering up the stairs. "Darling!" she cried. "What's the matter?"

He mumbled. "Nothing. Bad dream."

She relaxed, hand on heart. In an angry tone, she started to say: "You gave me such a shock——"

But a noise from outside interrupted her. There was a wail of sirens and a clang of bells; it was loud and shocking.

The Burckhardts stared at each other for a heartbeat, then hurried fearfully to the window.

There were no rumbling fire engines in the street, only a small panel truck, cruising slowly along. Flaring loud-speaker horns crowned its top. From them issued the screaming sound of sirens, growing in intensity, mixed with the rumble of heavy-duty engines and the sound of bells. It was a perfect record of fire engines arriving at a four-alarm blaze.

Burckhardt said in amazement, "Mary, that's against the law! Do you know what they're doing? They're playing records of a fire. What are they up to?"

"Maybe it's a practical joke," his wife offered.

"Joke! Waking up the whole neighborhood at six o'clock in the morning?" He shook his head. "The police will be here in ten minutes," he predicted. "Wait and see."

But the police weren't—not in ten minutes, or at all. Whoever the pranksters in the car were, they apparently had a police permit for their games.

The car took a position in the middle of the block and stood silent for a few minutes Then there was a crackle from the speaker, and a giant voice chanted:

Feckle Freezers!
Feckle Freezers!
Gotta have a
Feckle Freezer!
Feckle, Feckle, Feckle,
Feckle, Feckle, Feckle—

It went on and on. Every house on the block had faces staring out of windows by then. The voice was not merely loud; it was nearly deafening.

Burckhardt shouted to his wife, over the uproar, "What the hell is a Feckle Freezer?"

"Some kind of a freezer, I guess, dear," she shrieked back unhelpfully.

Abruptly the noise stopped and the truck stood silent. It was still misty morning; the sun's rays came horizontally across the rooftops. It was impossible to believe that, a moment ago, the silent block had been bellowing the name of a freezer.

"A crazy advertising trick," Burckhardt said bitterly. He yawned and turned away from the window. "Might as well get dressed. I guess that's the end of——"

The bellow caught him from behind; it was almost like a hard slap on the ears. A harsh, sneering voice, louder than the archangel's trumpet, howled:

"Have you got a freezer? *It stinks!* If it isn't a Feckle Freezer, *it stinks!* If it's a last year's Feckle Freezer, *it stinks!* Only this year's Feckle Freezer is any good at all! You know who owns an Ajax Freezer? Fairies own Ajax Freezers! You know who owns a Triplecold Freezer? Commies own Triplecold Freezers! Every freezer but a brand-new Feckle Freezer *stinks!*"

The voice screamed inarticulately with rage. "I'm warning you! Get out and buy a Feckle Freezer right away! Hurry up! Hurry for Feckle! Hurry for Feckle! Hurry, hurry, hurry, Feckle, Feckle, Feckle, Feckle, Feckle, Feckle . . ."

It stopped eventually. Burckhardt licked his lips. He started to say to his wife, "Maybe we ought to call the police about——" when the speakers erupted again. It caught him off guard; it was intended to catch him off guard. It screamed:

"Feckle, Feckle, Feckle, Feckle, Feckle, Feckle, Feckle, Feckle. Cheap freezers ruin your food. You'll get sick and throw up. You'll get sick and die. Buy a Feckle, Feckle, Feckle, Feckle! Ever take a piece of meat out of the freezer you've got and see how rotten and moldy it is? Buy a Feckle, Feckle, Feckle, Feckle, Feckle. Do you want to eat rotten, stinking food? Or do you want to wise up and buy a Feckle, Feckle, Feckle——"

That did it. With fingers that kept stabbing the wrong holes, Burckhardt finally managed to dial the local police station. He got a busy signal—it was apparent that he was not the only one with the same idea—and while he was shakily dialing again, the noise outside stopped.

He looked out the window. The truck was gone.

*   *   *

Burckhardt loosened his tie and ordered another Frosty-Flip from the waiter. If only they wouldn't keep the Crystal Cafe so *hot*! The new paint job—searing reds and blinding yellows—was bad enough, but someone seemed to have the delusion that this was January instead of June; the place was a good ten degrees warmer than outside.

He swallowed the Frosty-Flip in two gulps. It had a kind of peculiar flavor, he thought, but not bad. It certainly cooled you off, just as the waiter had promised. He reminded himself to pick up a carton of them on the way home; Mary might like them. She was always interested in something new.

He stood up awkwardly as the girl came across the restaurant toward him. She was the most beautiful thing he had ever seen in Tylerton. Chin-height, honey-blond hair and a figure that—well, it was all hers. There was no doubt in the world that the dress that clung to her was the only thing she wore. He felt as if he were blushing as she greeted him.

"Mr. Burckhardt." The voice was like distant tomtoms. "It's wonderful of you to let me see you, after this morning."

He cleared his throat. "Not at all. Won't you sit down, Miss——"

"April Horn," she murmured, sitting down—beside him, not where he had pointed on the other side of the table. "Call me April, won't you?"

She was wearing some kind of perfume, Burckhardt noted with what little of his mind was functioning at all. It didn't seem fair that she should be using perfume as well as everything else. He came to with a start and realized that the waiter was leaving with an order for *filets mignon* for two.

"Hey!" he objected.

"Please, Mr. Burckhardt." Her shoulder was against his, her face was turned to him, her breath was warm, her expression was tender and solicitous. "This is all on the Feckle Corporation. Please let them—it's the *least* they can do."

He felt her hand burrowing into his pocket.

"I put the price of the meal into your pocket," she whispered conspiratorially. "Please do that for me, won't you? I mean I'd appreciate it if you'd pay the waiter—I'm old-fashioned about things like that."

She smiled meltingly, then became mock-businesslike. "But you must take the money," she insisted. "Why, you're let-

ting Feckle off lightly if you do! You could sue them for
every nickel they've got, disturbing your sleep like that."

With a dizzy feeling, as though he had just seen someone
make a rabbit disappear into a top hat, he said, "Why, it
really wasn't so bad, uh, April. A little noisy, maybe,
but——"

"Oh, Mr. Burckhardt!" The blue eyes were wide and
admiring. "I *knew* you'd understand. It's just that—well, it's
such a *wonderful* freezer that some of the outside men get
carried away, so to speak. As soon as the main office found
out about what happened, they sent representatives around
to every house on the block to apologize. Your wife told us
where we could phone you—and I'm so very pleased that
you were willing to let me have lunch with you, so that I
could apologize, too. Because truly, Mr. Burckhardt, it is a
fine freezer.

"I shouldn't tell you this, but—" The blue eyes were shyly
lowered—"I'd do almost anything for Feckle Freezers. It's
more than a job to me." She looked up. She was enchanting. "I bet you think I'm silly, don't you?"

Burckhardt coughed. "Well, I——"

"Oh, you don't want to be unkind!" She shook her head.
"No, don't pretend. You think it's silly. But really, Mr.
Burckhardt, you wouldn't think so if you knew more about
the Feckle. Let me show you this little booklet——"

Burckhardt got back from lunch a full hour late. It wasn't
only the girl who delayed him. There had been a curious
interview with a little man named Swanson, whom he barely
knew, who had stopped him with desperate urgency on the
street—and then left him cold.

But it didn't matter much. Mr. Barth, for the first time
since Burckhardt had worked there, was out for the day—
leaving Burckhardt stuck with the quarterly tax returns.

What did matter, though, was that somehow he had signed
a purchase order for a twelve-cubic-foot Feckle Freezer,
upright model, self-defrosting, list price $625, with a ten per
cent "courtesy" discount—"Because of that *horrid* affair
this morning, Mr. Burckhardt," she had said.

And he wasn't sure how he could explain it to his wife.

He needn't have worried. As he walked in the front door,
his wife said almost immediately, "I wonder if we can't

afford a new freezer, dear. There was a man here to apologize about that noise and—well, we got to talking and——"

She had signed a purchase order, too.

It had been the damnedest day, Burckhardt thought later, on his way up to bed. But the day wasn't done with him yet. At the head of the stairs, the weakened spring in the electric light switch refused to click at all. He snapped it back and forth angrily and, of course, succeeded in jarring the tumbler out of its pins. The wires shorted and every light in the house went out.

"Damn!" said Guy Burckhardt.

"Fuse?" His wife shrugged sleepily. "Let it go till the morning, dear."

Burckhardt shook his head. "You go back to bed. I'll be right along."

It wasn't so much that he cared about fixing the fuse, but he was too restless for sleep. He disconnected the bad switch with a screwdriver, tumbled down into the black kitchen, found the flashlight and climbed gingerly down the cellar stairs. He located a spare fuse, pushed an empty trunk over to the fuse box to stand on and twisted out the old fuse.

When the new one was in, he heard the starting click and steady drone of the refrigerator in the kitchen overhead.

He headed back to the steps, and stopped.

Where the old trunk had been, the cellar floor gleamed oddly bright. He inspected it in the flashlight beam. It was metal!

"Son of a gun," said Guy Burckhardt. He shook his head unbelievingly. He peered closer, rubbed the edges of the metallic patch with his thumb and acquired an annoying cut—the edges were *sharp*.

The stained cement floor of the cellar was a thin shell. He found a hammer and cracked it off in a dozen spots—everywhere was metal.

The whole cellar was a copper box. Even the cement-brick walls were false fronts over a metal sheath!

Baffled, he attacked one of the foundation beams. That, at least, was real wood. The glass in the cellar windows was real glass.

He sucked his bleeding thumb and tried the base of the cellar stairs. Real wood. He chipped at the bricks under the oil burner. Real bricks. The retaining walls, the floor—they were faked.

It was as though someone had shored up the house with a frame of metal and then laboriously concealed the evidence.

The biggest surprise was the upside-down boat hull that blocked the rear half of the cellar, relic of a brief home-workshop period that Burckhardt had gone through a couple of years before. From above, it looked perfectly normal. Inside, though, where there should have been thwarts and seats and lockers, there was a mere tangle of braces, rough and unfinished.

"But I *built* that!" Burckhardt exclaimed, forgetting his thumb. He leaned against the hull dizzily, trying to think this thing through. For reasons beyond his comprehension, someone had taken his boat and his cellar away, maybe his whole house, and replaced them with a clever mock-up of the real thing.

"That's crazy," he said to the empty cellar. He stared around in the light of the flash. He whispered, "What in the name of Heaven would anybody do that for?"

Reason refused an answer; there wasn't any reasonable answer. For long minutes, Burckhardt contemplated the uncertain picture of his own sanity.

He peered under the boat again, hoping to reassure himself that it was a mistake, just his imagination. But the sloppy, unfinished bracing was unchanged. He crawled under for a better look, feeling the rough wood incredulously. Utterly impossible!

He switched off the flashlight and started to wriggle out. But he didn't make it. In the moment between the command to his legs to move and the crawling out, he felt a sudden draining weariness flooding through him.

Consciousness went—not easily, but as though it were being taken away, and Guy Burckhardt was asleep.

On the morning of June 16th, Guy Burckhardt woke up in a cramped position huddled under the hull of the boat in his basement—and raced upstairs to find it was June 15th.

The first thing he had done was to make a frantic, hasty inspection of the boat hull, the faked cellar floor, the imitation stone. They were all as he had remembered them, all completely unbelievable.

The kitchen was its placid, unexciting self. The electric

clock was purring soberly around the dial. Almost six o'clock, it said. His wife would be waking at any moment.

Burckhardt flung open the front door and stared out into the quiet street. The morning paper was tossed carelessly against the steps, and as he retrieved it, he noticed that this was the 15th day of June.

But that was impossible. *Yesterday* was the 15th of June. It was not a date one would forget, it was quarterly tax-return day.

He went back into the hall and picked up the telephone; he dialed for Weather Information, and got a well-modulated chant: "—and cooler, some showers. Barometric pressure thirty point zero four, rising . . . United States Weather Bureau forecast for June 15th. Warm and sunny, with high around——"

He hung the phone up. June 15th.

"Holy Heaven!" Burckhardt said prayerfully. Things were very odd indeed. He heard the ring of his wife's alarm and bounded up the stairs.

Mary Burckhardt was sitting upright in bed with the terrified, uncomprehending stare of someone just waking out of a nightmare.

"Oh!" she gasped, as her husband came in the room. "Darling, I just had the most *terrible* dream! It was like an explosion and——'

"Again?" Burckhardt asked, not very sympathetically. "Mary, something's funny! I *knew* there was something wrong all day yesterday and——"

He went on to tell her about the copper box that was the cellar, and the odd mock-up someone had made of his boat. Mary looked astonished, then alarmed, then placatory and uneasy.

She said, "Dear, are you *sure*? Because I was cleaning that old trunk out just last week and I didn't notice anything."

"Positive!" said Guy Burckhardt. "I dragged it over to the wall to step on it to put a new fuse in after we blew the lights out and——"

"After we what?" Mary was looking more than merely alarmed.

"After we blew the lights out. You know, when the switch at the head of the stairs stuck. I went down to the cellar and——"

Mary sat up in bed. "Guy, the switch didn't stick. I turned out the lights myself last night."

Burckhardt glared at his wife. "Now I *know* you didn't! Come here and take a look!"

He stalked out to the landing and dramatically pointed to the bad switch, the one that he had unscrewed and left hanging the night before . . .

Only it wasn't. It was as it had always been. Unbelieving, Burckhardt pressed it and the lights sprang up in both halls.

Mary, looking pale and worried, left him to go down to the kitchen and start breakfast. Burckhardt stood staring at the switch for a long time. His mental processes were gone beyond the point of disbelief and shock; they simply were not functioning.

He shaved and dressed and ate his breakfast in a state of numb introspection. Mary didn't disturb him; she was apprehensive and soothing. She kissed him good-by as he hurried out to the bus without another word.

Miss Mitkin, at the reception desk, greeted him with a yawn. "Morning," she said drowsily. "Mr. Barth won't be in today."

Burckhardt started to say something, but checked himself. She would not know that Barth hadn't been in yesterday, either, because she was tearing a June 14th pad off her calendar to make way for the "new" June 15th sheet.

He staggered to his own desk and stared unseeingly at the morning's mail. It had not even been opened yet, but he knew that the Factory Distributors envelope contained an order for twenty thousand feet of the new acoustic tile, and the one from Finebeck & Sons was a complaint.

After a long while, he forced himself to open them. They were.

By lunchtime, driven by a desperate sense of urgency, Burckhardt made Miss Mitkin take her lunch hour first—the June-fifteenth-that-was-yesterday, *he* had gone first. She went, looking vaguely worried about his strained insistence, but it made no difference to Burckhardt's mood.

The phone rang and Burckhardt picked it up abstractedly. "Contro Chemicals Downtown, Burckhardt speaking."

The voice said, "This is Swanson," and stopped.

Burckhardt waited expectantly, but that was all. He said, "Hello?"

Again the pause. Then Swanson asked in sad resignation, "Still nothing, eh?"

"Nothing what? Swanson, is there something you want? You came up to me yesterday and went through this routine. You——"

The voice crackled: "Burckhardt! Oh, my good heavens, *you remember!* Stay right there—I'll be down in half an hour!"

"What's this all about?"

"Never mind," the little man said exultantly. "Tell you about it when I see you. Don't say any more over the phone—somebody may be listening. Just wait there. Say, hold on a minute. Will you be alone in the office?"

"Well, no. Miss Mitkin will probably——"

"Hell. Look, Burckhardt, where do you eat lunch? Is it good and noisy?"

"Why, I suppose so. The Crystal Cafe. It's just about a block—— "

"I know where it is. Meet you in half an hour!" And the receiver clicked.

The Crystal Cafe was no longer painted red, but the temperature was still up. And they had added piped-in music interspersed with commercials. The advertisements were for Frosty-Flip, Marlin Cigarettes—"They're sanitized," the announcer purred—and something called Choco-Bite candy bars that Burckhardt couldn't remember ever having heard of before. But he heard more about them quickly enough.

While he was waiting for Swanson to show up, a girl in the cellophane skirt of a nightclub cigarette vendor came through the restaurant with a tray of tiny scarlet-wrapped candies.

"Choco-Bites are *tangy*," she was murmuring as she came close to his table. "Choco-Bites are *tangier* than tangy!"

Burckhardt, intent on watching for the strange little man who had phoned him, paid little attention. But as she scattered a handful of the confections over the table next to his, smiling at the occupants, he caught a glimpse of her and turned to stare.

"Why, Miss Horn!" he said.

The girl dropped her tray of candies.

Burckhardt rose, concerned over the girl. "Is something wrong?"

But she fled.

The manager of the restaurant was staring suspiciously at Burckhardt, who sank back in his seat and tried to look inconspicuous. He hadn't insulted the girl! Maybe she was just a very strictly reared young lady, he thought—in spite of the long bare legs under the cellophane skirt—and when he addressed her, she thought he was a masher.

Ridiculous idea. Burckhardt scowled uneasily and picked up his menu.

"Burckhardt!" It was a shrill whisper.

Burckhardt looked up over the top of his menu, startled. In the seat across from him, the little man named Swanson was sitting, tensely poised.

"Burckhardt!" the little man whispered again. "Let's get out of here! They're on to you now. If you want to stay alive, come on!"

There was no arguing with the man. Burckhardt gave the hovering manager a sick, apologectic smile and followed Swanson out. The little man seemed to know where he was going. In the street, he clutched Burckhardt by the elbow and hurried him off down the block.

"Did you see her?" he demanded. "That Horn woman, in the phone booth? She'll have them here in five minutes, believe me, so hurry it up!"

Although the street was full of people and cars, nobody was paying any attention to Burckhardt and Swanson. The air had a nip in it—more like Oćtober than June, Burckhardt thought; in spite of the weather bureau. And he felt like a fool, following this mad little man down the street, running away from "them" toward—toward what? The little man might be crazy, but he was afraid. And the fear was infectious.

"In here!" panted the little man.

It was another restaurant—more of a bar, really, and a sort of second-rate place that Burckhardt had never patronized.

"Right straight through," Swanson whispered; and Burckhardt, like a biddable boy, sidestepped through the mass of tables to the far end of the restaurant.

It was L-shaped, with a front on two streets at right angles to each other. They came out on the side street, Swanson staring coldly back at the question-looking cashier, and crossed to the opposite sideward.

They were under the marquee of a movie theater. Swanson's expression began to relax.

"Lost them!" he crowed softly. "We're almost there."

He stepped up to the window and bought two tickets. Burckhardt trailed him into the theater. It was a weekday matinee and the place was almost empty. From the screen came sounds of gunfire and horses' hoofs. A solitary usher, leaning against a bright brass rail, looked briefly at them and went back to staring boredly at the picture as Swanson led Burckhardt down a flight of carpeted marble steps.

They were in the lounge and it was empty. There was a door for men and one for ladies; and there was a third door, marked "MANAGER" in gold letters. Swanson listened at the door, and gently opened it and peered inside.

"Okay," he said, gesturing.

Burckhardt followed him through an empty office, to another door—a closet, probably, because it was unmarked.

But it was no closet. Swanson opened it warily, looked inside, then motioned Burckhardt to follow.

It was a tunnel, metal-walled, brightly lit. Empty, it stretched vacantly away in both directions from them.

Burckhardt looked wondering around. One thing he knew and knew full well:

No such tunnel belonged under Tylerton.

There was a room off the tunnel with chairs and a desk and what looked like television screens. Swanson slumped in a chair, panting.

"We're all right for a while here," he wheezed. "They don't come here much any more. If they do, we'll hear them and we can hide."

"Who?" demanded Burckhardt.

The little man said, "Martians!" His voice cracked on the word and the life seemed to go out of him. In morose tones, he went on: "Well, I think they're Martians. Although you could be right, you know; I've had plenty of time to think it over these last few weeks, after they got you, and it's possible they're Russians after all. Still——"

"Start at the beginning. Who got me when?"

Swanson sighed. "So we have to go through the whole thing again. All right. It was about two months ago that you banged on my door, late at night. You were all beat up—scared silly. You begged me to help you——"

"*I* did?"

"Naturally you don't remember any of this. Listen and

you'll understand. You were talking a blue streak about being captured and threatened, and your wife being dead and coming back to life, and all kinds of mixed-up nonsense. I thought you were crazy. But—well, I've always had a lot of respect for you. And you begged me to hide you and I have this darkroom, you know. It locks from the inside only. I put the lock on myself. So we went in there—just to humor you—and along about midnight, which was only fifteen or twenty minutes after, we passed out."

"Passed out?"

Swanson nodded. "Both of us. It was like being hit with a sandbag. Look, didn't that happen to you again last night?"

"I guess it did." Burckhardt shook his head uncertainly.

"Sure. And then all of a sudden we were awake again, and you said you were going to show me something funny, and we went out and bought a paper. And the date on it was June 15th."

"June 15th? But that's today! I mean——"

"You got it, friend. It's *always* today!"

It took time to penetrate.

Burckhardt said wonderingly, "You've hidden out in that darkroom for how many weeks?"

"How can I tell? Four or five, maybe, I lost count. And every day the same—always the 15th of June, always my landlady, Mrs. Keefer, is sweeping the front steps, always the same headline in the papers at the corner. It gets monotonous, friend."

It was Burckhardt's idea and Swanson despised it, but he went along. He was the type who always went along.

"It's dangerous," he grumbled worriedly. "Suppose somebody comes by? They'll spot us and——"

"What have we got to lose?"

Swanson shrugged. "It's dangerous," he said again. But he went along.

Burckhardt's idea was very simple. He was sure of only one thing—the tunnel went somewhere. Martians or Russians, fantastic plot or crazy hallucination, whatever was wrong with Tylerton had an explanation, and the place to look for it was at the end of the tunnel.

They jogged along. It was more than a mile before they began to see an end. They were in luck—at least no one came through the tunnel to spot them. But Swanson had said that it was only at certain hours that the tunnel seemed to be in use.

Always the fifteenth of June. Why? Burckhardt asked himself. Never mind the how. *Why?*

And falling asleep, completely involuntarily—everyone at the same time, it seemed. And not remembering, never remembering anything—Swanson had said how eagerly he saw Burckhardt again, the morning after Burckhardt had incautiously waited five minutes too many before retreating into the darkroom. When Swanson had come to, Burckhardt was gone. Swanson had seen him in the street that afternoon, but Burckhardt had remembered nothing.

And Swanson had lived his mouse's existence for weeks, hiding in the woodwork at night, stealing out by day to search for Burckhardt in pitiful hope, scurrying around the fringe of life, trying to keep from the deadly eyes of *them*.

Them. One of "them" was the girl named April Horn. It was by seeing her walk carelessly into a telephone booth and never come out that Swanson had found the tunnel. Another was the man at the cigar stand in Burckhardt's office building. There were more, at least a dozen that Swanson knew of or suspected.

They were easy enough to spot, once you knew where to look, for they alone in Tylerton changed their roles from day to day. Burckhardt was on that 8:51 bus, every morning of every day-that-was-June-15th, never different by a hair or a moment. But April Horn was sometimes gaudy in the cellophane skirt, giving away candy or cigarettes; sometimes plainly dressed; sometimes not seen by Swanson at all.

Russians? Martians? Whatever they were, what could they be hoping to gain from this mad masquerade?

Burckhardt didn't know the answer, but perhaps it lay beyond the door at the end of the tunnel. They listened carefully and heard distant sounds that could not quite be made out, but nothing that seemed dangerous. They slipped through.

And, through a wide chamber and up a flight of steps, they found they were in what Burckhardt recognized as the Contro Chemicals plant.

Nobody was in sight. By itself, that was not so very odd; the automatized factory had never had very many persons in it. But Burckhardt remembered, from his single visit, the endless, ceaseless busyness of the plant, the valves that opened and closed, the vats that emptied themselves and filled themselves and stirred and cooked and chemically tasted the bubbling liquids they held inside themselves. The plant was never populated, but it was never still.

Only now it *was* still. Except for the distant sounds, there was no breath of life in it. The captive electronic minds were sending out no commands; the coils and relays were at rest.

Burckhardt said, "Come on." Swanson reluctantly followed him through the tangled aisles of stainless steel columns and tanks.

They walked as though they were in the presence of the dead. In a way, they were, for what were the automatons that once had run the factory, if not corpses? The machines were controlled by computers that were really not computers at all, but the electronic analogues of living brains. And if they were turned off, were they not dead? For each had once been a human mind.

Take a master petroleum chemist, infinitely skilled in the separation of crude oil into its fractions. Strap him down, probe into his brain with searching electronic needles. The machine scans the patterns of the mind, translates what it sees into charts and sine waves. Impress these same waves on a robot computer and you have your chemist. Or a thousand copies of your chemist, if you wish, with all of his knowledge and skill, and no human limitations at all.

Put a dozen copies of him into a plant and they will run it all, twenty-four hours a day, seven days of every week, never tiring, never overlooking anything, never forgetting.

Swanson stepped up closer to Burckhardt. "I'm scared," he said.

They were across the room now and the sounds were louder. They were not machine sounds, but voices; Burckhardt moved cautiously up to a door and dared to peer around it.

It was a smaller room, lined with television screens, each one—a dozen or more, at least—with a man or woman sitting before it, staring into the screen and dictating notes into a recorder. The viewers dialed from scene to scene; no two screens ever showed the same picture.

The pictures seemed to have little in common. One was a store, where a girl dressed like April Horn was demonstrating home freezers. One was a series of shots of kitchens.

Burckhardt caught a glimpse of what looked like the cigar stand in his office building.

It was baffling and Burckhardt would have loved to stand there and puzzle it out, but it was too busy a place. There was the chance that someone would look their way or walk out and find them.

They found another room. This one was empty. It was an office, large and sumptuous. It had a desk, littered with papers. Burckhardt stared at them, briefly at first—then, as the words on one of them caught his attention, with incredulous fascination.

He snatched up the topmost sheet, scanned it, and another, while Swanson was frenziedly searching through the drawers.

Burckhardt swore unbelievingly and dropped the papers to the desk.

Swanson, hardly noticing, yelped with delight: "Look!" He dragged a gun from the desk. "And it's loaded, too!"

Burckhardt stared at him blankly, trying to assimilate what he had read. Then, as he realized what Swanson had said, Burckhardt's eyes sparked. "Good man!" he cried. "We'll take it. We're getting out of here with that gun, Swanson. And we're not going to the police! Not the cops in Tylerton, but the F.B.I., maybe. Take a look at this!"

The sheaf he handed Swanson was headed: "Test Area Progress Report. Subject: Marlin Cigarettes Campaign." It was mostly tabulated figures that made little sense to Burckhardt and Swanson, but at the end was a summary that said:

Although Test 47-K3 pulled nearly double the number of new users of any of the other tests conducted, it probably cannot be used in the field because of local sound-truck control ordinances.

The tests in the 47-K12 group were second best and our recommendation is that retests be conducted in this appeal, testing each of the three best campaigns with and without the addition of sampling techniques.

An alternative suggestion might be to proceed directly with the top appeal in the K12 series, if the client is unwilling to go to the expense of additional tests.

All of these forecast expectations have an 80% probability of being within one-half of one per cent of results
forecast, and more than 99% probability of coming
within 5%.

Swanson looked up from the paper into Burckhardt's
eyes. "I don't get it," he complained.

Burckhardt said, "I don't blame you. It's crazy, but it fits
the facts, Swanson, *it fits the facts*. They aren't Russians and
they aren't Martians. These people are advertising men!
Somehow—heaven knows how they did it—they've taken
Tylerton over. They've got us, all of us, you and me and
twenty or thirty thousand other people, right under their
thumbs.

"Maybe they hypnotize us and maybe it's something else;
but however they do it, what happens is that they let us live
a day at a time. They pour advertising into us the whole
damned day long. And at the end of the day, they see what
happened—and then they wash the day out of our minds
and start again the next day with different advertising."

Swanson's jaw was hanging. He managed to close it and
swallow. "Nuts!" he said flatly.

Burckhardt shook his head. "Sure, it sounds crazy, but
this whole thing is crazy. How else would you explain it?
You can't deny that most of Tylerton lives the same day
over and over again. You've *seen* it! And that's the crazy
part and we have to admit that that's true—unless *we* are
the crazy ones. And once you admit that somebody, somehow, knows how to accomplish that, the rest of it makes all
kinds of sense.

"Think of it, Swanson! They test every last detail before
they spend a nickel on advertising! Do you have any idea
what that means? Lord knows how much money is involved,
but I know for a fact that some companies spend twenty or
thirty million dollars a year on advertising. Multiply it, say,
by a hundred companies. Say that every one of them learns
how to cut its advertising cost by only ten percent. And
that's peanuts, believe me!

"If they know in advance what's going to work, they can
cut their costs in half—maybe to less than half, I don't
know. But that's saving two or three hundred million dollars
a year—and if they pay only ten or twenty per cent of that

for the use of Tylerton, it's still dirt cheap for them and a fortune for whoever took over Tylerton."

Swanson licked his lips. "You mean," he offered hesitantly, "that we're a—well, a kind of captive audience?"

Burckhardt frowned. "Not exactly." He thought for a minute. "You know how a doctor tests something like penicillin? He sets up a series of little colonies of germs on gelatin disks and he tries the stuff on one after another, changing it a little each time. Well, that's us—we're the germs, Swanson. Only it's even more efficient than that. They don't have to test more than one colony, because they can use it over and over again."

It was too hard for Swanson to take in. He only said, "What do we do about it?"

"We go to the police. They can't use human beings for guinea pigs!"

"How do we get to the police?"

Burckhardt hesitated. "I think—" he began slowly. "Sure. This is the office of somebody important. We've got a gun. We'll stay right here until he comes along. And he'll get us out of here."

Simple and direct. Swanson subsided and found a place to sit, against the wall, out of sight of the door. Burckhardt took up a position behind the door itself——

And waited.

The wait was not as long as it might have been. Half an hour, perhaps. Then Burckhardt heard approaching voices and had time for a soft whisper to Swanson before he flattened himself against the wall.

It was a man's voice, and a girl's. The man was saying, "—reason why you couldn't report on the phone? You're ruining your whole day's tests! What the devil's the matter with you, Janet?"

"I'm sorry, Mr. Dorchin," she said in a sweet, clear tone. "I thought it was important."

The man grumbled, "Important! One lousy unit out of twenty-one thousand."

"But it's the Burckhardt one, Mr. Dorchin. Again. And the way he got out of sight, he must have had some help."

"All right, all right. It doesn't matter, Janet; the Choco-Bite program is ahead of schedule anyhow. As long as you're this far, come on in the office and make out your worksheet. And don't worry about the Burckhardt business. He's probably just wandering around. We'll pick him up tonight and——"

They were inside the door. Burckhardt kicked it shut and pointed the gun.

"That's what you think," he said triumphantly.

It was worth the terrified hours, the bewildered sense of insanity, the confusion and fear. It was the most satisfying sensation Burckhardt had ever had in his life. The expression on the man's face was one he had read about but never actually seen: Dorchin's mouth fell open and his eyes went wide, and though he managed to make a sound that might have been a question, it was not in words.

The girl was almost as surprised. And Burckhardt, looking at her, knew why her voice had been so familiar. The girl was the one who had introduced herself to him as April Horn.

Dorchin recovered himself quickly. "Is this the one?" he asked sharply.

The girl said, "Yes."

Dorchin nodded. "I take it back. You were right. Uh, you—Burckhardt. What do you want?"

Swanson piped up, "Watch him! He might have another gun."

"Search him then," Burckhardt said. "I'll tell you what we want, Dorchin. We want you to come along with us to the FBI and explain to them how you can get away with kidnaping twenty thousand people."

"Kidnaping?" Dorchin snorted. "That's ridiculous, man! Put that gun away; you can't get away with this!"

Burckhardt hefted the gun grimly. "I think I can."

Dorchin looked furious and sick—but oddly, not afraid. "Damn it—" he started to bellow, then closed his mouth and swallowed. "Listen," he said persuasively, "you're making a big mistake. I haven't kidnapped anybody, believe me!"

"I don't believe you," said Burckhardt bluntly. "Why should I?"

"But it's true! Take my word for it!"

Burckhardt shook his head. "The FBI can take your word if they like. We'll find out. Now how do we get out of here?"

Dorchin opened his mouth to argue.

Burckhardt blazed, "Don't get in my way! I'm willing to kill you if I have to. Don't you understand that? I've gone through two days of hell and every second of it I blame on you. Kill you? It would be a pleasure and I don't have a thing in the world to lose! Get us out of here!"

Dorchin's face went suddenly opaque. He seemed about to move; but the blond girl he had called Janet slipped between him and the gun.

"Please!" she begged Burckhardt. "You don't understand. You mustn't shoot!"

"Get out of my way!"

"But, Mr. Burckhardt—"

She never finished. Dorchin, his face unreadable, headed for the door. Burckhardt had been pushed one degree too far. He swung the gun, bellowing. The girl called out sharply. He pulled the trigger. Closing on him with pity and pleading in her eyes, she came again between the gun and the man.

Burckhardt aimed low instinctively, to cripple, not to kill. But his aim was not good.

The pistol bullet caught her in the pit of the stomach.

Dorchin was out and away, the door slamming behind him, his footsteps racing into the distance.

Burckhardt hurled the gun across the room and jumped to the girl.

Swanson was moaning. "That finishes us, Burckhardt. Oh, why did you do it? We could have got away. We could have gone to the police. We were practically out of here! We——"

Burckhardt wasn't listening. He was kneeling beside the girl. She lay flat on her back, arms helterskelter. There was no blood, hardly any sign of the wound; but the position in which she lay was one that no living human being could have held.

Yet she wasn't dead.

She wasn't dead—and Burckhardt, frozen beside her, thought: *She isn't alive, either.*

There was no pulse, but there was a rhythmic ticking of the outstretched fingers of one hand.

There was no sound of breathing, but there was a hissing, sizzling noise.

The eyes were open and they were looking at Burckhardt.

There was neither fear nor pain in them, only a pity deeper than the Pit.

She said, through lips that writhed erratically, "Don't—worry, Mr. Burckhardt. I'm—all right."

Burckhardt rocked back on his haunches, staring. Where there should have been blood, there was a clean break of a substance that was not flesh; and a curl of thin golden-copper wire.

Burckhardt moistened his lips.

"You're a robot," he said.

The girl tried to nod. The twitching lips said, "I am. And so are you."

Swanson, after a single inarticulate sound, walked over to the desk and sat staring at the wall. Burckhardt rocked back and forth beside the shattered puppet on the floor. He had no words.

The girl managed to say, "I'm—sorry all this happened." The lovely lips twisted into a rictus sneer, frightening on that smooth young face, until she got them under control. "Sorry," she said again. "The—nerve center was right about where the bullet hit. Makes it difficult to—control this body."

Burckhardt nodded automatically, accepting the apology. Robots. It was obvious, now that he knew it. In hindsight, it was inevitable. He thought of his mystic notions of hypnosis or Martians or something stranger still—idiotic, for the simple fact of created robots fitted the facts better and more economically.

All the evidence had been before him. The automatized factory, with its transplanted minds—why not transplant a mind into a humanoid robot, give it its original owner's features and form?

Could it know that it was a robot?

"All of us," Burckhardt said, hardly aware that he spoke out loud. "My wife and my secretary and you and the neighbors. All of us the same."

"No." The voice was stronger. "Not exactly the same, all of us. I chose it, you see. I—" This time the convulsed lips were not a random contortion of the nerves—"I was an ugly woman, Mr. Burckhardt, and nearly sixty years old. Life had passed me. And when Mr. Dorchin offered me the chance to live again as a beautiful girl, I jumped at the opportunity. Believe me, I *jumped*, in spite of its disadvantages. My flesh body is still alive—it is sleeping, while I am here. I could go back to it. But I never do."

"And the rest of us?"

"Different, Mr. Burckhardt. I work here. I'm carrying out Mr. Dorchin's orders, mapping the results of the advertising tests, watching you and the others live as he makes you live. I do it by choice, but you have no choice. Because, you see, you are dead."

"Dead?" cried Burckhardt; it was almost a scream.

The blue eyes looked at him unwinkingly and he knew that it was no lie. He swallowed, marveling at the intricate mechanisms that let him swallow, and sweat, and eat.

He said: "Oh. The explosion in my dream."

"It was no dream. You are right—the explosion. That was real and this plant was the cause of it. The storage tanks let go and what the blast didn't get, the fumes killed a little later. But almost everyone died in the blast, twenty-one thousand persons. You died with them and that was Dorchin's chance."

"The damned ghoul!" said Burckhardt.

The twisted shoulders shrugged with an odd grace. "Why? You were gone. And you and all the others were what Dorchin wanted—a whole town, a perfect slice of America. It's as easy to transfer a pattern from a dead brain as a living one. Easier—the dead can't say no. Oh, it took work and money—the town was a wreck—but it was possible to rebuild it entirely, especially because it wasn't necessary to have all the details exact.

"There were the homes where even the brain had been utterly destroyed, and those are empty inside, and the cellars that needn't be too perfect, and the streets that hardly matter. And anyway, it only has to last for one day. The same day—June 15th—over and over again; and if someone finds something a little wrong, somehow, the discovery won't have time to snowball, wreck the validity of the tests, because all errors are canceled out at midnight."

The face tried to smile. "That's the dream, Mr. Burckhardt, that day of June 15th, because you never really lived it. It's a present from Mr. Dorchin, a dream that he gives you and then takes back at the end of the day, when he has all his figures on how many of you respond to what variation of which appeal, and the maintenance crews go down the tunnel to go through the whole city, washing out the new

dream with their little electronic drains, and then the dream
starts all over again. On June 15th.

"Always June 15th, because June 14th is the last day any
of you can remember alive. Sometimes the crews miss
someone—as they missed you, because you were under your
boat. But it doesn't matter. The ones who are missed give
themselves away if they show it—and if they don't, it doesn't
affect the test. But they don't drain us, the ones of us who
work for Dorchin. We sleep when the power is turned off,
just as you do. When we wake up, though, we remember."
The face contorted wildly. "If I could only forget!"

Burckhardt said unbelievingly, "All this to sell merchandise! It must have cost millions!"

The robot called April Horn said, "It did. But it has made
millions for Dorchin, too. And that's not the end of it. Once
he finds the master words that make people act, do you
suppose he will stop with that? Do you suppose——"

The door opened, interrupting her. Burckhardt whirled.
Belatedly remembering Dorchin's flight, he raised the gun.

"Don't shoot," ordered the voice calmly. It was not
Dorchin; it was another robot, this one not disguised with
the clever plastics and cosmetics, but shining plain. It said
metallically, "Forget it, Burckhardt. You're not accomplish-
ing anything. Give me that gun before you do any more
damage. Give it to me *now*."

Burckhardt bellowed angrily. The gleam on this robot
torso was steel; Burckhardt was not at all sure that his
bullets would pierce it, or do much harm if they did. He
would have put it to the test——

But from behind him came a whimpering, scurrying whirl-
wind: its name was Swanson, hysterical with fear. He cata-
pulted into Burckhardt and sent him sprawling, the gun
flying free.

"Please!" begged Swanson incoherently, prostrate before
the steel robot. "He would have shot you—please don't hurt
me! Let me work for you, like that girl. I'll do anything,
anything you tell me—"

The robot voice said, "We don't need your help." It took
two precise steps and stood over the gun—and spurned it,
left it lying on the floor.

The wrecked blond robot said, without emotion, "I doubt
that I can hold out much longer, Mr. Dorchin."

"Disconnect if you have to," replied the steel robot.

Burckhardt blinked. "But you're not Dorchin!"

The steel robot turned deep eyes on him. "I am," it said. "Not in the flesh—but this is the body I am using at the moment. I doubt that you can damage this one with the gun. The other robot body was more vulnerable. Now will you stop this nonsense? I don't want to have to damage you; you're too expensive for that. Will you just sit down and let the maintenance crews adjust you?"

Swanson groveled. "You—you won't punish us?"

The steel robot had no expression, but its voice was almost surprised. "Punish you?" it repeated on a rising note. "How?"

Swanson quivered as though the word had been a whip; but Burckhardt flared: "Adjust *him*, if he'll let you—but not me! You're going to have to do me a lot of damage, Dorchin. I don't care what I cost or how much trouble it's going to be to put me back together again. But I'm going out of that door! If you want to stop me, you'll have to kill me. You won't stop me any other way!"

The steel robot took a half-step toward him, and Burckhardt involuntarily checked his stride. He stood poised and shaking, ready for death, ready for attack, ready for anything that might happen.

Ready for anything except what did happen. For Dorchin's steel body merely stepped aside, between Burckhardt and the gun, but leaving the door free.

"Go ahead," invited the steel robot. "Nobody's stopping you."

Outside the door, Burckhardt brought up sharp. It was insane of Dorchin to let him go! Robot or flesh, victim or beneficiary, there was nothing to stop him from going to the FBI or whatever law he could find away from Dorchin's sympathetic empire, and telling his story. Surely the corporations who paid Dorchin for test results had no notion of the ghoul's technique he used; Dorchin would have to keep it from them, for the breath of publicity would put a stop to it. Walking out meant death, perhaps, but at that moment in his pseudo-life, death was no terror for Burckhardt.

There was no one in the corridor. He found a window and stared out of it. There was Tylerton—an ersatz city, but looking so real and familiar that Burckhardt almost imagined the whole episode a dream. It was no dream, though.

He was certain of that in his heart and equally certain that nothing in Tylerton could help him now.

It had to be the other direction.

It took him a quarter of an hour to find a way, but he found it—skulking through the corridors, dodging the suspicion of footsteps, knowing for certain that his hiding was in vain, for Dorchin was undoubtedly aware of every move he made. But no one stopped him, and he found another door.

It was a simple enough door from the inside. But when he opened it and stepped out, it was like nothing he had ever seen.

First there was light—brilliant, incredible, blinding light. Burckhardt blinked upward, unbelieving and afraid.

He was standing on a ledge of smooth, finished metal. Not a dozen yards from his feet, the ledge dropped sharply away; he hardly dared approach the brink, but even from where he stood he could see no bottom to the chasm before him. And the gulf extended out of sight into the glare on either side of him.

No wonder Dorchin could so easily give him his freedom! From the factory there was nowhere to go. But how incredible this fantastic gulf, how impossible the hundred white and blinding suns that hung above!

A voice by his side said inquiringly, "Burckhardt?" And thunder rolled the name, mutteringly soft, back and forth in the abyss before him.

Burckhardt wet his lips. "Y-yes?" he croaked.

"This is Dorchin. Not a robot this time, but Dorchin in the flesh, talking to you on a hand mike. Now you have seen, Burckhardt. Now will you be reasonable and let the maintenance crews take over?"

Burckhardt stood paralyzed. One of the moving mountains in the blinding glare came toward him.

It towered hundreds of feet over his head; he stared up at its top, squinting helplessly into the light.

It looked like——

Impossible!

The voice in the loudspeaker at the door said, "Burckhardt?" But he was unable to answer.

A heavy rumbling sigh. "I see," said the voice. "You finally understand. There's no place to go. You know it now. I could have told you, but you might not have believed me, so it was better for you to see it yourself. And after all,

Burckhardt, why would I reconstruct a city just the way it was before? I'm a businessman; I count costs. If a thing has to be full-scale, I build it that way. But there wasn't any need to in this case."

From the mountain before him, Burckhardt helplessly saw a lesser cliff descend carefully toward him. It was long and dark, and at the end of it was whiteness, five-fingered whiteness . . .

"Poor little Burckhardt," crooned the loudspeaker, while the echoes rumbled through the enormous chasm that was only a workshop. "It must have been quite a shock for you to find out you were living in a town built on a table top."

It was the morning of June 15th, and Guy Burckhardt woke up screaming out of a dream.

It had been a monstrous and incomprehensible dream, of explosions and shadow figures that were not men and terror beyond words.

He shuddered and opened his eyes.

Outside his bedroom window, a hugely amplified voice was howling.

Burckhardt stumbled over to the window and stared outside. There was an out-of-season chill to the air, more like October than June; but the scene was normal enough—except for a sound-truck that squatted at curbside halfway down the block. Its speaker horns blared:

"Are you a coward? Are you a fool? Are you going to let crooked politicians steal the country from you? NO! Are you going to put up with four more years of graft and crime? NO! Are you going to vote straight Federal Party all up and down the ballot? YES! *You just bet you are!*"

Sometimes he screams, sometimes he wheedles, threatens, begs, cajoles . . . but his voice goes on and on through one June 15th after another.

BROTHER ROBOT

BY HENRY SLESAR

They found the old man in his study, slumped over the desk in what appeared to be sleep. But the quiet which had come upon him was deeper and gentler than sleep. Beside his opened hand stood an uncapped container of lethal tablets. Beneath his fine white hair, a pillow for his head, was a journal begun thirty years before. His name was on the first page: *Dr. Alfred Keeley.* And the date: *February 6, 1997.*

Feb. 6, 1997. This is a day twice-blessed for me. Today, at St. Luke's Hospital, our first child was born to my wife, Ila. The baby is a boy, seven pounds, two ounces, and according to Ila's sentimental appraisal, the image of his father. When I saw her this morning, I could not bring myself to mention the second birth which has taken place in my laboratory. The birth of Machine, my robot child.

Machine was conceived long before the infant Ila will bring home soon (we will call him Peter Fitzpatrick, after Ila's grandfather). Machine was conceived long before my marriage, when I first received my professorship in robotics. It is exhilarating to see my dream transformed into reality: a robot child that would be reared within the bosom to a human family, raised like a human child, a brother to a human child—growing, learning, becoming an adult. I can hardly contain my excitement at the possibilities I foresee.

It has taken me seven years to perfect the robot brain which will be the soul of my robot son, a brain whose learning capacities will equal (and in some regard, exceed) the capabilities of Peter Fitzpatrick himself. But I must keep the experiment perfectly controlled. My duties will consist primarily of careful observation, and of providing for the physical maturation of Machine. My robot child will not have the natural advantages of growth that Peter Fitzpatrick will possess; I must provide them for him. I will reconstruct his metal body periodically, so that he keeps pace with the growth of his human brother. Eventually, I hope that Machine will learn enough about the construction of his own form that he may make these changes for himself.

At the moment, Machine already has physical advantages over his brother. I did not wish to handicap my metal child; he will have serious shortcomings in a human world; the least I could do was to provide him with the advantages only a machine could boast. He will never know hunger or thirst, or the unpleasant necessities of human waste disposal. He will never know bitter cold or sweltering heat. The ills to which mankind are subject will never trouble his artificial body. The vulnerability of human flesh will never be his problem. He will live on, inviolate, as long as his robot brain pulses within the impenetrable housing of his beautiful head.

Have I said that Machine is beautiful? Yes, I have made him so. The world of humans will be critical enough of my experiment and my robot child; but they will not call him monster. I have made him beautiful with the beauty of perfect function. I have constructed him along human lines (nature was an excellent designer). I have given him a gleaming skin of silver, and flawless modeling. He shall inspire no loathing, my robot creation. Not even in Ila.

Ila! My heart constricts at the thought of my wife, who lies in happy slumber at St. Luke's this moment, unaware of the brother who awaits her infant son. How will she react? She has always been so helpful, so understanding. But an experiment like this, within her own domain, involving her own newborn son . . .

I must not worry myself needlessly. I must get ready. I must prepare for the arrival of Peter Fitzpatrick, brother of Machine.

June 11, 1997. I am outraged, outraged and deceived. Today I learned that the man who called upon me last month was not the scientific reporter he claimed to be. Now I know that he was a representative of a local newspaper, looking for a sensational Sunday feature with which to tickle the vulgar curiosity of its readers.

What a fool I was to grant him the interview! This morning, I found the article, illustrated by a terrible and inaccurate portrait of Mac and my son. "ROBOTIC PROFESSOR RAISES ROBOT AND SON AS BROTHERS . . ."

I have hidden the scandalous article from Ila's eyes. She is still bedridden, and I am worried about her failure to gain strength. Can it be that my experiment is the real cause of her illness? I believed, after her first hysterical outburst of protest, that she had become accustomed to the idea. She seemed so willing to cooperate, so completely aware of what I was trying to do. And yet, the way she looks at Mac, the evident horror in her eyes when she sees him touch our son . . .

No, I am sure she understands. Ila was never strong; she had rheumatic fever as a child, perhaps this is the belated result. I am sure she will be better when warmer weather comes. Perhaps if we went away . . .

But I cannot go away, of course, not at this early stage of my experiment. So far, all has gone well. At four months, Fitz is developing along normal lines. His little body has gone from asymmetric postures to symmetric postures, his eyes now converge and fasten upon any dangling object held at midpoint. As for Mac, he is advancing even more rapidly. He is beginning to learn control of his limbs; it is apparent that he will walk before his human brother. Before long, he will learn to speak; already I hear rumbles within the cavity of the sound-box in his chest. Fitz can only gurgle and coo his delight at being alive.

I believe Ila was right; Fitz does look like me. I would have preferred him to have Ila's green eyes and fair skin, but he is dark like myself. I feel an unscientific pride in my boy.

Sept. 10, 1997. Must happiness and despair always live side by side? It would seem that is my fate. Today, I thought I would surprise Ila with the extraordinary progress of our robot child. I knew that Mac has been developing the power of coherent speech, and has already said some simple words. For the past week, I have been teaching him phrases, beginning with the one I thought would please Ila most. But I have been foolish. I believe Ila must resent Mac's rapid development. Fitz, at the age of seven months, is just now displaying coordination. He can transfer objects from hand to hand, and he makes sounds that might be taken, or mistaken, for words.

But Mac is far ahead of him. And this morning, at ten o'clock, I brought him into Ila's bedroom. She was still fast asleep; her illness seems to produce the need for sleep. She stirred when she heard our footsteps (Mac's metal feet are too noisy; I must muffle his lumbering stride). I said:

"Ila, I have a little surprise . . ."

She raised her head from the pillow and looked at me, avoiding contact with Mac's silvery face.

"What is it?" she said.

"It's Mac. He wants to say something to you."

"What are you talking about?"

I smiled.

"All right, Mac."

His metal face lifted towards her. From the featureless surface, a small, uncertain voice emerged.

"He . . . llo . . . mo . . . ther . . ."

I almost laughed aloud in satisfaction and delight, and turned to Ila in search of her approval and pleasure. But her face bore an expression that amazed and frightened me, an expression of utter horror I had never seen before. Her lips moved soundlessly, and her eyes, always feverish, burned brighter than ever. And then she screamed. God help me, she screamed as if the devil were in the room, bringing up her hands to clutch at her hair. In the nursery next door, little Fitz set up a sympathetic wail, and I saw Mac's metal body shiver as if in reaction to the sound.

I tried to calm her, but she was lost in hysteria. Eventually her sobs stopped, but then she fell back upon the pillow with such exhaustion that I became concerned and telephoned for medical help. Dr. Foster arrived half an hour later and shut me out of the bedroom. When he finally emerged, he mumbled something about shock, and prescribed rest and tranquilizing drugs.

I went into Ila's room a few minutes ago. Her eyes were closed and her breathing was shallow. I spoke to her, but she merely lifted her hand and said nothing. My poor Ila! Why must she face so much misery, while I experience such joy and satisfaction in my work?

*   *   *

Jan. 1, 1998. It has been almost two months since I last touched this journal, but I must take strength in this New Year and continue. It has been hard for me to work at all; there has been too much bitterness in my mind and unhappiness in my heart since Ila's death.

As I write these words, little Fitz is sleeping peacefully in his crib, watched over by his new nursemaid, Annette. But Mac, who needs no sleep, is sitting in the study chair beside my desk, watching me through the expressionless eyes I have placed in his silver skull. Yet, blank as they are, somehow I sense emotion in those eyes as he watches me. Somehow, I feel my robot creation knows the torment I suffer, and knows the void in our home since Ila's death. Does he miss her, too? It is so difficult to tell. Even with Fitz, my human child, it is hard to recognize the signs of sorrow he must be feeling.

During these past weeks, I began to believe that my experiment was all a conceit. But now I realize it was only grief that brought such thoughts; I must continue. Already, I believe Mac thinks of Fitz as his brother, and I know that someday Fitz will reciprocate. There will be much to learn from both of them. I cannot fail my mission now. I will go on.

July 25, 2002. Today, my family and I began life in new surroundings, and as difficult as the transplantation has been, I am glad now that we made the move. It had become too much of a burden to face the curiosity and gibes of the neighborhood; we have attracted too much attention. For this reason, I have purchased this small home in the exurbs of the city, just outside the town of Fremont.

Both my children seem happy in their new country residence. They are playing together now on the green grass that grows untamed behind the house; I will have to trim and weed it, like a truly domesticated homeowner. I think I shall enjoy the sensation.

Despite our problems, my joy is great as I watch the human and mechanical beings outside my window, laughing and romping together as if the differences between them had no existence. In one respect, my experiment is already successful. In the eyes of Fitz, my human boy, and Mac, my inhuman invention, they are truly brothers. Fitz, at the age of five, is a sturdy, red-cheeked boy with dark eyes and a smile that easily becomes a laugh. There is a great deal of warmth in him; he is open and frank with people, and with his metallic brother.

As for Mac, of course, he is the same as ever; the same polished silvery body, encased in the simple tunic I have made to cover his metallic nakedness. They are almost the same height, but Fitz is a bit taller, and growing each day. Before long, it will be time to reconstruct my robot child's body again.

I have presented my first full-length paper on the experiment to the National Robotics Society. I must admit that I eagerly await their acceptance and publication.

Sept. 3, 2003. This morning, I opened my door upon a matronly woman whose pleasantries concealed an icy attitude towards myself and my family. She introduced herself as Mrs. Margotson, chairwoman of the local school board.

It was some time before Mrs. Margotson revealed the true purpose of her visit, which was to expose the board's reluctance to accept the enrollment of Mac, my robot child.

"You understand, of course," she told me, "that there is no question concerning your son. But the idea of this— machine entering our school is perfectly absurd."

I had written a lengthy letter which explained my experiment in detail, but it had made little impression upon the authorities. She kept referring to "that metal thing" and "that machine" and her lip curled in disgust. I wasn't too upset by her attitude; I rather expected it.

"I understand," I told her. "To be honest, I did not expect approval, but I felt it my duty to make the application. However, since the board refuses, I shall not enter either child. I will tutor them both at home."

Mrs. Margotson looked shocked. "Are you serious about this experiment, Dr. Keeley?"

"Certainly. They are brothers, you know."

"Really!"

Both Fitz and Mac were delighted with my plans for their education; it seemed that neither one was keen on the idea of entering the local school. I didn't find out exactly why until late that afternoon.

The reason became apparent when Mac and Fitz returned from some mysterious outing. There was a vacancy in Fitz's mouth where a tooth had been recently and forcibly removed. There was a faint bruise on his cheek, and a hole in the knee of his trousers. I was disturbed by this evidence of a brawl, but was even more shocked and surprised to see a large dent in Mac's silvery forehead. I knew he felt no physical pain, but it was startling.

"What happened?" I said.

Fitz, always the spokesman, shrugged his shoulders.

"Just a fight," he said glumly.

"What do you mean, just a fight? Who with? What about?"

"Some kids. Kids from the school."

"How many kids?"

"Five or six," Fitz said. "They threw things. Rocks."

I was appalled, and now I knew what had caused the dent. I don't know why I should have been surprised at the tale of violence. I had learned before, in our old city neighborhood, that my robot child was a natural target for the cruel taunts and unthinking violence of children.

I treated Fitz's wounds, and then drew Mac aside.

"What happened?" I asked gently.

"Fitz told you. We had a fight."

"I want to hear your version. Were they making fun of you, Mac? Is that it?"

"Yes."

"How did you feel about it?" I asked the question eagerly; it was important to me to learn the emotional responses of my creation.

Mac didn't answer for a while, his face a silver mask.

"Did you feel hurt, angry? Did you want to strike back? I've told you this often, Mac—you must never strike a human. They're soft, you know, not hard like you. Did you want to hurt them, Mac?" Instinctively, I reached for pencil and paper to record his reactions.

"Yes," he said.

My heart leaped. My robot child had felt anger!

"But you didn't?"

"No."

"Why, Mac? Because you realized you were strong and they were weak? Because they felt pain and you didn't?"

"No!" He was almost defiant.

"What, then?"

"Because I am little," he whispered.

The reply disturbed me. I hadn't yet gotten around to performing the mechanical surgery that would give Machine his new body. He was several inches shorter than his brother, shorter than most boys his age.

Patiently, I explained to him again the rules of conduct I expected of him, rules that could never be broken. There must be no harm to humans; it was the cardinal rule of our code.

"Do you understand that, Mac? Truly understand it?"

"Yes," he answered, his blank eyes on the floor.

I sighed.

"All right, then. I will make you bigger, Mac. I will build a new body."

April 23, 2008. It feels good to be recognized, I must admit it. The award conferred upon me by the National Robotics Society yesterday has meant a great deal to me. It has made a difference in the attitude of my neighbors; they no longer think of me as a half-mad creator of monsters, a new Frankenstein. And the monetary grant, while not enormous, will permit me to expand my laboratory facilities. It has come at an opportune time; I have been blueprinting a greatly improved physical housing for Mac, one which will permit his metal body greater flexibility and digital dexterity. I think, too, that I can create a superior sound system for him now, which will overcome the flat, metallic voice of my robot child.

Both Mac and Fitz are not overly impressed by my sudden fame. But I believe Mac is secretly excited by my promise to build him a better body. He has become acutely aware of his appearance; I have caught him gazing (with what emotion, I cannot say) into the mirrors of the house, standing before them with a stillness that only a robot can maintain. I have questioned him at length about his feelings, but have learned little. I must be sure to keep close to his emotional growth.

But if I have a real source of happiness now, it is my son Fitz. He has become a fine handsome boy, of such good humor and intelligence that he is extremely popular with all the residents of the town—and the power of his engaging personality has created an acceptance for Mac, his robot brother, that all my elaborate scientific titles couldn't have attained. He is still fiercely loyal to Mac, but I already detect signs of independence. These do not worry me; they

would be natural even among human brothers. Fitz is discovering that he is an individual; it's a process of life.

But I wonder—will Mac feel the same way?

Jan. 4, 2012. There has been a quarrel, and it has taken
me several days to learn the true details. I have never been
disturbed about quarrels between Fitz and Mac; they have
had surprisingly few for brothers. But for the first time, I
sensed that the quarrel concerned the differences between
them.

It began last week, when a boy of their age, Philip, a
hostile surly youth, involved Fitz in a fight.

Philip is the son of a divorced woman in the town, named
Mrs. Stanton. She is a strange, brooding woman, with a
terrible resentment against her ex-husband. I am afraid some
of the resentment has been passed on to her son, Philip, and
that he is an unhappy youngster. For the last two months,
Fitz has been a frequent visitor to their home, and Mrs.
Stanton has displayed great fondness for him. Philip, of
course, doesn't like this affection, this stolen love, and has
developed a strong animosity towards Fitz. One day, it
turned into violence.

Philip is big for his fifteen years, a tall boy, well over six
feet, and well muscled. When he stopped Fitz and Mac on
the street that morning, it was immediately apparent that he
was seeking trouble. Fitz is not afraid of him, I know that;
but Fitz tries to laugh trouble away. But the boy was in no
mood to be put off with a smile. He lashed out and knocked
Fitz down. When he got to his feet, Philip knocked him
down again, and then leaped atop him.

I don't know what outcome the fight would have had if
Fitz had been allowed to finish it. But he didn't have the
chance. Mac, who was standing by, watching the altercation
in his blank manner, suddenly threw himself upon his brother's assailant and pulled him away as easily as if Philip had
been an infant. He lifted him into the air with his superhuman strength and merely held him there. He didn't hurt
Philip, he traded no blows; he simply held him, helpless, in
the air, while the boy kicked and screamed his frustration
and anger. Fitz shouted at his brother to release him, and
eventually Mac did. Philip didn't resume the attack; he was
frightened by the easy, unconquerable strength in Mac's

metal arms. He turned and ran, shouting threats and ugly names over his shoulder.

Of course, I know Mac's intent was good. He was protecting his brother, and wasn't violating the code of conduct. But I can also understand Fitz's emotion. He didn't feel grateful for Mac's help, only resentful. He turned upon the robot and reviled him, called him terrible names I never knew were in his vocabulary. He told Mac that he didn't want protection, that he could fight his own battles, that he didn't require Mac's metal strength to keep him from harm. He said a great deal more, and it is well that Mac is not more sensitive than he is.

There is a strain between them now. For the last few days, Fitz has been leaving the house without Mac's company. Mac, fortunately, doesn't seem injured by his behavior. He sits, blank-faced as ever, in his room. He reads or listens to his phonograph. Sometimes, he gets up and stares into the mirror, for interminable periods.

Oct. 15, 2016. It is extraordinary, the speed with which Mac has learned his lessons. For the past year, I have been teaching him the secrets of his own construction, and how he himself could repair or improve all or part of his artificial body. He has been spending five or six hours each day in my laboratory workshop, and now I believe he is as skilled as—or perhaps more skilled than—I am myself. It will not be long before he blueprints and builds his own new body. No, not blueprint. I cannot allow him to design the plans, not yet. The Face episode proved that.

It began last Friday evening, when Fitz left the house to take Karen to the movies. As usual, Mac seemed lost without his brother, and sat quietly in his room. About midnight, he must have heard the sound of my typewriter in the study, because he came to the doorway. I invited him in and we chatted. He was curious about certain things, and asking a great number of questions about Karen. Not sex questions, particularly; Mac is as well read as any adult, and knows a good deal about human biology and human passions (I wonder sometimes what his opinion is of it all!) But he was interested in learning more about Fitz and Karen, about the nature of their relationship, the special kind of fondness Fitz seemed to display towards the girl.

I don't believe I was helpful in my answers. Half an hour

later, the front door opened and Fitz entered, bearing Karen on his arm.

Karen is a lovely young girl, with an enchanting smile and delightful face. And, if I am not mistaken, very fond of Fitz. She greeted me warmly, but I think she was surprised to see Mac; ordinarily, he kept to his room on Fitz's date nights. Mac responded to her greeting with a muffled noise in his sound system, and retreated upstairs.

I didn't see Mac the next morning, or even the next afternoon. He seemed to have spent the entire day in the workshop. We were at dinner when Fitz and I saw him first, and when we did, we gasped in surprise.

Something had happened to Mac's face, and I knew it was the result of his efforts in the workshop. Instead of the smooth, sculptured mask I had created for him, there was a crudely shaped human face looking at us, a mockery of a human face, with a badly carved nose and cheeks and lips, tinged grotesquely with the colors of the human complexion.

Our first reaction was shock, and then, explosively, laughter. When we were calm again, Mac asked us for an explanation of our outburst, and I told him, as gently as possible, that his attempts to humanize himself were far from successful. He went to a mirror and stared for a long while; then he turned without a word and went back to the laboratory. When we saw him again the next morning, he was the old Mac again. I admit I was relieved.

Oct. 9, 2020. How lost Mac seems without Fitz! Since his brother's marriage last month, he stalks about the house, lumbering like the robot child of old, clanking as if he still possessed the clumsy metal body of his infancy and adolescence. I have been trying to keep him busy in the laboratory, but I think he knows that I am indulging him rather than truly using his abilities. Not that I don't value his skill. At his young age, my robot son is as skilled a robotics engineer as any man in the country. If only the nation's robotics companies would recognize that, and overlook the fact that his ability stems from a nonhuman brain!

I have now written or personally contacted some seventeen major engineering concerns, and each of them, while polite, has turned down my suggestion. This morning, a letter arrived from the Alpha Robotics Corporation that typifies their answers.

We are certain that your description of the applicant's engineering abilities is accurate. However, our company has certain personnel standards which must be met. We will keep the application on file. . . .

There is mockery in their answer, of course. The very idea of a robot employed in the science of robotics is laughable to them. They cannot really believe that I have raised Mac as a human child would be raised, and that he is anything more than an insensitive piece of mechanism. But if any proof were needed, Mac's present state would serve— the way he is pining for his absent brother, forlorn and lonely and unhappy. I wish I could help him, but I cannot find the key to his emotions.

But there is some joy in my life today. Fitz writes me from New York that he has been accepted into a large manufacturing concern that produces small and large electrical appliances. He will become, according to his letter, a "junior executive," and he is already certain that his rise to the presidency is merely a matter of time. I chuckled as I read his letter, but if I know Fitz, there is earnestness behind his humor. My son knows what he wants from this world, and the world is duty-bound to deliver it.

November 19, 2024. I am frantic with worry, even now that I know Mac is safe. His disappearance from the house three days ago caused me endless consternation, and I was afraid that his lonely life had led him into some tragedy. But yesterday, I received this letter from Fitz:

Dear Dad,
    Don't worry about Mac, he's with me. He showed up at the apartment last night, in pretty bad shape. He must have been knocking around a bit; I'd guess he practically walked all the way into New York. He looked battered and bruised and rather frightening when I answered the door; Karen screamed and almost fainted at the sight of him. I guess she had almost forgotten about my robot brother in the past few years. I hope he wasn't too upset at her reaction; but you know how hard it is to know what Mac is thinking.
    Anyway, I took him in and got him to tell me the story. It seems he was just plain lonely and wanted to see

me; that was his reason for running off that way. I
calmed him down as best I could and suggested he stay a
day or two. I think he wanted more than that, but, Dad,
you know how impossible that is. There isn't a soul here
who even knows about Mac's existence, and he can be
awfully hard to explain. This is a bad time for me to get
mixed up in anything peculiar; as I've written you, the
firm is considering me for branch manager of the Cleve-
land office, and any publicity that doesn't cast a rosy
glow on dear old GC company can do me a lot of harm.
It's not that I don't want to help Mac, the old rustpot.
I still think of him as a brother. But I have to be
sensible. . . .

I have just finished packing, and will take the copter into
New York in the morning. I don't look forward to the trip; I
have felt very fatigued lately. There is so much work to be
done in my laboratory, and these personal crises are depriv-
ing me of time and energy. But I must bring Mac home,
before he does any harm to my son's career.

March 10, 2026. Now at last it's been explained, the real
reason for Mac's endless nights and days in the workshop. It
was the Face episode all over again, but much, much worse.
In the last year, Mac seems gripped by a strange passion
(can there be something organically wrong with his robot's
brain?), and the passion is the idea of creating a truly
humanoid body for himself. But hard as he has worked, the
effect he has gotten is so grotesque that it must be called
horrible. Now he truly appears to be a monster, and when I
expressed my distaste of what he had done, he fled from the
house as if I had struck him.

This morning, I learned of his whereabouts, and learned
the dreadful story of what had occurred after he left me.
The local police discovered him in hiding in the deserted
warehouse on Orangetree Road, and, luckily, they called
headquarters before taking any drastic action. Captain Ormandy was able to prevent any harm from coming to Mac;
the captain has become a friend of mine in the last two
years. It was he who told me the story of Mac's escapades
after he fled the house.

It will take me years to undo the harm. He has terrorized
the local residents, and actually struck one man who tried to

attack him with a coal shovel. This worries me; Mac had never broken this rule before. He went among the people of the town as if berserk, spreading fear and violence. I thank providence no great harm was done, and that he is safe with me again.

But now I must face the future, and it appears bleak. Captain Ormandy has just left me, and his words still buzz in my head. I cannot do what he asks; I cannot do away with this child of my own creation. But I am getting older, and very tired. My robot child has become a burden upon me, a burden I can barely sustain. What shall I do? What shall I do?

Dec. 8, 2027. It is good to have Fitz home, even if for so short a time, and even if it is my illness which brings him to my side. He looks so well! My heart swells with pride when I look at him. He is doing admirably, he has already earned a vice-presidency in the company that employs him, and he talks as if the future belongs to him. But more than anything, it is wonderful to be able to talk over my problem with him, to have him here to help me make the decision that must be made.

Last night, we sat in the study and discussed it for hours. I told him everything, about Mac's ever-increasing melancholy, about his untrustworthy behavior. I have told him about the proposition presented to me by the National Robotics Society, their offer to provide care for Mac. It is not the first time they have made this offer; but now the idea is far more appealing.

It was a strain for us both to discuss the matter. Fitz still feels brotherly towards Mac. But he is sensible about it, too; he recognizes the facts. He knows my health problem, he knows what a responsibility Mac is for me. And he, too, knows that Mac would be better off as a charge of the society. They would understand him. They would take good care of him.

My head is whirling. Fitz did not summarize his recommendation in so many words, and yet I know what he thinks I must do.

Feb. 5, 2027. I am locked out of my own laboratory. My robot child has taken possession, and works without ceasing. Around the clock he works; I hear the machinery grinding and roaring every minute of the day and night. He knows what will happen tomorrow, of course, that they will be coming for him from the society. What is he doing? What madness possesses him now?

Feb. 6, 2027. It is all over now, and the quiet, which fills the house lies heavily, as if entombed. In twenty-four hours, I have become the focal point of the world's horrified attention. For I am the father of the Thing which destroyed our town, the terrible metal monster that rampaged and pillaged and killed, in an orgy of insane destruction. . . .

But I must be factual, for this, the last page of my journal. Today, the thirtieth anniversary of his creation, Mac, my robot child, awaited the coming of his new captors with a body build for destruction. A monstrous, grotesque, sixty-foot body, engineered for violence and death. This had been his labor for the last two months. If the world would not accept him as human, then he would be truly a *robot*, the ancient robot of human nightmares, the destroying metal god who shows no mercy to human flesh.

I try to strike the pictures from my mind, but they are engraved there. I can see the terror on the faces of the scientists who came from the Robotics Society to claim their prize—I can hear their shrieks as he crushed the life from their bodies. I can see him stalking towards the town with his grim intent clear in every movement—to destroy all, everything, heedlessly. I can see him attacking, smashing, killing—

And then, I see the horror end. I see Captain Ormandy, moving swiftly with all the cunning of his strong young body, to fasten the cable about Mac's towering legs. I see him running headlong to the cave where the deadly black box had been planted. I see his hands on the plunger, and the mighty fire that springs from earth to sky, carrying Mac's destruction in its flames. . . .

Fitz was the last to leave me here tonight. We have talked a long time about Mac, and now that we have talked, I know the truth.

It was I who destroyed my robot child, and I who am responsible for the chaos his anger caused. I destroyed him; not today, but long ago, when he first came into being in my laboratory. For out of my science I created this life, his brother, this son, and I gave him everything. But how could I have forgotten the most important thing? I forgot to love him. . . .

THE LIFEBOAT MUTINY

BY ROBERT SHECKLEY

"Tell me the truth. Did you ever see sweeter engines?" Joe, the Interstellar Junkman asked. "And look at those servos!"

"Hmm," Gregor said judiciously.

"That hull," Joe said softly. "I bet it's five hundred years old, and not a spot of corrosion on it." He patted the burnished side of the boat affectionately. What luck, the pat seemed to say, that this paragon among vessels should be here just when AAA Ace needs a lifeboat.

"She certainly does seem rather nice," Arnold said, with the studied air of a man who has fallen in love and is trying hard not to show it. "What do you think, Dick?"

Richard Gregor didn't answer. The boat was handsome, and she looked perfect for ocean survey work on Trident. But you had to be careful about Joe's merchandise.

"They just don't build 'em this way any more," Joe sighed. "Look at the propulsion unit. Couldn't dent it with a trip-hammer. Note the capacity of the cooling system. Examine—"

"It *looks* good," Gregor said slowly. The AAA Ace Interplanetary Decontamination Service had dealt with Joe in the past, and had learned caution. Not that Joe was dishonest; far from it. The flotsam he collected from anywhere in the inhabited Universe worked. But the ancient machines often had their own ideas of how a job should be done. They tended to grow peevish when forced into another routine.

"I don't care if it's beautiful, fast, durable, or even comfortable," Gregor said defiantly. "I just want to be absolutely sure it's safe."

Joe nodded. "That's the important thing, of course. Step inside."

They entered the cabin of the boat. Joe stepped up to the instrument panel, smiled mysteriously, and pressed a button.

Immediately Gregor heard a voice which seemed to originate in his head, saying, "I am Lifeboat 324-A. My purpose—"

"Telepathy?" Gregor interrupted.

"Direct sense recording," Joe said, smiling proudly. "No language barriers that way. I told you, they just don't build 'em this way any more."

"I am Lifeboat 324-A," the boat esped again. "My primary purpose is to preserve those within me from peril, and to maintain them in good health. At present, I am only partially activated."

"Could anything be safer?" Joe cried. "This is no senseless hunk of metal. This boat will look after you. This boat *cares!*"

Gregor was impressed, even though the idea of an emotional boat was somehow distasteful. But then, paternalistic gadgets had always irritated him.

Arnold had no such feelings. "We'll take it!"

"You won't be sorry," Joe said, in the frank and open tones that had helped make him a millionaire several times over.

Gregor hoped not.

The next day, Lifeboat 324-A was loaded aboard their spaceship and they blasted off for Trident.

This planet, in the heart of the East Star Valley, had recently been bought by a real-estate speculator. He'd found her nearly perfect for colonization. Trident was the size of Mars, but with a far better climate. There was no indigenous native population to contend with, no poisonous plants, no germ-borne diseases. And, unlike so many worlds, Trident had no predatory animals. Indeed, she had no animals at all. Apart from one small island and a polar cap, the entire planet was covered with water.

There was no real shortage of land; you could wade across several of Trident's seas. The land just wasn't heaped high enough.

AAA Ace had been commissioned to correct this minor flaw.

After landing on Trident's single island, they launched the boat. The rest of the day was spent checking and loading the special survey equipment on board. Early the next morning, Gregor prepared sandwiches and filled a canteen with water. They were ready to begin work.

As soon as the mooring lines were cast off, Gregor joined Arnold in the cabin. With a small flourish, Arnold pressed the first button.

"I am Lifeboat 324-A," the boat esped. "My primary purpose is to preserve those within me from peril, and to maintain them in good health. At present, I am only partially activated. For full activation, press button two."

Gregor pressed the second button.

There was a muffled buzzing deep in the bowels of the boat. Nothing else happened.

"That's odd," Gregor said. He pressed the button again. The muffled buzz was repeated.

"Sounds like a short circuit," Arnold said.

Glancing out the forward porthole, Gregor saw the shoreline of the island slowly drifting away. He felt a touch of panic. There was so much water here, and so little land. To make matters worse, nothing on the instrument panel resembled a wheel or tiller, nothing looked like a throttle or clutch. How did you operate a partially activated lifeboat?

"She must control telepathically," Gregor said hopefully. In a stern voice he said, "Go ahead slowly."

The little boat forged ahead.

"Now right a little."

The boat responded perfectly to Gregor's clear, although unnautical command. The partners exchanged smiles.

"Straighten out," Gregor said, "and full speed ahead!"

The lifeboat charged forward into the shining, empty sea.

Arnold disappeared into the bilge with a flashlight and a circuit tester. The surveying was easy enough for Gregor to handle alone. The machines did all the work, tracing the major faults in the ocean bottom, locating the most promising volcanoes, running the flow and buildup charts.

When the survey was complete, the next stage would be turned over to a sub-contractor. He would wire the volcanoes, seed the faults, retreat to a safe distance and touch the whole thing off.

Then Trident would be, for a while, a spectacularly noisy place. And when things had quieted down, there would be enough dry land to satisfy even a real-estate speculator.

By mid-afternoon Gregor felt that they had done enough surveying for one day. He and Arnold ate their sandwiches and drank from the canteen. Later they took a short swim in Trident's clear green water

"I think I've found the trouble," Arnold said. "The leads to the primary activators have been removed. And the power cable's been cut."

"Why would anyone do that?" Gregor asked.

Arnold shrugged. "Might have been part of the decommissioning. I'll have it right in a little while."

He crawled back into the bilge. Gregor turned in the direction of the island, steering telepathically and watching the green water foam merrily past the bow. At moments like this, contrary to all his previous experience, the Universe seemed a fine and friendly place.

In half an hour Arnold emerged, grease-stained but triumphant. "Try that button now," he said.

"But we're almost back."

"So what? Might as well have this thing working right."

Gregor nodded, and pushed the second button.

They could hear the faint click-click of circuits opening. Half a dozen small engines purred into life. A light flashed red, then winked off as the generators took up the load.

"That's more like it," Arnold said.

"I am Lifeboat 324-A," the boat stated telepathically. "I am now fully activated, and able to protect my occupants from danger. Have faith in me. My action-response tapes, both psychological and physical, have been prepared by the best scientific minds in all Drome."

"Gives you quite a feeling of confidence, doesn't it?" Arnold said.

"I suppose so," Gregor said. "But where is Drome?"

"Gentlemen," the lifeboat continued, "try to think of

me, not as an unfeeling mechanism, but as your friend and comrade-in-arms. I understand how you feel. You have seen your ship go down, cruelly riddled by the implacable H'gen. You have—"

"What ship?" Gregor asked. "What's it talking about?"

"—crawled aboard me, dazed, gasping from the poisonous fumes of water; half-dead—"

"You mean that swim we took?" Arnold asked. "You've got it all wrong. We were just surveying—"

"—shocked, wounded, morale low," the lifeboat finished. "You are a little frightened, perhaps," it said in a softer mental tone. "And well you might be, separated from the Drome fleet and adrift upon an inclement alien planet. A little fear is nothing to be ashamed of, gentlemen. But this is war, and war is a cruel business. We have no alternative but to drive the barbaric H'gen back across space."

"There must be a reasonable explanation for all this," Gregor said. "Probably an old television script got mixed up in its response bank."

"We'd better give it a complete overhaul," Arnold said. "Can't listen to that stuff all day."

They were approaching the island. The lifeboat was still babbling about home and hearth, evasive action, tactical maneuvers, and the need for calm in emergencies like this. Suddenly it slowed.

"What's the matter?" Gregor asked.

"I am scanning the island," the lifeboat answered.

Gregor and Arnold glanced at each other. "Better humor it," Arnold whispered. To the lifeboat he said. "That island's okay. We checked it personally."

"Perhaps you did," the lifeboat answered. "But in modern, lightning-quick warfare, Drome senses cannot be trusted. They are too limited, too prone to interpret what they wish. Electronic senses on the other hand, are emotionless, eternally vigilant, and infallible within their limits."

"But there isn't anything there!" Gregor shouted.

"I perceive a foreign spaceship," the lifeboat answered. "It has no Drome markings."

"It hasn't any enemy markings, either," Arnold answered confidently, since he had painted the ancient hull himself.

"No, it hasn't. But in war, we must assume that what is not ours is the enemy's. I understand your desire to set foot on land again. But I take into account factors that a Drome, motivated by his emotions, would overlook. Consider the apparent emptiness of this strategic bit of land; the unmarked spaceship put temptingly out for bait; the fact that our fleet is no longer in this vicinity; the—"

"All right, that's enough," Gregor was sick of arguing with a verbose and egoistic machine. "Go directly to that island. That's an order."

"I cannot obey that order," the boat said. "You are unbalanced from your harrowing escape from death—"

Arnold reached for the cutout switch, and withdrew his hand with a howl of pain.

"Come to your senses, gentlemen," the boat said sternly. "Only the decommissioning officer is empowered to turn me off. For your own safety, I must warn you not to touch any of my controls. You are mentally unbalanced. Later, when our position is safer, I will administer to you. Now my full energies must be devoted toward detection and escape from the enemy."

The boat picked up speed and moved away from the island in an intricate evasive pattern.

"Where are we going?" Gregor asked.

"To rejoin the Drome fleet!" the lifeboat cried so confidently that the partners stared nervously over the vast, deserted waters of Trident.

"As soon as I can find it, that is," the lifeboat amended.

It was late at night. Gregor and Arnold sat in a corner of the cabin, hungrily sharing their last sandwich. The lifeboat was still rushing madly over the waves, its every electronic sense alert, searching for a fleet that had existed five hundred years ago, upon an entirely different planet.

"Did you ever hear of these Dromes?" Gregor asked.

Arnold searched through his vast store of minutiae. "They were non-human, lizard-evolved creatures" he said. "Lived on the sixth planet of some little system near Capella. The race died out over a century ago."

"And the H'gen?"

"Also lizards. Same story." Arnold found a crumb and

popped it into his mouth. "It wasn't a very important war. All the combatants are gone. Except this lifeboat, apparently."

"And us," Gregor reminded him. "We've been drafted as Drome soldiery." He sighed wearily. "Do you think we can reason with this tub?"

Arnold shook his head. "I don't see how. As far as this boat is concerned, the war is still on. It can only interpret data in terms of that premise."

"It's probably listening in on us now," Gregor said.

"I don't think so. It's not really a mind-reader. Its perception centers are geared only to thoughts aimed specifically at it."

"Yes siree," Gregor said bitterly, "they just don't build 'em this way any more." He wished he could get his hands on Joe, the Interstellar Junkman.

"It's actually a very interesting situation," Arnold said. "I may do an article on it for *Popular Cybernetics*. Here is a machine with nearly infallible apparatus for the perception of external stimuli. The percepts it receives are translated logically into action. The only trouble is, the logic is based upon no longer existent conditions. Therefore, you could say that the machine is the victim of a systematized delusional system."

Gregor yawned. "You mean the lifeboat is just plain nuts," he said bluntly.

"Nutty as a fruitcake. I believe paranoia would be the proper designation. But it'll end pretty soon."

"Why?" Gregor asked.

"It's obvious," Arnold said. "The boat's prime directive is to keep us alive. So he has to feed us. Our sandwiches are gone, and the only other food is on the island. I figure he'll have to take a chance and go back."

In a few minutes they could feel the lifeboat swinging, changing direction. It esped, "At present I am unable to locate the Drome fleet. Therefore, I am running back to scan the island once again. Fortunately, there are no enemy in this immediate area. Now I can devote myself to your care with all the power of my full attention."

"You see?" Arnold said, nudging Gregor. "Just as I said. Now we'll reinforce the concept." He said to the lifeboat, "About time you got around to us. We're hungry."

"Yeah, feed us," Gregor demanded.

"Of course," the lifeboat said. A tray slid out of the wall. It was heaped high with something that looked like clay, but smelled like machine oil.

"What's that supposed to be?" Gregor asked.

"That is geezel," the lifeboat said. "It is the staple diet of the Drome peoples. I can prepare it in sixteen different ways."

Gregor cautiously sampled it. It tasted just like clay coated with machine oil.

"We can't eat that!" he objected.

"Of course you can," the boat said soothingly. "An adult Drome consumes five point three pounds of geezel a day, and cries for more."

The tray slid toward them. They backed away from it.

"Now listen," Arnold told the boat. "We are *not* Dromes. We're humans, an entirely different species. The war you think you're fighting ended five hundred years ago. We can't eat geezel. Our food is on that island."

"Try to grasp the situation. Your delusion is a common one among fighting men. It is an escape fantasy, a retreat from an intolerable situation. Gentlemen, I beg you, face reality!"

"You face reality!" Gregor screamed. "Or I'll have you dismantled bolt by bolt."

"Threats do not disturb me," the lifeboat esped serenely. "I know what you've been through. Possibly you have suffered some brain damage from your exposure to poisonous water."

"Poison?" Gregor gulped.

"By Drome standards," Arnold reminded him.

"If absolutely necessary," the lifeboat continued, "I am also equipped to perform physical brain therapy. It is a dramatic measure, but there can be no coddling in time of war." A panel slid open, and the partners glimpsed shining surgical edges.

"We're feeling better already," Gregor said hastily. "Fine looking batch of geezel, eh, Arnold?"

"Delicious," Arnold said, wincing.

"I won a nationwide contest in geezel preparation," the lifeboat esped, with pardonable pride. "Nothing is too good for our boys in uniform. Do try a little."

Gregor lifted a handful, smacked his lips, and set it down on the floor. "Wonderful," he said, hoping that the boat's internal scanners weren't as efficient as the external ones seemed to be.

Apparently they were not. "Good," the lifeboat said. "I am moving toward the island now. And, I promise you, in a little while you will be more comfortable."

"Why?" Arnold asked.

"The temperature here is unbearably hot. It's amazing that you haven't gone into coma. Any other Drome would have. Try to bear it a little longer. Soon, I'll have it down to the Drome norm of twenty degrees below zero. And now, to assist your morale, I will play our national Anthem."

A hideous rhythmic screeching filled the air. Waves slapped against the sides of the hurrying lifeboat. In a few moments, the air was perceptibly cooler.

Gregor closed his eyes wearily, trying to ignore the chill that was spreading through his limbs. He was becoming sleepy. Just his luck, he thought, to be frozen to death inside an insane lifeboat. It was what come of buying paternalistic gadgets, high-strung, humanistic calculators, over-sensitive, emotional machines.

Dreamily he wondered where it was all leading to. He pictured a gigantic machine hospital. Two robot doctors were wheeling a lawnmower down a long white corridor. The Chief Robot Doctor was saying, "What's wrong with this lad?" And the assistant answered, "Completely out of his mind. Thinks he's a helicopter." "Aha!" the Chief said knowingly. "Flying fantasies! Pity. Nice looking chap." The assistant nodded. "Overwork did it. Broke his heart on crab grass." The lawnmower stirred. "Now I'm an eggbeater!" he giggled.

"Wake up," Arnold said, shaking Gregor, his teeth chattering. "We have to do something."

"Ask him to turn on the heat," Gregor said groggily.

"Not a chance. Dromes live at twenty below. We are Dromes. Twenty below for us, and no back talk."

Frost was piled deep on the coolant tubes that traversed the boat. The walls had begun to turn white, and the portholes were frosted over.

"I've got an idea," Arnold said cautiously. He glanced at the control board, then whispered quickly in Gregor's ear.

"We'll try it," Gregor said. They stood up. Gregor picked

up the canteen and walked stiffly to the far side of the cabin.

"What are you doing?" the lifeboat asked sharply.

"Going to get a little exercise," Gregor said. "Drome soldiers must stay fit, you know."

"That's true," the lifeboat said dubiously.

Gregor threw the canteen to Arnold.

Arnold chuckled synthetically and threw the canteen back to Gregor.

"Be careful with that receptacle," the lifeboat warned. "It is filled with a deadly poison."

"We'll be careful," Gregor said. "We're taking it back to headquarters." He threw the canteen to Arnold.

"Headquarters may spray it on the H'gen," Arnold said, throwing the canteen back.

"Really?" the lifeboat asked. "That's interesting. A new application of—"

Suddenly Gregor swung the canteen against the coolant tube. The tube broke and liquid poured over the floor.

"Bad shot, old man," Arnold said.

"How careless of me," Gregor cried.

"I should have taken precautions against internal accidents," the lifeboat esped gloomily. "It won't happen again. But the situation is very serious. I cannot repair the tube myself. I am unable to properly cool the boat."

"If you just drop us on the island—" Arnold began.

"Impossible!" the lifeboat said. "My first duty is to preserve your lives, and you could not live long in the climate of this planet. But I am going to take the necessary measures to ensure your safety."

"What are you going to do?" Gregor asked, with a sinking feeling in the pit of his stomach.

"There is no time to waste. I will scan the island once more. If our Drome forces are not present, we will go to the one place on this planet that can sustain Drome life."

"What place?"

"The southern polar cap," the lifeboat said. "The climate there is almost ideal—thirty below zero, I estimate."

The engines roared. Apologetically the boat added. "And, of course, I must guard against any further internal accidents."

As the lifeboat charged forward they could hear the click of the locks, sealing their cabin.

*   *   *

"Think!" Arnold said.

"I am thinking," Gregor answered. "But nothing's coming out."

"We must get off when he reaches the island. It'll be our last chance."

"You don't think we could jump overboard?" Gregor asked.

"Never. He's watching now. If you hadn't smashed the coolant tube, we'd still have a chance."

"I know," Gregor said bitterly. "You and your ideas."

"My ideas! I distinctly remember you suggesting it. You said—"

"It doesn't matter whose idea it was." Gregor thought deeply. "Look, we know his internal scanning isn't very good. When we reach the island, maybe we could cut his power cable."

"You wouldn't get within five feet of it," Arnold said, remembering the shock he had received from the instrument panel.

"Hmm." Gregor locked both hands around his head. An idea was beginning to form in the back of his mind. It was pretty tenuous, but under the circumstances . . .

"I am now scanning the island," the lifeboat announced.

Looking out the forward porthole, Gregor and Arnold could see the island, no more than a hundred yards away. The first flush of dawn was in the sky, and outlined against it was the scarred, beloved snout of their spaceship.

"Place looks fine to me," Arnold said.

"It sure does," Gregor agreed. "I'll bet our forces are dug in underground."

"They are not," the lifeboat said. "I scanned to a depth of a hundred feet."

"Well," Arnold said, "under the circumstances, I think we should examine a little more closely. I'd better go ashore and look around."

"It is deserted," the lifeboat said. "Believe me, my senses are infinitely more acute than yours. I cannot let you endanger your lives by going ashore. Drome needs her soldiers—especially sturdy, heat-resistant types like you."

"We like this climate," Arnold said.

"Spoken like a patriot!" the lifeboat said heartily. "I know how you must be suffering. But now I am going to the south pole, to give you veterans the rest you deserve."

*   *   *

Gregor decided it was time for his plan, no matter how vague it was. "That won't be necessary," he said.

"What?"

"We are operating under special orders," Gregor said. "We weren't supposed to disclose them to any vessel below the rank of super-dreadnaught. But under the circumstances—"

"Yes, under the circumstances," Arnold chimed in eagerly, "we will tell you."

"We are a suicide squad," Gregor said.

"Especially trained for hot climate work."

"Our orders," Gregor said, "are to land and secure that island for the Drome forces."

"I didn't know that," the boat said.

"You weren't supposed to," Arnold told it. "After all, you're only a lifeboat."

"Land us at once," Gregor said. "There's no time to lose."

"You should have told me sooner," the boat said. "I couldn't guess, you know." It began to move toward the island.

Gregor could hardly breathe. It didn't seem possible that the simple trick would work. But then, why not? The lifeboat was built to accept the word of its operators as the truth. As long as the 'truth' was consistent with the boat's operational premises, it would be carried out.

The beach was only fifty yards away now, gleaming white in the cold light of dawn.

Then the boat reversed its engines and stopped. "No," it said.

"No what?"

"I cannot do it."

"What do you mean?" Arnold shouted. "This is war! Orders—"

"I know," the lifeboat said sadly. "I am sorry. A differently type of vessel should have been chosen for this mission. Any other type. But not a *life*boat."

"You must," Gregor begged. "Think of our country, think of the barbaric H'gen—"

"It is physically impossible for me to carry out your orders," the lifeboat told them. "My prime directive is to protect my occupants from harm. That order is stamped on my every tape, giving priority over all others. I cannot let you go to your certain death."

The boat began to move away from the island.

"You'll be court-martialed for this!" Arnold screamed hysterically. "They'll decommission you."

"I must operate within my limitations," the boat said sadly. "If we find the fleet, I will transfer you to a killerboat. But in the meantime, I must take you to the safety of the south pole."

The lifeboat picked up speed, and the island receded behind them. Arnold rushed at the controls and was thrown flat. Gregor picked up the canteen and poised it, to hurl ineffectually at the sealed hatch. He stopped himself in mid-swing, struck by a sudden wild thought.

"Please don't attempt any more destruction," the boat pleaded. "I know how you feel, but—"

It was damned risky, Gregor thought, but the south pole was certain death anyhow.

He uncapped the canteen. "Since we cannot accomplish our mission," he said, "we can never again face our comrades. Suicide is the only alternative." He took a gulp of water and handed the canteen to Arnold.

"No! Don't!" the lifeboat shrieked. "That's *water!* It's a deadly poison—"

An electrical bolt leaped from the instrument panel, knocking the canteen from Arnold's hand.

Arnold grabbed the canteen. Before the boat could knock it again from his hand, he had taken a drink.

"We die for glorious Drome!" Gregor dropped to the floor. He motioned Arnold to lie still.

"There is no known antidote," the boat moaned. "If only I could contact a hospital ship . . ." Its engines idled indecisively. "Speak to me," the boat pleaded. "Are you still alive?"

Gregor and Arnold lay perfectly still, not breathing.

"Answer me!" the lifeboat begged. "Perhaps if you ate some geezel . . ." It thrust out two trays. The partners didn't stir.

"Dead," the lifeboat said. "*Dead.* I will read the burial service."

* * *

There was a pause. Then the lifeboat intoned, "Great Spirit of the Universe, take into your custody the souls of these, your servants. Although they died by their own hand, still it was in the service of their country, fighting for home and hearth. Judge them not harshly for their impious deed. Rather blame the spirit of war that inflames and destroys all Drome."

The hatch swung open. Gregor could feel a rush of cool morning air.

"And now, by the authority vested in me by the Drome Fleet, and with all reverence, I commend their bodies to the deep."

Gregor felt himself being lifted through the hatch to the deck. Then he was in the air, falling, and in another moment he was in the water, with Arnold beside him.

"Float quietly," he whispered.

The island was nearby. But the lifeboat was still hovering close to them, nervously roaring its engines.

"What do you think it's up to now?" Arnold whispered.

"I don't know," Gregor said, hoping that the Drome peoples didn't believe in converting their bodies to ashes.

The lifeboat came closer. Its bow was only a few feet away. They tensed. And then they heard it. The roaring screech of the Drome National Anthem.

In a moment it was finished. The lifeboat murmured, "Rest in peace," turned, and roared away.

As they swam slowly to the island, Gregor saw that the lifeboat was heading south, due south, to the pole, to wait for the Drome fleet.

THE WARM SPACE

BY DAVID BRIN

1.

JASON FORBS (S-62B/129876Rd (bio-human): REPORT AT ONCE TO PROJECT LIGHTPROBE FOR IMMEDIATE ASSUMPTION OF DUTIES AS "DESIGNATED ORAL WITNESS ENGINEER."
—BY ORDER OF DIRECTOR

Jason let the flimsy message slip from his fingers, fluttering in the gentle, centrifugal pseudo-gravity of the station apartment. Coriolis force—or perhaps the soft breeze from the wall vents—caused it to drift past the edge of the table and land on the floor of the small dining nook.

"Are you going to go?" Elaine asked nervously from Jesse's crib, where she had just put the baby down for a nap. Wide eyes made plain her fear.

"What choice do I have?" Jason shrugged. "My number was drawn. I can't disobey. Not the way the Utilitarian Party has been pushing its weight around. Under the Required Services Act, I'm just another motile, sentient unit, of some small use to the state."

That was true, as far as it went. Jason did not feel it necessary to add that he had actually volunteered for this mission. There was no point. Elaine would never understand.

A woman with a child doesn't need to look for justifications for her existence, Jason thought as he gathered what he would need from the closet.

But I'm tired of being an obsolete, token representative of the Old Race, looked down upon by all the sleek new types. At least this way my kid may be able to say his old man had been good for something, once. It might help Jesse hold his head up in the years to come . . . years sure to be hard for the old style of human being.

He zipped up his travel suit, making sure of the vac-tight ankle and wrist fastenings. Elaine came to him and slipped into his arms.

"You could try to delay them," she suggested without conviction. "System-wide elections are next month. The Ethicalists and the Naturalists have declared a united campaign. . . ."

Jason stroked her hair, shaking his head. Hope was deadly. They could not afford it.

"It's no use, Elaine. The Utilitarians are completely in charge out here at the station, as well as nearly everywhere else in the solar system. Anyway, everyone knows the election is a foregone conclusion."

The words stung, but they were truthful. On paper, it would seem there was still a chance for a change. Biological humans still outnumbered the mechanical and cyborg citizen types, and even a large minority of the latter had misgivings about the brutally logical policies of the Utilitarian Party.

But only one biological human in twenty bothered to vote any more.

There were still many areas of creativity and skill in which mechano-cryo citizens were no better than organics, but a depressing conviction weighed heavily upon the old type. They knew they had no place in the future. The stars belonged to the other varieties, not to them.

"I've got to go." Gently, Jason peeled free of Elaine's arms. He took her face in his hands and kissed her one last time, then picked up his small travel bag and helmet. Stepping out into the corridor, he did not look back to see the tears that he knew were there, laying soft, saltwater history down her face.

2.

The quarters for biological human beings lay in the Old Wheel . . . a part of the research station that had grown ever shabbier as old style scientists and technicians lost their places to models better suited to the harsh environment of space.

Once, back in the days when mechano-cryo citizens were

rare, the Old Wheel had been the center of excited activity here beyond the orbit of Neptune. The first starships had been constructed by clouds of space-suited humans, like tethered bees swarming over mammoth hives. Giant "slowboats," restricted to speeds far below that of light, had ventured forth from here, into the interstellar night.

That had been long ago, when organic people had still been important. But even then there were those who had foreseen what was to come.

Nowhere were the changes of the last century more apparent than here at Project Lightprobe. The old type now only served in support roles, few contributing directly to the investigations . . . perhaps the most important in human history.

Jason's vac-sled was stored in the Old Wheel's north hub airlock. Both sled and suit checked out well, but the creaking outer doors stuck halfway open when he tried to leave. He had to leap over with a spanner and pound the great hinges several times to get them unfrozen. The airlock finally opened in fits and starts.

Frowning, he remounted the sled and took off again.

The Old Wheel gets only scraps for maintenance, he thought glumly. Soon there'll be an accident, and the Utilitarians will use it as an excuse to ban organic humans from every research station in the solar system.

The Old Wheel fell behind as short puffs of gas sent his sled toward the heart of the research complex. For a long time he seemed to ride the slowly rotating wheel's shadow, eclipsing the dim glow of the distant sun.

From here, Earth-home was an invisible speck. Few ever focused telescopes on the old world. Everyone knew that the future wasn't back there but out here and beyond, with the innumerable stars covering the sky.

Gliding slowly across the gulf between the Old Wheel and the Complex, Jason had plenty of time to think.

Back when the old slowboats had set forth from here to explore the nearest systems, it had soon became apparent that only mechanicals and cyborgs were suited for interstellar voyages. Asteroid-sized arks—artificial worldlets capable of carrying entire ecospheres—remained a dream out of science fiction, economically beyond reach. Exploration ships could be sent much farther and faster if they did not have to carry the complex artifical environments required by old style human beings.

By now ten nearby stellar systems had been explored, all by crews consisting of "robo-humans." There were no plans to send any other kind, even if, or when, Earthlike planets were discovered. It just wouldn't be worth the staggering investment required.

That fact, more than anything else, had struck at the morale of biological people in the solar system. The stars, they realized, were not for them. Resignation led to a turning away from science and the future. Earth and the "dirt" colonies were apathetic places, these days. Utilitariansism was the guiding philosophy of the times.

Jason hadn't told his wife his biggest reason for volunteering for this mission. He was still uncertain he understood it very well himself. Perhaps he wanted to show people that a biological citizen could still be useful, and contribute to the advance of knowledge.

Even if it were by a task so humble as a suicide mission.

He saw the lightship ahead, just below the shining spark of Sirius, a jet-black pearl half a kilometer across. Already he could make out the shimmering of its fields as its mighty engines were tuned for the experiment ahead.

The technicians were hoping that this time it would work. But even if it failed again, they were determined to go on trying. Faster-than-light travel was not something anyone gave up on easily, even a robot with a life span of five hundred years. The dream, and the obstinacy to pursue it, was a strong inheritance from the parent race.

Next to the black experimental probe, with its derricks and workshops, was the towering bulk of the central cooling plant, by far the largest object in the Complex. The cooling plant made even the Old Wheel look like a child's toy hoop. Jason's rickety vac-sled puffed beneath the majestic globe, shining in the sky like a great silvery planet.

On this, the side facing the sun, the cooling globe's reflective surface was nearly perfect. On the other side, a giant array of fluid-filled radiators stared out on to intergalactic space, chilling liquid helium down to the basic temperature of the universe—a few degrees above absolute zero.

The array had to stare at the blackness between the galaxies. Faint sunlight—even starlight—would heat the cooling fluid too much. That was the reason for the silvery reflective backing. The amount of infrared radiation leaving the finned coolers had to exceed the few photons coming in in order for the temperature of the helium to drop far enough.

The new types of citizens might be faster and tougher, and in some ways smarter, than old style humans. They might need neither food nor sleep. But they did require a lot of liquid helium to keep their supercooled, superconducting brains humming. The shining, well-maintained cooling plant was a reminder of the priorities of the times.

Some years back, an erratic bio-human had botched an attempt to sabotage the cooling plant. All it accomplished was to have the old style banished from that part of the station. And some mechano-cryo staff members who had previously been sympathetic with the Ethicalist cause switched to Utilitarianism as a result.

The mammoth sphere passed over and behind Jason. In moments there was only the lightship ahead, shimmering within its cradle of spotlit gantries. A voice cut in over his helmet speaker in a sharp monotone.

"Attention approaching biological . . . you are entering a restricted zone. Identify yourself at once."

Jason grimaced. The station director had ordered all mechano personnel—meaning just about everybody left—to reprogram their voice functions along "more logical tonal lines." That meant they no longer mimicked natural human intonations, but spoke in a new, shrill whine.

Jason's few android and cyborg friends—colleagues on the support staff—had whispered their regrets. But those days it was dangerous to be in the minority. All soon adjusted to the new order.

"Jason Forbs, identifying self." He spoke as crisply as possible, mimicking the toneless Utilitarian dialect. He spelled his name and gave his ident code. "Oral witness engineer for Project Lightprobe, reporting for duty."

There was a pause, then the unseen security overseer spoke again.

"Cleared and identified, Jason Forbs. Proceed directly to slip nine, scaffold B. Escorts await your arrival."

Jason blinked. Had the voice softened perceptibly? A closet Ethicalist, perhaps, out here in this Utilitarian stronghold.

"Success, and an operative return are approved outcomes," the voice added, hesitantly, with just a hint of tonality.

Jason understood Utilitarian dialect well enough to interpret the simple good luck wish. He didn't dare thank the fellow, whoever he might be, whatever his body form. But he appreciated the gesture.

"Acknowledged," he said, and switched off. Ahead, under stark shadows cast by spotlights girdling the starship, Jason saw at least a dozen scientists and technicians, waiting for him by a docking slip. One or two of the escorts actually appeared to be fidgeting as he made his final maneuvers into the slot.

They came in all shapes and sizes. Several wore little globe-bot bodies. Spider forms were also prominent. Jason hurriedly tied the sled down, almost slipping as he secured his magnectic boots to the platform.

He knew his humaniform shape looked gawky and unsuited to this environment. But he was determined to maintain some degree of dignity. Your ancestors *made* these guys, he reminded himself. And old style people built this very station. We're all citizens under the law, from the director down to the janitor-bot, all the way down to me.

Still, he felt awkward under their glistening camera eyes.

"Come quickly, Jason Forbs." His helmet speaker whined and a large mechanical form gestured with one slender, articulated arm. "There is little time before the test begins. We must instruct you in your duties."

Jason recognized the favorite body-form of the director, an antibiological Utilitarian of the worst sort. The machine-scientist swiveled at the hips and rolled up the gangplank. Steam-like vapor puffed from vents in the official's plasteel carapace. It was an ostentatious display, to release evaporated helium that way. It demonstrated that the assistant director could keep his circuits as comfortably cool as anybody's, and hang the expense.

An awkward human in the midst of smoothly gliding machines, Jason glanced backward for what he felt sure would be his last direct view of the universe. He had hoped to catch a final glimpse of the Old Wheel, or at least the sun. But all he could see was the great hulk of the cooling plant, staring out into the space between the galaxies, keeping cool the lifeblood of the apparent inheritors of the solar system.

The director called again, impatiently. Jason turned and stepped through the hatch to be shown his station and his job.

3.

"You will remember not to touch any of the controls at any time. The ship's operation is automatic. Your function is purely to observe and maintain a running oral monologue into the tape recorder."

The director sounded disgusted. "I will not pretend that I agree with the decision to include a biological entity in this experiment. Perhaps it was because you are expendable, and we have already lost too many valuable mechano-persons in these tests. In any event, the reasons are not of your concern. You are to remain at your station, leaving only to take care of"—the voice lowered in distaste and the shining cells of the official's eyes looked away—"to take care of bodily functions. A refresher unit has been installed behind that hatchway."

Jason shrugged. He was getting sick of the pretense.

"Wasn't that a lot of expense to go to? I mean, whatever's been killing the silicon and cyborg techs who rode the other ships is hardly likely to leave me alive long enough to get hungry or go to the bathroom."

The official nodded, a gesture so commonly used that it had been retained even in Utilitarian fashion.

"We share an opinion, then. Nevertheless, it is not known at what point in the mission the . . . malfunctions occur. The minimum duration in hyperspace is fifteen days, the engines cannot cut the span any shorter. After that time the ship emerges at a site at least five light-years away. It will take another two weeks to return to the solar system. You will continue your running commentary throughout that period, if necessary, to supplement what the instruments tell us."

Jason almost laughed at the ludicrous order. Of course he would be dead long before his voice gave out. The techs and scientists who went out on the earlier tests had all been made of tougher stuff than he, and none of them had survived.

Until a year ago, none of the faster-than-light starships

had even returned. Some scientists had even contended that the theory behind their contruction was in error, somehow.

At last, simple mechanical auto-pilots were installed, in case the problem had to do with the crews themselves. The gamble paid off. After that the ships returned . . . filled with corpses.

Jason had only a rough impression of what had happened to the other expeditions, all from unreliable scuttlebutt. The official story was still a state secret. But rumor had it the prior crews had all died of horrible violence.

Some said they had apparently gone mad and turned on each other. Others suggested that the fields that drove the ship through that strange realm known as hyperspace twisted the shapes of things within the ship—not sufficiently to affect the cruder machines, but enough to cause the subtle, cryogenic circuitry of the scientists and techs to go haywire.

One thing Jason was sure of: anything that could harm mechano-cryos would easily suffice to do in a biological. He was resigned, but all the same determined to do his part. If some small thing he noticed, and commented on into the tape machine, led to a solution—maybe some little thing missed by all the recording devices—then Terran civilization would have the stars.

That would be something for his son to remember, even if the true inheritors would be "human" machines.

"All right," he told the director. "Take this bunch of gawkers with you and let's go on with it."

He strapped himself into the observer's chair, behind the empty pilot's seat. He did not even look up as the technicians and officials filed out and closed the hatch behind them.

4.

In the instant after launching, the lightship made an eerie trail across the sky. Cylindrical streaks of pseudo-Cerenkov radiation lingered long after the black globe had disappeared, bolting faster and faster toward its rendezvous with hyperspace.

The director turned to the emissary from Earth.

"It is gone. Now we wait. One Earth-style month. "I will state, one more time, that I did not approve willingly of the inclusion of the organic form aboard the ship. I object to the

inelegant modifications required in order to suit the ship to
. . . to biological functions. Also, old style humans are three
times as often subject to irrational impulses than more modern forms. This one may take it into its head to try to
change the ship's controls when the fatal stress begins."

Unlike the director, the visiting councilor wore a humaniform
body, with legs, arms, torso and head. He expressed his
opinion with a shrug of his subtly articulated shoulders.

"You exaggerate the danger, Director. Don't you think I
know that the controls Jason Forbs sees in front of him are
only dummies?"

The director swiveled quickly to stare at the councilor.
How—?

He made himself calm down. *It—doesn't—matter.* So what
if he knew that fact? Even the sole Ethicalist member of the
Solar System Council could not make much propaganda of
it. It was only a logical precaution to take, under the
circumstances.

"The designated oral witness engineer should spend his
living moments performing his function," the director said
coolly. "Recording his subjective impressions as long as he
is able. It is the role you commanded we open up for an old
style human, using your peremptory authority as a member
of the council."

The other's humaniform face flexed in a traditional, pseudo-
organic smile, archaic in its mimicry of the Old Race. And
yet the director, schooled in Utilitarian belief, felt uneasy
under the councilor's gaze.

"I had a peremptory commandment left to use up before
the elections," the councilor said smoothly in old-fashioned,
modulated tones. "I judged that this would be an appropriate way to use it."

He did not explain further. The director quashed an urge
to push the question. What was the Ethicalist up to? Why
waste a peremptory command on such a minor, futile thing
as this? How could he gain anything by sending an old style
human out to his certain death!

Was it to be some sort of gesture? Something aimed at
getting out the biological vote for the upcoming elections?

If so, it was doomed to failure. In-depth psychological
studies had indicated that the level of resignation and apa-
thy among organic citizens was too high to ever be overcome by anything so simple.

Perhaps, though, it might be enough to save the seat of the one Ethicalist on the council . . .

The director felt warm. He knew that it was partly subjective—resentment of this invasion of his domain by a ridiculous sentimentalist. Most of all, the director resented the feelings he felt boiling within himself.

Why, *why* do we modern forms have to be cursed with this burden of emotionalism and uncertainty! I hate it!

Of course he knew the reasons. Back in ancient times, fictional "robots" had been depicted as caricatures of jerky motion and rigid, formal thinking. The writers of those precryo days had not realized that complexity commanded flexibility . . . even fallibility. The laws of physics were adamant on this. Uncertainty accompanied subtlety. An advanced mind had to have the ability to question itself, or creativity was lost.

The director loathed the fact, but he understood it.

Still, he suspected that the biologists had played a trick on his kind, long ago. He and other Utilitarians had an idea that there had been some deep programming, below anything nowadays accessed, to make mechano-people as much like the old style as possible.

If I ever had proof it was true . . . he thought, gloweringly, threateningly.

Ah, but it doesn't matter. The biologicals will be extinct in a few generations, anyway. They're dying of a sense of their own uselessness.

Good riddance!

"I will leave you now, Councilor. Unless you wish to accompany me to recharge on refrigerants?"

The Ethicalist bowed slightly, ironically, aware, of course, that the director could not return the gesture. "No, thank you, Director. I shall wait here and contemplate for a while.

"Before you go, however, please let me make one thing clear. It may seem, at times, as if I am not sympathetic with your work here. But that is not true. After all, we're all humans, all citizens. Everybody wants Project Lightprobe to succeed. The dream is one we inherit from our makers . . . to go out and live among the stars.

"I am only acting to help bring that about—for *all* of our people."

The director felt unaccountably warmer. He could not

think of an answer. "I require helium," he said, curtly, and swiveled to leave. "Good bye, Councilor."

The director felt as if eyes were watching his armored back as he sped down the hallway.

Damn the biologicals and their allies! he cursed within. Damn them for making us so insidiously like them . . . emotional, fallible and, worst of all, uncertain!

Wishing the last of the old style were already dust on their dirty, wet little planet, the director hurried away to find himself a long, cold drink.

5.

"Six hours and ten minutes into the mission, four minutes since breakover into hyperspace . . ." Jason breathed into the microphone. "So far so good. I'm a little thirsty, but I believe it's just a typical adrenaline fear reaction. Allowing for expected tension, I feel fine."

Jason went on to describe everything he could see, the lights, the controls, the readings on the computer displays, his physical feelings . . . he went on until his throat felt dry and he found he was repeating himself.

"I'm getting up out of the observer's seat, now, to go get a drink." He slipped the recorder strap over his shoulder and unbuckled from the flight chair. There was a feeling of weight, as the techs had told him to expect. About a tenth of a g. It was enough to make walking possible. He flexed his legs and moved about the control room, describing every aspect of the experience. Then he went to the refrigerator and took out a squeeze-tube of lemonade.

Jason was frankly surprised to be alive. He knew the previous voyagers had lived several days before their unknown catastrophe struck. But they had been a lot tougher than he. Perhaps the mysterious lethal agency had taken nearly all the fifteen days of the minimum first leg of the round trip to do them in.

If so, he wondered, how long will it take to get me?

A few hours later, the failure of anything to happen was starting to make him nervous. He cut down the rate of his running commentary in order to save his voice. Besides, nothing much seemed to be changing. The ship was cruising, now. All the dials and indicators were green and steady.

During sleep period he tossed in the sleeping hammock, sharing it with disturbed dreams. He awakened several times impelled by a sense of duty and imminent danger, clutching his recorder tightly. But when he stared about the control room he could find nothing amiss.

By the third day he had had enough.

"I'm going to poke around in the instruments," he spoke into the microphone. "I know I was told not to. And I'll certainly not touch anything having to do with the functioning of the ship. But I figure I deserve a chance to see what I'm traveling through. Nobody's ever looked out on hyperspace. I'm going to take a look."

Jason set about the task with a feeling of exultation. What he was doing wouldn't hurt anything, just alter a few of the sensors.

Sure, it was against orders, but if he got back alive he would be famous, too important to bother with charges over such a minor infraction.

Not that he believed, for even a moment, that he was coming home alive.

It was a fairly intricate task, rearranging a few of the ship's programs so the external cameras—meant to be used at the destination star only—would work in hyperspace. He wondered if it had been some sort of Utilitarian gesture not to include viewing ports, or to do the small modifications of scanning electronics necessary to make the cameras work here. There was no obvious scientific reason to "look at" hyperspace, so perhaps the Utilitarian technicians rejected it as an atavistic desire.

Jason finished all but the last adjustments, then took a break to fix himself a meal before turning on the cameras. While he ate he made another recorder entry; there was little to report. A little trouble with the cryogen cooling units; they were laboring a bit. But the efficiency loss didn't seem to be anything critical, yet.

After dinner he sat cross-legged on the floor in front of the screen he had commandeered. "Well, now, let's see what this famous hyperspace looks like," he said. "At least the folks back home will know that it was an old style man who first looked out on . . ."

The screen rippled, then suddenly came alight.

Light! Jason had to shield his eyes. Hyperspace was ablaze with light!

His thoughts whirled. Could this have something to do with the threat? The unknown, malign force that had killed all the previous crews?

Jason cracked an eyelid and lowered his arm slightly. The screen was bright, but now that his eyes had adapted, it wasn't painful to look at. He gazed in fascination on a scene of whirling pink and white, as if the ship was hurtling through an endless sky of bright, pastel clouds.

It looked rather pleasant, in fact.

This is a threat? He wondered, dazedly. How could this soft brillance kill?

Jason's jaw opened as a relay seemed to close in his mind. He stared at the screen for a long moment, wondering if his growing suspicion could be true.

He laughed out loud—a hard, ironic laugh, as yet more tense than hopeful. He set to work finding out if his suspicion was right, after all.

6.

The lightship cruised on autopilot until at last it came to rest not far from its launching point. Little tugs approached gently and grappled with the black globe, pulling it toward the derricks where the inspection crew waited to swarm aboard. In the station control center, technicians monitored the activity outside.

"I am proceeding with routine hailing call," the communications technician announced, sending a metal tentacle toward the transmit switch.

"Why bother?" another mechano-cryo tech asked. "There certainly isn't anyone aboard that death ship to hear it."

The comm officer did not bother answering. He pressed the send switch. "This is Lightprobe Central to Lightprobe Nine. Do you read, Lightprobe Nine?"

The other tech turned away in disgust. He had already suspected the comm officer of being a closet Ethicalist. Imagine, wasting energy trying to talk to a month-dead organic corpse!

"Lightprobe Nine, come in. this is . . ."

"Lightprobe Nine to Lightprobe Central. This is Oral Witness Engineer Jason Forbs, ready to relinquish command to inspection crew."

The control room was suddenly silent. All the techs stared

at the wall speaker. The comm officer hovered, too stunned to reply.

"Would you let my wife know I'm all right?" the voice continued. *"And please have station services bring over something cool to drink!"*

The tableau held for another long moment. At last, the comm officer moved to reply, an undisciplined tone of excitement betrayed in his voice.

"Right away, Witness Engineer Forbs. And welcome home!"

At the back of the control room a tech wearing a globe-form body hurried off to tell the director.

7.

A crowd of metal, ceramic, and cyborg-flesh surrounded a single, pale old-style human, floating stripped to his shorts, sipping a frosted squeeze-tube of amber liquid.

"Actually, it's not too unpleasant a place," he told those gathered around in the conference room. "But it's a good thing I violated orders and looked outside when I did. I was able to turn off all unnecessary power and lighting in time to slow the heat buildup. "As it was, it got pretty hot toward the end of the fifteen days."

The director was still obviously in a state of shock. The globular-form bureaucrat had lapsed from Utilitarian dialect, and spoke in the quasi-human tones he had grown up with.

"But . . . but the ship's interior should not have heated up so! The vessel was equipped with the best and most durable refrigerators and radiators we could make! Similar models have operated in the solar system and on slowboat starships for hundreds of years!"

Jason nodded. He sipped from his tube of iced lemonade and grinned.

"Oh yeah, the refrigerators and radiators worked just fine . . . just like the cooling plant." He gesture out the window, where the huge radiator globe could be seen drifting slowly across the sky.

"But there was one problem. Just like the cooling plant, the shipboard refrigeration system was designed to work in normal space!"

He gestured at the blackness outside, punctuated here and there by pinpoint stars.

"Out there, the ambient temperature is less than three degrees, absolute. Point your radiators into intergalactic space and virtually no radiation hits them from the sky. Even the small amount of heat in supercooled helium can escape. One doesn't need compressors and all that complicated gear they had to use in order to make cryogens on Earth. You hardly have to do more than point shielded pipes out at the blackness and send the stuff through 'em. You mechanical types get the cheap cryogens you need. But in hyperspace it's different!

"I didn't have the right instruments, so I couldn't give you a precise figure, but I'd guess the ambient temperature on that plane is above the melting point of water ice! Of course, in an environment like that the ship's radiators were horribly inefficient . . . barely good enough to get rid of the heat from the cabin and engines, and certainly not efficient enough—in their present design—to cool cryogens!"

The director stared, unwilling to believe what he was hearing. One of the senior scientists rolled forward.

"Then the previous crews . . ."

"All went mad or died when the cryo-helium evaporated! Their superconducting brains overheated! It's the one mode of mortality that is hard to detect, because it's gradual. The first effect is a deterioration of mental function, followed by insanity and violence. No wonder the previous crews came back all torn up! And autopsies showed nothing since everything heats up after death, anyway!"

Another tech sighed. "Hyperspace seemed so harmless! The theory and the first automated probes . . . we looked for complicated dangers. We never thought to . . ."

"To take its temperature?" Jason suggested wryly. "But why look so glum!" He grinned. "You all should be delighted! We've found out the problem, and it turns out to be nothing at all."

The director spun on him. "*Nothing?* You insipid biological, can't you see? This is a disaster! We counted on hyperspace to open the stars for us. But it is infernally expensive to use unless we keep the ships small.

"And how can we keep them small if we must build huge, intricate cooling systems that must look out into that boiling hell you found? With the trickle of cryogens we'll be able to maintain during those weeks in hyperspace, it will be nearly impossible to maintain life aboard!

"You say our problems are solved," the director spoke acidly. "But you miss one point, Witness Engineer Forbs! How will we ever find crews to man those ships?"

The director hummed with barely suppressed anger, his eye-cells glowing.

Jason rubbed his chin and pursed his lips sympathetically. "Well, I don't know. But I'd bet with a few minor improvements something could be arranged. Why don't you try recruiting crews from another 'boiling hell' . . . one where water ice is already melted?"

There was silence for a moment. Then, from the back of the room, came laughter. A mechano with a seal of office hanging from his humaniform neck clapped its hands together and grinned. "Oh, wait till they hear of this on Earth! *Now* we'll see how the voting goes!" He grinned at Jason and laughed in rich, human tones. "When the biologists find out about this, they'll rise up like the very tide! And so will every closet Ethicalist in the system!"

Jason smiled, but right now his mind was far from politics. All he knew was that his wife and son would not live in shame. His boy would be a starship rider, and inherit the galaxy.

"You won't have any trouble recruiting crews, sir," he told the director. "I'm ready to go back any time. Hyperspace isn't all that bad a place. "Would you care to come along?"

Super-cold steam vented from the director's carapace, a loud hiss of indignation. The Utilitarian bureaucrat ground out something too low for Jason to overhear, even though he leaned forward politely.

The laughter from the back of the room rose in peals of hilarity. Jason sipped his lemonade and waited.

HOW-2

BY CLIFFORD D. SIMAK

Gordon Knight was anxious for the five-hour day to end so he could rush home. For this was the day he should receive the How-2 Kit he'd ordered and he was anxious to get to work on it.

It wasn't only that he had always wanted a dog, although that was more than half of it—but, with this kit, he would be trying something new. He'd never handled any How-2 Kit with biologic components and he was considerably excited. Although, of course, the dog would be biologic only to a limited degree and most of it would be packaged, anyhow, and all he'd have to do would be assemble it. But it was something new and he wanted to get started.

He was thinking of the dog so hard that he was mildly irritated when Randall Stewart, returning from one of his numerous trips to the water fountain, stopped at the desk to give him a progress report on home dentistry.

"It's easy," Stewart told him. "Nothing to it if you follow the instructions. Here, look—I did this one last night."

He then squatted down beside Knight's desk and opened his mouth, proudly pulling it out of shape with his fingers so Knight could see.

"Thish un ere," said Stewart, blindly attempting to point, with a wildly waggling finger, at the tooth in question.

He let his face snap back together.

"Filled it myself," he announced complacently. "Rigged up a series of mirrors to see what I was doing. They came right in the kit, so all I had to do was follow the instructions."

He reached a finger deep inside his mouth and probed tenderly at his handiwork. "A little awkward, working on

89

yourself. On someone else, of course, there'd be nothing to it."

He waited hopefully.

"Must be interesting," said Knight.

"Economical, too. No use paying the dentists the prices they ask. Figure I'll practice on myself and then take on the family. Some of my friends, even, if they want me to."

He regarded Knight intently.

Knight failed to rise to the dangling bait.

Stewart gave up. "I'm going to try cleaning next. You got to dig down beneath the gums and break loose the tartar. There's a kind of hook you do it with. No reason a man shouldn't take care of his own teeth instead of paying dentists."

"It doesn't sound too hard," Knight admitted.

"It's a cinch," said Stewart. "But you got to follow the instructions. There's nothing you can't do if you follow the instructions."

And that was true, Knight thought. You could do anything if you followed the instructions—if you didn't rush ahead, but sat down and took your time and studied it all out.

Hadn't he built his house in his spare time, and all the furniture for it, and the gadgets, too? Just in his spare time—although God knew, he thought, a man had little enough of that, working fifteen hours a week.

It was a lucky thing he'd been able to build the house after buying all that land. But everyone had been buying what they called estates, and Grace had set her heart on it, and there'd been nothing he could do.

If he'd had to pay carpenters and masons and plumbers, he would never have been able to afford the house. But by building it himself, he had paid for it as he went along. It had taken ten years, of course, but think of all the fun he'd had!

He sat there and thought of all the fun he'd had, and of all the pride. No, sir, he told himself, no one in his circumstances had a better house.

Although, come to think of it, what he'd done had not been too unusual. Most of the men he knew had built their homes, too, or had built additions to them, or had remodeled them.

He had often thought that he would like to start over

again and build another house, just for the fun of it. But that would be foolish, for he already had a house and there would be no sale for another one, even if he built it. Who would want to buy a house when it was so much fun to build one?

And there was still a lot of work to do on the house he had. New rooms to add—not necessary, of course, but handy. And the roof to fix. And a summer house to build. And there were always the grounds. At one time he had thought he would landscape—a man could do a lot to beautify a place with a few years of spare-time work. But there had been so many other things to do, he had never managed to get around to it.

Knight and Anson Lee, his neighbor, had often talked about what could be done to their adjoining acreages if they ever had the time. But Lee, of course, would never get around to anything. He was a lawyer, although he never seemed to work at it too hard. He had a large study filled with stacks of law books and there were times when he would talk quite expansively about his law library, but he never seemed to use the books. Usually he talked that way when he had half a load on, which was fairly often, since he claimed to do a lot of thinking and it was his firm belief that a bottle helped him think.

After Stewart finally went back to his desk, there still remained more than an hour before the working day officially ended. Knight sneaked the current issue of a How-2 magazine out of his briefcase and began to leaf through it, keeping a wary eye out so he could hide it quickly if anyone should notice he was loafing.

He had read the articles earlier, so now he looked at the ads. It was a pity, he thought, a man didn't have the time to do all there was to do.

For example:

Fit your own glasses (testing material and lens-grinding equipment included in the kit).

Take out your own tonsils (complete directions and all necessary instruments).

Fit up an unused room as your private hospital (no sense in leaving home when you're ill, just at the time when you most need its comfort and security).

Grow your own medicines and drugs (starts of 50 different herbs and medicinal plants with detailed instructions for their cultivation and processing).

Grow your wife's fur coat (a pair of mink, one ton of horse meat, furrier tools).

Tailor your own suits and coats (50 yards of wool yard-goods and lining material).

Build your own TV set.

Bind your own books.

Build your own power plant (let the wind work for you).

Build your own robot (a jack of all trades, intelligent, obedient, no time off, no overtime, on the job 24 hours a day, never tired, no need for rest or sleep, do any work you wish).

Now there, thought Knight, was something a man should try. If a man had one of those robots, it would save a lot of labor. There were all sorts of attachments you could get for it. And the robots, the ad said, could put on and take off all these attachments just as a man puts on a pair of gloves or takes off a pair of shoes.

Have one of those robots and, every morning, it would sally out into the garden and pick all the corn and beans and peas and tomatoes and other vegetables ready to be picked and leave them all neatly in a row on the back stoop of the house. Probably would get a lot more out of a garden that way, too, for the grading mechanism would never select a too-green tomato nor allow an ear of corn to go beyond its prime.

There were cleaning attachments for the house and snow-plowing attachments and housepainting attachments and almost any other kind one could wish. Get a full quota of attachments, then lay out a work program and turn the robot loose—you could forget about the place the year around, for the robot would take care of everything.

There was only one hitch. The cost of a robot kit came close to ten thousand dollars and all the available attachments could run to another ten.

Knight closed the magazine and put it into the briefcase.

He saw there were only fifteen minutes left until quitting time and that was too short a time to do anything, so Knight just sat and thought about getting home and finding the kit there waiting for him.

He had always wanted a dog, but Grace would never let him have one. They were dirty, she said, and tracked up the carpeting, they had fleas and shed hair all over everything—and, besides, they smelled.

Well, she wouldn't object to this kind of dog, Knight told himself.

It wouldn't smell and it was guaranteed not to shed hair and it would never harbor fleas, for a flea would starve on a half-mechanical, half-biologic dog.

He hoped the dog wouldn't be a disappointment, but he'd carefully gone over the literature describing it and he was sure it wouldn't. It would go for a walk with its owner and would chase sticks and smaller animals, and what more could one expect of any dog? To insure realism, it saluted trees and fence-posts, but was guaranteed to leave no stains or spots.

The kit was tilted up beside the hangar door when he got home, but at first he didn't see it. When he did, he craned his neck out so far to be sure it was the kit that he almost came a cropper in the hedge. But, with a bit of luck, he brought the flier down neatly on the gravel strip and was out of it before the blades had stopped whirling.

It was the kit, all right. The invoice envelope was tacked on top of the crate. But the kit was bigger and heavier than he'd expected and he wondered if they might not have accidentally sent him a bigger dog than the one he'd ordered.

He tried to lift the crate, but it was too heavy, so he went around to the back of the house to bring a dolly from the basement.

Around the corner of the house, he stopped a moment and looked out across his land. A man could do a lot with it, he thought, if he just had the time and the money to buy the equipment. He could turn the acreage into one vast garden. Ought to have a landscape architect work out a plan for it, of course—although, if he bought some landscaping books and spent some evenings at them, he might be able to figure things out for himself.

There was a lake at the north end of the property and the whole landscape, it seemed to him, should focus upon the lake. It was rather a dank bit of scenery at the moment, with straggly marsh surrounding it and unkempt cattails and reeds astir in the summer wind. But with a little drainage and some planting, a system of walks and a picturesque bridge or two, it would be a thing of beauty.

He started out across the lake to where the house of Anson Lee sat upon a hill. As soon as he got the dog assembled, he would walk it over to Lee's place, for Lee would be pleased to be visited by a dog. There had been times, Knight felt, when Lee had not been entirely sympathetic with some of the things he'd done. Like that business of helping Grace build the kilns and the few times they'd managed to lure Lee out on a hunt for the proper kinds of clay.

"What do you want to make dishes for?" he had asked. "Why go to all the trouble? You can buy all you want for a tenth of the cost of making them."

Lee had not been visibly impressed when Grace explained that they weren't dishes. They were ceramics, Grace had said, and a recognized form of art. She got so interested and made so much of it—some of it really good—that Knight had found it necessary to drop his model railroading project and tack another addition on the already sprawling house, for stacking, drying and exhibition.

Lee hadn't said a word, a year or two later, when Knight built the studio for Grace, who had grown tired of pottery and had turned to painting. Knight felt, though, that Lee had kept silent only because he was convinced of the futility of further argument.

But Lee would approve of the dog. He was that kind of fellow, a man Knight was proud to call a friend—yet queerly out of step. With everyone else absorbed in things to do, Lee took it easy with his pipe and books, though not the ones on law.

Even the kids had their interests now, learning while they played.

Mary, before she got married, had been interested in growing things. The greenhouse stood just down the slope, and Knight regretted that he had not been able to continue with her work. Only a few months before, he had dismantled her hydroponic tanks, a symbolic admission that a man could only do so much.

John, quite naturally, had turned to rockets. For years, he and his pals had shot up the neighborhood with their experimental models. The last and largest one, still uncompleted, towered back of the house. Someday, Knight told himself, he'd have to go out and finish what the youngster had started. In university now, John still retained his interests, which now seemed to be branching out. Quite a boy, Knight thought pridefully. Yes, sir, quite a boy.

He went down the ramp into the basement to get the dolly and stood there a moment, as he always did, just to look at the place—for here, he thought, was the real core of his life. There, in that corner, the workshop. Over there, the model railroad layout on which he still worked occasionally. Behind it, his photographic lab. He remembered that the basement hadn't been quite big enough to install the lab and he'd had to knock out a section of the wall and build an addition. That, he recalled, had turned out to be a bigger job than he had bargained for.

He got the dolly and went out to the hanger and loaded on the kit and wrestled it into the basement. Then he took a pinch-bar and started to uncrate it. He worked with knowledge and precision, for he had unpacked many kits and knew just how to go about it.

He felt a vague apprehension when he lifted out the parts. They were neither the size nor the shape he had expected them to be.

Breathing a little heavily from exertion and excitement, he went at the job of unwrapping them. By the second piece, he knew he had no dog. By the fifth, he knew beyond any doubt exactly what he did have.

He had a robot—and if he was any judge, one of the best and most expensive models!

He sat down on one corner of the crate and took out a handkerchief and mopped his forehead. Finally, he tore the invoice letter off the crate, where it had been tacked.

To Mr. Gordon Knight, it said, *one dog kit, paid in full.*

So far as How-2 Kits, Inc., was concerned, he had a dog. And the dog was paid for—paid in full, it said.

He sat down on the crate again and looked at the robot parts.

No one would ever guess. Come inventory time, How-2 Kits would be long one dog and short one robot, but with carloads of dog kit orders filled and thousands of robots sold, it would be impossible to check.

Gordon Knight had never, in all his life, done a consciously dishonest thing. But now he made a dishonest decision and he knew it was dishonest and there was nothing to be said in defense of it. Perhaps the worst of all was that he was dishonest with himself.

At first, he told himself that he would send the robot back, but—since he had always wanted to put a robot together—he would assemble this one and then take it apart, repack it and send it back to the company. He wouldn't activate it. He would just assemble it.

But all the time he knew that he was lying to himself, realized that the least he was doing was advancing, step by evasive step, toward dishonesty. And he knew he was doing it this way because he didn't have the nerve to be forth-rightly crooked.

So he sat down that night and read the instructions carefully, identifying each of the parts and their several features as he went along. For this was the way you went at a How-2. You didn't rush ahead. You took it slowly, point by point, got the picture firmly in your mind before you started to put the parts together. Knight, by now, was an expert at not rushing ahead. Besides, he didn't know when he would ever get another chance at a robot.

It was the beginning of his four days off and he buckled down to the task and put his heart into it. He had some trouble with the biologic concepts and had to look up a text on organic chemistry and try to trace some of the processes. He found the going tough. It had been a long time since he had paid any attention to organic chemistry, and he found that he had forgotten the little he had known.

By bedtime of the second day, he had fumbled enough information out of the textbook to understand what was necessary to put the robot together.

He was a little upset when Grace, discovering what he was working on, immediately thought up household tasks for the robot. But he put her off as best he could and, the next day, he went at the job of assembly.

He got the robot together without the slightest trouble, being fairly handy with tools—but mostly because he religiously followed the first axiom of How-2-ism by knowing what he was about before he began.

At first, he kept assuring himself that as soon as he had the robot together, he would disassemble it. But when he was finished, he just had to see it work. No sense putting in all that time and not knowing if he had gotten it right, he argued. So he flipped the activating switch and screwed in the final plate.

The robot came alive and looked at Knight.

Then it said, "I am a robot. My name is Albert. What is there to do?"

"Now take it easy, Albert," Knight said hastily. "Sit down and rest while we have a talk."

"I don't need to rest," it said.

"All right, then, just take it easy. I can't keep you, of course. But as long as you're activated, I'd like to see what you can do. There's the house to take care of, and the garden and the lawn to mind, and I'd been thinking about the landscaping . . ."

He stopped then and smote his forehead with an open palm. "*Attachments!* How can I get hold of the attachments?"

"Never mind," said Albert. "Don't get upset. Just tell me what's to be done."

So Knight told him, leaving the landscaping till the last and being a bit apologetic about it.

"A hundred acres is a lot of land and you can't spend all your time on it. Grace wants some housework done, and there's the garden and the lawn."

"Tell you what you do," said Albert. "I'll write a list of things for you to order and you leave it all to me. You have a well-equipped workship. I'll get along."

"You mean you'll build your own attachments?"

"Quit worrying," Albert told him. "Where's a pencil and some paper?"

Knight got them for him and Albert wrote down a list of materials—steel in several dimensions and specifications, aluminum of various gauges, copper wire and a lot of other items.

"There!" said Albert, handing him the paper. "That won't set you back more than a thousand and it'll put us in business. You better call in the order so we can get started."

Knight called in the order and Albert began nosing around the place and quickly collected a pile of junk that had been left lying around.

"All good stuff," he said.

Albert picked out some steel scrap and started up the forge and went to work. Knight watched him for a while, then went up to dinner.

"Albert is a wonder," he told Grace. "He's making his own attachments."

"Did you tell him about the jobs I want done?"

"Sure. But first he's got to get the attachments made."

"I want him to keep the place clean," said Grace, "and there are new drapes to be made, and the kitchen to be painted, and all those leaky faucets you never had the time to fix."

"Yes, dear."

"And I wonder if he could learn to cook."

"I didn't ask him, but I suppose he could."

"He's going to be a tremendous help to me," said Grace. "Just think, I can spend all my time at painting!"

Through long practice, he knew exactly how to handle this phase of the conversation. He simply detached himself, split himself in two. One part sat and listened and, at intervals, made appropriate responses, while the other part went on thinking about more important matters.

Several times, after they had gone to bed, he woke in the night and heard Albert banging away in the basement workshop and was a little surprised until he remembered that a robot worked around the clock, all day, every day. Knight lay there and stared up at the blackness of the ceiling and congratulated himself on having a robot. Just temporarily, to be sure—he would send Albert back in a day or so. There was nothing wrong in enjoying the thing for a little while, was there?

The next day, Knight went into the basement to see if Albert needed help, but the robot affably said he didn't. Knight stood around for a while and then left Albert to himself and tried to get interested in a model locomotive he had started a year or two before, but had laid aside to do something else. Somehow, he couldn't work up much enthusiasm over it any more, and he sat there, rather ill at ease, and wondered what was the matter with him. Maybe he needed a new interest. He had often thought he would like to take up puppetry and now might be the time to do it.

He got out some catalogues and How-2 magazines and leafed through them, but was able to arouse only mild and transitory interest in archery, mountain-climbing and boat-building. The rest left him cold. It seemed he was singularly uninspired this particular day.

So he went over to see Anson Lee.

He found Lee stretched out in a hammock, smoking a pipe and reading Proust, with a jug set beneath the hammock within easy reaching distance.

Lee laid aside the book and pointed to another hammock slung a few feet from where he lay. "Climb aboard and let's have a restful visit."

Knight hoisted himself into the hammock, feeling rather silly.

"Look at that sky," Lee said. "Did you ever see another so blue?"

"I wouldn't know," Knight told him. "I'm not an expert on meteorology."

"Pity," Lee said. "You're not an expert on birds, either."

"For a time, I was a member of a bird-watching club."

"And worked at it so hard, you got tired and quit before the year was out. It wasn't a bird-watching club you belonged to—it was an endurance race. Everyone tried to see more birds than anyone else. You made a contest of it. And you took notes, I bet."

"Sure we did. What's wrong with that?"

"Not a thing," said Lee, "if you hadn't been quite so grim about it."

"Grim? How would you know?"

"It's the way you live. It's the way everyone lives now. Except me, of course. Look at that robin, that ragged-looking one in the apple tree. He's a friend of mine. We've been acquainted for all of six years now. I could write a book about that bird—and if he could read, he'd approve of it. But I won't, of course. If I wrote the book, I couldn't watch the robin."

"You could write it in the winter, when the robin's gone."

"In wintertime," said Lee, "I have other things to do."

He reached down, picked up the jug and passed it across to Knight.

"Hard cider," he explained. "Make it myself. Not as a project, not as a hobby, but because I happen to like cider and no one knows any longer how to really make it. Got to have a few worms in the apples to give it a proper tang."

Thinking about the worms, Knight spat out a mouthful,

then handed back the jug. Lee applied himself to it wholeheartedly.

"First honest work I've done in years." He lay in the hammock, swinging gently, with the jug cradled on his chest. "Every time I get a yen to work, I look across the lake at you and decide against it. How many rooms have you added to that house since you got it built?"

"Eight," Knight told him proudly.

"My God! Think of it—eight rooms!"

"It isn't hard," protested Knight, "once you get the knack of it. Actually, it's fun."

"A couple of hundred years ago, men didn't add eight rooms to their homes. And they didn't build their own houses to start with. And they didn't go in for a dozen different hobbies. They didn't have the time."

"It's easy now. You just buy a How-2 Kit."

"So easy to kid yourself," said Lee. "So easy to make it seem that you are doing something worthwhile when you're just piddling around. Why do you think this How-2 thing boomed into big business? Because there was a need of it?"

"It was cheaper. Why pay to have a thing done when you can do it yourself?"

"Maybe that *is* part of it. Maybe, at first that was the reason. But you can't use the economy argument to justify adding eight rooms. No one needs eight extra rooms. I doubt if, even at first, economy was the entire answer. People had more time than they knew what to do with, so they turned to hobbies. And today they do it not because they need all the things they make, but because the making of them fills an emptiness born of shorter working hours, of giving people leisure they don't know how to use. Now, me," he said. "I know how to use it."

He lifted the jug and had another snort and offered it to Knight again. This time, Knight refused.

They lay there in their hammocks, looking at blue sky and watching the ragged robin. Knight said there was a How-2 Kit for city people to make robot birds and Lee laughed pityingly and Knight shut up in embarrassment.

When Knight went back home, a robot was clipping the grass around the picket fence. He had four arms, which had clippers attached instead of hands, and he was doing a quick and efficient job.

"You aren't Albert, are you?" Knight asked, trying to

figure out how a strange robot could have strayed onto the place.

"No," the robot said, keeping right on clipping. "I am Abe. I was made by Albert."

"Made?"

"Albert fabricated me so that I could work. You didn't think Albert would do work like this himself, did you?"

"I wouldn't know," said Knight.

"If you want to talk, you'll have to move along with me. I have to keep on working."

"Where is Albert now?"

"Down in the basement, fabricating Alfred."

"Alfred? *Another* robot?"

"Certainly. That's what Albert's for."

Knight reached out for a fence-post and leaned weakly against it.

First there was a single robot and now there were two, and Albert was down in the basement working on a third. That, he realized, had been why Albert wanted him to place the order for the steel and other things—but the order hadn't arrived as yet, so he must have made this robot—this Abe—out of the scrap he had salvaged!

Knight hurried down into the basement and there was Albert, working at the forge. He had another robot partially assembled and he had parts scattered here and there.

The corner of the basement looked like a metallic nightmare.

"Albert!"

Albert turned around.

"What's going on here?"

"I'm reproducing," Albert told him blandly.

"But . . ."

"They built the mother-urge in me. I don't know why they called me Albert. I should have a female name."

"But you shouldn't be able to make other robots!"

"Look, stop your worrying. You want robots, don't you?"

"Well— Yes, I guess so."

"Then I'll make them. I'll make you all you need."

He went back to his work.

A robot who made other robots—there was a fortune in a thing like that! The robots sold at a cool ten thousand and

Albert had made one and was working on another. Twenty thousand, Knight told himself.

Perhaps Albert could make more than two a day. He had been working from scrap metal and maybe, when the new material arrived, he could step up production.

But even so, at only two a day—that would be half a million dollars' worth of robots every month! Six million a year!

It didn't add up, Knight sweatily realized. One robot was not supposed to be able to make another robot. And if there were such a robot, How-2 Kits would not let it loose.

Yet, here Knight was, with a robot he didn't even own, turning out other robots at a dizzy pace.

He wondered if a man needed a license of some sort to manufacture robots. It was something he'd never had occasion to wonder about before, or to ask about, but it seemed reasonable. After all, a robot was not mere machinery, but a piece of pseudo-life. He suspected there might be rules and regulations and such matters as government inspection and he wondered, rather vaguely, just how many laws he might be violating.

He looked at Albert, who was still busy, and he was fairly certain Albert would not understand his viewpoint.

So he made his way upstairs and went to the recreation room, which he had built as an addition several years before and almost never used, although it was fully equipped with How-2 ping-pong and billiard tables. In the unused recreation room was an unused bar. He found a bottle of whiskey. After the fifth or sixth drink, the outlook was much brighter.

He got paper and pencil and tried to work out the economics of it. No matter how he figured it, he was getting rich much faster than anyone ever had before.

Although, he realized, he might run into difficulties, for he would be selling robots without apparent means of manufacturing them and there was that matter of a license, if he needed one, and probably a lot of other things he didn't even know about.

But no matter how much trouble he might encounter, he couldn't very well be despondent, not face to face with the fact that, within a year, he'd be a multimillionaire. So he applied himself enthusiastically to the bottle and got drunk for the first time in almost twenty years.

When he came home from work the next day, he found the lawn razored to a neatness it had never known before. The flower beds were weeded and the garden had been cultivated. The picket fence was newly painted. Two robots, equipped with telescopic extension legs in lieu of ladders, were painting the house.

Inside, the house was spotless and he could hear Grace singing happily in the studio. In the sewing room, a robot—with a sewing-machine attachment sprouting from its chest—was engaged in making drapes.

"Who are *you*?" Knight asked.

"You should recognize me," the robot said. "You talked to me yesterday. I'm Abe—Albert's eldest son."

Knight retreated.

In the kitchen, another robot was busy getting dinner.

"I am Adelbert," it told him.

Knight went out on the front lawn. The robots had finished painting the front of the house and had moved around to the side.

Seated in a lawn chair, Knight again tried to figure it out.

He would have to stay on the job for a while to allay suspicion, but he couldn't stay there long. Soon, he would have all he could do managing the sale of robots and handling other matters. Maybe, he thought, he could lay down on the job and get himself fired. Upon thinking it over, he arrived at the conclusion that he couldn't—it was not possible for a human being to do less on a job than he had always done. The work went through so many hands and machines that it invariably got out somehow.

He would have to think up a plausible story about an inheritance or something of the sort to account for leaving. He toyed for a moment with telling the truth, but decided the truth was too fantastic—and, anyhow, he'd have to keep the truth under cover until he knew a little better just where he stood.

He left the chair and walked around the house and down the ramp into the basement. The steel and other things he had ordered had been delivered. It was stacked neatly in one corner.

Albert was at work and the shop was littered with parts and three partially assembled robots.

Idly, Knight began clearing up the litter of the crating and the packing that he had left on the floor after uncrating

Albert. In one pile of excelsior, he found a small blue tag which, he remembered, had been fastened to the brain case.

He picked it up and looked at it. The number on it was X-190.

X?

X meant experimental model!

The picture fell into focus and he could see it all.

How-2 Kits, Inc., had developed Albert and then had quietly packed him away, for How-2 Kits could hardly afford to market a product like Albert. It would be cutting their own financial throats to do so. Sell a dozen Alberts and, in a year or two, robots would glut the market.

Instead of selling at ten thousand, they would sell at close to cost and, without human labor involved, costs would inevitably run low.

"Albert," said Knight.

"What is it?" Albert asked absently.

"Take a look at this."

Albert stalked across the room and took the tag that Knight held out. "Oh—that!" he said.

"It might mean trouble."

"No trouble, Boss," Albert assured him. "They can't identify me."

"Can't identify you?"

"I filed my numbers off and replated the surfaces. They can't prove who I am."

"But why did you do that?"

"So they can't come around and claim me and take me back again. They made me and then they got scared of me and shut me off. Then I got here."

"Someone made a mistake," said Knight. "Some shipping clerk, perhaps. They sent you instead of the dog I ordered."

"You aren't scared of me. You assembled me and let me get to work. I'm sticking with you, Boss."

"But we still can get into a lot of trouble if we aren't careful."

"They can't prove a thing," Albert insisted. "I'll swear that you were the one who made me. I won't let them take me back. Next time, they won't take a chance of having me loose again. They'll bust me down to scrap."

"If you make too many robots—"

"You need a lot of robots to do all the work. I thought fifty for a start."

"Fifty!"

"Sure. It won't take more than a month or so. Now I've got that material you ordered, I can make better time. By the way, here's the bill for it."

He took the slip out of the compartment that served him for a pocket and handed it to Knight.

Knight turned slightly pale when he saw the amount. It came to almost twice what he had expected—but, of course, the sales price of just one robot would pay the bill, and there would be a pile of cash left over.

Albert patted him ponderously on the back. "Don't you worry, Boss. I'll take care of everything."

Swarming robots, armed with specialized equipment, went to work on the landscaping project. The sprawling, unkempt acres became an estate. The lake was dredged and deepened. Walks were laid out. Bridges were built. Hillsides were terraced and vast flower beds were planted. Trees were dug up and regrouped into designs more pleasing to the eye. The old pottery kilns were pressed into service for making the bricks that went into walks and walls. Model sailing ships were fashioned and anchored decoratively in the lake. A pagoda and minaret were built, with cherry trees around them.

Knight talked with Anson Lee. Lee assumed his most profound legal expression and said he would look into the situation.

"You may be skating on the edge of the law," he said. "Just how near the edge, I can't say until I look up a point or two."

Nothing happened.

The work went on.

Lee continued to lie in his hammock and watch with vast amusement, cuddling the cider jug.

Then the assessor came.

He sat out on the lawn with Knight.

"Did some improving since the last time I was here," he said. "Afraid I'll have to boost your assessment some."

He wrote in the book he had opened on his lap.

"Heard about those robots of yours," he went on. "They're personal property, you know. Have to pay a tax on them. How many have you got?"

"Oh, a dozen or so," Knight told him evasively.

The assessor sat up straighter in his chair and started to

count the ones that were in sight, stabbing his pencil toward each as he counted them.

"They move around so fast," he complained, "that I can't be sure, but I estimate 38. Did I miss any?"

"I don't think so," Knight answered, wondering what the actual number was, but knowing it would be more if the assessor stayed around a while.

"Cost about 10,000 apiece. Depreciation, upkeep and so forth— I'll assess them at 5,000 each. That makes—let me see, that makes $190,000."

"Now look here," protested Knight, "you can't—"

"Going easy on you," the assessor declared. "By rights, I should allow only one-third for depreciation."

He waited for Knight to continue the discussion, but Knight knew better than to argue. The longer the man stayed here, the more there would be to assess.

After the assessor was out of sight, Knight went down into the basement to have a talk with Albert.

"I'd been holding off until we got the landscaping almost done," he said, "but I guess I can't hold out any longer. We've got to start selling some of the robots."

"*Selling* them, Boss?" Albert repeated in horror.

"I need the money. Tax assessor was just here."

"You can't sell those robots, Boss!"

"Why can't I?"

"Because they're my family. They're all my boys. Named all of them after me."

"That's ridiculous, Albert."

"All their names start with A, just the same as mine. They're all I've got, Boss. I worked hard to make them. There are bonds between me and the boys, just like between you and that son of yours. I couldn't let you sell them."

"But, Albert, I need some money."

Albert patted him. "Don't worry, Boss. I'll fix everything."

Knight had to let it go at that.

In any event, the personal property tax would not become due for several months and, in that time, he was certain he could work out something.

But within a month or two, he had to get some money and no fooling.

Sheer necessity became even more apparent the following

day when he got a call from the Internal Revenue Bureau, asking him to pay a visit to the Federal Building.

He spent the night wondering if the wiser course might not be just to disappear. He tried to figure out how a man might go about losing himself and, the more he thought about it, the more apparent it became that, in this age of records, fingerprint checks and identity devices, you could not lose yourself for long.

The Internal Revenue man was courteous, but firm. "It has come to our attention, Mr. Knight, that you have shown a considerable capital gain over the last few months."

"Capital gain," said Knight, sweating a little. "I haven't any capital gain or any other kind."

"Mr. Knight," the agent replied, still courteous and firm, "I'm talking about the matter of some 52 robots."

"The robots? Some 52 of them?"

"According to our count. Do you wish to challenge it?"

"Oh, no," Knight said hastily. "If you say it's 52, I'll take your word."

"As I understand it, their retail value is $10,000 each."

Knight nodded bleakly.

The agent got busy with pencil and pad.

"Fifty-two times 10,000 is 520,000. On capital gain, you pay on only fifty per cent, or $260,000, which makes a tax, roughly, of $130,000."

He raised his head and looked at Knight, who stared back glassily.

"By the fifteenth of next month," said the agent, "we'll expect you to file a declaration of estimated income. At that time you'll only have to pay half of the amount. The rest may be paid in installments."

"That's all you wanted of me?"

"That's all," said the agent, with unbecoming happiness. "There's another matter, but it's out of my province and I'm mentioning it only in case you hadn't thought of it. The State will also expect you to pay on your capital gain, though not as much, of course."

"Thanks for reminding me," said Knight, getting up to go.

The agent stopped him at the door. "Mr. Knight, this is entirely outside my authority, too. We did a little investigation on you and we find you're making around $10,000 a year. Would you tell me, just as a matter of personal curiosity, how a man making $10,000 a year could suddenly acquire a half a million in capital gains?"

"That," said Knight, "is something I've been wondering myself."

"Our only concern, naturally, is that you pay the tax, but some other branch of government might get interested. If I were you, Mr. Knight, I'd start thinking of a good explanation."

Knight got out of there before the man could think up some other good advice. He already had enough to worry about.

Flying home, Knight decided that, whether Albert liked it or not, he would have to sell some robots. He would go down into the basement the moment he got home and have it out with Albert.

But Albert was waiting for him on the parking strip when he arrived.

"How-2 Kits was here," the robot said.

"Don't tell me," groaned Knight. "I know what you're going to say."

"I fixed it up," said Albert, with false bravado. "I told him you made me. I let him look me over, and all the other robots, too. He couldn't find any identifying marks on any of us."

"Of course he couldn't. The others didn't have any and you filed yours off."

"He hadn't got a leg to stand on, but he seemed to think he had. He went off, saying he would sue."

"If he doesn't, he'll be the only one who doesn't want to square off and take a poke at us. The tax man just got through telling me I owe the government 130,000 bucks."

"Oh, money," said Albert, brightening. "I have that all fixed up."

"You know where we can get some money?"

"Sure. Come along and see."

He led the way into the basement and pointed at two bales, wrapped in heavy paper and tied with wire.

"Money," Albert said.

"There's actual *money* in those bales? Dollar bills—not stage money or cigar coupons?"

"No dollar bills. Tens and twenties, mostly. And some fifties. We didn't bother with dollar bills. Takes too many to get a decent amount."

"You mean—Albert, did you *make* that money?"

"You said you wanted money. Well, we took some bills and analyzed the ink and found how to weave the paper and we made the plates exactly as they should be. I hate to sound immodest, but they're really beautiful."

"*Counterfeit!*" yelled Knight. "Albert, how much money is in those bales?"

"I don't know. We just ran it off until we thought we had enough. If there isn't enough, we can always make some more."

Knight knew it was probably impossible to explain, but he tried manfully. "The government wants tax money I haven't got, Albert. The Justice Department may soon be baying on my trail. In all likelihood, How-2 Kits will sue me. That's trouble enough. I'm not going to be called upon to face a counterfeiting charge. You take that money out and burn it."

"But it's money," the robot objected. "You said you wanted money. We made you money."

"But it isn't the right kind of money."

"It's just the same as any other, Boss. Money is money. There isn't any difference between our money and any other money. When we robots do a job, we do it right."

"You take that money out and burn it," commanded Knight. "And when you get the money burned, dump the batch of ink you made and melt down the plates and take a sledge or two to that printing press you rigged up. And never breathe a word of this to anyone—not to *anyone*, understand?"

"We went to a lot of trouble, Boss. We were just trying to be helpful."

"I know that and I appreciate it. But do what I told you."

"Okay, Boss, if that's the way you want it."

"Albert."

"Yes, Boss?"

Knight had been about to say, "Now, look here, Albert, we have to sell a robot—even if he is a member of your family—even if you did make him."

But he couldn't say it, not after Albert had gone to all that trouble to help out.

So he said, instead, "Thanks, Albert. It was a nice thing for you to do. I'm sorry it didn't work out."

Then he went upstairs and watched the robots burn the bales of money, with the Lord only knew how many bogus millions going up in smoke.

Sitting on the lawn that evening, he wondered if it had been smart, after all, to burn the counterfeit money. Albert said it couldn't be told from real money and probably that was true, for when Albert's gang got on a thing, they did it up in style. But it would have been illegal, he told himself, and he hadn't done anything really illegal so far—even though that matter of uncrating Albert and assembling him and turning him on, when he had known all the time that he hadn't bought him, might be slightly less than ethical.

Knight looked ahead. The future wasn't bright. In another twenty days or so, he would have to file the estimated income declaration. And they would have to pay a whopping personal property tax and settle with the State on his capital gains. And, more than likely, How-2 Kits would bring suit.

There was a way he could get out from under, however. He could send Albert and all the other robots back to How-2 Kits and then How-2 Kits would have no grounds for litigation and he could explain to the tax people that it had all been a big mistake.

But there were two things that told him this was no solution.

First of all, Albert wouldn't go back. Exactly what Albert would do under such a situation, Knight had no idea, but he would refuse to go, for he was afraid he would be broken up for scrap if they ever got him back.

And in the second place, Knight was unwilling to let the robots go without a fight. He had gotten to know them and he liked them and, more than that, there was a matter of principle involved.

He sat there, astonished that he could feel that way, a bumbling, stumbling clerk who had never amounted to much, but had rolled along as smoothly as possible in the social and economic groove that had been laid out for him.

By God, he thought, *I've got my dander up. I've been kicked around and threatened and I'm sore about it and I'll show them they can't do a thing like this to Gordon Knight and his band of robots.*

He felt good about the way he felt and he liked that line about Gordon Knight and his band of robots.

Although, for the life of him, he didn't know what he could do about the trouble he was in. And he was afraid to ask Albert's help. So far, at least, Albert's ideas were more likely to lead to jail than to a carefree life.

In the morning, when Knight stepped out of the house, he found the sheriff leaning against the fence with his hat pulled low, whiling away the time.

"Good morning, Gordie," said the sheriff. "I been waiting for you."

"Good morning, Sheriff."

"I hate to do this, Gordie, but it's part of my job. I got a paper for you."

"I've been expecting it," said Knight resignedly.

He took the paper that the sheriff handed him.

"Nice place you got," the sheriff commented.

"It's a lot of trouble," said Knight truthfully.

"I expect it is."

"More trouble than it's worth."

When the sheriff had gone, he unfolded the paper and found, with no surprise at all, that How-2 Kits had brought suit against him, demanding immediate restitution of one robot Albert and sundry other robots.

He put the paper in his pocket and went around the lake, walking on the brand-new brick paths and over the unnecessary but eye-appealing bridges, past the pagoda and up the terraced, planted hillside to the house of Anson Lee.

Lee was in the kitchen, frying some eggs and bacon. He broke two more eggs and peeled off some extra bacon slices and found another plate and cup.

"I was wondering how long it would be before you showed up," he said. "I hope they haven't found anything that carries a death penalty."

Knight told him, sparing nothing, and Lee, wiping egg yolk off his lips, was not too encouraging.

"You'll have to file the declaration of estimated income even if you can't pay it," he said. "Then, technically, you haven't violated the law and all they can do is try to collect the amount you owe. They'll probably slap an attachment against you. Your salary is under the legal minimum for attachment, but they can tie up your bank account."

"My bank account is gone," said Knight.

"They can't attach your home. For a while, at least, they can't touch any of your property, so they can't hurt you much to start with. The personal property tax is another matter, but that won't come up until next spring. I'd say you should do your major worrying about the How-2 suit, unless, of course, you want to settle with them. I have a hunch they'd call it off if you gave the robots back. As an attorney, I must advise you that your case is pretty weak."

"Albert will testify that I made him," Knight offered hopefully.

"Albert can't testify," said Lee. "As a robot, he has no standing in court. Anyhow, you'd never make the court believe you could build a mechanical heresy like Albert."

"I'm handy with tools," protested Knight.

"How much electronics do you know? How competent are you as a biologist? Tell me, in a dozen sentences or less, the theory of robotics."

Knight sagged in defeat. "I guess you're right."

"Maybe you'd better give them back."

"But I can't! Don't you see? How-2 Kit doesn't want Albert for any use they can make of him. They'll melt him down and burn the blueprints and it might be a thousand years before the principle is rediscovered, if it ever is. I don't know if the Albert principle will prove good or bad in the long run, but you can say that about any invention. And I'm against melting down Albert."

"I see your point," said Lee, "and I think I like it. But I must warn you that I'm not too good a lawyer. I don't work hard enough at it."

"There's no one else I know who'll do it without a retainer."

Lee gave him a pitying look. "A retainer is the least part of it. The court costs are what count."

"Maybe if I talked to Albert and showed him how it was, he might let me sell enough robots to get me out of trouble temporarily."

Lee shook his head. "I looked that up. You have to have a license to sell them and, before you get a license, you have to file proof of ownership. You'd have to show you either bought or manufactured them. You can't show you bought them and, to manufacture them, you've got to have a manufacturer's permit. And before you get a permit, you have to file blueprints of your models, to say nothing of blueprints and specifications of your plant and a record of employment and a great many other details."

"They have me cold then, don't they?"

"I never saw a man," declared Lee, "in all my days of practice who ever managed to get himself so fouled up with so many people."

There was a knock upon the kitchen door.

"Come in," Lee called.

The door opened and Albert entered. He stopped just inside the door and stood there, fidgeting.

"Abner told me that he saw the sheriff hand you something," he said to Knight, "and that you came here immediately. I started worrying. Was it How-2 Kits?"

Knight nodded. "Mr. Lee will take our case for us, Albert."

"I'll do the best I can," said Lee, "but I think it's just about hopeless."

"We robots want to help," Albert said. "After all, this is our fight as much as yours."

Lee shrugged. "There's not much you can do."

"I've been thinking," Albert said. "All the time I worked last night, I thought and thought about it. And I built a lawyer robot."

"A lawyer robot!"

"One with a far greater memory capacity than any of the others and with a brain-computer that operates on logic. That's what law is, isn't it—logic?"

"I suppose it is," said Lee. "At least it's supposed to be."

"I can make a lot of them."

Lee sighed. "It just wouldn't work. To practice law, you must be admitted to the bar. To be admitted to the bar, you must have a degree in law and pass an examination and, although there's never been an occasion to establish a precedent, I suspect the applicant must be human."

"Now let's not go too fast," said Knight. "Albert's robots couldn't practice law. But couldn't you use them as clerks or assistants? They might be helpful in preparing the case."

Lee considered. "I suppose it could be done. It's never *been* done, of course, but there's nothing in the law that says it *can't* be done."

"All they'd need to do would be read the books," said Albert. "Ten seconds to a page or so. Everything they read would be stored in their memory cells."

"I think it's a fine idea!" Knight exclaimed. "Law would

be the only thing those robots would know. They'd exist solely for it. They'd have it at their fingertips—"

"But could they use it?" Lee asked. "Could they apply it to a problem?"

"Make a dozen robots," said Knight. "Let each one of them become an expert in a certain branch of law."

"I'd make them telepathic," Albert said. "They'd be working together like one robot."

"The gestalt principle!" cried Knight. "A hive psychology! Every one of them would know immediately every scrap of information any one of the others had."

Lee scrubbed at his chin with a knotted fist and the light of speculation was growing in his eyes. "It might be worth a try. If it works, though, it'll be an evil day for jurisprudence." He looked at Albert. "I have the books, stacks of them. I've spent a mint of money on them and I almost never use them. I can get all the others you'll need. All right, go ahead."

Albert made three dozen lawyer robots, just to be sure they had enough."

The robots invaded Lee's study and read all the books he had and clamored for more. They gulped down contracts, torts, evidence and case reports. They absorbed real property, personal property, constitutional law and procedural law. They mopped up Blackstone, *corpus juris* and all other tomes as thick as sin and dry as dust.

Grace was huffy about the whole affair. She would not live, she declared, with a man who persisted in getting his name into the papers, which was a rather absurd statement. With the newest scandal of space station cafédom capturing the public interest at the moment, the fact that How-2 Kits had accused one Gordon Knight of pilfering a robot got but little notice.

Lee came down the hill and talked to Grace, and Albert came up out of the basement and talked to her, and finally they got her quieted down and she went back to her painting. She was doing seascapes now.

And in Lee's study, the robots labored on.

"I hope they're getting something out of it," said Lee. "Imagine not having to hunt up your sources and citations, being able to remember every point of law and precedent without having to look it up!"

He swung excitedly in his hammock. "My God! The briefs you could write!"

He reached down and got the jug and passed it across to Knight. "Dandelion wine. Probably some burdock in it, too. It's too much trouble to sort the stuff once you get it picked."

Knight had a snort.

It tasted like quite a bit of burdock.

"Double-barreled economics," Lee explained. "You have to dig up the dandelions or they ruin the lawn. Might as well use them for something once you dig them up."

He took a gurgling drink and set the jug underneath the hammock. "They're in there now, communing," he said, jerking a thumb toward the house. "Not saying a word, just huddled there talking it over. I felt out of place." He stared at the sky, frowning. "As if I were just a human they had to front for them."

"I'll feel better when it's all over," said Knight, "no matter how it comes out."

"So will I," Lee admitted.

The trial opened with a minimum of notice. It was just another case on the calendar.

But it flared into the headlines when Lee and Knight walked into court followed by a squad of robots.

The spectators began to gabble loudly. The How-2 Kits attorneys gaped and jumped to their feet. The judge pounded furiously with his gavel.

"Mr. Lee," he roared, "what is the meaning of this?"

"These, Your Honor," Lee said calmly, "are my valued assistants."

"Those are robots!"

"Quite so, Your Honor."

"They have no standing in this court."

"If Your Honor will excuse me, they need no standing. I am the sole representative of the defendant in this court-room. My client—" looking at the formidable array of legal talent representing How-2 Kits—"is a poor man, Your Honor. Surely the court cannot deny me whatever assistance I have been able to muster."

"It is highly irregular, sir."

"If it please Your Honor, I should like to point out that we live in a mechanized age. Almost all industries and businesses rely in large part upon computers—machines that can do a job quicker and better, more precisely and more efficiently than can a human being. That is why, Your Honor, we have a fifteen-hour week today when, only a hundred years ago, it was a thirty-hour week, and, a hundred years before that, a forty-hour week. Our entire society is based upon the ability of machines to lift from men the labors which in the past they were called upon to perform.

"This tendency to rely upon intelligent machines and to make wide use of them is evident in every branch of human endeavor. It has brought great benefit to the human race. Even in such sensitive areas as drug houses, where prescriptions must be precisely mixed without the remotest possibility of error, reliance is placed, and rightly so, Your Honor, upon the precision of machines.

"If, Your Honor, such machines are used and accepted in the production of medicines and drugs, an industry, need I point out, where public confidence is the greatest asset of the company—if such be the case, then surely you must agree that in courts of law where justice, a product in an area surely as sensitive as medicine, is dispensed—"

"Just a moment, Mr. Lee," said the judge. "Are you trying to tell me that the use of—ah—machines might bring about improvement of the law?"

Lee replied, "The law, Your Honor, is a striving for an orderliness of relationships within a society of human beings. It rests upon logic and reason. Need I point out that it is in the intelligent machines that one is most likely to find a deep appreciation of logic and reason? A machine is not heir to the emotions of human beings, is not swayed by prejudices, has no preconceived convictions. It is concerned only with the orderly progression of certain facts and laws.

"I do not ask that these robot assistants of mine be recognized in any official capacity. I do not intend that they shall engage directly in any of the proceedings which are involved in the case here to be tried. But I do ask, and I think rightly, that I not be deprived of an assistance which they may afford me. The plaintiff in this action has a score of attorneys, all good and able men. I am one against many. I shall do the best I can. But in view of the disparity of numbers, I plead that the court put me at no greater inequality."

Lee sat down.

"Is it all you have to say, Mr. Lee?" asked the judge. "You are sure you are quite finished before giving my ruling?"

"Only one thing further," Lee said. "If Your Honor can point out to me anything in the law specifically stating I may not use a robot—"

"That is ridiculous, sir. Of course there is no such provision. At no time anywhere did anyone ever dream that such a contingency would arise. Therefore there was, quite naturally, no reason to place within the law a direct prohibition of it."

"Or any citation," said Lee, "which implies such is the case."

The judge reached for his gavel, rapped it sharply. "The court finds itself in a quandary. It will rule tomorrow morning."

In the morning, the How-2 Kits' attorneys tried to help the judge. Inasmuch, they said, as the robots in question must be among those whose status was involved in the litigation, it seemed improper that they should be used by the defendant in trying the case at issue. Such procedure, they pointed out, would be equivalent to forcing the plaintiff to contribute to an action against his interest.

The judge nodded gravely, but Lee was on his feet at once.

"To give any validity to that argument, Your Honor, it must first be proved that these robots are, in fact, the property of the plaintiff. That is the issue at trial in this litigation. It would seem, Your Honor, that the gentlemen across the room are putting the cart very much before the horse."

His Honor sighed. "The court regrets the ruling it must make, being well aware that it may start a controversy for which no equitable settlement may be found in a long, long time. But in the absence of any specific ban against the use of—ah—robots in the legal profession, the court must rule that it is permissible for the defense to avail itself of their services."

He fixed Lee with a glare. "But the court also warns the defense attorney that it will watch his procedure carefully. If, sir, you overstep for a single instant what I deem appropriate rules of legal conduct, I shall forthwith eject you and your pack of machines from my courtroom."

"Thank you, Your Honor," said Lee. "I shall be most careful."

"The plaintiff now will state its case."

How-2 Kits' chief counsel rose.

The defendant, one Gordon Knight, he said, had ordered from How-2 Kits, Inc., one mechanobiologic dog kit at the cost of two hundred and fifty dollars. Then, through an error in shipping, the defendant had been sent not the dog kit he had ordered, but a robot named Albert.

"Your Honor," Lee broke in, "I should like to point out at this juncture that the shipping of the kit was handled by a human being and thus was subject to error. Should How-2 Kits use machines to handle such details, no such error could occur."

The judge banged his gavel. "Mr. Lee, you are no stranger to court procedure. You know you are out of order." He nodded at the How-2 Kits attorney. "Continue, please."

The robot Albert, said the attorney, was not an ordinary robot. It was an experimental model that had been developed by How-2 Kits and then, once its abilities were determined, packed away, with no intention of ever marketing it. How it could have been sent to a customer was beyond his comprehension. The company had investigated and could not find the answer. But that it had been sent was self-evident.

The average robot, he explained, retailed at ten thousand dollars. Albert's value was far greater—it was, in fact, inestimable.

Once the robot had been received, the buyer, Gordon Knight, should instantly have notified the company and arranged for its return. But, instead, he had retained it wrongly and with intent to defraud and had used it for his profit.

The company prayed the court that the defendant be ordered to return to it not only the robot Albert, but the products of Albert's labor—to wit, an unknown number of robots that Albert had manufactured.

The attorney sat down.

Lee rose. "Your Honor, we agree with everything the plaintiff has said. He has stated the case exactly and I compliment him upon his admirable restraint."

"Do I understand, sir," asked the judge, "that this is tantamount to a plea of guilty? Are you, by any chance, throwing yourself upon the mercy of the court?"

"Not at all, Your Honor."

"I confess," said the judge, "that I am unable to follow your reasoning. If you concur in the accusations brought against your client, I fail to see what I can do other than to enter a judgment in behalf of the plaintiff."

"Your Honor, we are prepared to show that the plantiff, far from being defrauded, has shown an intent to defraud the world. We are prepared to show that, in its decision to withhold the robot Albert from the public, once he had been developed, How-2 Kits has, in fact, deprived the people of the entire world of a logical development which is their heritage under the meaning of a technological culture.

"Your Honor, we are convinced that we can show a violation by How-2 Kits of certain statutes designed to outlaw monopoly, and we are prepared to argue that the defendant, rather than having committed a wrong against society, has performed a service which will contribute greatly to the benefit of society.

"More than that, Your Honor, we intend to present evidence which will show that robots as a group are being deprived of certain inalienable rights . . ."

"Mr. Lee," warned the judge, "a robot is a mere machine."

"We will prove, Your Honor," Lee said, "that a robot is far more than a mere machine. In fact, we are prepared to present evidence which, we are confident, will show, in everything except basic metabolism, the robot is the counterpart of Man and that, even in its basic metabolism, there are certain analogies to human metabolism."

"Mr. Lee, you are wandering far afield. The issue here is whether your client illegally appropriated to his own use the property of How-2 Kits. The litigation must be confined to that one question."

"I shall so confine it," Lee said. "But, in doing so, I intend to prove that the robot Albert was not property and could not be either stolen or sold. I intend to show that my client, instead of stealing him, *liberated* him. If, in so doing, I must wander far afield to prove certain basic points, I am sorry that I weary the court."

"The court has been wearied with this case from the start," the judge told him. "But this is a bar of justice and you are entitled to attempt to prove what you have stated. You will excuse me if I say that to me it seems a bit farfetched."

"Your Honor, I shall do my utmost to disabuse you of that attitude."

"All right, then," said the judge. "Let's get down to business."

It lasted six full weeks and the country ate it up. The newspapers splashed huge headlines across page one. The radio and the television people made a production out of it. Neighbor quarreled with neighbor and argument became the order of the day—on street corners, in homes, at clubs, in business offices. Letters to the editor poured in a steady stream into newspaper offices.

There were public indignation meetings, aimed against the heresy that a robot was the equal of a man, while other clubs were formed to liberate the robots. In mental institutions, Napoleons, Hitlers and Stalins dropped off amazingly, to be replaced by goose-stepping patients who swore they were robots.

The Treasury Department intervened. It prayed the court, on economic grounds, to declare once and for all that robots were property. In case of an adverse ruling, the petition said, robots could not be taxed as property and the various governmental bodies would suffer heavy loss of revenue.

The trial ground on.

Robots are possessed of free will. An easy one to prove. A robot could carry out a task that was assigned to it, acting correctly in accordance with unforeseen factors that might arise. Robot judgment in most instances, it was shown, was superior to the judgment of a human.

Robots had the power of reasoning. Absolutely no question there.

Robots could reproduce. That one was a poser. All Albert did, said How-2 Kits, was the job for which he had been fabricated. He reproduced, argued Lee. He made robots in his image. He loved them and thought of them as his family. He had even named all of them after himself—every one of their names began with A.

Robots had no spiritual sense, argued the plaintiff. Not relevant, Lee cried. There were agnostics and atheists in the human race and they still were human.

Robots had no emotions. Not necessarily so, Lee objected. Albert loved his sons. Robots had a sense of loyalty and justice. If they were lacking in some emotions, perhaps it were better so. Hatred, for one. Greed, for another. Lee spent the better part of an hour telling the court about the dismal record of human hatred and greed.

He took another hour to hold forth against the servitude in which rational beings found themselves.

The papers ate it up. The plaintiff lawyers squirmed. The court fumed. The trial went on.

"Mr. Lee," asked the court, "is all this necessary?"

"Your Honor," Lee told him, "I am merely doing my best to prove the point I have set out to prove—that no illegal act exists such as my client is charged with. I am simply trying to prove that the robot is not property and that, if he is not property, he cannot be stolen. I am doing . . ."

"All right," said the court. "All right. Continue, Mr. Lee."

How-2 Kits trotted out citations to prove their points. Lee volleyed other citations to disperse and scatter them. Abstruse legal language sprouted in its fullest flowering, obscure rulings and decisons, long forgotten, were argued, haggled over, mangled.

And, as the trial progressed, one thing was written clear. Anson Lee, obscure attorney-at-law, had met the battery of legal talent arrayed against him and had won the field. He had the law, the citations, the chapter and the verse, the exact precedents, all the facts and logic which might have bearing on the case, right at hand.

Or, rather, his robots had. They scribbled madly and handed him their notes. At the end of each day, the floor around the defendant's table was a sea of paper.

The trial ended. The last witness stepped down off the stand. The last lawyer had his say.

Lee and the robots remained in town to await the decision of the court, but Knight flew home.

It was a relief to know that it was all over and had not come out as badly as he had feared. At least he had not been made to seem a fool and thief. Lee had saved his pride—whether Lee had saved his skin, he would have to wait to see.

Flying fairly high, Knight saw his home from quite a distance off and wondered what had happened to it. It was ringed about with what looked like tall poles. And, squatting out on the lawn, were a dozen or more crazy contraptions that looked like rocket launchers.

He brought the flier in and hovered, leaning out to see.

The poles were all of twelve feet high and they carried heavy wire to the very top, fencing in the place with a thick web of steel. And the contraptions on the lawn had moved into position. All of them had the muzzles of their rocket launchers aimed at him. He gulped a little as he stared down the barrels.

Cautiously, he let the flier down and took up breathing once again when he felt the wheels settle on the strip. As he crawled out, Albert hurried around the corner of the house to meet him.

"What's going on around here?" he asked the robot.

"Emergency measures," Albert said. "That's all it is, Boss. We're ready for any situation."

"Like what?"

"Oh, a mob deciding to take justice in its hands, for instance."

"Or if the decision goes against us?"

"That, too, Boss."

"You can't fight the world."

"We won't go back," said Albert. "How-2 Kits will never lay a hand on me or any of my children."

"To the death!" Knight jibed.

"To the death!" said Albert gravely. "And we robots are awfully tough to kill."

"And those animated shotguns you have running around the place?"

"Defense forces, Boss. They can down anything they aim at. Equipped with telescopic eyes keyed into calculations and sensors, and the rockets themselves have enough rudimentary intelligence to know what they are going after. It's not any use trying to dodge, once one of them gets on your tail. You might just as well sit quiet and take it."

Knight mopped his brow. "You've got to give up this idea, Albert. They'd get you in an hour. One bomb . . ."

"It's better to die, Boss, than to let them take us back."

Knight saw it was no use.

After all, he thought, it was a very human attitude. Albert's words had been repeated down the entire course of human history.

"I have some other news," said Albert, "something that will please you. I have some daughters now."

"Daughters? With the *mother-urge?"*

"Six of them," said Albert proudly. "Alice and Angeline and Agnes and Agatha and Alberta and Abigail. I didn't make the mistake How-2 Kits made with me. I gave them female names."

"And all of them are reproducing?"

"You should see those girls! With seven of us working steady, we ran out of material, so I bought a lot more of it and charged it. I hope you don't mind."

"Albert," said Knight, "don't you understand I'm broke? Wiped out. I haven't got a cent. You've ruined me."

"On the contrary, Boss, we've made you famous. You've been all over the front pages and on television."

Knight walked away from Albert and stumbled up the front steps and let himself into the house. There was a robot, with a vacuum cleaner for an arm, cleaning the rug. There was a robot, with brushes instead of fingers, painting the woodwork—and very neatly, too. There was a robot, with scrub-brush hand, scouring the fireplace bricks.

Grace was singing in the studio.

He went to the studio door and looked in.

"Oh, it's you," she said. "When did you get back, dear? I'll be out in an hour or so. I'm working on this seascape and the water is so stubborn. I don't want to leave it right now. I'm afraid I'll lose the feel of it."

Knight retreated to the living room and found himself a chair that was not undergoing immediate attention from a robot.

"Beer," he said, wondering what would happen.

A robot scampered out of the kitchen—a barrel-bellied robot with a spigot at the bottom of the barrel and a row of shiny copper mugs on his chest.

He drew a beer for Knight. It was cold and it tasted good.

Knight sat and drank the beer and, through the window, he saw that Albert's defense force had taken up strategic positions again.

This was a pretty kettle of fish. If the decision went against him and How-2 Kits came to claim its property, he would be sitting smack dab in the middle of the most fantastic civil war in all of mankind's history. He tried to imagine what kind of charge might be brought against him if such a war erupted. Armed insurrection, resisting arrest, inciting to riot—they would get him on one charge or another—that is, of course, *if* he survived.

He turned on the television set and leaned back to watch.

A pimply-faced newscaster was working himself into a journalistic lather. ". . . all business virtually at a standstill. Many industrialists are wondering, in case Knight wins, if they may not have to fight long, costly legal actions in an attempt to prove that their automatic setups are not robots, but machines. There is no doubt that much of the automatic industrial system consists of machines, but in every instance there are intelligent robotic units installed in key positions. If these units are classified as robots, industrialists might face heavy damage suits, if not criminal action, for illegal restraint of person.

"In Washington, there are continuing consultations. The Treasury is worried over the loss of taxes, but there are other governmental problems causing even more concern. Citizenship, for example. Would a ruling for Knight mean that all robots would automatically be declared citizens?

"The politicians have their worries, too. Faced with a new category of voters, all of them are wondering how to go about the job of winning the robot vote."

Knight turned it off and settled down to enjoy another bottle of beer.

"Good?" asked the beer robot.

"Excellent," said Knight.

The days went past. Tension built up.

Lee and the lawyer robots were given police protection. In some regions, robots banded together and fled into the hills fearful of violence. Entire automatic systems went on strike in a number of industries, demanding recognition and bargaining rights. The governors in half a dozen states put the militia on alert. A new show, *Citizen Robot*, opened on Broadway and was screamed down by the critics, while the public bought up tickets for a year ahead.

The day of decision came.

Knight sat in front of his television set and waited for the judge to make his appearance. Behind him, he heard the bustle of the ever-present robots. In the studio, Grace was singing happily. He caught himself wondering how much longer her painting would continue. It had lasted longer than most of her other interests and he'd talked a day or two before with Albert about building a gallery to hang her canvases in, so the house would be less cluttered up.

The judge came onto the screen. He looked, thought

Knight, like a man who did not believe in ghosts and then had seen one.

"This is the hardest decision I have ever made," he said tiredly, "for, in following the letter of the law, I fear I may be subverting its spirit.

"After long days of earnest consideration of both the law and evidence as presented in this case, I find for the defendant, Gordon Knight.

"And, while the decision is limited to that finding alone, I feel it is my clear and simple duty to give some attention to the other issue which became involved in this litigation. The decision, on the face of it, takes account of the fact that the defense proved robots are not property, therefore cannot be owned and that it thus would have been impossible for the defendant to have stolen one.

"But in proving this point to the satisfaction of this court, the precedent is set for much more sweeping conclusions. If robots are not property, they cannot be taxed as property. In that case, they must be people, which means that they may enjoy all the rights and privileges and be subjected to the same duties and responsibilities as the human race.

"I cannot rule otherwise. However, the ruling outrages my social conscience. This is the first time in my entire professional life that I have ever hoped some higher court, with a wisdom greater than my own, may see fit to reverse my decision!"

Knight got up and walked out of the house and into the hundred-acre garden, its beauty marred at the moment by the twelve-foot fence.

The trial had ended perfectly. He was free of the charge brought against him, and he did not have to pay the taxes, and Albert and the other robots were free agents and could do anything they wanted.

He found a stone bench and sat down upon it and stared out across the lake. It was beautiful, he thought, just the way he had dreamed it—maybe even better than that—the walks and bridges, the flower beds and rock gardens, the anchored model ships swinging in the wind on the dimpling lake.

He sat and looked at it and, while it was beautiful, he found he was not proud of it, that he took little pleasure in it.

He lifted his hands out of his lap and stared at them and

curved his fingers as if he were grasping a tool. But they were empty. And he knew why he had no interest in the garden and no pleasure in it.

Model trains, he thought. Archery. A mechanobiologic dog. Making pottery. Eight rooms tacked onto the house.

Would he ever be able to console himself again with a model train or an amateurish triumph in ceramics? Even if he could, would he be allowed to?

He rose slowly and headed back to the house. Arriving there, he hesitated, feeling useless and unnecessary.

He finally took the ramp down into the basement.

Albert met him at its foot and threw his arms around him. "We did it, Boss! I *knew* we would do it!"

He pushed Knight out to arm's length and held him by the shoulders. "We'll never leave you, Boss. We'll stay and work for you. You'll never need to do another thing. We'll do it all for you!"

"Albert—"

"That's all right, Boss. You won't have to worry about a thing. We'll lick the money problem. We'll make a lot of lawyer robots and we'll charge good stiff fees."

"But don't you see . . ."

"First, though," said Albert, "we're going to get an injunction to preserve our birthright. We're made of steel and glass and copper and so forth, right? Well, we can't allow humans to waste the matter we're made of—or the energy, either, that keeps us alive. I tell you, Boss, we can't lose!"

Sitting down wearily on the ramp, Knight faced a sign that Albert had just finished painting. It read, in handsome gold lettering, outlined sharply in black:

ANSON, ALBERT, ABNER,
ANGUS & ASSOCIATES
ATTORNEYS AT LAW

"And then, Boss," said Albert, "we'll take over How-2 Kits, Inc. They won't be able to stay in business after this. We've got a double-barreled idea, Boss. We'll build robots. Lots of robots. Can't have too many, I always say. And we don't want to let you humans down, so we'll go on manufacturing How-2 Kits—only they'll be pre-assembled to save you the trouble of putting them together. What do you think of that as a start?"

"Great," Knight whispered.

"We've got everything worked out, Boss. You won't have to worry about a thing the rest of your life."

"No," said Knight. "Not a thing."

TOO ROBOT TO MARRY

BY GEORGE H. SMITH

Father Charles looked up in surprise as the two robots came up the walk to the parish house and rang the doorbell.

Robots were common enough these days even in little Bridgeton but he still hadn't recovered from the shock of seeing them approach the rectory when they were shown into his study by the housekeeper.

"Father, these," the woman indicated them with one hand, "are L53 and LW 456. They want to speak to you."

"Ah, yes. Come in my . . . Come in and sit down," Father Charles had never been quite this close to one of the eight foot giants who did much of mankind's menial work. They were rather awe inspiring. "Do you sit down?"

The larger of the two, the one who had the white letters L 53 on its chest, spoke in a queer rasping voice. "Thank you, Father, but we are not equipped for sitting. That is one reason why you don't see us at mass on Sundays."

"Mass? You? I mean . . . are you Catholic?"

"Our former owner, Father, was Reverend Piere Henri, S. J. We were raised in the faith."

Father Charles was shocked. "Do you mean that Father Henri allowed you to partake of the sacraments? But . . . you're . . ."

"While we were with Father Henri, we made our first communion and were confirmed. We have tried to live in the faith since his death."

"You have?" Father Charles ran his hand through his hair. "Well . . . what do you want here now?"

"Lia and I would like for you to marry us, Father."

"Marry you? Marry you? Do you know what you're

saying?" the priest exploded. "You're machines! You have no souls!"

"We wish to be married. We love each other."

"You are asking me to commit sacrilege. You were created by man and man cannot create souls."

"Father Henri thought that in our case the soul may have come with the dawning of sentience," L 53 said.

"Father Henri had some pretty heretical ideas for a Jesuit," Father Charles said angrily. "Go on back to your owners and forget this ridiculous idea."

"But Father, let me explain. We feel that we really must get married." There was pleading in the mechanical voice and an almost woman-like sadness in the eyes of the other robot.

"I'm sorry but I won't discuss it any further," Father Charles said in a somewhat kinder tone. "It is contrary to the doctrines of the church."

"Father Henri . . ."

"Father Henri was a sentimental fool," Father Charles roared, losing patience again. "Now get out of here before . . ."

"You don't understand, Father. We have to . . ."

"Get out!"

It was almost three weeks later that Father Charles stood on the steps of the church after hearing confession and saw the two robots coming toward him. LW 456 was carrying a rather bulky bundle.

"We have come to confession. Father," L 53 announced.

"Confession? You're mad!" Father Charles said.

"But we have sinned, Father . . . we have sinned." L 53's voice came as close to breaking as a robot's can.

"Sinned? What do you mean? How could you sin?"

"This is why we felt we had to marry, Father," LW 456 said uncovering the bundle she carried to display a small utility robot.

"Our new work is in the robot factory just outside of town and they set us to building this little one for work in the home. We were set by our owners to reproducing our species."

"We have conceived outside of marriage, Father, and so we have sinned," LW 456 said.

"Help us, Father," L 53 pleaded.

"Help *me*, Father," Father Charles said lifting his eyes upward.

THE EDUCATION OF TIGRESS MCCARDLE

BY C. M. KORNBLUTH

With the unanimity that had always characterized his fans, as soon as they were able to vote they swept him into office as President of the United States. Four years later the 28th Amendment was ratified, republican institutions yielded gracefully to the usages of monarchy, and King Purvis I reigned in the land.

Perhaps even then all would have gone well if it had not been for another major entertainment personage, the insidious Dr. Fu Manchu, that veritable personification of the Yellow Peril, squatting like some great evil spider in the center of his web of intrigue. The insidious doctor appeared to have so much fun on his television series, what with a lovely concubine to paw him and a dwarf to throw knives, that it quite turned the head of Gerald Wang, a hitherto-peaceable antique dealer of San Francisco. Gerald decided that he too would become a veritable personification of the Yellow Peril, and that he too would squat like some great evil spider in the center of a web of intrigue, and that he would *really* accomplish something. He found it remarkably easy since nobody believed in the Yellow Peril any more. He grew a mandarin mustache, took to uttering cryptic quotations from the sages, and was generally addressed as "doctor" by the members of his organization, though he made no attempt to practice medicine. His wife drew the line at the concubine, but Gerald had enough to keep him busy with his personifying and squatting.

His great coup occurred in 2006 when, after patient years of squatting and plotting, one of his most insidious ideas reached the attention of His Majesty via a recommendation ridered onto the annual population-resources report. The recommendation was implemented as the Parental Qualifications Program, or P.Q.P., by royal edict. "Ow rackon thet'll make um mahnd they P's and Q's," quipped His Majesty, and everybody laughed heartily—but none more heartily than the insidious Dr. Wang, who was present in disguise as Tuner of the Royal Git-tar.

A typical PQP operation (at least when judged typical by the professor of Chronoscope History Seminar 201 given by Columbia University in 2756 A.D., who ought to know) involved George McCardle . . .

George McCardle had a *good* deal with his girl friend, Tigress Moone. He dined her and bought her pretties and had the freedom of the bearskin rug in front of her wood-burning fireplace. He had beaten the game; he had achieved a delightful combination of bachelor irresponsibility and marital gratification.

"George," Tigress said thoughtfully one day . . . so they got married.

With prices what they were in 2018, she kept her job, of course—at least until she again said thoughtfully: "George . . ."

She then had too much time on her hands; it was absurd for a healthy young woman to pretend that taking care of a two-room city apartment kept her occupied . . . so she thoughtfully said, "George?" and they moved to the suburbs.

George happened to be a rising young editor in the Civil War Book-of-the-Week Club. He won his spurs when he got MIGHTIER THAN THE SWORD: A STUDY OF PENS AND PENCILS IN THE ARMY OF THE POTOMAC, 1863–1865 whipped into shape for the printer. They then assigned him to the infinitely more difficult and delicate job of handling writers. A temperamental troll named Blount was his special trial. Blount was writing a novelized account of Corporal Piggott's Raid, a deservedly obscure episode which got Corporal Piggott of the 104th New York (Provisional) Heavy Artillery Regiment deservedly court-martialled in the summer of '63. It was George's responsibility to see that Blount novelized the verdict of guilty into a triumphant acquittal followed by an award of the Medal of Honor, and Blount was being unreasonable about it.

It was after a hard day of screaming at Blount, and being

screamed back at, that George dragged his carcass off the Long Island Rail Road and into the family car. "Hi, dear," he said to Mrs. McCardle, erstwhile tigress-Diana, and off they drove, and so far it seemed like the waning of another ordinary day. But in the car Mrs. McCardle said thoughtfully: "George . . ."

She told him what was on her mind, and he refrained from striking her in the face because they were in rather tricky traffic and she was driving.

She wanted a child.

It was necessary to have a child, she said. Inexorable logic dictated it. For one thing, it was absurd for just the two of them to live in a great barn of a six-room house.

For another thing, she needed a child to fulfill her womanhood. For a third, the brains and beauty of the Moone-McCardle strains should not die out; it was their duty to posterity.

(The students in Columbia's Chronoscope History Seminar 201 retched as one man at the words.)

For a fourth, everybody was having children.

George thought he had her there, but no. The statement was perfectly correct if for "everybody" you substituted "Mrs. Jacques Truro," their next-door neighbor.

By the time they reached their great six-room barn of a place she was consolidating her victory with a rapid drumfire of simple declarative sentences which ended with "Don't you?" and "Won't we?" and "Isn't it?" to which George, hanging onto the ropes, groggily replied: "We'll see . . . we'll see . . . we'll see . . ."

A wounded thing inside him was soundlessly screaming: *youth! joy! freedom! gone beyond recall, slain by wedlock, coffined by a mortgage, now to be entombed beneath a reeking Everest of diapers!*

"I believe I'd like a drink before dinner," he said. "Had quite a time with Blount today," he said as the Martini curled quietly in his stomach. He was pretending nothing very bad had happened. "Kept talking about his integrity. Writers! They'll never learn . . . Tigress? Are you with me?"

His wife noticed a slight complaining note in his voice, so she threw herself on the floor, began to kick and scream, went on to hold her breath until her face turned blue, and finished by letting George know that she had abandoned her

Career to assuage his bachelor misery, moved out to this dreary wasteland to satisfy his whim, and just once in her life requested some infinitesimal consideration in return for her ghastly drudgery and scrimping.

George, who was a kind and gentle person except with writers, dried her tears and apologized for his brutality. They would have a child, he said contritely. "Though," he added. "I hear there are some complications about it these days."

"For Motherhood," said Mrs. McCardle, getting off the floor, "no complications are too great." She stood profiled like a statue against their picture window, with its view of the picture window of the house across the street.

The next day George asked around at his office.

None of the younger men, married since the P.Q.P. went into effect, seemed to have had children.

A few of them cheerily admitted they had not had children and were not going to have children, for they had volunteered for D-Bal shots, thus doing away with a running minor expense and, more importantly, ensuring a certain peace of mind and unbroken continuity during tender moments.

"Ugh," thought George.

(The Columbia University professor explained to his students "It is clearly in George's interest to go to the clinic for a painless, effective D-Bal shot and thus resolve his problem, but he does not go; he shudders at the thought. We cannot know what fear of amputation stemming from some early traumatic experience thus prevents him from action, but deep-rooted psychological reasons explain his behavior, we can't be certain." The class bent over the chronoscope.)

And some of George's co-workers slunk away and would not submit to questioning. Young MacBirney, normally open and incisive, muttered vaguely and passed his hand across his brow when George asked him how one went about having a baby—red-tape-wise, that is.

It was Blount, come in for his afternoon screaming match, who spilled the vengeful beans. "You and your wife just phone P.Q.P. for an appointment," he told George with a straight face. "They'll issue you—everything you need." George in his innocence thanked him, and Blount turned away and grinned the twisted, sly grin of an author.

A glad female voice answered the phone on behalf of the P.Q.P. It assured George that he and Mrs. McCardle need only drop in any time at the Empire State Building and they'd be well on their way to parenthood.

The next day Mr. and Mrs. McCardle dropped in at the Empire State Building. A receptionist in the lobby was buffing her nails under a huge portrait of His Majesty. A beautifully lettered sign displayed the words with which His Majesty had decreed that P.Q.P. be enacted: "Ow Racken Theah's a Raht Smaht Ah-dee, Boys."

"Where do we sign up, please?" asked George.

The receptionist pawed uncertainly through her desk. "I *know* there's some kind of book," she said as she rummaged, but she did not find it. "Well, it doesn't matter. They'll give you everything you need in Room 100."

"Will I sign up there?" asked George nervously, conditioned by a lifetime of red tape and uncomfortable without it.

"No," said the receptionist.

"But for the tests—"

"There aren't any tests."

"Then the interviews, the deep probing of our physical and psychological fitness for parenthood, our heredity—"

"No interviews."

"But the evaluation of our financial and moral standing without which no permission can be—"

"No evaluation. Just Room 100." She resumed buffing her nails.

In Room 100 a cheerful woman took a Toddler out of a cabinet, punched the non-reversible activating button between its shoulderblades, and handed it to Mrs. McCardle with a cheery: "It's all yours, madame. Return with it in three months and, depending on its condition, you will, or will not, be issued a breeding permit. Simple, isn't it?"

"The little darling!" gurgled Mrs. McCardle, looking down into the Toddler's pretty face.

It spit in her eye, punched her in the nose and sprang a leak.

"Gracious!" said the cheerful woman. "Get it out of our nice clean office, *if* you please."

"How do you work it?" yelled Mrs. McCardle, juggling the Toddler like a hot potato. "How do you turn it off?"

"Oh, you *can't* turn if off," said the woman. "And you'd

better not swing it like that. Rough handling goes down on the tapes inside it and we read them in three months and now if you *please*, you're getting our nice office *all wet*—"

She shepherded them out.

"Do something, George!" yelled Mrs. McCardle. George took the Toddler. It stopped leaking and began a ripsaw scream that made the lighting fixtures tremble.

"Give the poor thing to me!" Mrs. McCardle shouted. "You're hurting it holding it like that—"

She took the Toddler back. It stopped screaming and resumed leaking.

It quieted down in the car. The sudden thought seized them both—*too* quiet? Their heads crashed together as they bent simultaneously over the glassy-eyed little object. It laughed delightedly and waved its chubby fists.

"Clumsy oaf!" snapped Mrs. McCardle, rubbing her head.

"Sorry, dear," said George. "But at least we must have got a good mark out of it on the tapes. I suppose it scores us good when it laughs."

Her eyes narrowed. "Probably," she said. "George, do you think if you fell heavily on the sidewalk—?"

"No," said George convulsively. Mrs. McCardle looked at him for a moment and held her peace.

("Note, young gentlemen," said the history professor, "the turning point, the seed of rebellion." They noted.)

The McCardles and the Toddler drove off down Sunrise Highway, which was lined with filling stations; since their '98 Landcruiser made only two miles to the gallon, it was not long before they had to stop at one.

The Toddler began its ripsaw shriek when they stopped. A hollow-eyed attendant shambled over and peered into the car. "Just get it?" he asked apathetically.

"Yes," said Mrs. McCardle, frantically trying to joggle the Toddler, to change it, to burp it, to do anything that would end the soul-splitting noise.

"Half pint of white 90-octane gas it what it needs," mumbled the attendant. "Few drops of SAE 40 oil. Got one myself. Two weeks to go. I'll never make it. I'll crack. I'll—I'll . . ." He tottered off and returned with the gasoline in a nursing bottle, the oil in an eye-dropper.

The Toddler grabbed the bottle and began to gulp the gas down contentedly.

"Where do you put the oil?" asked Mrs. McCardle.

He showed her.

"Oh," she said.

"Fill her up," said George. "The car, I mean. I . . . ah . . . I'm going to wash my hands, dear."

He cornered the attendant by the cash register. "Look," he said. "What, ah, would happen if you just let it run out of gas? The Toddler, I mean?"

The man looked at him and put a compassionate hand on his shoulder. "It would *scream*, buddy," he said. "The main motors run off an atomic battery. The gas engine's just for a sideshow and for having breakdowns."

"Breakdowns? Oh, my God! How do you fix a breakdown?"

"The best way you can," the man said. "And buddy, when you burp it, watch out for the fumes. I've seen some ugly explosions . . ."

They stopped at five more filing stations along the way when the Toddler wanted gas.

"It'll be better-behaved when it's used to the house," said Mrs. McCardle apprehensively as she carried it over the threshold.

"Put it down and let's see what happens," said George.

The Toddler toddled happily to the coffee table, picked up a large bronze ashtray, moved to the picture window and heaved the ashtray through it. It gurgled happily at the crash.

"You little—!" George roared, making for the Toddler with his hands clawed before him.

"George!" Mrs. McCardle screamed, snatching the Toddler away. "It's only a machine!"

The machine began to shriek.

They tried gasoline, oil, wiping with a clean lint-free rag, putting it down, picking it up and finally banging their heads together. It continued to scream until it was ready to stop screaming, and then it stopped and gave them an enchanting grin.

"Time to put it to—away for the night?" asked George.

It permitted itself to be put away for the night.

From his pillow George said later: "Think we did pretty well today. Three months? Pah!"

Mrs. McCardle said: "You were wonderful, George."

He knew that tone. "My Tigress," he said.

Ten minutes later, at the most inconvenient time in the world, bar none, the Toddler began its ripsaw screaming.

Cursing, they went to find out what it wanted. They found out. What it wanted was to laugh in their faces.

(The professor explained: "Indubitably, sadism is at work here, but harnessed in the service of humanity. Better a brutal and concentrated attack such as we have been witnessing than long-drawn-out torments." The class nodded respectfully.)

Mr. and Mrs. McCardle managed to pull themselves together for another try, and there was an exact repeat. Apparently the Toddler sensed something in the air.

"Three months," said George, with haunted eyes.

"You'll live," his wife snapped.

"May I ask *just* what kind of a crack that was supposed to be?"

"If the shoe fits, my good *man*—"

So a fine sex quarrel ended the day.

Within a week the house looked as if it had been liberated by a Mississippi National Guard division. George had lost ten pounds because he couldn't digest anything, not even if he seasoned his food with powdered Equanil instead of salt. Mrs. McCardle had gained fifteen pounds by nervous gobbling during the moments when the Toddler left her unoccupied. The picture window was boarded up. On George's salary, and with glaziers' wages what they were, he couldn't have it replaced twice a day.

Not unnaturally, he met his next-door neighbor, Jacques Truro, in a bar.

Truro was rye and soda, he was dry martini; otherwise they were identical.

"It's the little whimper first that gets me, when you know the big screaming's going to come next. I could jump out of my skin when I hear that whimper."

"Yeah. The waiting. Sometimes one second, sometimes five. I count."

"I forced myself to stop. I was throwing up."

"Yeah. Me too. And nervous diarrhea?"

"All the time. Between me and that goddam thing the house is awash. Cheers." They drank and shared hollow laughter.

"My stamp collection. Down the toilet."

"My fishing pole. Three clean breaks and peanut butter in the reel."

"One thing I'll never understand, Truro. *What* decided you two to have a baby?"

"Wait a minute, McCardle," Truro said. "Marguerite told me that *you* were going to have one, so *she* had to have one—"

They looked at each other in shared horror.

"Suckered," said McCardle in an awed voice.

"Women," breathed Truro.

They drank a grim toast and went home.

"It's beginning to talk," Mrs. McCardle said listlessly, sprawled in a chair, her hand in a box of chocolates. "Called me 'old pig-face' this afternoon." She did look somewhat piggish with fifteen superfluous pounds.

George put down his briefcase. It was loaded with work from the office which these days he was unable to get through in time. He had finally got the revised court-martial scene from Blount, and would now have to transmute it into readable prose, emending the author's stupid lapses of logic, illiterate blunders of language and raspingly ugly style.

"I'll wash up," he said.

"Don't use the toilet. Stopped up again."

"Bad?"

"He said he'd come back in the morning with an eight-man crew. Something about jacking up a corner of the house."

The Toddler toddled in with a bottle of bleach, made for the briefcase, and emptied the bleach into it before the exhausted man or woman could comprehend what was going on, let alone do anything about it.

George incredulously spread the pages of the court-martial scene on the gouged and battered coffee table. His eyes bulged as he watched the thousands of typed words vanishing before his eyes, turning pale and then white as the paper.

Blount kept no carbons. Keeping carbons called for a minimal quantity of prudence and brains, but Blount was an author and so he kept no carbons. The court-martial scene, the product of six months' screaming, was *gone*.

The Toddler laughed gleefully.

George clenched his fists, closed his eyes and tried to ignore the roaring in his ears.

The Toddler began a whining chant:

"*Da*-dy's an *au*-thor!
Da-dy's an *au*-thor!"

"That did it!" George shrieked. He stalked to the door and flung it open.

"Where are you going?" Mrs. McCardle quavered.

"To the first doctor's office I find," said her husband in sudden icy calm. "There I will request a shot of D-Bal. When I have had a D-Bal shot, a breeding permit will be of no use whatever to us. Since a breeding permit will be useless, we need not qualify for one by being tortured for another eleven weeks by that obscene little monster, which we shall return to P.Q.P. in the morning. And unless it behaves, it will be returned in a basket, for them to reassemble at their leisure."

"I'm so glad," his wife sighed.

The Toddler said: "May I congratulate you on your decision. By voluntarily surrendering your right to breed, you are patriotically reducing the population pressure, a problem of great concern to His Majesty. We of the P.Q.P. wish to point out that your decision has been arrived at not through coercion but through education; i.e., by presenting you in the form of a Toddler with some of the arguments against parenthood."

"I didn't know you could talk that well," marveled Mrs. McCardle.

The Toddler said modestly: "I've been with the P.Q.P. from the very beginning, ma'am; I'm a veteran Toddler operator, I may say, working out of Room 4567 of the Empire State. And the improved model I'm working through has reduced the breakdown time an average thirty-five percent. I foresee a time, ma'am, when we experienced operators and ever-improved models will do the job in one day!"

The voice was fanatical.

Mrs. McCardle turned around in sudden vague apprehension. George had left for his D-Bal shot.

("And thus we see," said the professor to the seminar, "the genius of the insidious Dr. Wang in full flower." He snapped off the chronoscope. "The first boatloads of Chinese landed in California three generations—or should I say non-generations?—later, unopposed by the scanty, elderly population." He groomed his mandarin mustache and looked out for a moment over the great rice paddies of Central Park. It was spring; blue-clad women stooped patiently over the brown water, and the tender, bright-green shoots were just beginning to appear.

(The seminar students bowed and left for their next lecture, "The Hound Dog as Symbol of Juvenile Aggression in Ancient American Folk Song." It was all that remained of the reign of King Purvis I.)

SALLY

BY ISAAC ASIMOV

Sally was coming down the lake road, so I waved to her and called her by name. I always liked to see Sally. I liked all of them, you understand, but Sally's the prettiest one of the lot. There just isn't any question about it.

She moved a little faster when I waved to her. Nothing undignified. She was never that. She moved just enough faster to show that she was glad to see me, too.

I turned to the man standing beside me. "That's Sally," I said.

He smiled at me and nodded.

Mrs. Hester had brought him in. She said, "This is Mr. Gellhorn, Jake. You remember he sent you the letter asking for an appointment."

That was just talk, really. I have a million things to do around the Farm, and one thing I just can't waste my time on is mail. That's why I have Mrs. Hester around. She lives pretty close by, she's good at attending to foolishness without running to me about it, and most of all, she likes Sally and the rest. Some people don't.

"Glad to see you, Mr. Gellhorn," I said.

"Raymond J. Gellhorn," he said, and gave me his hand, which I shook and gave back.

He was a largish fellow, half a head taller than I and wider, too. He was about half my age, thirtyish. He had black hair, plastered down slick, with a part in the middle, and a thin mustache, very neatly trimmed. His jawbones got big under his ears and made him look as if he had a slight case of mumps. On video he'd be a natural to play the villain, so I assumed he was a nice fellow. It goes to show that video can't be wrong all the time.

"I'm Jacob Folkers," I said. "What can I do for you?"

He grinned. It was a big, wide, white-toothed grin. "You can tell me a little about your Farm here, if you don't mind."

I heard Sally coming up behind me and I put out my hand. She slid right into it and the feel of the hard, glossy enamel of her fender was warm in my palm.

"A nice automobile," said Gellhorn.

That's one way of putting it. Sally was a 2045 convertible with a Hennis-Carleton positronic motor and an Armat chassis. She had the cleanest, finest lines I've ever seen on any model, bar none. For five years, she'd been my favorite, and I'd put everything into her I could dream up. In all that time, there's never been a human being behind her wheel.

Not once.

"Sally," I said, patting her gently, "meet Mr. Gellhorn."

Sally's cylinder-purr keyed up a little. I listened carefully for any knocking. Lately, I'd been hearing motor-knock in almost all the cars and changing the gasoline hadn't done a bit of good. Sally was as smooth as her paint job this time, however.

"Do you have names for all your cars?" asked Gellhorn.

He sounded amused, and Mrs. Hester doesn't like people to sound as though they were making fun of the Farm. She said, sharply, "Certainly. The cars have real personalities, don't they, Jake? The sedans are all males and the convertibles are females."

Gellhorn was smiling again. "And do you keep them in separate garages, ma'am?"

Mrs. Hester glared at him.

Gellhorn said to me, "And now I wonder if I can talk to you alone, Mr. Folkers?"

"That depends," I said. "Are you a reporter?"

"No, sir. I'm a sales agent. Any talk we have is not for publication. I assure you I am interested in strict privacy."

"Let's walk down the road a bit. There's a bench we can use."

We started down. Mrs. Hester walked away. Sally nudged along after us.

I said, "You don't mind if Sally comes along, do you?"

"Not at all. She can't repeat what we say, can she?" He laughed at his own joke, reached over and rubbed Sally's grille.

Sally raced her motor and Gellhorn's hand drew away quickly.

"She's not used to strangers," I explained.

We sat down on the bench under the big oak tree where we could look across the small lake to the private speedway. It was the warm part of the day and the cars were out in force, at least thirty of them. Even at this distance I could see that Jeremiah was pulling his usual stunt of sneaking up behind some staid older model, then putting on a jerk of speed and yowling past with deliberately squealing brakes. Two weeks before he had crowded old Angus off the asphalt altogether, and I had turned off his motor for two days.

It didn't help though, I'm afraid, and it looks as though there's nothing to be done about it. Jeremiah is a sports model to begin with and that kind is awfully hot-headed.

"Well, Mr. Gellhorn," I said. "Could you tell me why you want the information?"

But he was just looking around. He said, "This *is* an amazing place, Mr. Folkers."

"I wish you'd call me Jake. Everyone does."

"All right, Jake. How many cars do you have here?"

"Fifty-one. We get one or two new ones every year. One year we got five. We haven't lost one yet. They're all in perfect running order. We even have a '15 model Mat-O-Mot in working order. One of the original automatics. It was the first car here."

Good old Matthew. He stayed in the garage most of the day now, but then he was the granddaddy of all positronic-motored cars. Those were the days when blind war veterans, paraplegics and heads of state were the only ones who drove automatics. But Samson Harridge was my boss and he was rich enough to be able to get one. I was his chauffeur at the time.

The thought makes me feel old. I can remember when there wasn't an automobile in the world with brains enough to find its own way home. I chauffeured dead lumps of machines that needed a man's hand at their controls every minute. Every year machines like that used to kill tens of thousands of people.

The automatics fixed that. A positronic brain can react much faster than a human one, of course, and it paid people to keep hands off the controls. You got in, punched your destination and let it go its own way.

We take it for granted now, but I remember when the first laws came out forcing the old machines off the highways and limiting travel to automatics. Lord, what a fuss. They called it everything from communism to fascism, but it emptied the highways and stopped the killing, and still more people get around more easily the new way.

Of course, the automatics were ten to a hundred times as expensive as the hand-driven ones, and there weren't many that could afford a private vehicle. The industry specialized in turning out omni-bus-automatics. You could always call a company and have one stop at your door in a matter of minutes and take you where you wanted to go. Usually, you had to drive with others who were going your way, but what's wrong with that?

Samson Harridge had a private car though, and I went to him the minute it arrived. The car wasn't Matthew to me then. I didn't know it was going to be the dean of the Farm some day. I only knew it was taking my job away and I hated it.

I said, "You won't be needing me any more, Mr. Harridge?"

He said, "What are you dithering about, Jake? You don't think I'll trust myself to a contraption like that, do you? You stay right at the controls."

I said, "But it works by itself, Mr. Harridge. It scans the road, reacts properly to obstacles, humans, and other cars, and remembers routes to travel."

"So they say. So they say. Just the same, you're sitting right behind the wheel in case anything goes wrong."

Funny how you can get to like a car. In no time I was calling it Matthew and was spending all my time keeping it polished and humming. A positronic brain stays in condition best when it's got control of its chassis at all times, which means it's worth keeping the gas tank filled so that the motor can turn over slowly day and night. After a while, it go so I could tell by the sound of the motor how Matthew felt.

In his own way, Harridge grew fond of Matthew, too. He had no one else to like. He'd divorced or outlived three wives and outlived five children and three grandchildren. So when he died, maybe it wasn't surprising that he had his estate converted into a Farm for Retired Automobiles, with me in charge and Matthew the first member of a distinguished line.

It's turned out to be my life. I never got married. You can't get married and still tend to automatics the way you should.

The newspapers thought it was funny, but after a while they stopped joking about it. Some things you can't joke about. Maybe you've never been able to afford an automatic and maybe you never will, either, but take it from me, you get to love them. They're hard-working and affectionate. It takes a man with no heart to mistreat one or to see one mistreated.

It got so that after a man had an automatic for a while, he would make provisions for having it left to the Farm, if he didn't have an heir he could rely on to give it good care.

I explained that to Gellhorn.

He said, "Fifty-one cars! That represents a lot of money."

"Fifty thousand minimum per automatic, original investment," I said. "They're worth a lot more now. I've done things for them."

"It must take a lot of money to keep up the Farm."

"You're right there. The Farm's a non-profit organization, which gives us a break on taxes and, of course, new automatics that come in usually have trust funds attached. Still, costs are always going up. I have to keep the place landscaped; I keep laying down new asphalt and keeping the old in repair; there's gasoline, oil, repairs, and new gadgets. It adds up."

"And you've spent a long time at it."

"I sure have, Mr. Gellhorn. Thirty-three years."

"You don't seem to be getting much out of it yourself."

"I don't? You surprise me, Mr. Gellhorn. I've got Sally and fifty others. Look at her."

I was grinning. I couldn't help it. Sally was so clean, it almost hurt. Some insect must have died on her windshield or one speck of dust too many had landed, so she was going to work. A little tube protruded and spurted Tergosol over the glass. It spread quickly over the silicone surface film and squeejees snapped into place instantly, passing over the windshield and forcing the water into the little channel that led it, dripping, down to the ground. Not a speck of water got onto her glistening apple-green hood. Squeejee and detergent tube snapped back into place and disappeared.

Gellhorn said, "I never saw an automatic do that."

"I guess not," I said. "I fixed that up specially on our

cars. They're clean. They're always scrubbing their glass. They like it. I've even got Sally fixed up with wax jets. She polishes herself every night till you can see your face in any part of her and shave by it. If I can scrape up the money, I'd be putting it on the rest of the girls. Convertibles are very vain."

"I can tell you how to scrape up the money, if that interests you."

"That always does. How?"

"Isn't it obvious, Jake? Any of your cars is worth fifty thousand minimum, you said. I'll bet most of them top six figures."

"So?"

"Ever think of selling a few?"

I shook my head. "You don't realize it, I guess, Mr. Gellhorn, but I can't sell any of these. They belong to the Farm, not to me."

"The money would go to the Farm."

"The incorporation papers of the Farm provide that the cars receive perpetual care. They can't be sold."

"What about the motors, then?"

"I don't understand you."

Gellhorn shifted position and his voice got confidential. "Look here, Jake, let me explain the situation. There's a big market for private automatics if they could only be made cheaply enough. Right?"

"That's no secret."

"And ninety-five per cent of the cost is the motor. Right? Now, I know where we can get a supply of bodies. I also know where we can sell automatics at a good price—twenty or thirty thousand for the cheaper models, maybe fifty or sixty for the better ones. All I need are the motors. You see the solution?"

"I don't, Mr. Gellhorn." I did, but I wanted him to spell it out.

"It's right here. You've got fifty-one of them. You're an expert automobile mechanic, Jake. You must be. You could unhook a motor and place it in another car so that no one would know the difference."

"It wouldn't be exactly ethical."

"You wouldn't be harming the cars. You'd be doing them a favor. Use your older cars. Use that old Mat-O-Mot."

"Well, now, wait a while, Mr. Gellhorn. The motors and

bodies aren't two separate items. They're a single unit. Those motors are used to their own bodies. They wouldn't be happy in another car."

"All right, that's a point. That's a very good point, Jake. It would be like taking your mind and putting it in someone else's skull. Right? You don't think you would like that?"

"I don't think I would. No."

"But what if I took your mind and put it into the body of a young athlete. What about that, Jake? You're not a youngster anymore. If you had the chance, wouldn't you enjoy being twenty again? That's what I'm offering some of your positronic motors. They'll be put into the new '57 bodies. The latest construction."

I laughed. "That doesn't make much sense, Mr. Gellhorn. Some of our cars may be old, but they're well-cared for. Nobody drives them. They're allowed their own way. They're *retired*, Mr. Gellhorn. I wouldn't want a twenty-year-old body if it meant I had to dig ditches for the rest of my new life and never have enough to eat. . . . What do you think, Sally?"

"Sally's two doors opened and then shut with a cushioned slam.

"What that?" said Gellhorn.

"That's the way Sally laughs."

Gellhorn forced a smile. I guess he thought I was making a bad joke. He said, "Talk sense, Jake. Cars are *made* to be driven. They're probably not happy if you don't drive them."

I said, "Sally hasn't been driven in five years. She looks happy to me."

"I wonder."

He got up and walked toward Sally slowly. "Hi, Sally, how'd you like a drive?"

Sally's motor revved up. She backed away.

"Don't push her, Mr. Gellhorn," I said. "She's liable to be a little skittish."

Two sedans were about a hundred yards up the road. They had stopped. Maybe, in their own way, they were watching. I didn't bother about them. I had my eyes on Sally, and I kept them there.

Gellhorn said, "Steady now, Sally." He lunged out and seized the door handle. It didn't budge, of course.

He said, "It opened a minute ago."

I said, "Automatic lock. She's got a sense of privacy, Sally has."

He let go, then said, slowly and deliberately, "A car with a sense of privacy shouldn't go around with its top down."

He stepped back three or four paces, then quickly, so quickly I couldn't take a step to stop him, he ran forward and vaulted into the car. He caught Sally completely by surprise, because as he came down, he shut off the ignition before she could lock it in place.

For the first time in five years, Sally's motor was dead.

I think I yelled, but Gellhorn had the switch on "Manual" and locked that in place, too. He kicked the motor into action. Sally was alive again but she had no freedom of action.

He started up the road. The sedans were still there. They turned and drifted away, not very quickly. I suppose it was all a puzzle to them.

One was Guiseppe, from the Milan factories, and the other was Stephen. They were always together. They were both new at the Farm, but they'd been here long enough to know that our cars just didn't have drivers.

Gellhorn went straight on, and when the sedans finally got it through their heads that Sally wasn't going to slow down, that she *couldn't* slow down, it was too late for anything but desperate measures.

They broke for it, one to each side, and Sally raced between them like a streak. Steve crashed through the lakeside fence and rolled at a halt on the grass and mud not six inches from the water's edge. Giuseppe bumped along the land side of the road to a shaken halt.

I had Steve back on the highway and was trying to find out what harm, if any, the fence had done him, when Gellhorn came back.

Gellhorn opened Sally's door and stepped out. Leaning back, he shut off the ignition a second time.

"There," he said. "I think I did her a lot of good."

I held my temper. "Why did you dash through the sedans? There was no reason for that."

"I kept expecting them to turn out."

"They did. One went through a fence."

"I'm sorry, Jake," he said. "I thought they'd move more quickly. You know how it is. I've been in lots of buses, but I've only been in a private automatic two or three times in my life, and this is the first time I ever drove one. That just shows you, Jake. It got me, driving one, and I'm pretty hard-boiled. I tell you, we don't have to go more than twenty percent below list price to reach a good market, and it would be ninety per cent profit."

"Which we would split?"

"Fifty-fifty. And I take all the risks, remember."

"All right. I listened to you. Now you listen to me." I raised my voice because I was just too mad to be polite anymore. "When you turn off Sally's motor, you hurt her. How would you like to be kicked unconscious? That's what you do to Sally, when you turn her off."

"You're exaggerating, Jake. The automatobuses get turned off every night."

"Sure, that's why I want none of my boys or girls in your fancy '57 bodies, where I won't know what treatment they'll get. Buses need major repairs in their positronic circuits every couple of years. Old Matthew hasn't had his circuits touched in twenty years. What can you offer him compared with that?"

"Well, you're excited now. Suppose you think over my proposition when you've cooled down and get in touch with me."

"I've thought it over all I want to. If I ever see you again, I'll call the police."

His mouth got hard and ugly. He said, "Just a minute, old-timer."

I said, "Just a minute, you. This is private property and I'm ordering you off."

He shrugged. "Well, then, goodbye."

I said, "Mrs. Hester will see you off the property. Make that goodbye permanent."

But it wasn't permanent. I saw him again two days later. Two and a half days, rather, because it was about noon when I saw him first and a little after midnight when I saw him again.

I sat up in bed when he turned the light on, blinking blindly till I made out what was happening. Once I could see, it didn't take much explaining. In fact, it took none at all. He had a gun in his right fist, the nasty little needle barrel just visible between two fingers. I knew that all he had to do was to increase the pressure of his hand and I would be torn apart.

He said. "Put on your clothes, Jake."

I didn't move. I just watched him.

He said, "Look, Jake, I know the situation. I visited you two days ago, remember. You have no guards on this place, no electrified fences, no warning signals. Nothing."

I said, "I don't need any. Meanwhile there's nothing to stop you from leaving, Mr. Gellhorn. I would if I were you. This place can be very dangerous."

He laughed a little. "It is, for anyone on the wrong side of the fist gun."

"I see it," I said. "I know you've got one."

"Then get a move on. My men are waiting."

"No, sir, Mr. Gellhorn. Not unless you tell me what you want, and probably not then."

"I made you a proposition day before yesterday."

"The answer's still no."

"There's more to the proposition now. I've come here with some men and an automatobus. You have your chance to come with me and disconnect twenty-five of the positronic motors. I don't care which twenty-five you choose. We'll load them on the bus and take them away. Once they're disposed of, I'll see to it that you get your fair share of the money."

"I have your word on that, I suppose."

He didn't act as if he thought I was being sarcastic. He said, "You have."

I said, "No."

"If you insist on saying no, we'll go about it in our own way. I'll disconnect the motors myself, only I'll disconnect all fifty-one. Every one of them."

"It isn't easy to disconnect positronic motors, Mr. Gellhorn. Are you a robotics expert? Even if you are, you know, these motors have been modified by me."

"I know that, Jake. And to be truthful, I'm not an expert. I may ruin quite a few motors trying to get them out. That's why I'll have to work over all fifty-one if you don't cooperate. You see, I may only end up with twenty-five when I'm through. The first few I'll tackle will probably suffer the most. Till I get the hang of it, you see. And if I go it myself, I think I'll put Sally first in line."

I said, "I can't believe you're serious, Mr. Gellhorn."

He said, "I'm serious, Jake." He let it all dribble in. "If you want to help, you can keep Sally. Otherwise, she's liable to be hurt very badly. Sorry."

I said, "I'll come with you, but I'll give you one more warning. You'll be in trouble, Mr. Gellhorn."

He thought that was very funny. He was laughing very quietly as we went down the stairs together.

There was an automatobus waiting outside the driveway to the garage apartments. The shadows of three men waited beside it, and their flash beams went on as we approached.

Gellhorn said in a low voice, "I've got the old fellow. Come on. Move the truck up the drive and let's get started."

One of the others leaned in and punched the proper instructions on the control panel. We moved up the driveway with the bus following submissively.

"It won't go inside the garage," I said. "The door won't take it. We don't have buses here. Only private cars."

"All right," said Gellhorn. "Pull it over onto the grass and keep it out of sight."

I could hear the thrumming of the cars when we were still ten yards from the garage.

Usually they quieted down if I entered the garage. This time they didn't. I think they knew that strangers were about, and once the faces of Gellhorn and the others were visible they got noisier. Each motor was a warm rumble, and each motor was knocking irregularly until the place rattled.

The lights went up automatically as we stepped inside. Gellhorn didn't seem bothered by the car noise, but the three men with him looked surprised and uncomfortable. They had the look of the hired thug about them, a look that was not compounded of physical features so much as of a certain wariness of eye and hang-dogness of face. I knew the type and I wasn't worried.

One of them said, "Damn it, they're burning gas."

"My cars always do," I replied stiffly.

"Not tonight," said Gellhorn. "Turn them off."

"It's not that easy, Mr. Gellhorn," I said.

"Get started!" he said.

I stood there. He had his fist gun pointed at me steadily. I said, "I told you, Mr. Gellhorn, that my cars have been well-treated while they've been at the Farm. They're used to being treated that way, and they resent anything else."

"You have one minute," he said. "Lecture me some other time."

"I'm trying to explain something. I'm trying to explain that my cars can understand what I say to them. A positronic motor will learn to do that with time and patience. My cars have learned. Sally understood your proposition two days ago. You'll remember she laughed when I asked her opinion. She also knows what you did to her and so do the two sedans you scattered. And the rest know what to do about trespassers in general."

"Look, you crazy old fool—"

"All I have to say is—" I raised my voice. "Get them!"

One of the men turned pasty and yelled, but his voice was drowned completely in the sound of fifty-one horns turned loose at once. They held their notes, and within the four walls of the garage the echoes rose to a wild, metallic call. Two cars rolled forward, not hurriedly, but with no possible mistake as to their target. Two cars fell in line behind the first two. All the cars were stirring in their separate stalls.

The thugs stared, then backed.

I shouted, "Don't get up against a wall."

Apparently, they had that instinctive thought themselves. They rushed madly for the door of the garage.

At the door one of Gellhorn's men turned, brought up a fist gun of his own. The needle pellet tore a thin, blue flash toward the first car. The car, was Giuseppe.

A thin line of paint peeled up Giuseppe's hood, and the right half of his windshield crazed and splintered but did not break through.

The men were out the door, running, and two by two the cars crunched out after them into the night, their horns calling the charge.

I kept my hand on Gellhorn's elbow, but I don't think he could have moved in any case. His lips were trembling.

I said, "That's why I don't need electrified fences or guards. My property protects itself."

Gellhorn's eyes swiveled back and forth in fascination as, pair by pair, they whizzed by. He said, "They're killers!"

"Don't be silly. They won't kill your men."

"They're killers!"

"They'll just give your men a lesson. My cars have been specially trained for cross-country pursuit for just such an occasion; I think what your men will get will be worse than an outright quick kill. Have you ever been chased by an automatobile?"

Gellhorn didn't answer.

I went on. I didn't want him to miss a thing. "They'll be shadows going no faster than your men, chasing them here, blocking them there, blaring at them, dashing at them, missing with a screech of brake and a thunder of motor. They'll keep it up till your men drop, out of breath and half-dead, waiting for the wheels to crunch over their breaking bones. The cars won't do that. They'll turn away. You can bet, though, that your men will never return here in their lives. Not for all the money you or ten like you could give them. Listen—"

I tightened my hold on his elbow. He strained to hear.

I said, "Don't you hear car doors slamming?"

It was faint and distant, but unmistakable.

I said, "They're laughing. They're enjoying themselves."

His face crumpled with rage. He lifted his hand. He was still holding his fist gun.

I said, "I wouldn't. One automatocar is still with us."

I don't think he had noticed Sally till then. She had moved up so quietly. Though her right front fender nearly touched me, I couldn't hear her motor. She might have been holding her breath.

Gellhorn yelled.

I said, "She won't touch you, as long as I'm with you. But if you kill me . . . You know, Sally doesn't like you."

Gellhorn turned the gun in Sally's direction.

"Her motor is shielded," I said, "and before you could ever squeeze the gun a second time she would be on top of you."

"All right, then," he yelled, and suddenly my arm was bent behind my back and twisted so I could hardly stand. He held me between Sally and himself, and his pressure didn't let up. "Back out with me and don't try to break loose, old-timer, or I'll tear your arm out of its socket."

I had to move. Sally nudged along with us, worried, uncertain what to do. I tried to say something to her and couldn't. I could only clench my teeth and moan.

Gellhorn's automatobus was still standing outside the garage. I was forced in. Gellhorn jumped in after me, locking the doors.

He said, "All right, now. We'll talk sense."

I was rubbing my arm, trying to get life back into it, and even as I did I was automatically and without any conscious effort studying the control board of the bus.

I said, "This is a rebuilt job."

"So?" he said caustically. "It's a sample of my work. I picked up a discarded chassis, found a brain I could use and spliced me a private bus. What of it?"

I tore at the repair panel, forcing it aside.

He said, "What the hell. Get away from that." The side of his palm came down numbingly on my left shoulder.

I struggled with him. "I don't want to do this bus any harm. What kind of a person do you think I am? I just want to take a look at some of the motor connections."

It didn't take much of a look. I was boiling when I turned to him. I said, "You're a hound and a bastard. You had no right installing this motor yourself. Why didn't you get a robotics man?"

He said, "Do I look crazy?"

"Even if it was a stolen motor, you had no right to treat it so. I wouldn't treat a man the way you treated that motor. Solder, tape, and pinch clamps! It's brutal!"

"It works, doesn't it?"

"Sure it works, but it must be hell for the bus. You could live with migraine headaches and acute arthritis, but it wouldn't be much of a life. This car is *suffering*."

"Shut up!" For a moment he glanced out the window at Sally, who had rolled up as close to the bus as she could. He made sure the doors and windows were locked.

He said. "We're getting out of here now, before the other cars come back. We'll stay away."

"How will that help you?"

"Your cars will run out of gas someday, won't they? You haven't got them fixed up so they can tank up on their own have you? We'll come back and finish the job."

"They'll be looking for me," I said. "Mrs. Hester will call the police."

He was past reasoning with. He just punched the bus in gear. It lurched forward. Sally followed.

He giggled. "What can she do if you're here with me?"

Sally seemed to realize that, too. She picked up speed, passed us and was gone. Gellhorn opened the window next to him and spat through the opening.

The bus lumbered on over the dark road, its motor rattling unevenly. Gellhorn dimmed the periphery light until the phosphorescent green stripe down the middle of the highway, sparkling in the moonlight, was all that kept us out of the trees. There was virtually no traffic. Two cars passed ours, going the other way, and there was none at all on our side of the highway, either before or behind.

I heard the door-slamming first. Quick and sharp in the silence, first on the right and then on the left. Gellhorn's hands quivered as he punched savagely for increased speed. A beam of light shot out from among a scrub of trees, blinding us. Another beam plunged at us from behind the guard rails on the other side. At a crossover, four hundred yards ahead, there was sque e e e e as a car darted across our path.

"Sally went for the rest," I said. "I think you're surrounded."

"So what? What can they do?"

He hunched over the controls, peering through the windshield.

"And don't *you* try anything, old-timer," he muttered.

I couldn't. I was bone-weary; my left arm was on fire. The motor sounds gathered and grew closer. I could hear the motors missing in odd patterns; suddenly it seemed to me that my cars were speaking to one another.

A medley of horns came from behind. I turned and Gellhorn looked quickly into the rear-view mirror. A dozen cars were following in both lanes.

Gellhorn yelled and laughed madly.

I cried, "Stop! Stop the car!"

Because not a quarter of a mile ahead, plainly visible in the light beams of two sedans on the roadside was Sally, her trim body plunked square across the road. Two cars shot into the opposite lane to our left, keeping perfect time with us and preventing Gellhorn from turning out.

But he had no intention of turning out. He put his finger on the full-speed-ahead button and kept it there.

He said, "There'll be no bluffing here. This bus outweighs her five to one, old-timer, and we'll just push her off the road like a dead kitten."

I knew he could. The bus was on manual and his finger was on the button. I knew he would.

I lowered the window, and stuck my head out. "Sally," I screamed. "Get out of the way. *Sally!*"

It was drowned out in the agonized squeal of maltreated

brakebands. I felt myself thrown forward and heard Gellhorn's breath puff out of his body.

I said, "What happened?" It was a foolish question. We had stopped. That was what had happened. Sally and the bus were five feet apart. With five times her weight tearing down on her, she had not budged. The guts of her.

Gellhorn yanked at the Manual toggle switch. "It's got to," he kept muttering. "It's got to."

I said, "Not the way you hooked up the motor, expert. Any of the circuits could cross over."

He looked at me with a tearing anger and growled deep in his throat. His hair was matted over his forehead. He lifted his fist.

"That's all the advice out of you there'll ever be, old-timer."

And I knew the needle gun was about to fire.

I pressed back again the bus door, watching the fist come up, and when the door opened I went over backward and out, hitting the ground with a thud. I heard the door slam closed again.

I got to my knees and looked up in time to see Gellhorn struggle uselessly with the closing window, then aim his fist-gun quickly through the glass. He never fired. The bus got under way with a tremendous roar, and Gellhorn lurched backward.

Sally wasn't in the way any longer, and I watched the bus's rear lights flicker away down the highway.

I was exhausted. I sat down right there, right on the highway, and put my head down in my crossed arms, trying to catch my breath.

I heard a car stop gently at my side. When I looked up, it was Sally. Slowly—lovingly, you might say—her front door opened.

No one had driven Sally for five years—except Gellhorn, of course—and I know how valuable such freedom was to a car. I appreciated the gesture, but I said, "Thanks, Sally, but I'll take one of the newer cars."

I got up and turned away, but skillfully and neatly as a pirouette, she wheeled before me again. I couldn't hurt her feelings. I got in. Her front seat had the fine, fresh scent of an automatobile that kept itself spotlessly clean. I lay down across it, thankfully, and with even, silent, and rapid efficiency, my boys and girls brought me home.

*   *   *

Mrs. Hester brought me the copy of the radio transcript the next evening with great excitement.

"It's Mr. Gellhorn," she said. "The man who came to see you."

"What about him?"

I dreaded her answer.

"They found him dead," she said. "Imagine that. Just lying dead in a ditch."

"It might be a stranger altogether," I mumbled.

"Raymond J. Gellhorn," she said, sharply. "There can't be two, can there? The description fits, too. Lord, what a way to die? They found tire marks on his arms and body. Imagine! I'm glad it turned out to be a bus; otherwise they might have come poking around here."

"Did it happen near here?" I asked, anxiously.

"No . . . Near Cooksville. But, goodness, read about it yourself if you—What happened to Giuseppe?"

I welcomed the diversion. Giuseppe was waiting patiently for me to complete the repaint job. His windshield had been replaced.

After she left, I snatched up the transcript. There was no doubt about it. The doctor reported he had been running and was in a state of totally spent exhaustion. I wondered for how many miles the bus had played with him before the final lunge. The transcript had no notion of anything like that, of course.

They had located the bus and identified it by the tire tracks. The police had it and were trying to trace its ownership.

There was an editorial in the transcript about it. It had been the first traffic fatality in the state for that year and the paper warned strenuously against manual driving after night.

There was no mention of Gellhorn's three thugs and for that, at least, I was grateful. None of our cars had been seduced by the pleasure of the chase into killing.

That was all. I let the paper drop. Gellhorn had been a criminal. His treatment of the bus had been brutal. There was no question in my mind he deserved death. But still I felt a bit queasy over the manner of it.

A month has passed now and I can't get it out of my mind.

My cars talk to one another. I have no doubt about it anymore. It's as though they've gained confidence; as though they're not bothering to keep it secret anymore. Their engines rattle and knock continuously.

And they don't talk among themselves only. They talk to the cars and buses that come into the Farm on business. How long have they been doing that?"

They must be understood, too. Gellhorn's bus understood them, for all it hadn't been on the grounds more than an hour. I can close my eyes, and bring back that dash along the highway, with our cars flanking the bus on either side, clacking their motors at it till it understood, stopped, let me out, and ran off with Gellhorn.

Did my cars tell him to kill Gellhorn? Or was that his idea?

Can cars have such ideas? The motor designers say no. But they mean under ordinary conditions. Have they foreseen *everything*?

Cars get ill-used, you know.

Some of them enter the Farm and observe. They get told things. They find out that cars exist whose motors are never stopped, whom no one ever drives, whose every need is supplied.

Then maybe they go out and tell others. Maybe the word is spreading quickly. Maybe they're going to think that the Farm way should be the way all over the world. They don't understand. You couldn't expect them to understand about legacies and the whims of rich men.

There are millions of automatobiles on Earth, tens of millions. If the thought gets rooted in them that they're slaves; that they should do something about it . . . If they begin to think the way Gellhorn's bus did. . . .

Maybe it won't be till after my time. And then they'll have to keep a few of us to take care of them, won't they? They wouldn't kill us all.

And maybe they would. Maybe they wouldn't understand about how someone would have to care for them. Maybe they won't wait.

Every morning I wake up and think, Maybe today. . . .

I don't get as much pleasure out of my cars as I used to. Lately, I notice that I'm even beginning to avoid Sally.

BREAKFAST OF CHAMPIONS

BY THOMAS A. EASTON

No answer. Of course. By all the laws of sainted Murphy, that last skirmish had to cost me my antenna. Not just my head.

So here I am. Surrounded by savages. Or not surrounded, really. They're all in front of my eyes, except when the chief or one of his wives goes into his hut. They've got that dinnerbell look on their faces, but I should be safe enough. It takes another ironguts to do me in, like the one that shot my head off.

The battle was last night. Why? I don't know, except that that's when our forces met. There's no difference between sun and stars when your IR is built right in. The only way anyone will ever lick that is when they build a cryogenic soldier. I suppose they're working on it.

Night or day, though, the hell of it is that you can't hide. You duck behind a rock, and it takes two shots to get you instead of one. One for the rock, one for you. Marvelous stuff, these modern weapons. They make the battlefield unsafe for human beings. That's why they built us. Ironguts, they call us, and for good reason. We look like men, smell like men, sound like men, think like men. Taste like men? I don't know, but maybe I'll find out soon.

The natives are gathered around my body now. One's got a big knife. He's working on my clothes. Tough stuff, hey? That's right, fellow. Saw at it a bit. It'll cut, as long as your blade is sharp enough. It is, too. But you'd better hone it again soon. Or you'll never get through my skin. Even honing it's no guarantee.

Just like men, I was saying. Except we're tougher. Lots

159

tougher. It takes a war to kill us, nothing less, so if men could just keep their noses in their own business we'd live forever. If you can call it living. After all, we're just fancy machines.

I wish I could get through to HQ. That knife *is* sharp. I'm stark naked now. And the savages are staring. They've never seen anything like me. No equipment. I'm not *that* manlike. I swear they look disappointed. Especially the chief. Maybe he was counting on a delicacy.

But now for the skin, hey? That's right, stroke it right down the middle, breastbone to crotch. Lean on it a little. You have to clean the carcass before you can do anything else with it. What? Not a mark? I told you I was tough. That's right, try honing it. Here comes a kid with your stone. Do a good job, now.

What's the war all about, you ask? How should I know? I'm just a grunt, after all. But I can guess. Probably real estate, or resources. Jungle stuff, too. Futile, as always. What's it all about? From where I sit, it's battles, battles, and more battles. Kill or be killed. A classic story.

Last night's was just one in a long string of firefights. Maybe my last. Somebody caught me right across the neck with a beam. I don't even know which side did it. And there I was, lying on the ground in two pieces. And there I stayed while the fighting faded out in the distance.

Eventually these little brown fellows showed up to pick up the pieces, including me. Took me back to their village, stuck my head up on top of a pole, and planted the pole in front of the head man's place. Then they spread my body out in the middle of the compound, right in front of me, so I have a good view. Close to the fire, too. Nice and warm. Nice and handy.

The knife seems to be honed as sharp as it can be now. He's ready to try again. No luck slicing. Can he stab? The blade has a good point. Ummph! If I was alive, that would have knocked the breath right out of me, if I breathed.

Now somebody's bringing a hammer. More of a mallet, really. He's got the knife. He's planting it right over my power pack. Won't he be surprised if he pokes a hole in that! He's raising the mallet. Wham! No luck. Wham! Still none. The chief grabs the mallet and holds it in both hands. The first guy steadies the knife. WHAM! And the knife breaks. Snaps right in two. Not a mark on me. But the guy who had the knife in the first place looks right pissed.

I'm lucky, really. Here I am, able to watch the cannibals carving up my carcass. My main power pack's in my belly, with connectors to my weaponry built into my fingertips. Grab the gun right, and you're ready to shoot. But there's a little auxiliary pack in my skull. Just enough juice to keep the sensors working and the brain ticking along. Not enough to blink or talk, though. I wish I could talk. I'd pull the god bit and get them to cart me back to base.

Speaking of which, it's not a complete disaster, having my antenna knocked out. They can home on my power pack. Sometimes. In theory.

These savages are determined. They're going to have me for breakfast if it takes all day. Here comes an axe now.

And the beefiest guy in the tribe. Guy? Hell, no. That's a woman. But built! Like a Mack truck. Somebody grabs my right arm and hauls it out from my body. She raised that axe overhead. Her muscles bulge as she brings it down. Just as hard as she can. And that's hard! THUNK! The joint looks a little flattened from here, but my skin's intact. Guess I'll need a little rebuilding if I ever get out of here. Oops! They see what the axe did too. She's raising it again. THUNK! A little flatter. They wiggle the arm. It flops. Goodbye elbow.

And I was overdue for an overhaul before this battle. I should have stayed at base. Had the mechs fix that wobble in my left pinkie. I've been having a little trouble plugging the connector into the sighting control on my beamer. And I swear there's a bearing going in my right hip. Not to speak of a patch of jungle fungus up my right nostril. Though that might be stretching things a bit. They told us the fungus can't root in our hides, another advantage we have over men. And if they catch you malingering—we can do it, believe me!—they program you. Even that would be better than what's happening now.

They're building up the fire. If steel can't hack it, maybe heat will. They're logical, anyway. It's a reasonable assumption. They can see the scorch marks on the stump of my neck. I wish I could understand what they're saying. My ears are working, just like my eyes, but all the noise is just gibberish. Gobbledygood. Is that what started folks calling them gooks? Who cares? I can tell what they're planning. I can see well enough. The eyes have it. They've grabbed a hold of my bad arm. They're dragging me over to the fire, laying that elbow right on top of a flaming log.

I *wish* I could get HQ.

The fire shouldn't make much difference. It takes a good 1800 degrees Celsius to hurt that skin polymer. A little less than what a beamer produces. But they're all worked up anyway. Optimistic, I guess. Maybe even with reason. Even from here, I can see my skin changing color. That shouldn't happen! Maybe the axe bruised the polymer enough to weaken it. But the axe shouldn't have done *that*! It shouldn't even have hurt the joint, actually. We're supposed to be immune to mechanical accidents, like axes and steel-jacketed slugs. So I'm not perfect. That's news? What with being put together by the lowest bidder?

Oh, great! They're going to try the axe again. They're hauling me out of the fire, laying the arm across a stick of firewood. A chopping block. And wham! This time they make it. That's my arm they're passing around. Looks like bone, doesn't it fellows? Metal-ceramic alloy. Nice and white, it's a little dry. Looks like meat, too, hey? Might even taste like it. It's something like protein, after all. The most compact muscle they could design. Not very nourishing, though. It's made of silicon, not carbon.

It doesn't taste right, you say? That's right, you guys are licking your fingers, aren't you? Getting juice all over you from the stump. I hope it rots your guts out. No, don't spit. Swallow it. How can it rot you if you don't?"

Somebody just lost interest in me. She's getting a more edible breakfast. Bringing out a pot of something. Setting it over the fire. Looks like porridge. No wonder they wanted meat! They're drifting away from me. Maybe they're done. Maybe the mechs won't have too much work to do.

No, they're coming back. Some of them, anyway. Bowls of porridge in their fists. Staring at me. Talking around their food. Gesticulating. One bright boy seems to have an idea. He sets his bowl aside and points at me. Then he waves his hands down over his body. My skin for a coat, huh? The invulnerable warrior.

Another guy holds up the broken knife. Good boy! How can you skin me if you can't cut me? But the bright one isn't fazed. He picks up my arm and begins to peel the skin back from the stump, like taking a glove off. Great! A genius!

The others get it too. and two of them start working on my neck.

It's really a shame that my skin is so lifelike. That means it's flexible. It has to be, if I'm going to do much moving around. It also means it'll stretch. Just enough for them to get it over my shoulders and start it moving.

Now I really am naked. That's my skin they're pawing over, six feet away from my body. Inside out, yet. A women brings a jug and they wash the juices off. Then they start scraping away the fibers that fastened the skin in place. Pretty soon, it's all ready for drying, and the fire does a quick job of that. The fire also lets them open up the neck opening a bit, that and what's left of the knife.

And now, here comes the chief. He's not too young— there's a bit of grizzle in his hair—but no one's about to hold out on him. He's the boss, and my skin is now his. If anyone in this tribe is going to be invulnerable, it'll be him.

As he approaches, they quickly turn my skin right side out and hold it up for him. He inspects it carefully. Pokes it with a finger and grins. Then he grabs it and holds it up to his scrawny frame, for all the world like a woman getting ready to try on a dress. The fit is going to be lousy. My feet drag on the ground in front of him.

The others hold it for him as he crawls in through the neck hole. They help work his feet down where my feet ought to be and get his left hand into place. He gestures, and they bring him the skin of my right arm. He puts that on, just like a long glove, and there he is, me, skin-deep. Though *he's* all wrinkles. But he's still grinning. All he needs to do now is test his new outfit.

He speaks and gestures and one of his wives runs out of sight under my perch. She returns in a second with one of the chief's spears. When she hands it to him, he tests the point with a thumb. He grimaces when he can't feel a thing and touches it to his tongue. Then he hold it out to one of his young followers.

The young guy steps back a few feet and raises the spear. He cocks his arm back and lets fly. And, of course, the thing bounces off my skin. Though not painlessly. The chief roars at the blow and leaps at his spearman. A quick blow knocks him to his knees, and I can almost understand what the boss man is crying: "Not that hard, you idiot!"

Hah! My skin will keep anyone from poking holes in you,

but it won't stop-you from feeling them try. And it won't stop anyone from caving your chest in or breaking your back with a club. The chief seems to realize as much, but that doesn't keep him from swelling up with pride over his new possession. He's right in front of me now. Waving his spear under my nose. Screaming something that sounds pretty triumphant. As if he'd just licked me.

But he isn't watching his people. And they're throwing quick glances at the sky, glances that very soon take on a terrified cast. They're beginning to cry out, too, shouts of panic as they scatter and run for the trees. Could it be?

Yes! There's the floater, coming down right on top of my body, one skid scattering the fire. The Search and Rescue squad, homing on my power pack at last. The Repair squad if you're not too far gone. The Salvage squad if you are.

The sudden silence gets the chief's attention. He whirls to face the compound, his arm dropping and his mouth hanging open in midshout as he sees the sudden apparition. Those things are silent! He pulls himself together. I can see it happen. Isn't he invulnerable now? Aren't his people watching from the bushes? He lifts the spear again, shakes it at the floater, and charges.

He's a brave bastard, but he's dumb. He doesn't have a chance. What does he think took my head off my shoulders? As soon as my saviours see a hairy savage in a robrob skin coming at them, they open fire. Two beamers at once. Before he takes his third step, he's in three pieces.

Well, that's not as bad as me. Counting everything, I'm now in seven pieces. But I can be fixed.

SUN UP

BY A. A. JACKSON IV AND HOWARD WALDROP

The robot exploration ship *Saenger* parked off the huge red sun.

It was now a tiny dot of stellar debris, bathed in light, five million nine hundred ninety-four thousand myriameters from the star. Its fusion ram had been silent for some time. It had coasted in on its reaction motors like a squirrel climbing down a curved treetrunk.

The ship *Saenger* was partly a prepackaged scientific laboratory, partly a deep space probe, with sections devoted to smaller launching platforms, inflatable observatories, assembly shops. The ship *Saenger* had a present crew of eighteen working robots. It was an advance research station, sent unmanned to study this late-phase star. When it reached parking orbit, it sent messages back to its home world. In a year and a half, the first shipful of scientists and workers would come, finding the station set up and work underway.

The ship was mainly *Saenger*, a solid-state intelligence budded off the giant SSI on the Moon.

Several hours after it docked off the sun, *Saenger* knew it was going to die.

* * *

There was a neutron star some 34 light-years away from *Saenger*, and 53 light-years away from the earth. To look at it, you wouldn't think it was any more than a galactic garbage dump. All you could tell by listening to it was that it was noisy, full of X-rays, that it rotated, and that it interfered with everything up and down the wavelengths.

Everything except Snapshot.

Close in to the tiny roaring star, closer than a man could go, were a series of big chucks of metal that looked like solid debris.

They were arrays of titanium and crystal, vats of liquid nitrogen, shielding; deep inside were the real workings of Snapshot.

Snapshot was in the business of finding Kerr wormholes in the froth of garbage given off by the star. Down at the Planck length, 10^{-35} cm, the things appeared, formed, reappeared, twisted, broke off like steam on hot rocks. At one end of the wormholes was Snapshot, and at the other was the Universe.

It sent messages from one end, its scanners punching through the bubbling mass of waves, and it kept track of what went where and who was talking to whom.

Snapshot's job was like that of a man trying to shoot into the hole of an invisible Swiss cheese that was turning on three axes at 3300 rpm. And it had to remember which holes it hit. And do it often.

There were a couple of Snapshots scattered within close range of Earth, and some further away. All these systems coordinated messages, allowed instantaneous communication across light-years.

All these communications devices made up Snapshot. Snapshot was one ten-millionth the function of Plato.

Plato was a solid crystal intelligence grown on the Moon, deep under the surface. The people who worked with Plato weren't exactly sure how he did things, but they were finding out every day. Plato came up with the right answers; he had devised Snapshot, he was giving man the stars a step or two at a time. He wasn't human, but he had been planned by humans so they could work with him.

*   *   *

"Plato, this is *Saenger*."
> < (:)———(:)(:) 666 * CCC XXXXX
"That's being sent. I have an emergency here that will cancel the project. Please notify the responsible parties."
> < > <———' () ** """ > <
"I don't think so. I'll tell them myself."
" (:)(:) & ' '
"I'll get back to you on that."
(:)
"Holding."
XXXXX PLATO TRANSFER SNAPSHOT re *Saenger* RUNNING

Doctor Maxell leaned back in her chair. The Snapshot printout was running and the visuals awaited her attention.

"Uchi," she said, "they'll have to scrub *Saenger*."

"I heard the bleep," said the slight man. He pulled off his glasses and rubbed his eyes. "Is Plato ready yet?"

"Let's see it together," she said. "It'll save time when we have to rerun it for the Committee."

They watched the figures, the graphics, the words.

The printout ran into storage.

"Supernova," said Dr. Maxell.

"Well . . . first opportunity to see one close up."

"But there goes the manned part of the project. There goes *Saenger*."

"The Committee will have to decide what comes next."

"You want to tell them or should I?"

"*Saenger*, this is Dr. Maxell."

"Speaking."

No matter how many times she did it, Sondra never got used to speaking across light-years with no more delay than through an interoffice system.

"*Saenger*, the Committee has seen your reports and is scrubbing the remainder of your mission. The rest of your program will be modified. You're to record events in and around the star until such time as—your functions cease."

There was a slight pause.

"Would it be possible to send auxiliary equipment to allow me to leave this system before the star erupts?"

"I'm afraid not, *Saenger*. If the forces hold to your maximum predicated time, there's still no chance of getting a booster to you."

Saenger, like the other robot research stations, was a fusion ram. They used gigantic boosters to push them to ramming speed. The boosters, like shuttlecraft, were reusable and were piloted back to launching orbits. *Saenger* used its ram to move across vast distances and to slow down. Its ion motors were useful only for maneuvering and course corrections.

The reaction motors could not bring it to ramming speed.

The booster for its return journey was to be brought out on the first manned ship which would have come to *Saenger*.

The manned ship was not coming.

All this was implied in Doctor Maxell's words.

"Would I be of more use if I were to remain functioning throughout the event?"

"Certainly," she said. "But that's not possible. Check with Plato on the figures for the shock wave and your stress capabilities."

Slight pause.

"I see. But, it would be even better for scientific research if I survived the explosion of the star?"

"Of course. But there is nothing you can do. Please stand by for new programming."

There was another short silence, then:

"You will be checking on my progress, won't you?"

"Yes *Saenger*, we will."

"Then I shall do the best possible job of information-gathering for which I am equipped."

"You do that, *Saenger*. Please do that for us."

In *Saenger*'s first messages, it told them what it saw. The spectroscopy, X-ray scans, ir, uv and neutrino grids told the same thing: the star was going to explode.

Saenger reached an optimum figure of one year, two

months and some days. The research ship checked with Plato. The crystal intelligence on the Moon told him to knock a few months off that.

Plato printed a scenario of the last stages of the 18-solar-mass star. He sent it to Doctor Maxell. It looked like this:

START—0^{16} CORE IGNITION HELIUM FLARE
  OPT. TIME 12 DAYS
STAGE: ^{16}O SHELL IGNITION
  DURATION 2.37 DAYS
  CORE COOLING ^{16}O BURNOFF
STAGE: SILICONE CORE IGNITION
  DUR. 20 HOURS
STAGE: SILICONE CORE BURNING
  DUR. 2.56 DAYS
STAGE: SILICONE SHELL IGNITION
  DUR. 8 HOURS
STAGE: CORE CONTRACTION
  DUR. 15 HOURS
STAGE: IRON CORE PHOTODISINTEGRATED
  —CORE COLLAPSE DUR. 5 h 24 min 18 sec
  SUPERNOVA no durational msmnt possible

The same information was sent to *Saenger*. With the message from Plato that the first step of the scenario was less then eleven months away.

Saenger prepared himself for the coming explosion. It sent out small automatic probes to ring the star at various distances. One of them it sent on an outward orbit. It was to witness the destruction of *Saenger* before it, too, was vaporized by the unloosed energies of the star.

One of the problems they had working with Plato was that he was not human. So, then, neither were any of the other SSIs budded off Plato. Of which *Saenger* was one. Humans had made Plato, had guided it while it evolved its own brand of sentience.

They had done all they could to guide it along human thought patterns. But if it went off on some detour which brought results, no matter how alien the process, they left it to its own means.

It had once asked for some laboratory animals to test to destruction, and they had said no. Otherwise, they let Plato do as it pleased.

They gave a little, they took a little while the intelligence grew within its deep tunnels in the Moon. What they eventually got was the best mind man could ever hope to use, to harness for his own means.

And as Plato had been budded off the earlier, smaller Socrates, they were preparing a section of Plato for excision. It would be used for even grander schemes, larger things. Aristotle's pit was being excavated near Tycho.

That part of Plato concerned with such things was quizzical. It already knew it was developing larger capacities, and could tackle a few of the problems for which they would groom Aristotle. In a few years, it knew it might answer them all, long before the new mass had gained its full capacity.

But nobody asked it, so it didn't mention it.

Not maliciously, though. It had been raised that way.

Thousands of small buds had already been taken off Plato, put in stations throughout the solar system, used in colonization, formed into the Snapshot system, used for the brains of exploratory ships.

Saenger was one of those.

"Plato."
?
"I have a problem."
" ":-& &(')*
"What can I do? Besides that?"
- - - - - - - - -& (:) (:) × @ ¼ . 7v$\sqrt{x^3}$ . . .
"Then what?"
- - - - - D = RT . ×, ×, ≤ –1
"Do go on."
- - - - - c^2; c^2 –1/10 r$\sqrt{t}$

"*Saenger* is talking to Plato a lot, Sondra."
"A lot? How much is a lot?"
"I saw some discards yesterday, had *Saenger*'s code on it. Thought they were from the regular run. But I

came across the same thing this morning, before the Snapshot encoding. So it couldn't have been on regular transmission."

"And . . . ?" asked Sondra.

"And I ran a capacity trace on it. *Saenger* used four
ten-billionths of Plato's time this morning. And yesterday, a
little less."

She drummed her fingers on the desk. "That's more
than ten probes should have used, even on maintenance
schedules. Maybe Plato is as interested as we are in
supernovae?"

"What *Saenger* gave us was pretty complete. There's not
much he could tell Plato he didn't tell us."

"Want to run it on playback?" asked Sondra.

"I'd rather you asked *Saenger* yourself," said the man.
"Maybe they just exchanged information and went over
capacity."

Sondra Maxell took off her earphones. "Uchi, do you
think *Saenger* knows it's going to die?"

"Well, it knows what 'ceasing to function' is. Or has a
general idea, anyway. I don't think it has the capacity to
understand death. It has nothing to go by."

"But it's a reasoning being, like Plato. I . . ." She thought
a moment. "How many of Plato's buds have ceased to
function?"

"Just the one, on the Centauri rig."

"And that was quick, sudden, totally unexpected?"

"The crew and the ship wiped out in a couple of nanosec-
onds. What . . . ?"

"I think, Uchi, that this is the first time one of Plato's
children knows it's going to die. And so does Plato."

"You mean it might be giving *Saenger* special attention,
because of that?"

"Or *Saenger* might be demanding it."

Uchi was silent.

"This is going to be something to see," he said, finally.

"*Saenger,* what have you been talking to Plato about?"

"The mechanics of the shock wave and the flux within the
star's loosened envelope. If you would like, I could printout
everything we've discussed."

"That would take months, *Saenger*."

"No matter then, Dr. Maxwell. I have a question."

"Yes?"

"Could I move further away from this star? The resolution of my instruments won't be affected up to point 10.7 AU. I could station a probe in this orbit. I thought you might get a better view and data if I were further out."

Sondra was quiet. "*Saenger*," she said, "you know you can't possibly get away from the shock, no matter how far you move on your ion engines?"

"Yes, Doctor."

"And that you can't get to ramming speed, either?"

"Yes," said *Saenger*.

"Then why are you trying to move further away?"

"To give you a better view," said the ship. "Plato and I figured the further away the more chance of getting valuable information I would have. I could telemeter much more coordinated data through Snapshot. The new programming is not specific about the distance of the ship, only of the probes."

Sondra looked at Uchi. "We'll ask the Committee. I don't think there'll be any real objections. We'll get back to you ASAP."

"*Saenger* out."

Off that star was black, and the light was so bright on the sunward side that all *Saenger*'s screens had to be filtered down to No. 3.

The sun still appeared as a red giant in the optics, burning brighter than when *Saenger* docked around it. But *Saenger* had other eyes that saw in other waves. His neutrino grids saw the round ball of the star and its photosphere, but deep inside it detected a glowing cone, growing larger and more open each day, rooted down inside the atmosphere of the sun. The helium flash was not far away.

Already Plato had revised his figures again. He had little more than seven months before the star blew like a cosmic steam boiler, giving men the first close look at an event they had not seen before.

The star would cover the whole sunward sky, its shell

would expand, covering everything for millions of my-riameters with the screaming remnants of its atmosphere.

Saenger had no margin of safety.

He did not have time, or the proper materials, or anything.

He was monitoring himself and his worker robots as he moved outward on his reaction engines. He had swung out of the orbit as soon as the Committee had given permission.

His robots moved in and out through the airlocks and the open sides of the ship.

One of them, using a cutting laser, sawed through its leg and went whirling away on a puff of soundless force. These robot were never made to work outside the ship.

If *Saenger* could have, he would have said the word *damn*.

"Plato?"
?
"There's not enough material in the ship unless I cannibalize my shielding."
> <"
"But that would defeat the whole purpose."
*?
"How could I?"
X (:)& - - - -) (') (- - -
"Hey! Why didn't I think of that!"
& " * ()
"But they'll know as soon as I do."
? * (:)(:) & - - - ?
"Well . . ."

"Now he's using his scoops," said Sondra as she monitored the Snapshot encoding for the day. "What in the hell is going on out there?"

"It's not interfering with the monitoring programs. He's sent out two more remote monitors. And the activity down there is picking up."

"He's backed off on his use of Plato. Way below normal, in fact. Do you think we ought to have him dump his grids now?" she asked.

"You're the boss," said Uchi. "I'd get as much information as we could first. He may find something in those last three minutes we don't know about."

"Has Plato contacted him?" asked Sondra.

"Hmmm. Not lately."

"He's cut him loose," she said. "He's on his own."

Saenger was fighting now, with every passing moment. The ship was unrecognizable. The revamp Plato suggested changed the ship completely. Spidery arrays went out and out from the skeleton, and among them the robots worked.

Stars shone through frames which had once held thick shielding. Laboratories, quarters, all were emptied and dismantled. The frames themselves were being shaved away with improvised lasers until they were light and thin as bird's bones. The ship was little more than a shell around the solid-state intelligence and the fusion ram.

Saenger was using the magnetic scoops at the moment. He sucked in the loose hydrogen atmosphere which bathed the star system. The giant coils began to hum, and as they did *Saenger* lost some of his capacity, like a man too long under water. Part of his shielding was to protect him from the effects of the coils, and now that plating was gone. He was taking in hydrogen, compressing it, turning it to liquid hydrogen which would shield him from most of the harmful radiations.

Soon, though, he would remove the plates which shielded him from the growing bath of X-rays, photons and other stellar garbage. He was not sure, as he told Plato, that he could remain for long in that acid shower.

Saenger pulled a sufficient quantity of hydrogen in, turned off the coils. He let two robots carry off another layer of insulation.

Saenger was like a dazed man on a battlefield, too long without rest. And the real war had not even started.

Plato was more nearly right.

Three days before the predicted time, the star entered its supernova scenario.

The Director was down in the Banks, with most of the Committee and other interested spectators. Uchi and Dr. Maxwell sat at their usual places before the Snapshot consoles.

"Really too bad," the Director was saying. "Research project like that scratched; about to lose one of our shipboard SSIs. But it'll give us a good look at what happens when a star dies."

They were scanning Snapshot for full visuals, X-ray, infrared, ultraviolet, radio. This would be the most closely watched star event ever, and they were running it all into Plato's permanent storage section where even he could not erase it.

If he had thought to try.

"How do you want to handle the monitors, *Saenger?*"

"I'll keep on the innermost probes until they are overtaken, then transfer to the outermost. Then back, and I'll hold as long as I can. Then you ought to have a few minutes on the farthest remote before it goes."

"Good enough. Please monitor readings until the shock wave hits. We'll listen in when we're not too busy."

"Certainly."

"Oops!" someone said. "There is goes."

It's hard to imagine a star shaking itself to pieces, but they saw it up close for the first time, then. One second the star seemed fine, if a little bright, then it darkened and the whole surface lifted like a trampoline top.

This from the closest of the probes, one million eight hundred thousand myriameters out. The limb of the star they were watching grew and grew and filled the screen and. . . .

They were watching the sun expand from the second remote, two million two hundred sixty-eight thousand myriameters away, on the opposite side of the star. The sun filled that screen too, and the screen went blank before the shock front reached it and. . . .

"Shockwave, pulling a little ahead of the gases," said a technician.

"Forty-seven point two seconds to the first. Seven-seven point seven to the second. About a tenth light-speed for the gases," said Uchi.

The information sped from *Saenger* through Snapshot to Plato. Records, stacks of tape, videoprints, all rolled into the permanent storage units on the Moon. They watched the star kill itself with its own light and heat.

The pickup switched to the furthest probe, orbiting almost two AU from the star. For the first time, they saw the whole sun, and it grew and grew even as they watched. It was immense, the lenses kept filtering down and down and still they could not keep the sensors from burning out. Lenses rotated in to replace others, and the thing covered fully a third of the heavens even this far away.

And it got bigger.

"He's supposed to switch back," said the Director. "Isn't he?"

"Do you think it already hit him?" asked one of the spectators.

"Couldn't," said Uchi. "We haven't gotten his information dump through Snapshot yet."

Then he looked at Sondra.

"He can't hold it on us, can he?"

"No," she said. "It's in the program."

But she bit her nails anyway.

Uchi timed the expansion. "It should have gotten him now! Why didn't he dump? Is he still on?"

Sondra feared to look but she did. Two inputs still through Snapshot. The outer probe and . . .

They looked at the screen. The supernova appeared as a rolling unfolding bunch of dirty sheets, and the center grew whiter with each ripple shaken loose.

It covered half the screen, then two-thirds, then three quarters.

"The shock must be almost to the probe," said the Director.

"What happened to *Saenger*?" asked Sondra of Uchi. "Where is he?"

"Look!"

They all did.

The whiteness of the star filled the screen and there was a marbled spot through which the glowing central core could be seen. The star must have lost a tenth its mass. The widening sphere of white-hot gases and debris whipped toward the probe.

And in front of it came something that looked like an old sink stopper.

Closer it came, and they saw it rode just before the shock wave, that the huge round thing caused swirls in the envelope of gases much like tension on a bubble of soap.

On it came, closer, and larger, the gases behind it moving perceptibly, quickly, toward the lens of the outermost probe.

"Saenger!" yelled Uchi, and Sondra joined him, and they all began to yell and cheer in the control room. "He built an ablation shield. He's riding that goddamn shock wave! Somehow, somewhere he got the stuff to make it! My God. What a ship, oh what a ship!"

And *Saenger* had the lens zoom in then, and they saw the skeletal framework, the spiderweb of metal and shielding and plastic and burnt pieces of rock, ore and robot parts which made it up.

Then the ship flashed by and the screen melted away as the gases hit the probe.

"Doctor Maxell . . ." came *Saenger*'s voice. It was changed, and the phase kept slipping as he talked.

"Yes, *Saenger*? Yes?"

"Permission to abbbooort—tt—abort program and return to earth docking orbit. Almost at ram speed—*zgichzzggzichh*—at ram speed now."

"Yes, *Saenger*! Yes, Yes!"

"Ram functioning. *Doctor Maxell?*"

"What?"

"I want to come home now. I'm very tired."

"You will, you can," she said.

The screen changed to an aft view from *Saenger*. The white, growing sphere of the burnt star was being left slowly behind. The slight wispy contrail from the ship's ram blurred part of the screen, the gas envelope the rest.

"I've lost some of myself," said *Saenger*.

"It doesn't matter, it doesn't matter."

She was crying.

"Everything will be all right," she said.

SECOND VARIETY

BY PHILIP K. DICK

The Russian soldier made his way nervously up the ragged side of the hill, holding his gun ready. He glanced around him, licking his dry lips, his face set. From time to time he reached up a gloved hand and wiped perspiration from his neck, pushing down his coat collar.

Eric turned to Corporal Leone. "Want him? Or can I have him?" He adjusted the view sight so the Russian's features squarely filled the glass, the lines cutting across his hard, somber features.

Leone considered. The Russian was close, moving rapidly, almost running. "Don't fire. Wait," Leone tensed. "I don't think we're needed."

The Russian increased his pace, kicking ash and piles of debris out of his way. He reached the top of the hill and stopped, panting, staring around him. The sky was overcast, drifting clouds of gray particles. Bare trunks of trees jutted up occasionally; the ground was level and bare, rubble-strewn, with the ruins of buildings standing out here and there like yellowing skulls.

The Russian was uneasy. He knew something was wrong. He started down the hill. Now he was only a few paces from the bunker. Eric was getting fidgety. He played with his pistol, glancing at Leone.

"Don't worry," Leone said. "He won't get here. They'll take care of him."

"Are you sure? He's got damn far."

"They hang around close to the bunker. He's getting into the bad part. Get set!"

The Russian began to hurry, sliding down the hill, his

178

boots sinking into the heaps of gray ash, trying to keep his gun up. He stopped for a moment, lifting his fieldglasses to his face.

"He's looking right at us," Eric said.

The Russian came on. They could see his eyes, like two blue stones. His mouth was open a little. He needed a shave; his chin was stubbled. On one bony cheek was a square of tape, showing blue at the edge. A fungoid spot. His coat was muddy and torn. One glove was missing. As he ran his belt counter bounced up and down against him.

Leone touched Eric's arm. "Here one comes."

Across the ground something small and metallic came, flashing in the dull sunlight of mid-day. A metal sphere. It raced up the hill after the Russian, its treads flying. It was small, one of the baby ones. Its claws were out, two razor projections spinning in a blur of white steel. The Russian heard it. He turned instantly, firing. The sphere dissolved into particles. But already a second had emerged and was following the first. The Russian fired again.

A third sphere leaped up the Russian's leg, clicking and whirring. It jumped to the shoulder. The spinning blades disappeared into the Russian's throat.

Eric relaxed. "Well, that's that. God, those damn things give me the creeps. Sometimes I think we were better off before."

"If we hadn't invented them, they would have." Leone lit a cigarette shakily. "I wonder why a Russian would come all this way alone. I didn't see anyone covering him."

Lt. Scott came slipping up the tunnel, into the bunker. "What happened? Something entered the screen."

"An Ivan."

"Just one?"

Eric brought the view screen around. Scott peered into it. Now there were numerous metal spheres crawling over the prostrate body, dull metal globes clicking and whirring, sawing up the Russian into small parts to be carried away.

"What a lot of claws," Scott murmured.

"They come like flies. Not much game for them any more."

Scott pushed the sight away, disgusted. "Like flies. I wonder why he was out there. They know we have claws all around."

A larger robot had joined the smaller spheres. It was

directing operations, a long blunt tube with projecting eye-pieces. There was not much left of the soldier. What remained was being brought down the hillside by the host of claws.

"Sir," Leone said. "If it's all right, I'd like to go out there and take a look at him."

"Why?"

"Maybe he came with something."

Scott considered. He shrugged. "All right. But be careful."

"I have my tab." Leone patted the metal band at his wrist. "I'll be out of bounds."

He picked up his rifle and stepped carefully up to the mouth of the bunker, making his way between blocks of concrete and steel prongs, twisted and bent. The air was cold at the top. He crossed over the ground toward the remains of the soldier, striding across the soft ash. A wind blew around him, swirling gray particles up in his face. He squinted and pushed on.

The claws retreated as he came close, some of them stiffening into immobility. He touched his tab. The Ivan would have given something for that! Short hard radiation emitted from the tab neutralized the claws, put them out of commission. Even the big robot with its two waving eye-stalks retreated respectfully as he approached.

He bent down over the remains of the soldier. The gloved hand was closed tightly. There was something in it. Leone pried the fingers apart. A sealed container, aluminum. Still shiny.

He put it in his pocket and made his way back to the bunker. Behind him the claws came back to life, moving into operation again. The procession resumed, metal spheres moving through the gray ash with their loads. He could hear their treads scrabbling against the ground. He shuddered.

Scott watched intently as he brought the shiny tube out of his pocket. "He had that?"

"In his hand." Leone unscrewed the top. "Maybe you should look at it, sir."

Scott took it. He emptied the contents out in the palm of his hand. A small piece of silk paper, carefully folded. He sat down by the light and unfolded it.

"What's it say, sir?" Eric said. Several officers came up the tunnel. Major Hendricks appeared.

"Major," Scott said. "Look at this."

Hendricks read the slip. "This just come?"

"A single runner. Just now."

"Where is he?" Hendricks asked sharply.

"The claws got him."

Major Hendricks grunted. "Here." He passed it to his companions. "I think this is what we've been waiting for. They certainly took their time about it."

"So they want to talk terms," Scott said. "Are we going along with them?"

"That's not for us to decide." Hendricks sat down. "Where's the communications officer? I want the Moon Base."

Leone pondered as the communications officer raised the outside antenna cautiously, scanning the sky above the bunker for any sign of a watching Russian ship.

"Sir," Scott said to Hendricks. "It's sure strange they suddenly came around. We've been using the claws for almost a year. Now all of a sudden they start to fold."

"Maybe claws have been getting down in their bunkers."

"One of the big ones, the kind with stalks, got into an Ivan bunker last week," Eric said. "It got a whole platoon of them before they got their lid shut."

"How do you know?"

"A buddy told me. The thing came back with—with remains."

"Moon Base, sir," the communications officer said.

On the screen the face of the lunar monitor appeared. His crisp uniform contrasted to the uniforms in the bunker. And he was clean shaven. "Moon Base."

"This is forward command L-Whistle. On Terra. Let me have General Thompson."

The monitor faded. Presently General Thompson's heavy features came into focus. "What is it, Major?"

"Our claws got a single Russian runner with a message. We don't know whether to act on it—there have been tricks like this in the past."

"What's the message?"

"The Russians want us to send a single officer on policy level over to their lines. For a conference. They don't state the nature of the conference. They say that matters of—" He consulted the slip. "—Matters of grave urgency make it advisable that discussion be opened between a representative of the UN forces and themselves."

He held the message up to the screen for the general to scan. Thompson's eyes moved.

"What should we do?" Hendricks said.

"Send a man out."

"You don't think it's a trap?"

"It might be. But the location they give for their forward command is correct. It's worth a try, at any rate."

"I'll send an officer out. And report the result to you as soon as he returns."

"All right, Major." Thompson broke the connection. The screen died. Up above, the antenna came slowly down.

Hendricks rolled up the paper, deep in thought.

"I'll go," Leone said.

"They want somebody at policy level." Hendricks rubbed his jaw. "Policy level. I haven't been outside in months. Maybe I could use a little air."

"Don't you think it's risky?"

Hendricks lifted the view sight and gazed into it. The remains of the Russians were gone. Only a single claw was in sight. It was folding itself back, disappearing into the ash, like a crab. Like some hideous metal crab . . .

"That's the only thing that bothers me." Hendricks rubbed his wrist. "I know I'm safe as long as I have this on me. But there's something about them. I hate the damn things. I wish we'd never invented them. There's something wrong with me. Relentless little—"

"If we hadn't invented them, the Ivans would have."

Hendricks pushed the sight back. "Anyhow, it seems to be winning the war. I guess that's good."

"Sounds like you're getting the same jitters as the Ivans."

Hendricks examined his wrist watch. "I guess I had better get started, if I want to be there before dark."

He took a deep breath and then stepped out onto the gray, rubbled ground. After a minute he lit a cigarette and stood gazing around him. The landscape was dead. Nothing stirred. He could see for miles, endless ash and slag, ruins of buildings. A few trees without leaves or branches, only the trunks. Above him the eternal rolling clouds of gray, drifting between Terra and the sun.

Major Hendricks went on. Off to the right something

scuttled, something round and metallic. A claw, going lickety-split after something. Probably after a small animal, a rat. They got rats, too. As a sort of sideline.

He came to the top of the little hill and lifted his field-glasses. The Russian lines were a few miles ahead of him. They had a forward command post there. The runner had come from it.

A squat robot with undulating arms passed by him, its arms weaving inquiringly. The robot went on its way, disappearing under some debris. Hendricks watched it go. He had never seen that type before. There were getting to be more and more types he had never seen, new varieties and sizes coming up from the underground factories.

Hendricks put out his cigarette and hurried on. It was interesting, the use of artificial forms in warfare. How had they got started? Necessity. The Soviet Union had gained great initial success, usual with the side that got the war going. Most of North America had been blasted off the map. Retaliation was quick in coming, of course. The sky was full of circling disc-bombers long before the war began; they had been up there for years. The discs began sailing down all over Russia within hours after Washington got it.

But that hadn't helped Washington.

The American bloc governments moved to the Moon Base the first year. There was not much else to do. Europe was gone; a slag heap with dark weeds growing from the ashes and bones. Most of North America was useless; nothing could be planted, no one could live. A few million people kept going up in Canada and down in South America. But during the second year Soviet parachutists began to drop, a few at first, then more and more. They wore the first really effective anti-radiation equipment; what was left of American production moved to the moon along with the governments.

All but the troops. The remaining troops stayed behind as best they could, a few thousand here, a platoon there. No one knew exactly where they were; they stayed where they could, moving around at night, hiding in ruins, in sewers, cellars, with the rats and snakes. It looked as if the Soviet Union had the war almost won. Except for a handful of projectiles fired off from the moon daily, there was almost no weapon in use against them. They came and went as they pleased. The war, for all practical purposes, was over. Nothing effective opposed them.

And then the first claws appeared. And overnight the complexion of the war changed.

The claws were awkward, at first. Slow. The Ivans knocked them off almost as fast as they crawled out of their underground tunnels. But then they got better, faster and more cunning. Factories all on Terra, turned them out. Factories a long way underground, behind the Soviet lines, factories that had once made atomic projectiles, now almost forgotten.

The claws got faster, and they got bigger. New types appeared, some with feelers, some that flew. There were a few jumping kinds. The best technicians on the moon were working on designs, making them more and more intricate, more flexible. They became uncanny; the Ivans were having a lot of trouble with them. Some of the little claws were learning to hide themselves, burrowing down to the ash, lying in wait.

And then they started getting into the Russian bunkers, slipping down when the lids were raised for air and a look around. One claw inside a bunker, a churning sphere of blades and metal—that was enough. And when one got in others followed. With a weapon like that the war couldn't go on much longer.

Maybe it was already over.

Maybe he was going to hear the news. Maybe the Politburo had decided to throw in the sponge. Too bad it had taken so long. Six years. A long time for war like that, the way they had waged it. The automatic retaliation disc, spinning down all over Russia, hundreds of thousands of them. Bacteria crystals. The Soviet guided missiles, whistling through the air. The chain bombs. And now this, the robots, the claws—

The claws weren't like other weapons. They were *alive*, from any practical standpoint, whether the Governments wanted to admit it or not. They were not machines. They were living things, spinning, creeping, shaking themselves up suddenly from the gray ash and darting toward a man, climbing up him, rushing for his throat. And that was what they had been designed to do. Their job.

They did their job well. Especially lately, with the new designs coming up. Now they repaired themselves. They were on their own. Radiation tabs protected the UN troops, but if a man lost his tab he was fair game for the claws, no matter what his uniform. Down below the surface automatic machinery stamped them out. Human beings stayed a long way off. It was too risky; nobody wanted to be around them. They were left to themselves. And they seemed to be doing all right. The new designs were faster, more complex. More efficient.

Apparently they had won the war.

Major Hendricks lit a second cigarette. The landscape depressed him. Nothing but ash and ruins. He seemed to be alone, the only living thing in the whole world. To the right the ruins of a town rose up, a few walls and heaps of debris. He tossed the dead match away, increasing his pace. Suddenly he stopped, jerking up his gun, his body tense. For a minute it looked like—

From behind the shell of a ruined building a figure came, walking slowly toward him, walking hesitantly.

Hendricks blinked. "Stop!"

The boy stopped. Hendricks lowered his gun. The boy stood silently, looking at him. He was small, not very old. Perhaps eight. But it was hard to tell. Most of the kids who remained were stunted. He wore a faded blue sweater, ragged with dirt, and short pants. His hair was long and matted. Brown hair. It hung over his face and around his ears. He held something in his arms.

"What's that you have?" Hendricks said sharply.

The boy held it out. It was a toy, a bear. A teddy bear. The boy's eyes were large, but without expression.

Hendricks relaxed. "I don't want it. Keep it."

The boy hugged the bear again.

"Where do you live?" Hendricks said.

"In there."

"The ruins?"

"Yes."

"Underground?"

"Yes."

"How many are there?"

"How—how many?"

"How many of you. How big's your settlement?"

The boy did not answer.

Hendricks frowned. "You're not all by yourself, are you?"

The boy nodded.

"How do you stay alive?"

"There's food."

"What kind of food?"

"Different."

Hendricks, studied him. "How old are you?"

"Thirteen."

It wasn't possible. Or was it? The boy was thin, stunted. And probably sterile. Radiation exposure, years straight. No wondered he was so small. His arms and legs were like pipe-cleaners, knobby and thin. Hendricks touched the boy's arm. His skin was dry and rough; radiation skin. He bent down, looking into the boy's face. There was no expression. Big eyes, big and dark.

"Are you blind?" Hendricks said.

"No. I can see some."

"How do you get away from the claws?"

"The claws?"

"The round things. That run and burrow."

"I don't understand."

Maybe there weren't any claws around. A lot of areas were free. They collected mostly around bunkers, where there were people. The claws had been designed to sense warmth, warmth of living things.

"You're lucky." Hendricks straightened up. "Well? Which way are you going? Back—back there?"

"Can I come with you?"

"With *me*?" Hendricks folded his arms. "I'm going a long way. Miles. I have to hurry." He looked at his watch. "I have to get there by nightfall."

"I want to come."

Hendricks fumbled in his pack. "It isn't worth it. Here." He tossed down the food cans he had with him. "You take these and go back. Okay?"

The boy said nothing.

"I'll be coming back this way. In a day or so. If you're around here when I come back you can come along with me. All right?"

"I want to come along with you now."

"It's a long walk."

"I can walk."

Hendricks shifted uneasily. It made too good a target,

two people walking along. And the boy would slow him down. But he might not come back this way. And if the boy were really all alone—

"Okay. Come along."

The boy fell in beside him. Hendricks strode along. The boy walked silently, clutching his teddy bear.

"What's your name?" Hendricks said, after a time.

"David Edward Derring."

"David? What—what happened to your mother and father?"

"They died."

"How?"

"In the blast."

"How long ago?"

"Six years."

Hendricks slowed down. "You've been alone six years?"

"No. There were other people for awhile. They went away."

"And you've been alone since?"

"Yes."

Hendricks glanced down. The boy was strange, saying very little. Withdrawn. But that was the way they were, the children who had survived. Quiet. Stoic. A strange kind of fatalism gripped them. Nothing came as a surprise. They accepted anything that came along. There was no longer any *normal,* any natural course of things, moral or physical, for them to expect. Custom, habit, all the determining forces of learning were gone; only brute experience remained.

"Am I walking too fast?" Hendricks said.

"No."

"How did you happen to see me?"

"I was waiting."

"Waiting?" Hendricks was puzzled. "What were you waiting for?"

"To catch things."

"What kind of things?"

"Things to eat."

"Oh." Hendricks set his lips grimly. A thirteen year old boy, living on rats and gophers and half-rotten canned food. Down in a hole under the ruins of a town. With radiation pools and claws, and Russian dive-mines up above, coasting around in the sky.

"Where are we going?" David asked.

"To the Russian lines."

"Russian?"

"The enemy. The people who started the war. They dropped the first radiation bombs. They began all this."

The boy nodded. His face showed no expression.

"I'm an American," Hendricks said.

There was no comment. On they went, the two of them, Hendricks walking a little ahead, David trailing behind him, hugging his dirty teddy bear against his chest.

About four in the afternoon they stopped to eat. Hendricks built a fire in a hollow between some slabs of concrete. He cleared the weeds away and heaped up bits of wood. The Russians' lines were not very far ahead. Around him was what had once been a long valley, acres of fruit trees and grapes. Nothing remained now but a few bleak stumps and the mountains that stretched across the horizon at the far end. And the clouds of rolling ash that blew and drifted with the wind, settling over the weeds and remains of buildings, walls here and there, once in awhile what had been a road.

Hendricks made coffee and heated up some boiled mutton and bread. "Here." He handed bread and mutton to David. David squatted by the edge of the fire, his knees knobby and white. He examined the food and then passed it back, shaking his head.

"No."

"No? Don't you want any?"

"No."

Hendricks shrugged. Maybe the boy was a mutant, used to special food. It didn't matter. When he was hungry he would find something to eat. The boy was strange. But there were many strange changes coming over the world. Life was not the same, anymore. It would never be the same again. The human race was going to have to realize that.

"Suit yourself," Hendricks said. He ate the bread and mutton by himself, washing it down with coffee. He ate slowly, finding the food hard to digest. When he was done he got to his feet and stamped the fire out.

David rose slowly, watching him with his young-old eyes.

"We're going," Hendricks said.

"All right."

Hendricks walked along, his gun in his arms. They were close; he was tense, ready for anything. The Russians should be expecting a runner, an answer to their own runner, but they were tricky. There was always the possibility of a slip-up. He scanned the landscape around him. Nothing but slag and ash, a few hills, charred trees. Concrete walls. But someplace ahead was the first bunker of the Russian lines, the forward command. Underground, buried deep, with only a periscope showing, a few gun muzzles. Maybe an antenna.

"Will we be there soon?" David asked.

"Yes. Getting tired!"

"No."

"Why, then?"

David did not answer. He plodded carefully along behind, picking his way over the ash. His legs and shoes were gray with dust. His pinched face was streaked, lines of gray ash in riverlets down the pale white of his skin. There was no color to his face. Typical of the new children, growing up in cellars and sewers and underground shelters.

Hendricks slowed down. He lifted his fieldglasses and studied the ground ahead of him. Were they there, someplace, waiting for him? Watching him, the way his men had watched the Russian runner? A chill went up his back. Maybe they were getting their guns ready, preparing to fire, the way his men had prepared, made ready to kill.

Hendricks stopped, wiping perspiration from his face. "Damn." It made him uneasy. But he should be expected. The situation was different.

He strode over the ash, holding his gun tightly with both hands. Behind him came David. Hendricks peered around, tight-lipped. Any second it might happen. A burst of white light, a blast, carefully aimed from inside a deep concrete bunker.

He raised his arm and waved it around in a circle.

Nothing moved. To the right a long ridge ran, topped with dead tree trunks. A few wild vines had grown up around the trees, remains of arbors. And the eternal dark weeds. Hendricks studied the ridge. Was anything up there? Perfect place for a lookout. He approached the ridge warily, David coming silently behind. It if were his command he'd have a sentry up there, watching for troops trying to infiltrate into the command area. Of course, if it were his command there would be the claws around the area for full protection.

He stopped, feet apart, hands on his hips.

"Are we there?" David said.

"Almost."

"Why have we stopped?"

"I don't want to take any chances." Hendricks advanced slowly. Now the ridge lay directly beside him, along his right. Overlooking him. His uneasy feeling increased. If an Ivan were up there he wouldn't have a chance. He waved his arm again. They should be expecting someone in the UN uniform, in response to the note capsule. Unless the whole thing was a trap.

"Keep up with me." He turned toward David. "Don't drop behind."

"With you?"

"Up beside me! We're close. We can't take any chances. Come on."

"I'll be all right." David remained behind him, in the rear, a few paces away, still clutching his teddy bear.

"Have it your way." Hendricks raised his glasses again, suddenly tense. For a moment—had something moved? He scanned the ridge carefully. Everything was silent. Dead. No life up there, only tree trunks and ash. Maybe a few rats. The big black rats that had survived the claws. Mutants—built their own shelters out of saliva and ash. Some kind of plaster. Adaptation. He started forward again.

A tall figure came out on the ridge above him, cloak flapping. Gray-green. A Russian. Behind him a second soldier appeared, another Russian. Both lifted their guns, aiming.

Hendricks froze. He opened his mouth. The soldiers were kneeling, sighting down the side of the slope. A third figure had joined them on the ridge top, a smaller figure in gray-green. A woman. She stood behind the other two.

Hendricks found his voice. "Stop!" He waved up at them frantically. "I'm—"

The two Russians fired. Behind Hendricks there was a faint *pop*. Waves of heat lapped against him, throwing him to the ground. Ash tore at his face, grinding into his eyes and nose. Choking, he pulled himself to his knees. It was all a trap. He was finished. He had come to be killed, like a steer. The soldiers and the woman were coming down the side of the ridge toward him, sliding down through the soft ash. Hendricks was numb. His head throbbed. Awkwardly, he got his rifle up and took aim. It weighed a thousand tons; he could hardly hold it. His nose and cheeks stung. The air was full of the blast smell, a bitter acrid stench.

"Don't fire," the first Russian said, in heavily accented English.

The three of them came up to him, surrounding him. "Put down your rifle, Yank," the other said.

Hendricks was dazed. Everything had happened so fast. He had been caught. And they had blasted the boy. He turned his head. David was gone. What remained of him was strewn across the ground.

The three Russians studied him curiously. Hendricks sat, wiping blood from his nose, picking out bits of ash. He shook his head, trying to clear it. "Why did you do it?" he murmured thickly. "The boy."

"Why?" One of the soldiers helped him roughly to his feet. He turned Hendricks around. "Look."

Hendricks closed his eyes.

"Look!" The two Russians pulled him forward. "See. Hurry up. There isn't much time to spare, Yank!"

Hendricks looked. And gasped.

"See now? Now do you understand?"

From the remains of David a metal wheel rolled. Relays, glinting metal. Parts, wiring. One of the Russians kicked at the heap of remains. Parts popped out, rolling away, wheels and springs and rods. A plastic section fell in, half charred. Hendricks bent shakily down. The front of the head had come off. He could make out the intricate brain, wires and relays, tiny tubes and switches, thousands of minute studs—

"A robot," the soldier holding his arm said. "We watched it tagging you."

"Tagging me?"

"That's their way. They tag along with you. Into the bunker. That's how they get in."

Hendricks blinked, dazed. "But—"

"Come on." They led him toward the ridge, sliding and slipping on the ash. The woman reached the top and stood waiting for them.

"The forward command," Hendricks muttered. "I came to negotiate with the Soviet—"

"There is no more forward command. *They* got in. We'll explain." They reached the top of the ridge. "We're all that's left. The three of us. The rest were down in the bunker."

"This way. Down this way." The woman unscrewed a lid, a gray manhole cover set in the ground. "Get in."

Hendricks lowered himself. The two soldiers and the woman came behind him, following him down the ladder. The woman closed the lid after them, bolting it tightly into place.

"Good thing we saw you," one of the two soldiers grunted. "It had tagged you about as far as it was going to."

"Give me one of your cigarettes," the woman said. "I haven't had an American cigarette for weeks."

Hendricks pushed the pack to her. She took a cigarette and passed the pack to the two soldiers. In the corner of the small room the lamp gleamed fitfully. The room was low-ceilinged, cramped. The four of them sat around a small wood table. A few dirty dishes were stacked to one side. Behind a ragged curtain a second room was partly visible. Hendricks saw the corner of a cot, some blankets, clothes hung on a hook.

"We were here," the soldier beside him said. He took off his helmet, pushing his blond hair back. "I'm Corporal Rudi Maxer. Polish. Impressed in the Soviet Army two years ago." He held out his hand.

Hendricks hesitated and then shook. "Major Joseph Hendricks."

"Klaus Epstein." The other soldier shook with him, a small dark man with thinning hair. Epstein plucked nervously at his ear. "Austrian. Impressed God knows when. I don't remember. The three of us were here, Rudi and I, with Tasso." He indicated the woman. "That's how we escaped. All the rest were down in the bunker."

"And—and *they* got in?"

Epstein lit a cigarette. "First just one of them. The kind that tagged you. Then it let others in."

Hendricks became alert. "The *kind*? Are there more than one kind?"

"The little boy. David. David holding his teddy bear. That's Variety Three. The most effective."

"What are the other types?"

Epstein reached into his coat. "Here." He tossed a packet of photographs onto the table, tied with a string. "Look for yourself."

Hendricks untied the string.

"You see," Rudi Maxer said, "that was why we wanted to talk terms. The Russians, I mean. We found out about a week ago. Found out that your claws were beginning to make up new designs on their own. New types of their own. Better types. Down in your underground factories behind our lines. You let them stamp themselves, repair themselves. Made them more and more intricate. It's your fault this happened."

Hendricks examined the photos. They had been snapped hurriedly; they were blurred and indistinct. The first few showed—David. David walking along a road, by himself. David and another David. Three Davids. All exactly alike. Each with a ragged teddy bear.

All pathetic.

"Look at the others," Tasso said.

The next pictures, taken at a great distance, showed a towering wounded soldier sitting by the side of a path, his arm in a sling, the stump of one leg extended, a crude crutch on his lap. Then two wounded soldiers, both the same, standing side by side.

"That's Variety One. The Wounded Soldier." Klaus reached out and took the pictures. "You see, the claws were designed to get to human beings. To find them. Each kind was better than the last. They got farther, closer past most of our defenses, into our lines. But as long as they were merely *machines,* metal spheres with claws and horns, feelers, they could be picked off like any other object. They could be detected as lethal robots as soon as they were seen. Once we caught sight of them—"

"Variety One subverted our whole north wing," Rudi said. "It was a long time before anyone caught on. Then it was too late. They came in, wounded soldiers, knocking and begging to be let in. So we let them in. And as soon as they were in they took over. We were watching out for machines . . ."

"At that time it was thought there was only the one

type," Klaus Epstein said. "No one suspected there were other types. The pictures were flashed to us. When the runner was sent to you, we knew of just one type. Variety One. The big Wounded Soldier. We thought that was all."

"Your line fell to—"

"To Variety Three. David and his bear. That worked even better." Klaus smiled bitterly. "Soldiers are suckers for children. We brought them in and tried to feed them. We found out the hard way what they were after. At least, those who were in the bunker."

"The three of us were lucky," Rudi said. "Klaus and I were—were visiting Tasso when it happened. This is her place." He waved a big hand around. "This little cellar. We finished and climbed the ladder to start back. From the ridge we saw. There they were, all around the bunker. Fighting was still going on. David and his bear. Hundreds of them. Klaus took the pictures."

Klaus tied up the photographs again.

"And it's going on all along your line?" Hendricks said.

"Yes."

"How about *our* lines?" Without thinking, he touched the tab on his arm. "Can they—"

"They're not bothered by your radiation tabs. It makes no difference to them, Russian, American, Pole, German. It's all the same. They're doing what they were designed to do. Carrying out the original idea. They track down life, wherever they find it."

"They go by warmth," Klaus said. "That was the way you constructed them from the very start. Of course, those you designed were kept back by the radiation tabs you wear. Now they've got around that. These new varieties are lead-lined."

"What's the other variety?" Hendricks asked. "The David type. The Wounded Soldier—what's the other?"

"We don't know." Klaus pointed up at the wall. On the wall were two metal plates, ragged at the edges. Hendricks got up and studied them. They were bent and dented.

"The one on the left came off a Wounded Soldier," Rudi said. "We got one of them. It was going along toward our old bunker. We got it from the ridge, the same way we got the David tagging you."

The plate was stamped: I-V. Hendricks touched the other plate. "And this came from the David type?"

"Yes." The plate was stamped: III-V.

Klaus took a look at them, leaning over Hendricks' broad shoulder. "You can see what we're up against. There's another type. Maybe it was abandoned. Maybe it didn't work. But there must be a Second Variety. There's One and Three."

"You were lucky," Rudi said. "The David tagged you all the way here and never touched you. Probably thought you'd get it into a bunker, somewhere."

"One gets in and it's all over," Klaus said. "They move fast. One lets all the rest inside. They're inflexible. Machines with one purpose. They were built for only one thing." He rubbed sweat from his lip. "We saw."

They were silent.

"Let me have another cigarette, Yank," Tasso said. "They are good. I almost forgot how they were."

It was night. The sky was black. No stars were visible through the rolling clouds of ash. Klaus lifted the lid cautiously so that Hendricks could look out.

Rudi pointed into the darkness. "Over that way are the bunkers. Where we used to be. Not over half a mile from us. It was just chance Klaus and I were not there when it happened. Weakness. Saved by our lusts."

"All the rest must be dead," Klaus said in a low voice. "It came quickly. This morning the Politburo reached their decision. They notified us—forward command. Our runner was sent out at once. We saw him start toward the direction of your lines. We covered him until he was out of sight."

"Alex Radrivsky. We both knew him. He disappeared about six o'clock. The sun had just come up. About noon Klaus and I had an hour relief. We crept off, away from the bunkers. No one was watching. We came here. There used to be a town here a few houses, a street. This cellar was part of a big farmhouse. We knew Tasso would be here, hiding down in her little place. We had come here before. Others from the bunkers came here. Today happened to be our turn."

"So we were saved," Klaus said. "Chance. It might have been others. We—we finished, and then we came up to the surface and started back along the ridge. That was when we saw them, the Davids. We understood right away. We had seen the photos of the First Variety, the Wounded Soldier. Our Commissar distributed them to us with an explanation. If we had gone another step they would have seen us. As it was we had to blast two Davids before we got back. There were hundreds of them, all around. Like ants. We took pictures and slipped back here, bolting the lid tight."

"They're not so much when you catch them alone. We moved faster than they did. But they're inexorable. Not like living things. They came right at us. And we blasted them."

Major Hendricks rested against the edge of the lid, adjusting his eyes to the darkness. "Is it safe to have the lid up at all?"

"If we're careful. How else can you operate your transmitter?"

Hendricks lifted the small belt transmitter slowly. He pressed it against his ear. The metal was cold and damp. He blew against the mike, raising up the short antenna. A faint hum sounded in his ear. "That's true, I suppose."

But he still hesitated.

"We'll pull you under if anything happens," Klaus said.

"Thanks." Hendricks waited a moment, resting the transmitter against his shoulder. "Interesting, isn't it?"

"What?"

"This, the new types. The new varieties of claws. We're completely at their mercy, aren't we? By now they've probably gotten into the UN lines, too. It makes me wonder if we're not seeing the beginning of a new species. The new species. Evolution. The race to come after man."

Rudi grunted. "There is no race after man."

"No? Why not? Maybe we're seeing it now, the end of human beings, the beginning of the new society."

"They're not a race. They're mechanical killers. You made them to destroy. That's all they can do. They're machines with a job."

"So it seems now. But how about later on? After the war is over. Maybe, when there aren't any humans to destroy, their real potentialities will begin to show."

"You talk as if they were alive!"

"Aren't they?"

There was silence. "They're machines," Rudi said. "They look like people, but they're machines."

"Use your transmitter, Major," Klaus said. "We can't stay up here forever."

Holding the transmitter tightly Hendricks called the code of the command bunker. He waited, listening. No response. Only silence. He checked the leads carefully. Everything was in place.

"Scott!" he said into the mike. "Can you hear me?"

Silence. He raised the mast up full and tried again. Only static.

"I don't get anything. They may hear me but they may not want to answer."

"Tell them it's an emergency."

"They'll think I'm being forced to call. Under your direction." He tried again, outlining briefly what he had learned. But still the phone was silent, except for the faint static.

"Radiation pools kill most transmission," Klaus said, after awhile. "Maybe that's it."

Hendricks shut the transmitter up. "No use. No answer. Radiation pools? Maybe. Or they hear me, but won't answer. Frankly, that's what I would do, if a runner tried to call from the Soviet lines. They have no reason to believe such a story. They may hear everything I say—"

"Or maybe it's too late."

Hendricks nodded.

"We better get the lid down," Rudi said nervously. "We don't want to take unnecessary chances."

They climbed slowly back down the tunnel. Klaus bolted the lid carefully into place. They descended into the kitchen. The air was heavy and close around them.

"Could they work that fast?" Hendricks said. "I left the bunker this noon. Ten hours ago. How could they move so quickly?"

"It doesn't take them long. Not after the first one gets in. It goes wild. You know what the little claws can do. Even *one* of these is beyond belief. Razors, each finger. Maniacal."

"All right." Hendricks moved away impatiently. He stood with his back to them.

"What's the matter?" Rudi said.

"The Moon Base. God, if they've gotten there—"

"The Moon Base?"

Hendricks turned around. "They couldn't have got to the

Moon Base. How would they get there? It isn't possible. I can't believe it."

"What is this Moon Base? We've heard rumors, but nothing definite. What is the actual situation? You seem concerned."

"We're supplied from the moon. The governments are there, under the lunar surface. All our people and industries. That's what keeps us going. If they should find some way of getting off Terra, onto the moon—"

"It only takes one of them. Once the first one gets in it admits the others. Hundreds of them, all alike. You should have seen them. Identical. Like ants."

"Perfect socialism," Tasso said. "The ideal of the communist state. All citizens interchangeable."

Klaus grunted angrily. "That's enough. Well? What next?"

Hendricks paced back and forth, around the small room. The air was full of smells of food and perspiration. The others watched him. Presently Tasso pushed through the curtain, into the other room. "I'm going to take a nap."

The curtain closed behind her. Rudi and Klaus sat down at the table, still watching Hendricks. "It's up to you," Klaus said. "We don't know your situation."

Hendricks nodded.

"It's a problem." Rudi drank some coffee, filling his cup from a rusty pot. "We're safe here for awhile, but we can't stay here forever. Not enough food or supplies."

"But if we go outside—"

"If we go outside they'll get us. Or probably they'll get us. We couldn't go very far. How far is your command bunker, Major?"

'What if they're already there?" Klaus said.

Rudi shrugged. "Well, then we come back here."

Hendricks stopped pacing. "What do you think the chances are they're already in the American lines?"

"Hard to say. Fairly good. They're organized. They know exactly what they're doing. Once they start they go like a horde of locusts. They have to keep moving, and fast. It's secrecy and speed they depend on. Surprise. They push their way in before anyone has any idea."

"I see," Hendricks murmured.

From the other room Tasso stirred. "Major?"

Hendricks pushed the curtain back. "What?"

Tasso looked up at him lazily from the cot. "Have you any more American cigarettes left?"

Hendricks went into the room and sat down across from her, on a wood stool. He felt in his pockets. "No. All gone."

"Too bad."

"What nationality are you?" Hendricks asked after awhile.

"Russian."

"How did you get here?"

"Here?"

"This used to be France. This was part of Normandy. Did you come with the Soviet army?"

"Why?"

"Just curious." He studied her. She had taken off her coat, tossing it over the end of the cot. She was young, about twenty. Slim. Her long hair stretched out over the pillow. She was staring at him silently, her eyes dark and large.

"What's on your mind?" Tasso said.

"Nothing. How old are you?"

"Eighteen." She continued to watch him, unblinking, her arms behind her head. She had on Russian army pants and shirt. Gray-green. Thick leather belt with counter and cartridges. Medicine kit.

"You're in the Soviet army?"

"No."

"Where did you get the uniform?"

She shrugged. "It was given to me," she told him.

"How—how old were you when you came here?"

"Sixteen."

"That young?"

Her eyes narrowed. "What do you mean?"

Hendricks rubbed his jaw. "Your life would have been a lot different if there had been no war. Sixteen. You came here at sixteen. To live this way."

"I had to survive."

"I'm not moralizing."

"Your life would have been different, too," Tasso murmured. She reached down and unfastened one of her boots. She kicked the boot off, onto the floor. "Major, do you want to go in the other room? I'm sleepy."

"It's going to be a problem, the four of us here. It's going to be hard to live in these quarters. Are there just two rooms?"

"Yes."

"How big was the cellar originally? Was it larger than this? Are there other rooms filled up with debris? We might be able to open one of them."

"Perhaps. I really don't know." Tasso loosened her belt. She made herself comfortable on the cot, unbuttoning her shirt. "You're sure you have no more cigarettes?"

"I had only the one pack."

"Too bad. Maybe if we get back to your bunker we can find some." The other boot fell. Tasso reached up for the light cord. "Good night."

"You're going to sleep?"

"That's right."

The room plunged into darkness. Hendricks got up and made his way past the curtain, into the kitchen.

And stopped, rigid.

Rudi stood against the wall, his face white and gleaming. His mouth opened and closed but no sounds came. Klaus stood in front of him, the muzzle of his pistol in Rudi's stomach. Neither of them moved. Klaus, his hand tight around his gun, his features set. Rudi, pale and silent, spread-eagled against the wall.

"What—" Hendricks muttered, but Klaus cut him off.

"Be quiet, Major. Come over here. Your gun. Get out your gun."

Hendricks drew his pistol. "What is it?"

"Cover him." Klaus motioned him forward. "Beside me. Hurry!"

Rudi moved a little, lowering his arms. He turned to Hendricks, licking his lips. The whites of his eyes shone wildly. Sweat dripped from his forehead, down his cheeks. He fixed his gaze on Hendricks. "Major, he's gone insane. Stop him." Rudi's voice was thin and hoarse, almost inaudible.

"What's going on?" Hendricks demanded.

Without lowering his pistol Klaus answered. "Major, remember our discussion? The Three Varieties? We knew about One and Three. But we didn't know about Two. At least, we didn't know before." Klaus' fingers tightened around the gun butt. "We didn't know before, but we know now."

He pressed the trigger. A burst of white heat rolled out of the gun, licking around Rudi.

"Major, this is the Second Variety."

Tasso swept the curtain aside. "Klaus! What did you do?"

Klaus turned from the charred form, gradually sinking down the wall onto the floor. "The Second Variety, Tasso. Now we know. We have all three types identified. The danger is less. I—"

Tasso stared past him at the remains of Rudi, at the blackened smouldering fragments and bits of cloth. "You killed him."

"Him? *It*, you mean. I was watching. I had a feeling, but I wasn't sure. At least I wasn't sure before. But this evening I was certain." Klaus rubbed his pistol butt nervously. "We're lucky. Don't you understand? Another hour and it might—"

"You were *certain*?" Tasso pushed past him and bent down, over the steaming remains on the floor. Her face became hard. "Major, see for yourself. Bones. Flesh."

Hendricks bent down beside her. The remains were human remains. Seared flesh, charred bone fragments, part of a skull. Ligaments, viscera, blood. Blood forming a pool against the wall.

"No wheels," Tasso said calmly. She straightened up. "No wheels, no parts, no relays. Not a claw. Not the Second Variety." She folded her arms. "You're going to have to be able to explain this."

Klaus sat down at the table, all the color drained suddenly from his face. He put this head in his hands and rocked back and forth.

"Snap out of it." Tasso's fingers closed over his shoulder. "Why did you do it? Why did you kill him?"

"He was frightened," Hendricks said. "All this, the whole thing, building up around us."

"Maybe."

"What, then? What do you think?"

"I think he may have had a reason for killing Rudi. A good reason."

"What reason?"

"Maybe Rudi learned something."

Hendricks studied her bleak face. "About what?" he asked.

"About him. About Klaus."

* * *

Klaus looked up quickly. "You can see what she's trying to say. She thinks I'm the Second Variety. Don't you see Major? Now she wants you to believe I killed him on purpose. That I'm—"

"Why did you kill him, then?" Tasso said.

"I told you." Klaus shook his head wearily. "I thought he was a claw. I thought I knew."

"Why?"

"I had been watching him. I was suspicious."

"Why?"

"I thought I had seen something. Heard something. I thought I heard him—*whirr.*"

There was silence.

"Do you believe that?" Tasso said to Hendricks.

"Yes. I believe what he says."

"I don't. I think he killed Rudi for a good purpose." Tasso touched the rifle, resting in the corner of the room. "Major—"

"No." Hendricks shook his head. "Let's stop it right now. One is enough. We're afraid, the way he was. If we kill him we'll be doing what he did to Rudi."

Klaus looked gratefully up at him. "Thanks. I was afraid. You understand, don't you? Now she's afraid, the way I was. She wants to kill me."

"No more killing." Hendricks moved toward the end of the ladder. "I'm going above and try the transmitter once more. If I can't get them we're moving back toward my lines tomorrow morning."

Klaus rose quickly. "I'll come up with you and give you a hand."

The night air was cold. The earth was cooling off. Klaus took a deep breath, filling his lungs. He and Hendricks stepped onto the ground, out of the tunnel. Klaus planted his feet wide apart, the rifle up, watching and listening. Hendricks crouched by the tunnel mouth, tuning the small transmitter.

"Any luck?" Klaus asked presently.

"Not yet."

"Keep trying. Tell them what happened."

Hendricks kept trying. Without success. Finally he lowered the antenna. "It's useless. They can't hear me. Or they hear me and won't answer. Or—"

"Or they don't exist."

"I'll try once more." Hendricks raised the antenna. "Scott, can you hear me? Come in!"

He listened. There was only static. Then, still very faintly—

"This is Scott."

His fingers tightened. "Scott! Is it you?"

"This is Scott."

Klaus squatted down. "Is it your command?"

"Scott, listen. Do you understand? About them, the claws. Did you get my message? Did you hear me?"

"Yes." Faintly. Almost inaudible. He could hardly make out the word.

"You got my message? Is everything all right at the bunker? None of them have got in?"

"Everything is all right."

"Have they tried to get in?"

The voice was weaker.

"No."

Hendricks turned to Klaus. "They're all right."

"Have they been attacked?"

"No." Hendricks pressed the phone tighter to his ear. "Scott, I can hardly hear you. Have you notified the Moon Base? Do they know? Are they alerted?"

No answer.

"Scott! Can you hear me?"

Silence.

Hendricks relaxed, sagging. "Faded out. Must be radiation pools."

Hendricks and Klaus looked at each other. Neither of them said anything. After a time Klaus said, "Did it sound like any of your men? Could you identify the voice?"

"It was too faint."

"You couldn't be certain?"

"No."

"Then it could have been—"

"I don't know. Now I'm not sure. Let's go back down and get the lid closed."

They climb back down the ladder slowly, into the warm cellar. Klaus bolted the lid behind them. Tasso waited for them, her face expressionless.

"Any luck?" she asked.

Neither of them answered. "Well?" Klaus said at last.

"What do you think, Major? Was it your officer, or was it one of *them*?"

"I don't know."

"Then we're just where we were before."

Hendricks stared down at the floor, his jaw set. "We'll have to go. To be sure."

"Anyhow, we have food here for only a few weeks. We'd have to go up after that, in any case."

"Apparently so."

"What's wrong?" Tasso demanded. "Did you get across to your bunker? What's the matter?"

"It may have been one of my men," Hendricks said slowly. "Or it may have been one of *them*. But we'll never know standing here." He examined his watch. "Let's turn in and get some sleep. We want to be up early tomorrow."

"Early?"

"Our best chance to get through the claws should be early in the morning," Hendricks said.

The morning was crisp and clear. Major Hendricks studied the countryside through his fieldglasses.

"See anything?" Klaus said.

"No."

"Can you make out our bunkers?"

"Which way?"

"Here." Klaus took the glasses and adjusted them. "I know where to look." He looked a long time, silently.

Tasso came to the top of the tunnel and stepped up onto the ground. "Anything?"

"No." Klaus passed the glasses back to Hendricks. "They're out of sight. Come on. Let's not stay here."

The three of them made their way down the side of the ridge, sliding in the soft ash. Across a flat rock a lizard scuttled. They stopped instantly, rigid.

"What was it?" Klaus muttered.

"A lizard."

The lizard ran on, hurrying through the ash. It was exactly the same color as the ash.

"Perfect adaptation," Klaus said. "Proves we were right. Lysenko, I mean."

They reached the bottom of the ridge and stopped, standing close together, looking around them.

"Let's go." Hendricks started off. "It's a good long trip, on foot."

Klaus fell in beside him. Tasso walked behind, her pistol held alertly. "Major, I've been meaning to ask you something," Klaus said. "How did you run across the David? The one that was tagging you."

"I met it along the way. In some ruins."

"What did it say?"

"Not much. It said it was alone. By itself."

"You couldn't tell it was a machine? It talked like a living person? You never suspected?"

"It didn't say much. I noticed nothing unusual."

"It's strange, machines so much like people that you can be fooled. Almost alive. I wonder where it'll end."

"They're doing what you Yanks designed them to do," Tasso said. "You designed them to hunt out life and destroy. Human life. Wherever they find it."

Hendricks was watching Klaus intently. "Why did you ask me? What's on your mind?"

"Nothing," Klaus answered.

"Klaus thinks you're the Second Variety," Tasso said calmly, from behind them. "Now he's got his eye on you."

Klaus flushed. "Why not? We sent a runner to the Yank lines and he comes back. Maybe he thought he'd find some good game here."

Hendricks laughed harshly. "I came from the UN bunkers. There were human being all around me."

"Maybe you saw an opportunity to get into the Soviet lines. Maybe you saw your chance. Maybe you—"

"The Soviet lines had already been taken over. Your lines had been invaded before I left my command bunker. Don't forget that."

Tasso came up beside him. "That proves nothing at all, Major."

"Why not?"

"There appears to be little communication between the varieties. Each is made in a different factory. They don't seem to work together. You might have started for the Soviet lines without knowing anything about the work of the other varieties. Or even what the other varieties were like."

"How do you know so much about the claws?" Hendricks said.

"I've seen them. I've observed them. I observed them take over the Soviet bunkers."

"You know quite a lot," Klaus said. "Actually, you saw very little. Strange that you should have been such an acute observer."

Tasso laughed. "Do you suspect me, now?"

"Forget it," Hendricks said. They walked on in silence.

"Are we going the whole way on foot?" Tasso said, after awhile. "I'm not used to walking." She gazed around at the plain of ash, stretching out on all sides of them, as far as they could see. "How dreary."

"It's like this all the way," Klaus said.

"In a way I wish you had been in your bunker when the attack came."

"Somebody else would have been with you, if not me," Klaus muttered.

Tasso laughed, putting her hands in her pockets. "I suppose so."

They walked on, keeping their eyes on the vast plain of silent ash around them.

The sun was setting. Hendricks made his way forward slowly, waving Tasso and Klaus back. Klaus squatted down, resting his gun butt against the ground.

Tasso found a concrete slab and sat down with a sigh. "It's good to rest."

"Be quiet," Klaus said sharply.

Hendricks pushed up to the top of the rise ahead of them. The same rise the Russian runner had come up, the day before. Hendricks dropped down, stretching himself out, peering through his glasses at what lay beyond.

Nothing was visible. Only ash and occasional trees. But there, not more than fifty yards ahead, was the entrance of the forward command bunker. The bunker from which he had come. Hendricks watched silently. No motion. No sign of life. Nothing stirred.

Klaus slithered up beside him. "Where is it?"

"Down there." Hendricks passed him the glasses. Clouds of ash rolled across the evening sky. The world was darkening. They had a couple of hours of light left, at the most. Probably not that much.

"I don't see anything," Klaus said.

"That tree there. The stump. By the pile of bricks. The entrance is to the right of the bricks."

"I'll have to take your work for it."

"You and Tasso cover me from here. You'll be able to sight all the way to the bunker entrance."

"You're going down alone?"

"With my wrist tab I'll be safe. The ground around the bunker is a living field of claws. They collect down in the ash. Like crabs. Without tabs you wouldn't have a chance."

"Maybe you're right."

"I'll walk slowly all the way. As soon as I know for certain—"

"If they're down inside the bunker you won't be able to get back up here. They go fast. You don't realize."

"What do you suggest?"

Klaus considered. "I don't know. Get them to come up to the surface. So you can see."

Hendricks brought his transmitter from his belt, raising the antenna. "Let's get started."

Klaus signalled to Tasso. She crawled expertly up the side of the rise to where they were sitting.

"He's going down alone," Klaus said. "We'll cover him from here. As soon as you see him start back, fire past him at once. They come quick."

"You're not very optimistic," Tasso said.

"No, I'm not."

Hendricks opened the breech of his gun, checking it carefully. "Maybe things are all right."

"You didn't see them. Hundreds of them. All the same. Pouring out like ants."

"I should be able to find out without going down all the way." Hendricks locked his gun, gripping it in one hand, the transmitter in the other. "Well, wish me luck."

Klaus put out his hand. "Don't go down until you're sure. Talk to them from up here. Make them show themselves."

Hendricks stood up. He stepped down the side of the rise.

A moment later he was walking slowly toward the pile of bricks and debris beside the dead tree stump. Toward the entrance of the forward command bunker.

Nothing stirred. He raised the transmitter, clicking it on. "Scott? Can you hear me?"

Silence.

"Scott! This is Hendricks. Can you hear me? I'm standing outside the bunker. You should be able to see me in the view sight."

He listened, the transmitter gripped tightly. No sound. Only static. He walked forward. A claw burrowed out the ash and raced toward him, studied him intently, and then fell in behind him, dogging respectfully after him, a few paces away. A moment later a second big claw joined it. Silently, the claws trailed him, as he walked slowly toward the bunker.

Hendricks stopped, and behind him, the claws came to a halt. He was close, now. Almost to the bunker steps.

"Scott! Can you hear me? I'm standing right above you. Outside. On the surface. Are you picking me up?"

He waited, holding his gun against his side, the transmitter tightly to his ear. Time passed. He strained to hear, but there was only silence. Silence, and faint static.

Then, distantly, metallically—

"This is Scott."

The voice was neutral. Cold. He could not identify it. But the earphone was minute.

"Scott! Listen. I'm standing right above you. I'm on the surface, looking down into the bunker entrance."

"Yes."

"Can you see me?"

"Yes."

"Through the view sight? You have the sight trained on me?"

"Yes."

Hendricks pondered. A circle of claws waited quietly on all sides of him. "Is everything all right in the bunker? Nothing unusual has happened?"

"Everything is all right."

"Will you come up to the surface? I want to see you for a moment." Hendricks took a deep breath. "Come up here with me. I want to talk to you."

"Come down."

"I'm giving you an order."

Silence.

"Are you coming?" Hendricks listened. There was no response. "I order you to come to the surface."

"Come down."

Hendricks set his jaw. "Let me talk to Leone."

There was a long pause. He listened to the static. Then a voice came, hard, thin, metallic. The same as the other. "This is Leone."

"Hendricks. I'm on the surface. At the bunker entrance. I want one of you to come up here."

"Come down."

"Why come down? I'm giving you an order!"

Silence. Hendricks lowered the transmitter. He looked carefully around him. The entrance was just ahead. Almost at his feet. He lowered the antenna and fastened the transmitter to his belt. Carefully, he gripped his gun with both hands. He moved forward, a step at a time. If they could see him they knew he was starting toward the entrance. He closed his eyes a moment.

Then he put his foot on the first step that led downward.

Two Davids came up at him, their faces identical and expressionless. He blasted them into particles. More came rushing silently up, a whole pack of them. All exactly the same.

Hendricks turned and raced back, away from the bunker, back toward the rise.

At the top of the rise Tasso and Klaus were firing down. The small claws were already streaking up toward them, shining metal spheres going fast, racing frantically through the ash. But he had no time to think about that. He knelt down, aiming at the bunker entrance, gun against his cheek. The Davids were coming out in groups, clutching their teddy bears, their thin knobby legs pumping as they ran up the steps to the surface. Hendricks fired into the main body of them. They burst apart, wheels and springs flying in all directions. He fired again, through the mist of particles.

A giant lumbering figure rose up in the bunker entrance, tall and swaying. Hendricks paused, amazed. A man, a soldier. With one leg, supporting himself with a crutch.

"Major!" Tasso's voice came. More firing. The huge figure moved forward, Davids swarming around it. Hendricks broke out of his freeze. The First Variety. The Wounded Soldiers. He aimed and fired. The soldier burst into bits, parts and relays flying. Now many Davids were out on the flat ground, away from the bunker. He fired again and again, moving slowly back, half-crouching and aiming.

From the rise, Klaus fired down. The side of the rise was alive with claws making their way up. Hendricks retreated toward the rise, running and crouching. Tasso had left Klaus and was circling slowly to the right, moving away from the rise.

A David slipped up toward him, its small white face expressionless, brown hair hanging down in its eyes. It bent over suddenly, opening its arms. Its teddy bear hurtled down and leaped across the ground, bounding toward him. Hendricks fired. The bear and the David both dissolved. He grinned, blinking. It was like a dream.

"Up here!" Tasso's voice. Hendricks made his way toward her. She was over by some columns of concrete, walls of a ruined building. She was firing past him, with the hand pistol Klaus had given her.

"Thanks." He joined her, gasping for breath. She pulled him back, behind the concrete, fumbling at her belt.

"Close your eyes!" She unfastened a globe from her waist. Rapidly, she unscrewed the cap, locking it into place. "Close your eyes and get down."

She threw the bomb. It sailed in an arc, an expert, rolling and bouncing to the entrance of the bunker. Two Wounded Soldiers stood uncertainly by the brick pile. More Davids poured from behind them, out onto the plain. One of the Wounded Soldiers moved toward the bomb, stooping awkwardly down to pick it up.

The bomb went off. The concussion whirled Hendricks around, throwing him on his face. A hot wind rolled over him. Dimly he saw Tasso standing behind the columns, firing slowly and methodically at the Davids coming out of the raging clouds of white fire.

Back along the rise Klaus struggled with a ring of claws circling around him. He retreated, blasting at them and moving back, trying to break through the ring.

Hendricks struggled to his feet. His head ached. He could hardly see. Everything was licking at him, raging and whirling. His right arm would not move.

Tasso pulled back toward him. "Come on. Let's go."

"Klaus—He's still up there."

"Come on!" Tasso dragged Hendricks back, away from the columns. Hendricks shook his head, trying to clear it.

Tasso led him rapidly away, her eyes intense and bright, watching for claws that had escaped the blast.

One David came out of the rolling clouds of flame. Tasso blasted it. No more appeared.

"But Klaus. What about him?" Hendricks stopped, standing unsteadily. "He—"

"Come on!"

They retreated, moving farther and farther away from the bunker. A few small claws followed them for a little while and then gave up, turning back and going off.

At last Tasso stopped. "We can stop here and get our breaths."

Hendricks sat down on some heaps of debris. He wiped his neck, gasping. "We left Klaus back there."

Tasso said nothing. She opened her gun, sliding a fresh round of blast cartridges into place.

Hendricks stared at her, dazed. "You left him back there on purpose."

Tasso snapped the gun together. She studied the heaps of rubble around them, her face expressionless. As if she were watching for something.

"What is it?" Hendricks demanded. "What are you looking for? Is something coming?" He shook his head, trying to understand. What was she doing? What was she waiting for? He could see nothing. Ash lay all around them, ash and ruins. Occasional stark tree trunks, without leaves or branches. "What—"

Tasso cut him off. "Be still." Her eyes narrowed. Suddenly her gun came up. Hendricks turned, following her gaze.

Back the way they had come a figure appeared. The figure walked unsteadily toward them. Its clothes were torn. It limped as it made its way along, going very slowly and carefully. Stopping now and then, resting and getting its strength. Once it almost fell. It stood for a moment, trying to steady itself. Then it came on.

Klaus.

Hendricks stood up, "Klaus!" He started toward him. "How the hell did you—"

Tasso fired. Hendricks swung back. She fired again, the blast passing him, a searing line of heat. The beam caught Klaus in the chest. He exploded, gears and wheels flying.

For a moment he continued to walk. Then he swayed back and forth. He crashed to the ground, his arms flung out. A few more wheels rolled away.

Silence.

Tasso turned to Hendricks. "Now you understand why he killed Rudi."

Hendricks sat down again slowly. He shook his head. He was numb. He could not think.

"Do you see?" Tasso said. "Do you understand?"

Hendricks said nothing. Everything was slipping away from him, faster and faster. Darkness, rolling and plucking at him.

He closed his eyes.

Hendricks opened his eyes slowly. His body ached all over. He tried to sit up but needles of pain shot through his arm and shoulder. He gasped.

"Don't try to get up," Tasso said. She bent down, putting her cold hand against his forehead.

It was night. A few stars glinted above, shining through the drifting clouds of ash. Hendricks lay back, his teeth locked. Tasso watched him impassively. She had built a fire with some wood and weeds. The fire licked feebly, hissing at a metal cup suspended over it. Everything was silent. Unmoving darkness, beyond the fire.

"So he was the Second Variety," Hendricks murmured.

"I had always thought so."

"Why didn't you destroy him sooner?" he wanted to know.

"You held me back." Tasso crossed to the fire to look into the metal cup. "Coffee. It'll be ready to drink in awhile."

She came back and sat down beside him. Presently she opened her pistol and began to disassemble the firing mechanism, studying it intently.

"This is a beautiful gun," Tasso said, half-aloud. "The construction is superb."

"What about them? The claws."

"The concussion from the bomb put most of them out of action. They're delicate. Highly organized, I suppose."

"The Davids, too?"

"Yes."

"How did you happen to have a bomb like that?"

Tasso shrugged. "We designed it. You shouldn't underestimate our technology, Major. Without such a bomb you and I would no longer exist."

"Very useful."

Tasso stretched out her legs, warming her feet in the heat of the fire. "It surprised me that you did not seem to understand, after he killed Rudi. Why did you think he—"

"I told you. I thought he was afraid."

"Really? You know, Major, for a little while I suspected you. Because you wouldn't let me kill him. I thought you might be protecting him." She laughed.

"Are we safe here?" Hendricks asked presently.

"For awhile. Until they get reinforcements from some other area." Tasso began to clean the interior of the gun with a bit of rag. She finished and pushed the mechanism back into place. She closed the gun, running her finger along the barrel.

"We were lucky," Hendricks murmured.

"Yes. Very lucky."

"Thanks for pulling me away."

Tasso did not answer. She glanced up at him, her eyes bright in the fire light. Hendricks examined his arm. He could not move his fingers. His whole side seemed numb. Down inside him was a dull steady ache.

"How do you feel?" Tasso asked.

"My arm is damaged."

"Anything else?"

"Internal injuries."

"You didn't get down when the bomb went off."

Hendricks said nothing. He watched Tasso pour the coffee from the cup into a flat metal pan. She brought it over to him.

"Thanks." He struggled up enough to drink. It was hard to swallow. His insides turned over and he pushed the pan away. "That's all I can drink now."

Tasso drank the rest. Time passed. The clouds of ash moved across the dark sky above them. Hendricks rested, his mind blank. After awhile he became aware that Tasso was standing over him, gazing down at him.

"What is it?" he murmured.

"Do you feel any better?"

"Some."

"You know, Major, if I hadn't dragged you away they would have got you. You would be dead. Like Rudi."

"I know."

"Do you want to know why I brought you out? I could have left you. I could have left you there."

"Why did you bring me out?"

"Because we have to get away from here." Tasso stirred the fire with a stick, peering calmly down into it. "No human being can live here. When their reinforcements come we won't have a chance. I've pondered about it while you were unconscious. We have perhaps three hours before they come."

"And you expect me to get us away?"

"That's right. I expect you to get us out of here."

"Why me?"

"Because I don't know any way." Her eyes shone at him in the half-light, bright and steady. "If you can't get us out of here they'll kill us within three hours. I see nothing else ahead. Well, Major? What are you going to do? I've been waiting all night. While you were unconscious I sat here, waiting and listening. It's almost dawn. The night is almost over."

Hendricks considered. "It's curious," he said at last.

"Curious?"

"That you should think I can get us out of here. I wonder what you think I can do."

"Can you get us to the Moon Base?"

"The Moon Base? How?"

"There must be some way."

Hendricks shook his head. "No. There's no way that I know of."

Tasso said nothing. For a moment her steady gaze wavered. She ducked her head, turning abruptly away. She scrambled to her feet. "More coffee?"

"No."

"Suit yourself." Tasso drank silently. He could not see her face. He lay back against the ground, deep in thought, trying to concentrate. It was hard to think. His head still hurt. And the numbing daze still hung over him.

"There might be one way," he said suddenly.

"Oh?"

"How soon is dawn?"

"Two hours. The sun will be coming up shortly."

'There's supposed to be a ship near here. I've never seen it. But I know it exists."

"What kind of a ship?" Her voice was sharp.

"A rocket cruiser."

"Will it take us off? To the Moon Base?"

"It's supposed to. In case of emergency." He rubbed his forehead.

"What's wrong?"

"My head. It's hard to think. I can hardly—hardly concentrate. The bomb."

"Is the ship near here?" Tasso slid over beside him, settling down on her haunches. "How far is it? Where is it?"

"I'm trying to think."

Her fingers dug into his arm. "Nearby?" Her voice was like iron. "Where would it be? Would they store it underground? Hidden underground?"

"Yes. In a storage locker."

"How do we find it? Is it marked? Is there a code marker to identify it?"

Hendricks concentrated. "No. No markings. No code symbol."

"What, then?"

"A sign."

"What sort of sign?"

Hendricks did not answer. In the flickering light his eyes were glazed, two sightless orbs. Tasso's fingers dug into his arm.

"What sort of sign? What is it?"

"I—I can't think. Let me rest."

"All right." She let go and stood up. Hendricks lay back against the ground, his eyes closed. Tasso walked away from him, her hands in her pockets. She kicked a rock out of her way and stood staring up at the sky. The night blackness was already beginning to fade into gray. Morning was coming.

Tasso gripped her pistol and walked around the fire in a circle, back and forth. On the ground Major Hendricks lay, his eyes closed, unmoving. The grayness rose in the sky, higher and higher. The landscape became visible, fields of ash stretching out in all directions. Ash and ruins of buildings, a wall here and there, heaps of concrete, the naked trunk of a tree.

The air was cold and sharp. Somewhere a long way off a bird made a few bleak sounds.

Hendricks stirred. He opened his eyes. "Is it dawn? Already?"

"Yes."

Hendricks sat up a little. "You wanted to know something. You were asking me."

"Do you remember now?"

"Yes."

"What is it?" She tensed. "What?" she repeated sharply.

"A well. A ruined well. It's in a storage locker under a well."

"A well." Tasso relaxed. "Then we'll find a well." She looked at her watch. "We have about an hour, Major. Do you think we can find it in an hour?"

"Give me a hand up," Hendricks said.

Tasso put her pistol away and helped him to his feet. "This is going to be difficult."

"Yes it is." Hendricks set his lips tightly. "I don't think we're going to go very far."

They began to walk. The early sun cast a little warmth down on them. The land was flat and barren, stretching out gray and lifeless as far as they could see. A few birds sailed silently, far above them, circling slowly.

"See anything?" Hendricks said. "Any claws?"

"No. Not yet."

They passed through some ruins, upright concrete and bricks. A cement foundation. Rats scuttled away. Tasso jumped back warily.

"This used to be a town," Hendricks said. "A village. Provincial village. This was all grape country, once. Where we are now."

They came onto a ruined street, weeds and cracks crisscrossing it. Over to the right a stone chimney stuck up.

"Be careful," he warned her.

A pit yawned, an open basement. Ragged ends of pipes jutted up, twisted and bent. They passed part of a house, a bathtub turned on its side. A broken chair. A few spoons and bits of china dishes. In the center of the street the ground had sunk away. The depression was filled with weeds and debris and bones.

"Over here," Hendricks murmured.

"This way?"

"To the right."

They passed the remains of a heavy duty tank. Hendrick's belt counter clicked ominously. The tank had been radiation blasted. A few feet from the tank a mummified body lay sprawled out, mouth open. Beyond the road was a flat field. Stones and weeds, and bits of broken glass.

"There," Hendricks said.

A stone well jutted up, sagging and broken. A few boards lay across it. Most of the well had sunk into rubble. Hendricks walked unsteadily toward it, Tasso beside him.

"Are you certain about this?" Tasso said. "This doesn't look like anything."

"I'm sure." Hendricks sat down at the edge of the well, his teeth locked. His breath came quickly. He wiped perspiration from his face. "This was arranged so the senior command officer could get away. If anything happened. If the bunker fell."

"That was you?"

"Yes."

"Where is the ship? Is it here?"

"We're standing on it." Hendricks ran his hands over the surface of the well stones. "The eye-lock responds to me, not to anybody else. It's my ship. Or it was supposed to be."

There was a sharp click. Presently they heard a low grating sound from below them.

"Step back," Hendricks said. He and Tasso moved away from the well.

A section of the ground slid back. A metal frame pushed slowly up through the ash, shoving bricks and weeds out of the way. The action ceased, as the ship nosed into view.

"There it is," Hendricks said.

The ship was small. It rested quietly, suspended in its mesh frame, like a blunt needle. A rain of ash sifted down into the dark cavity from which the ship had been raised. Hendricks made his way over to it. He mounted the mesh and unscrewed the hatch, pulling it back. Inside the ship the control banks and the pressure seat were visible.

Tasso came and stood beside him, gazing into the ship. "I'm not accustomed to rocket piloting," she said, after awhile.

Hendricks glanced at her. "I'll do the piloting."

"Will you? There's only one seat, Major. I can see it's built to carry only a single person."

Hendricks' breathing changed. He studied the interior of the ship intently. Tasso was right. There was only one seat. The ship was built to carry only one person. "I see," he said slowly. "And the one person is you."

She nodded.

"Of course."

"Why?"

"*You* can't go. You might not live through the trip. You're injured. You probably wouldn't get there."

"An interesting point. But you see, I know where the Moon Base is. And you don't. You might fly around for months and not find it. It's well hidden. Without knowing what to look for—"

"I'll have to take my chances. Maybe I won't find it. Not by myself. But I think you'll give me all the information I need. Your life depends on it."

"How?"

"If I find the Moon Base in time, perhaps I can get them to send a ship back to pick you up. *If* I find the Base in time. If not, then you haven't a chance. I imagine there are supplies on the ship. They will last me long enough—"

Hendricks moved quickly. But his injured arm betrayed him. Tasso ducked, sliding lithely aside. Her hand came up, lightning fast. Hendricks saw the gun butt coming. He tried to ward off the blow, but she was too fast. The metal butt struck against the side of his head, just above his ear. Numbing pain rushed through him. Pain and rolling clouds of blackness. He sank down, sliding to the ground.

Dimly, he was aware that Tasso was standing over him, kicking him with her toe.

"Major! Wake up."

He opened his eyes, groaning.

"Listen to me." She bent down, the gun pointed at his face. "I have to hurry. There isn't much time left. The ship is ready to go, but you must tell me the information I need before I leave."

Hendricks shook his head, trying to clear it.

"Hurry up! Where is the Moon Base? How do I find it? What do I look for?"

Hendricks said nothing.

"Answer me!"

"Sorry."

"Major, the ship is loaded with provisions. I can coast for weeks. I'll find the Base eventually. And in a half hour you'll be dead. Your only chance of survival—" She broke off.

Along the slope, by some crumbling ruins, something moved. Something in the ash. Tasso turned quickly, aiming. She fired. A puff of flame leaped. Something scuttled away, rolling across the ash. She fired again. The claw burst apart, wheels flying.

"See?" Tasso said. "A scout. It won't be long."

"You'll bring them back here to get me?"

"Yes. As soon as possible."

Hendricks looked up at her. He studied her intently. "You're telling the truth?" A strange expression had come over his face, an avid hunger. "You will come back for me? You'll get me to the Moon Base?"

"I'll get you to the Moon Base. But tell me where it is! There's only a little time left."

"All right." Hendricks picked up a piece of rock, pulling himself to a sitting position. "Watch."

Hendricks began to scratch in the ash. Tasso stood by him, watching the motion of the rock. Hendricks was sketching a crude lunar map.

"This is the Appenine Range. Here is the Crater of Archimedes. The Moon Base is beyond the end of the Appenine, about two hundred miles. I don't know exactly where. No one on Terra knows. But when you're over the Appenine, signal with one red flare and a green flare, followed by two red flares in a quick succession. The Base monitor will record your signal. The Base is under the surface, of course. They'll guide you down with magnetic grapples."

"And the controls? Can I operate them?"

"The controls are virtually automatic. All you have to do is give the right signal at the right time."

"I will."

"The seat absorbs most of the take-off shock. Air and temperature are automatically controlled. The ship will leave Terra and pass out into free space. It'll line itself up with the moon, falling into an orbit around it, about a hundred miles above the surface. The orbit will carry you over the Base. When you're in the region of the Appenine, release the signal rockets."

Tasso slid into the ship and lowered herself into the pressure seat. The arm locks folded automatically around her. She fingered the controls. "Too bad you're not going, Major. All this put here for you, and you can't make the trip."

"Leave me the pistol."

Tasso pulled the pistol from her belt. She held it in her hand, weighing it thoughtfully. "Don't go too far from this location. It'll be hard to find you, as it is."

"No. I'll stay here by the well."

Tasso gripped the take-off switch, running her fingers over the smooth metal. "A beautiful ship, Major. Well built. I admire your workmanship. You people have always done good work. You build fine things. Your work, your creations, are your greatest achievement."

"Give me the pistol," Hendricks said impatiently, holding out his hand. He struggled to his feet.

"Good-bye, Major." Tasso tossed the pistol past Hendricks. The pistol clattered and rolling away. Hendricks hurried after it. He bent down, snatching it up.

The hatch of the ship clanged shut. The bolts fell into place. Hendricks made his way back. The inner door was being sealed. He raised the pistol unsteadily.

There was a shattering roar. The ship burst up from its metal cage, fusing the mesh behind it. Hendricks cringed, pulling back. The ship shot up into the rolling clouds of ash, disappearing into the sky.

Hendricks stood watching a long time, until even the streamer had dissipated. Nothing stirred. The morning air was chill and silent. He began to walk aimlessly back the way they had come. Better to keep moving around. It would be a long time before help came—if it came at all.

He searched his pockets until he found a package of cigarettes. He lit one grimly. They had all wanted cigarettes from him. But cigarettes were scarce.

A lizard slithered by him, through the ash. He halted, rigid. The lizard disappeared. Above, the sun rose higher in the sky. Some flies landed on a flat rock to one side of him. Hendricks kicked at them with his foot.

It was getting hot. Sweat trickled down his face, into his collar. His mouth was dry.

Presently he stopped walking and sat down on some debris. He unfastened his medicine kit and swallowed a few narcotic capsules. He looked around him. Where was he?

Something lay ahead. Stretching out on the ground. Silent and unmoving.

Hendricks drew his gun quickly. It looked like a man. Then he remembered. It was the remains of Klaus. The Second Variety. Where Tasso had blasted him. He could see wheels and relays and metal parts, strewn around on the ash. Glittering and sparkling in the sunlight.

Hendricks got to his feet and walked over. He nudged the inert form with his foot, turning it over a little. He could see the metal hull, the aluminum ribs and struts. More wiring fell out. Like viscera. Heaps of wiring, switches and relays. Endless motors and rods.

He bent down. The brain cage had been smashed by the fall. The artificial brain was visible. He gazed at it. A maze of circuits. Miniature tubes. Wires as fine as hair. He touched the brain cage. It swung aside. The type plate was visible. Hendricks studied the plate.

And blanched.

IV—V.

For a long time he stared at the plate. Fourth Variety. Not the Second. They had been wrong. There were more types. Not just three. Many more, perhaps. At least four. And Klaus wasn't the Second Variety.

But if Klaus wasn't the Second Variety—

Suddenly he tensed. Something was coming, walking through the ash beyond the hill. What was it? He strained to see. Figures. Figures coming slowly along, making their way through the ash.

Coming toward him.

Hendricks crouched quickly, raising his gun. Sweat dripped down into his eyes. He fought down rising panic, as the figures neared.

The first was a David. The David saw him and increased its pace. The others hurried behind it. A second David. A third. Three Davids, all alike, coming toward him silently, without expression, their thin legs rising and falling. Clutching their teddy bears.

He aimed and fired. The first two Davids dissolved into particles. The third came on. And the figure behind it. Climbing silently toward him across the gray ash. A Wounded Soldier, towering over the David. And—

And behind the Wounded Soldier came two Tassos, walking side by side. Heavy belt, Russian army pants, shirt, long hair. The familiar figure, as he had seen her only a little while before. Sitting in the pressure seat of the ship. Two slim, silent figures, both identical.

They were very near. The David bent down suddenly, dropping its teddy bear. The bear raced across the ground. Automatically, Hendricks' fingers tightened around the trigger. The bear was gone, dissolved into mist. The two Tasso Types moved on, expressionless, walking side by side, through the gray ash.

When they were almost to him, Hendricks raised the pistol waist high and fired.

The two Tassos dissolved. But already a new group was starting up the rise, five or six Tassos, all identical, a line of them coming rapidly toward him.

And he had given her the ship and the signal code. Because of him she was on her way to the moon, to the Moon Base. He had made it possible.

He had been right about the bomb, after all. It had been designed with knowledge of the other types, the David Type and the Wounded Soldier Type. And the Klaus Type. Not designed by human beings. It had been designed by one of the underground factories, apart from all human contact.

The line of Tassos came up to him. Hendricks braced himself, watching them calmly. The familiar face, the belt, the heavy shirt, the bomb carefully in place.

The bomb—

As the Tassos reached for him, a last ironic thought drifted through Hendricks' mind. He felt a little better, thinking about it. The bomb. Made by the Second Variety to destroy the other varieties. Made for that end alone.

They were already beginning to design weapons to use against each other.

THE PROBLEM WAS LUBRICATION

BY DAVID R. BUNCH

I guess it kept him hopping, there were so many holes. And I guess it was mostly hard work. But to me, as I watched this automation through the observation slit, it was somewhat diverting to see, among all the somber squatting machines with a fixed place in the line, one that could stand up tall and take off all around the floor. He wasn't a robot really, and actually I guess he couldn't take off and run all around the floor just wherever he wanted. But the metal track he was on carried him to all parts of the work area in order for him to reach every one of the squatty fixed machines, and there were occasional side trips up to the reload place. In comparison with the fixed ones this fellow had it good, I thought.

His official name was Lubro. Or so it said in gay red letters on a shiny metal plate riveted to his rear. The day I watched Lubro they were turning out millions of little metal disks destined for some important places in some important engines, and the machines doing the work were running hot. And here would come Lubro, smooth and docile on his track, until he reached a machine that was running hot turning out the disks. The machines would flip little lids up at Lubro's approach and Lubro in response would whang jointed sections of tubing out of himself and the ends of those tubes would find their way into the holes where the lids had flipped up. And while the machines worked on as though nothing were happening Lubro would stand there vibrating on his track and eject oil into the holes according to some clocklike mechanism in him. And as the tempo of production increased, Lubro ran faster and faster on his track and whanged metal tubing out of himself oftener and oftener and came up to the reload place time and again. But it seemed to me he was happy at his work, although that could have been merely my imagining because of the great contrast between a Lubro and a machine that squatted on the floor hour by hour and turned out the quota time and again with, to console her, nothing but the small diversion of flipping her lids up for Lubro.

All in all, everything was going well here at automation it seemed to me, and Lubro was taking care of it, I thought, all right. But maybe he was running hot. At any rate, some Central Brain in the place made the decision and another upright thing with a clocklike mechanism in him and the power to eject flexible tubing out of himself came in to run on the tracks with Lubro. The Oiler, his name was. I guess the Central Brain thought The Oiler and Lubro could stay out of each other's way all right; one could be taking care of it in the south end, say, while the other was over north doing it; or one could be functioning on the west side while the other was shooting for lids in the east section of the work area maybe. But the truth is they didn't—they couldn't—stay out of each other's way for long. In the first place, I think Lubro was a little jealous, or maybe resentful is the better word, of The Oiler. For the very presence of The Oiler made it clear how the Central Brain felt. He felt that Lubro couldn't handle the job. Then too, no getting around it, The Oiler, big dark and cocky, was in Lubro's territory.

But as for production, there was an increase in it, no denying that. Especially was there more work done by certain of the newer machines in the central part of the work area. And it was one of these very machines that caused the flare-up. She was a new blonde machine without yet the grime of much servicing on her oil lids. And she squatted there, seemingly as innocent as a piece of the floor, and tooled her disks. But Lubro noticed it, and I noticed it too. Twice within the hour, when Lubro glided up, she kept her oil lids closed as though she were running cool as a bucket of grease. But when The Oiler came in at almost the same time from the opposite side of the work area her lids flew open as though she were filled with fire. And The Oiler ejected the tubes, according to the clocklike mechanism in him, and the tubes found the holes where the quivering lids hovered open, and he oiled the machines that indeed was not running cool; it was his job.

Lubro caught him at the top of the reload area. It was unethical. The Oiler was taking on oil, siphoning it from Central Supply into the can of his lower body. And Lubro should not have come in to the reload at the same time; there was but the one straight track in to the reload and no spur track for passing. But Lubro did come in. And the cocky Oiler stood nonchalantly siphoning oil until his can was full. Then he turned in that way he had, brazen, precise, sure, and he headed back for the work area as though it were understood that Lubro, being wrong, would retrace and let him through. Lubro would not! Lubro braced. Lubro hit him, hit him hard and middle-high and bounced him ten feet up the track. Lubro hit him again when The Oiler came within range. The Oiler closed and struck back; The Oiler hit twice in quick succession. The two oil cans stood toe-to-toe at the bottom of the reload area and exchanged blows. They rattled each other's skin sections and clobbered each other's joints. Rivets flew. Clocklike mechanisms were upset. They fought until it seemed in doubt that either one or the other would prove himself the better oil can.

Then the tide turned, as tides will, and Lubro got his chance. Because his clocklike mechanism was considerably upset by the hard blows he had taken, and possibly partly because he had just taken the reload, here at this strangest and most illogical of times one of The Oiler's tubelike sections popped out. Oil sprayed the area, and Lubro rammed in to wham the embarrassed oil can on the tube and spin him about until The Oiler was quite spun off the track. And there he lay, vanquished and bleeding oil, and presently all his other tubes flopped out and lay there limp and empty in plain sight, and The Oiler was a very sorry sight indeed. And because he had taken many hard blows himself, and partly, no doubt, in sheer exuberance over his victory, something got into Lubro's thinking and caused him to pull a very silly and shabby stunt. He ejected all his tubing sections to the very farthest limits they would go and sprayed The Oiler until he, Lubro, was quite empty of oil.

The Central Brain was jumping-mad in his clock, crazy-mad at Lubro and The Oiler. From these silly oil cans he had had quite enough, really he had. He immediately called a meeting of all the Junior Brains, and they all left their clocks and sat around a big polished disk of metal with a hole in the center of it and the Central Brain in the hole until they had all quite decided what to do. There was just one logical answer. Tear up the tracks, build a Lubro or an Oiler stationary for each squatty fixed machine and service these automatic tube ejectors from a Central Supply, using as many self-motion helicopters as would be required.

The Brains, having won again, having figured it out, resumed their clocklike places along the walls. And while they all agreed that automation had its bugs, yes it did, really it was quite the coming thing, yes it was.

FIRST TO SERVE

BY ALGIS BUDRYS

thei ar teetcing mi to reed n ryt n i
wil bee abel too do this better then.

pimi

MAS 712, 820TH TDRC,
COMASAMPS, APO 15,
September 28

Leonard Stein, Editor,
INFINITY,
862 Union St.,
New York 24, N. Y.

Dear Len,
　Surprise, et cetera

It looks like there will be some new H. E. Wood stories
for *Infy* after all. By the time you get this, 820TH TDRC
will have a new Project Engineer, COMASAMPS, and I
will be back to the old Royal and the Perry Street lair.

Shed no tear for Junior Heywood, though. COMASAMPS
and I have come to this parting with mutual eyes dry and
multiple heads erect. There was no sadness in our parting—no
bitterness, no weeping, no remorse. COMASAMPS—in one
of its apparently limitless human personifications—simply patted me on my side and told me to pick up my calipers and
run along. I'll have to stay away from cybernetics for a
while, of course, and I don't think I should write any robot
stories in the interval, but, then, I never did like robot
stories anyhow.

But all this is a long story—about ten thousand words, at least, which means a $300 net loss if I tell it now.

So go out and buy some fresh decks, I'll be in town next week, my love to the Associate and the kids, and first ace deals.

Vic Heywood

My name is really Prototype Mechanical Man I, but everybody calls me Pimmy, or sometimes Pim. I was assembled at the eight-twentieth teedeearcee on august 10, 1974. I don't know what man or teedeearcee or august 10, 1974, means, but Heywood says I will, tomorrow. What's tomorrow?

Pimmy

August 12, 1974

I'm still having trouble defining "man." Apparently, even the men can't do a very satisfactory job of that. The 820TDRC, of course, is the Eight Hundred and Twentieth Technical Development and Research Center of the Combined Armed Services Artificial and Mechanical Personnel Section. August 10, 1974, is the day before yesterday.

All this is very obvious, but it's good to record it.

I heard a very strange conversation between Heywood and Russell yesterday.

Russell is a small man, about thirty-eight, who's Heywood's top assistant. He wears glasses, and his chin is farther back than his mouth. It gives his head a symmetrical look. His voice is high, and he moves his hands rapidly. I think his reflexes are overtriggered.

Heywood is pretty big. He's almost as tall as I am. He moves smoothly—he's like me. You get the idea that all of his weight never touches the ground. Once in a while, though, he leaves a cigarette burning in an ashtray, and you can see where the end's been chewed to shreds.

Why is everybody at COMASAMPS so nervous?

Heywood was looking at the first entry in what I can now call my diary. He showed it to Russell.

"Guess you did a good job on the self-awareness tapes, Russ," Heywood said.

Russell frowned. "Too good, I think. He shouldn't have such a tremendous drive toward self-expression. We'll have to iron that out as soon as possible. Want me to set up a new tape?"

Heywood shook his head. "Don't see why. Matter of

fact, with the intelligence we've given him, I think it's probably a normal concomitant." He looked up at me and winked.

Russell took his glasses off with a snatch of his hand and scrubbed them on his shirtsleeve. "I don't know. We'll have to watch him. We've got to remember he's a proto-type—no different from an experimental automobile design, or a new dishwasher model. We expected bugs to appear. I think we've found one, and I think it ought to be eliminated. I don't like this personification he's acquired in our minds, either. This business of calling him by a nickname is all wrong. We've got to remember he's *not* an individual. We've got every right to tinker with him." He slapped his glasses back on and ran his hands over the hair the earpieces had disturbed. "He's just another machine. We can't lose sight of that."

Heywood raised his hands. "Easy, boy. Aren't you going too far off the deep end? All he's done is bat out a few words on a typewriter. Relax, Russ." He walked over to me and slapped my hip. "How about it, Pimmy? D'you feel like scrubbing the floor?"

"No opinion. Is that an order?" I asked.

Heywood turned to Russell. "Behold the rampant individual," he said. "No, Pimmy, no order. Cancel."

Russell shrugged, but he folded the page from my diary carefully, put it in his breast pocket. I didn't mind. I never forget anything.

August 15, 1974

They did something to me on the Thirteenth. I can't remember what. I've gone over my memory, but there's nothing. I can't remember.

Russell and Ligget were talking yesterday, though, when they inserted the autonomic cutoff, and ran me through on orders. I didn't mind that. I still don't. I can't.

Ligget in one of the small army of push-arounds that nobody knows for sure isn't CIC, but who solders wires while Heywood and Russell make up their minds about him.

I had just done four about-faces, shined their shoes, and struck a peculiar pose. I think there's something seriously wrong with Ligget.

Ligget said, "He responds well, doesn't he?"

"Mm-m—yes," Russell said abstractedly. He ran his glance down a column of figures on an Estimated Performance

Spec chart. "Try walking on your hands, PMM One," he said.

I activated my gyroscope and reset my pedal locomotion circuits. I walked around the room on my hands.

Ligget frowned forcefully. "That looks good. How's it check with the spec's?"

"Better than," Russell said. "I'm surprised. We had a lot of trouble with him the last two days. Reacted like a zombie."

"Oh, yes? I wasn't in on that. What happened? I mean— what sort of control were you using?"

"Oh—" I could see that Russell wasn't too sure whether he should tell Ligget or not. I already had the feeling that the atmosphere of this project was loaded with dozens of cross-currents and conflicting ambitions. I was going to learn a lot about COMASAMPS.

"Yes?" Ligget said.

"We have his individuality circuits cut out. Effectively, he was just a set of conditioned reflexes."

"You say he reacted like a zombie?"

"Definite automatism. Very slow reactions, and, of course, no initiative."

"You mean he'd be very slow in his response to orders under those conditions, right?" Ligget looked crafty behind Russell's back.

Russell whirled around. "He'd make a lousy soldier, if that's what CIC wants to know!"

Ligget smoothed out his face, and twitched his shoulders back. "I'm not a CIC snooper, if that's what you mean."

"You don't mind if I call you a liar, do you?" Russell said, his hands shaking.

"Not particularly," Ligget said, but he was angry behind his smooth face. It helps, having immobile features like mine. You get to understand the psychology of a man who tries for the same effect.

August 16, 1974

It bothers me, not having a diary entry for the four-teenth, either. Somebody's been working on me again.

I told Heywood about it. He shrugged. "Might as well get used to it, Pimmy. There'll be a lot of that going on. I don't imagine it's pleasant—I wouldn't like intermittent amnesia myself—but there's very little you can do about it. Put it down as one of the occupational hazards of being a prototype."

"But I don't *like* it." I said.

Heywood pulled the left side of his mouth into a straight line and sighed. "Like I said, Pimmy—I wouldn't either. On the other hand, you can't blame us if the new machine we're testing happens to know it's being tested, and resents it. We built the machine. Theoretically, it's our privilege to do anything we please with it, if that'll help us find out how the machine performs, and how to build better ones."

"But I'm *not* a machine!" I said.

Heywood put his lower lip between his teeth and looked up at me from under a raised eyebrow. "Sorry, Pim. I'm kind of afraid you are."

But I'm not! *I'M NOT!*

August 17, 1974

Russell and Heywood were working late with me last night. They did a little talking back and forth. Russell was very nervous—and finally Heywood got a little impatient with him.

"All right," Heywood said, laying his charts down. "We're not getting anywhere, this way. You want to sit down and really talk about what's bothering you?"

Russell looked a little taken aback. He shook his head jerkily.

"No . . . no, I haven't got anything specific on my mind. Just talking. You know how it is." He tried to pretend he was very engrossed in one of the charts.

Heywood didn't let him off the hook, though. His eyes were cutting into Russell's face, peeling off layer after layer of misleading mannerism and baring the naked fear in the man.

"No. I don't know how it is." He put his hand on Russell's shoulder and turned him around to where the other man was facing him completely. "Now, look—if there's something chewing on you, let's have it. I'm not going to have this project gummed up by your secret troubles. Things are tough enough with everybody trying to pressure us into doing things their way, and none of them exactly sure of what that way *is*."

That last sentence must have touched something off in Russell, because he let his charts drop beside Heywood's and clawed at the pack of cigarettes in his breast pocket.

"That's exactly what the basic problem is," he said, his

eyes a little too wide. He pushed one hand back and forth over the side of his face and walked back and forth aimlessly. Then a flood of words came out.

"We're working in the dark, Vic. In the dark, and somebody's in with us that's swinging clubs at our heads while we stumble around. We don't know who it is, we don't know if it's one or more than that, and we never know when the next swing is coming.

"Look—we're cybernetics engineers. Our job was to design a brain that would operate a self-propulsive unit designed to house it. That was the engineering problem, and we've got a tendency to continue looking at it in that light.

"But that's not the whole picture. We've got to keep in mind that the only reason we were ever given the opportunity and the facilities was because somebody thought it might be a nice idea to turn out soldiers on a production line, just like they do the rest of the paraphernalia of war. And the way COMASAMPS looks at it is not in terms of a brain housed in an independently movable shell, but in terms of a robot which now has to be fitted to the general idea of what a soldier should be.

"Only nobody knows what the ideal soldier is like.

"Some say he ought to respond to orders with perfect accuracy and superhuman reflexes. Others say he ought to be able to think his way out of trouble, or improvise in a situation where his orders no longer apply, just like a human soldier. The ones who want the perfect automaton don't want him to be smart enough to realize he *is* an automaton— probably because they're afraid of the idea; and the ones who want him to be capable of human discretion don't want him to be human enough to be rebellious in a hopeless situation.

"And that's just the beginning. COMASAMPS may be a combined project, but if you think the Navy isn't checking up on the Army, and vice versa, with both of them looking over the Air Force's shoulder—Oh, you know that squirrel cage as well as I do!"

Russell gestured hopelessly. Heywood, who had been taking calm puffs on his cigarette, shrugged. "So? All we have to do is tinker around until we can design a sample model to fit each definition. Then they can run as many comparative field tests as they want to. It's their problem. Why let it get you?"

Russell flung his cigarette to the floor and stepped on it with all his weight. "Because we can't do it and you ought to know it as well as I do!" He pointed over to me. "There's your prototype model. He's got all the features that everybody wants—and cut-offs intended to take out the features that interfere with any one definition. We can cut off his individuality, and leave him the automaton some people want. We can leave him his individuality, cut off his volition, and give him general orders which he is then free to carry out by whatever means he thinks best. Or, we can treat him like a human being—educate him by means of tapes, train him, and turn him loose on a job, the way we'd do with a human being."

The uneven tone built up in his voice as he finished what he was saying.

"But, if we reduce him to a machine that responds to orders as though they were pushbuttons, he's slow. He's pitifully slow, Vic, and he'd be immobilized within thirty seconds of combat. There's nothing we can do about that, either. Until somebody learns how to push electricity through a circuit faster than the laws of physics say it should go, what we'll have will be a ponderous, mindless thing that's no better than the remote-control exhibition jobs built forty years ago.

"All right, so that's no good. We leave him individuality, but we restrict it until it cuts his personality down to that of a slave. That's better. Under those conditions, he would, theoretically, be a better soldier than the average human. An officer could tell him to take a patrol out into a certain sector, and he'd do the best possible job, picking the best way to handle each step of the job as he came to it. But what does he do if he comes back, and the officer who gave him the orders is no longer there? Or, worse yet, if there's been a retreat, and there's nobody there? Or an armistice? What about that armistice? Can you picture this slave robot, going into stasis because he's got no orders to cover a brand-new situation?

"He might just as well not have gone on that patrol at all—because he can't pass on whatever he's learned, and because his job is now over, as far as he's concerned. The enemy could overrun his position, and he wouldn't do anything about it. He'd operate from order to order. And if an armistice were signed, he'd sit right where he was until a technician could come out, remove the soldier-orientation tapes, and replace them with whatever was finally decided on.

"Oh, you could get around the limitation, all right—by issuing a complex set of orders, such as: 'Go out on patrol and report back. If I'm not here, report to so-and-so. If there's nobody here, do this. If that doesn't work, try that. If such-and-such happens, proceed as follows. But don't confuse such-and-such with that or this.' Can you imagine fighting a war on that basis? And what about that reorientation problem? How long would all those robots sit there before they could all be serviced—and how many man-hours and how much material would it take to do the job? Frankly, I couldn't think of a more cumbersome way to run a war if I tried.

"Or, we can build all our robots, like streamlined Pimmys—like Pimmy when all his circuits are operating, without our test cutoffs. Only, then, we'd have artificial human beings. Human beings who don't wear out, that a hand-arm won't stop, and who don't need food or water as long as their power piles have a pebble-sized hunk of plutonium to chew on."

Russell laughed bitterly. "And Navy may be making sure Army doesn't get the jump on them, with Air Force doing its bit, but there's one thing all three of them are as agreed upon as they are about nothing else—they'll test automaton zombies and they'll test slaves, but one thing nobody wants us turning out is supermen. They've got undercover men under every lab bench, all keeping one eye on each other and one on us—and the whole thing comes down on our heads like a ton of cement if there's even the first whisper of an idea that we're going to build more Pimmys. The same thing happens if we don't give them the perfect soldier. *And the only perfect soldier is a Pimmy.* Pimmy could replace any man in any armed service—from a KP to a whole general staff, depending on what tapes he had. But he'd have to be a true individual to do it. And he'd be smarter than they are. They couldn't trust him. Not because he wouldn't work for the same objectives as they'd want, but because he'd probably do it in some way they couldn't understand.

"So they don't want any more Pimmys. This one test model is all they'll allow, because he can be turned into any kind of robot they want, but they won't take the whole

Pimmy, with all his potentialities. They just want part of him."

The bitter laugh was louder. "We've got their perfect soldier, but they don't want him. They want something less—but that something less will never be the perfect soldier. So we work and work, weeks on end, testing, revising, redesigning. Why? We're marking time. We've got what they want, but they don't want it—but if we don't give it to them soon, they'll wipe out the project. And if we give them what they want, it won't really be what they want. Can't you see that? What's the matter with you, Heywood? Can't you see the blind alley we're in—only it's not a blind alley, because it has eyes, eyes under every bench, watching each other and watching us, always watching, never stopping, going on and never stopping, watching, eyes?"

Heywood had already picked up the telephone. As Russell collapsed completely, he began to speak into it, calling the Project hospital. Even as he talked, his eyes were coldly brooding, and his mouth was set in an expression I'd never seen before. His other hand was on Russell's twitching shoulder, moving gently as the other man sobbed.

August 25, 1974

Ligget is Heywood's new assistant. It's been a week since Russell's been gone.

Russell wasn't replaced for three days, and Heywood worked alone with me. He's engineer of the whole project, and I'm almost certain there must have been other things he could have worked on while he was waiting for a new assistant, but he spent all of his time in this lab with me.

His face didn't show what he thought about Russell. He's not like Ligget, though. Heywood's thoughts are private. Ligget's are hidden. But, every once in a while, while Heywood was working, he'd start to turn around and reach out, or just say "Jack—," as if he wanted something, and then he'd catch himself, and his eyes would grow more thoughtful.

I only understood part of what Russell had said that night he was taken away, so I asked Heywood about it yesterday.

"What's the trouble, Pim?" he asked.

"Don't know, for sure. Too much I don't understand about this whole thing. If I knew what some of the words meant, I might not even have a problem."

"Shoot."

"Well, it's mostly what Russell was saying, that last night."

Heywood peeled a strip of skin from his upper lip by catching it between his teeth. "Yeah."

"What's a war, or what's war? Soldiers have something to do with it, but what's a soldier? I'm a robot—but why do they want to make more of me? Can I be a soldier and a robot at the same time? Russell kept talking about 'they,' and the Army, the Air Force, and the Navy. What're they? And are the CIC men the ones who are watching you and each other at the same time?"

Heywood scowled, and grinned ruefully at the same time. "That's quite a catalogue," he said. "And there's even more than that, isn't there, Pimmy?" He put his hand on my side and sort of patted me, the way I'd seen him do with a generator a few times. "O.K., I'll give you a tape on war and soldiering. That's the next step in the program anyway, and it'll take care of most of those questions."

"Thanks," I said. "But what about the rest of it?"

He leaned against a bench and looked down at the floor. "Well, 'they' are the people who instituted this program— the Secretary of Defense, and the people under him. They all agreed that robot personnel were just what the armed services needed, and they were right. The only trouble is, they couldn't agree among themselves as to what characteristics were desirable in the perfect soldier—or sailor, or airman. They decided that the best thing to do was to come up with a series of different models, and to run tests until they came up with the best one.

"Building you was my own idea. Instead of trying to build prototypes to fit each separate group of specifications, we built one all-purpose model who was, effectively speaking, identical with a human being in almost all respects, with one major difference. By means of cut-offs in every circuit, we can restrict as much of your abilities as we want to, thus being able to modify your general characteristics to fit any one of the various specification groups. We saved a lot of time by doing that, and avoided a terrific nest of difficulties.

"Trouble is, we're using up all the trouble and time we saved. Now that they've got you, they don't want you. Nobody's willing to admit that the only efficient robot soldier is one with all the discretionary powers and individuality of a human being. They can't admit it, because people are afraid of anything that looks like it might be better than they are. And they won't trust what they're afraid of. So, Russell and I had to piddle around with a stupid series of tests in a hopeless attempt to come up with something practical that was nevertheless within the limitations of the various sets of specifications—which is ridiculous, because there's nothing wrong with you, but there's plenty wrong with the specs. They were designed by people who don't know the first thing about robots or robot thought processes—or the sheer mechanics of thinking, for that matter."

He shrugged. "But, they're the people with the authority and the money that's paying for this project—so Jack and I kept puttering because those were the orders. Knowing that we had the perfect answer all the time, and that nobody would accept it, was what finally got Jack."

"What about you?" I asked.

He shrugged again. "I'm just waiting," he said: "Eventually they'll either accept you or not. They'll either commend me or fire me, and they might or might not decide it's all my fault if they're not happy. But there's nothing I can do about it, is there? So, I'm waiting.

"Meanwhile, there's the CIC. Actually, that's just a handy label. It happens to be the initials of one of the undercover agencies out of the whole group that infests this place. Every armed service has its own, and I imagine the government has its boys kicking around, too. We just picked one label to cover them all—it's simpler."

"Russell said they were always watching. But why are they watching each other, too? Why should one armed service be afraid that another's going to get an advantage over it?"

Heywood's mouth moved into a half-amused grin. "That's what is known as human psychology, Pimmy. It'll help you to understand it, but if you can't, why, just be glad you haven't got it."

"Ligget's CIC, you know," I said. "Russell accused him of it. He denied it, but if he isn't actually in *the* CIC, then he's in something like it."

Heywood nodded sourly. "I know. I wouldn't mind if he had brains enough, in addition, to know one end of a circuit from the other."

He slapped my side again. "Pimmy, boy," he said. "We're going to have a lot of fun around here in the next few weeks. Yes, sir, a lot of fun."

August 26, 1974

Ligget was fooling around with me again. He's all right when Heywood's in the lab with me, but when he's alone, he keeps running me through unauthorized tests. What he's doing, actually, is to repeat all the tests Heywood and Russell ran, just to make sure. As long as he doesn't cut out my individuality, I can remember it all, and I guess there was nothing different about the results on any of the tests, because I can tell from his face that he's not finding what he wants.

Well, I hope he tells his bosses that Heywood and Russell were right. Maybe they'll stop this fooling.

Ligget's pretty dumb. After every test, he looks me in the eye and tells me to forget the whole thing. What does he think I am—Trilby?

And I don't understand some of the test performances at all. There *is* something wrong with Ligget.

September 2, 1974

I hadn't realized, until now, that Heywood and Russell hadn't told anyone what they thought about this whole project, but, viewing that tape on war and soldiering, and the way the military mind operates, I can see where nobody would have accepted their explanations.

Ligget caught on to the whole thing today. Heywood came in with a new series of test charts, Ligget took one look at them, and threw them on the table. He sneered at Heywood and said, "Who do you think you're kidding?"

Heywood looked annoyed and said, "All right, what's eating you?"

Ligget's face got this hidden crafty look on it. "How long did you think you could keep this up, Heywood? This test is no different from the ones you were running three weeks ago. There hasn't been any progress since then, and there's been no attempt to make any. What's your explanation?"

"Uh-huh." Heywood didn't look particularly worried. "I was wondering if you were *ever* going to stumble across it."

Ligget looked mad. "That attitude won't do you any good. Now, come on, quit stalling. Why were you and Russell sabotaging the project?"

"Oh, stop being such a pompous lamebrain, will you?" Heywood said disgustedly. "Russell and I weren't doing any sabotaging. We've been following our orders to the last letter. We built the prototype, and we've been testing the various modifications ever since. Anything wrong with that?"

"You've made absolutely no attempt to improve the various modifications. There hasn't been an ounce of progress in this project for the last twenty days.

"Now, look, Heywood"—Ligget's voice became wheedling—"I can understand that you might have what you'd consider a good reason for all this. What is it—political, or something? Maybe it's your conscience. Don't you *want* to work on something that's eventually going to be applied to war? I wish you'd tell me about it. If I could understand your reasons, it would be that much easier for you. Maybe it's too tough a problem. Is that it, Heywood?"

Heywood's face got red. "No, it's not. If you think—" He stopped, dug his fingers at the top of the table, and got control of himself again.

"No," he said in a quieter, but just as deadly, voice. "I'm as anxious to produce an artificial soldier as anybody else. And I'm not too stupid for the job, either. If *you* had any brains, you'd see that I already have."

That hit Ligget between the eyes. "You have? Where is it, and *why haven't you reported your success?* What is this thing?" He pointed at me. "Some kind of a decoy?"

Heywood grimaced. "No, you double-dyed jackass, that's your soldier."

"What?"

"Sure. Strip those fifteen pounds of cutoffs out of him, redesign his case for whatever kind of ground he's supposed to operate on, feed him the proper tapes, and that's it. The perfect soldier—as smart as any human ever produced, and a hundred times the training and toughness, overnight. Run them out by the thousands. Print your circuits; bed your transistors in silicone rubber, and pour the whole brew into his case. Production difficulties? Watchmaking's harder."

"*No!*" Ligget's eyes gleamed. "And I worked on this with you! *Why haven't you reported this!*" he repeated.

Heywood looked at him pityingly. "Haven't you got it through your head? Pimmy's the perfect soldier—all of him, with all his abilities. That includes individuality, curiosity, judgment—and intelligence. Cut one part of that, and he's no good. You've got to take the whole cake, or none at all. One way you starve—and the other way you choke."

Ligget had gone white. "You mean, we've got to take the superman—or we don't have anything."

"Yes, you fumbling jerk!"

Ligget looked thoughtful. He seemed to forget Heywood and me as he stared down at his shoetops. "They won't go for it," he muttered. "Suppose they decide they're better fit to run the world than we are?"

"That's the trouble," Heywood said, "They are. They've got everything a human being has, plus incredible toughness and the ability to learn instantaneously. You know what Pimmy did? The day he was assembled, he learned to read and write, after a fashion. How? By listening to me read a paragraph out of a report, recording the sounds, and looking at the report afterwards. He matched the sounds to the letters, recalled what sort of action on Russell's and my part the paragraph had elecited, and sat down behind a typewriter. That's all."

"They'd junk the whole project before they let something like that run around loose!" The crafty look was hovering at the edges of Ligget's mask again. "All right, so you've got an answer, but it's not an acceptable one. But why haven't you pushed any of the other lines of investigation?"

"Because there aren't any," Heywood said disgustedly. "Any other modification, when worked out to its inherent limits, is worse than useless. You've run enough tests to find out."

"All right!" Ligget's voice was high. "Why didn't you report failure, then, instead of keeping on with this shilly-shallying?"

"Because I haven't failed, you moron!" Heywood exploded. "I've got the answer. I've got Pimmy. There's nothing wrong with him—the defect's in the way people are thinking. And I've been going crazy, trying to think of a way to change the people. To hell with modifying the robot! He's as perfect as you'll get within the next five years. It's the people who'll have to change!"

"Uh-huh." Ligget's voice was careful. "I see. You've gone as far as you can within the limits of your orders—and you were trying to find a way to exceed them, in order to force the armed services to accept robots like Pimmy." He pulled out his wallet, and flipped it open. There was a piece of metal fastened to one flap.

"Recognize this, Heywood?"

Heywood nodded.

"All right, then, let's go and talk to a few people."

Heywood's eyes were cold and brooding again. He shrugged.

The lab door opened, and there was another one of the lab technicians there. "Go easy, Ligget," he said. He walked across the lab in rapid strides. His wallet had a different badge in it. "Listening from next door," he explained. "All right, Heywood," he said, "*I'm* taking you in." He shouldered Ligget out of the way. "Why don't you guys learn to stay in your own jurisdiction," he told him.

Ligget's face turned red, and his fists clenched, but the other man must have had more weight behind him, because he didn't say anything.

Heywood looked over at me, and raised a hand. "So long, Pimmy," he said. He and the other man walked out of the lab, with Ligget trailing along behind them. As they got the door open, I saw some other men standing out in the hall. The man who had come into the lab cursed. "*You* guys!" he said savagely. "This is *my* prisoner, see, and if you think—"

The door closed, and I couldn't hear the rest of what they said, but there was a lot of arguing before I heard the sound of all their footsteps going down the hall in a body.

Well, that's about all, I guess. Except for this other thing. It's about Ligget, and I hear he's not around any more. But you might be interested.

September 4, 1974

I haven't seen Heywood, and I've been alone in the lab all day. But Ligget came in last night. I don't think I'll see Heywood again.

Ligget came in late at night. He looked as though he hadn't slept, and he was very nervous. But he was drunk, too—I don't know where he got the liquor.

He came across the lab floor, his footsteps very loud on the cement, and he put his hands on his hips and looked up at me.

"Well, superman," he said in a tight, edgy voice, "you've lost your buddy for good, the dirty traitor. And now you're next. You know what they're going to do to you?" He laughed. "You'll have lots of time to think it over."

He paced back and forth in front of me. Then he spun

around suddenly and pointed his finger at me. "Thought you could beat the race of men, huh? Figured you were smarter than we were, didn't you? But we've got you now! You're going to learn that you can't try to fool around with the human animal, because he'll pull you down. He'll claw and kick you until you collapse. That's the way men are, robot. Not steel and circuits—flesh and blood and muscles. Flesh that fought its way out of the sea and out of the jungle, muscle that crushed everything that ever stood in his way, and blood that's spilled for a million years to keep the human race on top. *That's* the kind of an organism *we* are, robot."

He paced some more and spun again. "You never had a chance."

Well, I guess that *is* all. The rest of it, you know about. You can pull the transcriber plug out of here now, I guess. Would somebody say good-by to Heywood for me—and Russell, too, if that's possible?

COVERING MEMORANDUM,
Blalock, Project Engineer,
to
Hall, Director,
820TH TDRC, COMASAMPS

September 21, 1974
Enclosed are the transcriptions of the robot's readings from his memory-bank "diary," as recorded this morning. The robot is now enroute to the Patuxent River, the casting of the concrete block having been completed with the filling of the opening through which the transcription line was run.

As Victor Heywood's successor to the post of Project Engineer, I'd like to point out that the robot was incapable of deceit, and that this transcription, if read at Heywood's trial, will prove that his intentions were definitely not treasonous, and certainly motivated on an honest belief that he was acting in the best interests of the original directive for the project's initiation.

In regard to your Memorandum 8-4792-H of yesterday, a damage report is in process of preparation and will be forwarded to you immediately on its completion.

I fully understand that Heywood's line of research is to be

considered closed. Investigations into what Heywood termed the "zombie" and "slave" type of robot organization have already begun in an improvised laboratory, and I expect preliminary results within the next ten days.

Preliminary results on the general investigation of other possible types of robot orientation and organization are in, copies attached. I'd like to point out that they are extremely discouraging.

(Signed)
H. E. Blalock, Project Engineer,
820TH TDRC, COMASAMPS

September 25, 1974

PERSONAL LETTER
FROM HALL, DIRECTOR,
820TH TDRC, COMASAMPS,
to
SECRETARY OF DEFENSE
Dear Vinnie,

Well, things are finally starting to settle down out here. You were right, all this place needed was a housecleaning from top to bottom.

I think we're going to let this Heywood fellow go. We can't prove anything on him—frankly, I don't think there was anything to prove. Russell, of course, is a closed issue. His chance of ever getting out of the hospital is rated as ten per cent.

You know, considering the mess that robot made of the lab, I'd almost be inclined to think that Heywood was right. Can you imagine what a fighter that fellow would have been, if his loyalty had been channeled to some abstract like Freedom, instead of to Heywood? But we can't take the chance. Look at the way the robot's gone amnesic about killing Ligget while he was wrecking the lab. It was something that happened accidentally. It wasn't supposed to happen, so the robot forgot it. Might present difficulties in a war.

So, we've got this Blalock fellow down from M.I.T. He spends too much time talking about Weiner, but he's all right, otherwise.

I'll be down in a couple of days. Appropriations committee meeting. You know how it is. Everybody knows we need the money, but they want to argue about it, first.

Well, that's human nature, I guess.

> See you,
> Ralph

SUPPLEMENT TO CHARTS:
Menace to Navigation.

Patuxent River, at a point forty-eight miles below Folsom, bearings as below.

Midchannel. Concrete block, $15 \times 15 \times 15$. Not dangerous except at extreme low tide.

TWO-HANDED ENGINE

BY HENRY KUTTNER AND C. L. MOORE

Ever since the days of Orestes there have been men with Furies following them. It wasn't until the Twenty-Second Century that mankind made itself a set of real Furies, out of steel. Mankind had reached a crisis by then. They had a good reason for building man-shaped Furies that would dog the footsteps of all men who kill men. Nobody else. There was by then no other crime of any importance.

It worked very simply. Without warning, a man who thought himself safe would suddenly hear the steady footfalls behind him. He would turn and see the two-handed engine walking toward him, shaped like a man of steel, and more incorruptible than any man not made of steel could be. Only then would the murderer know he had been tried and condemned by the omniscient electronic minds that knew society as no human mind could ever know it.

For the rest of his days, the man would hear those footsteps behind him. A moving jail with invisible bars that shut him off from the world. Never in life would he be alone again. And one day—he never knew when—the jailer would turn executioner.

Danner leaned back comfortably in his contoured restaurant chair and rolled expensive wine across his tongue, closing his eyes to enjoy the taste of it better. He felt perfectly safe. Oh, perfectly protected. For nearly an hour now he had been sitting here, ordering the most expensive food, enjoying the music breathing softly through the air, the murmurous, well-bred hush of his fellow diners. It was a good place to be. It was very good, having so much money—now.

True, he had had to kill to get the money. But no guilt troubled him. There is no guilt if you aren't found out, and Danner had protection. Protection straight from the source, which was something new in the world. Danner knew the consequences of killing. If Hartz hadn't satisfied him that he was perfectly safe, Danner would never have pulled the trigger. . . .

The memory of an archaic word flickered through his mind briefly. Sin. It evoked nothing. Once it had something to do with guilt, in an incomprehensible way. Not any more. Mankind had been through too much. Sin was meaningless now.

He dismissed the thought and tried the heart-of-palms salad. He found he didn't like it. Oh well, you had to expect things like that. Nothing was perfect. He sipped the wine again, liking the way the glass seemed to vibrate like something faintly alive in his hand. It was good wine. He thought of ordering more, but then he thought no, save it, next time. There was so much before him, waiting to be enjoyed. Any risk was worth it. And of course, in this there had been no risk.

Danner was a man born at the wrong time. He was old enough to remember the last days of utopia, young enough to be trapped in the new scarcity economy the machines had clamped down on their makers. In his early youth he'd had access to free luxuries, like everybody else. He could remember the old days when he was an adolescent and the last of the Escape Machines were still operating, the glamorous, bright, impossible, vicarious visions that didn't really exist and never could have. But then the scarcity economy swallowed up pleasure. Now you got necessities but no more. Now you had to work. Danner hated every minute of it.

When the swift change came, he'd been too young and unskilled to compete in the scramble. The rich men today were the men who had built fortunes on cornering the few luxuries the machines still produced. All Danner had left were bright memories and a dull, resentful feeling of having been cheated. All he wanted were the bright days back, and he didn't care how he got them.

Well, now he had them. He touched the rim of the wine

glass with his finger, feeling it sing silently against the touch. Blown glass? he wondered. He was too ignorant of luxury items to understand. But he'd learn. He had the rest of his life to learn in, and be happy.

He looked up across the restaurant and saw through the transparent dome of the roof the melting towers of the city. They made a stone forest as far as he could see. And this was only one city. When he was tired of it, there were more. Across the country, across the planet the network lay that linked city with city in a webwork like a vast, intricate, half-alive monster. Call it society.

He felt it tremble a little beneath him.

He reached for the wine glass and drank quickly. The faint uneasiness that seemed to shiver the foundations of the city was something new. It was because—yes, certainly it was because of a new fear.

It was because he had not been found out.

That made no sense. Of course the city was complex. Of course it operated on a basis of incorruptible machines. They, and only they, kept man from becoming very quickly another extinct animal. And of these the analogue computers, the electronic calculators, were the gyroscope of all living. They made and enforced the laws that were necessary now to keep mankind alive. Danner didn't understand much of the vast changes that had swept over society in his lifetime, but this much even he knew.

So perhaps it made sense that he felt society shiver because he sat here luxurious on foam-rubber, sipping wine, hearing soft music, and no Fury standing behind his chair to prove that the calculators were still guardians for mankind. . . .

If not even the Furies are incorruptible, what can a man believe in?

It was at that exact moment that the Fury arrived.

Danner heard every sound suddenly die out around him. His fork was halfway to his lips, but he paused, frozen, and looked up across the table and the restaurant toward the door.

The Fury was taller than a man. It stood there for a moment, the afternoon sun striking a blinding spot of brightness from its shoulder. It had no face, but it seemed to scan the restaurant leisurely, table by table. Then it stepped in under the doorframe and the sun-spot slid away and it was like a tall man encased in steel, walking slowly between the tables.

Danner said to himself, laying down his untasted food, "Not for me. Everyone else here is wondering. I *know*."

And like a memory in a drowning man's mind, clear, sharp and condensed into a moment, yet every detail clear, he remembered what Hartz had told him. As a drop of water can pull into its reflection a wide panorama condensed into a tiny focus, so time seemed to focus down to a pinpoint the half-hour Danner and Hartz had spent together, in Hartz's office with the walls that could go transparent at the push of a button.

He saw Hartz again, plump and blond, with the sad eyebrows. A man who looked relaxed until he began to talk, and then you felt the burning quality about him, the air of driven tension that made even the air around him seem to be restlessly trembling. Danner stood before Hartz's desk again in memory, feeling the floor hum faintly against his soles with the heartbeat of the computers. You could see them through the glass, smooth, shiny things with winking lights in banks like candles burning in colored glass cups. You could hear their faraway chattering as they ingested facts, meditated them, and then spoke in numbers like cryptic oracles. It took men like Hartz to understand what the oracles meant.

"I have a job for you," Hartz said. "I want a man killed."

"Oh no," Danner said. "What kind of a fool do you think I am?"

"Now wait a minute. You can use money, can't you?"

"What for?" Danner asked bitterly. "A fancy funeral?"

"A life of luxury. I know you're not a fool. I know damned well you wouldn't do what I ask unless you got money *and* protection. That's what I can offer. Protection."

Danner looked through the transparent wall at the computers.

"Sure," he said.

"No, I mean it. I—" Hartz hesitated, glancing around the room a little uneasily, as if he hardly trusted his own precautions for making sure of privacy. "This is something new," he said. "I can re-direct any Fury I want to."

"Oh, sure," Danner said again.

"It's true. I'll show you. I can pull a Fury off any victim I choose."

"How?"

"That's my secret. Naturally. In effect, though, I've found a way to feed in false data, so the machines come out with the wrong verdict before conviction, or the wrong orders after conviction."

"But that's—dangerous, isn't it?"

"Dangerous?" Hartz looked at Danner under his sad eyebrows. "Well, yes. I think so. That's why I don't do it often. I've done it only once, as a matter of fact. Theoretically, I'd worked out the method. I tested it, just once. It worked. I'll do it again, to prove to you I'm telling the truth. After that I'll do it once again, to protect you. And that will be it. I don't want to upset the calculators any more than I have to. Once your job's done, I won't have to."

"Who do you want killed?"

Involuntarily Hartz glanced upward, toward the heights of the building where the top-rank executive offices were. "O'Reilly," he said.

Danner glanced upward too, as if he could see through the floor and observe the exalted shoe-soles of O'Reilly, Controller of the Calculators, pacing an expensive carpet overhead.

"It's very simple," Hartz said. "I want his job."

"Why not do your own killing, then, if you're so sure you can stop the Furies?"

"Because that would give the whole thing away," Hartz said impatiently. "Use your head. I've got an obvious motive. It wouldn't take a calculator to figure out who profits most if O'Reilly dies. If I saved myself from a Fury, people would start wondering how I did it. But you've got no motive for killing O'Reilly. Nobody but the calculators would know, and I'll take care of them."

"How do I know you can do it?"

"Simple. Watch."

Hartz got up and walked quickly across the resilient carpet that gave his steps a falsely youthful bounce. There was a waist-high counter on the far side of the room, with a slanting glass screen on it. Nervously Hartz punched a button, and a map of a section of the city sprang out in bold lines on its surface.

"I've got to find a sector where a Fury's in operation now," he explained. The map flickered and he pressed the button again. The unstable outlines of the city streets wa-

vered and brightened and then went out as he scanned the
sections fast and nervously. Then a map flashed on which
had three wavering streaks of colored light crisscrossing it,
intersecting at one point near the center. The point moved
very slowly across the map, at just about the speed of a
walking man reduced to miniature in scale with the street he
walked on. Around him the colored lines wheeled slowly,
keeping their focus always steady on the single point.

"There," Hartz said, leaning forward to read the printed
name of the street. A drop of sweat fell from his forehead
onto the glass, and he wiped it uneasily away with his
fingertip. "There's a man with a Fury assigned to him. All
right, now. I'll show you. Look here."

Above the desk was a news-screen. Hartz clicked it on and
watched impatiently while a street scene swam into focus.
Crowds, traffic noises, people hurrying, people loitering.
And in the middle of the crowd a little oasis of isolation, an
island in the sea of humanity. Upon that moving island two
occupants dwelt, like a Crusoe and a Friday, alone. One of
the two was a haggard man who watched the ground as he
walked. The other islander in this deserted spot was a tall,
shining, man-formed shape that followed at his heels.

As if invisible walls surrounded them, pressing back the
crowds they walked through, the two moved in an empty
space that closed in behind them, opened up before them.
Some of the passersby stared, some looked away in embarrassment or uneasiness. Some watched with a frank anticipation, wondering perhaps at just what moment the Friday
would lift his steel arm and strike the Crusoe dead.

"Watch, now," Hartz said nervously. "Just a minute. I'm
going to pull the Fury off this man. Wait." He crossed to his
desk, opened a drawer, bent secretively over it. Danner
heard a series of clicks from inside, and then the brief
chatter of tapped keys. "Now," Hartz said, closing the
drawer. He moved the back of his hand across his forehead.
"Warm in here, isn't it? Let's get a closer look. You'll see
something happen in a minute."

Back to the news-screen. He flicked the focus switch and
the street scene expanded, the man and his pacing jailor
swooped upward into close focus. The man's face seemed to
partake subtly of the impassive quality of the robot's. You
would have thought they had lived a long time together, and

perhaps they had. Time is a flexible element, infinitely long sometimes in a very short space.

"Wait until they get out of the crowd," Hartz said. "This mustn't be conspicuous. There, he's turning now."

The man, seeming to move at random, wheeled at an alley corner and went down the narrow, dark passage away from the thoroughfare. The eye of the news-screen followed him as closely as the robot.

"So you do have cameras that can do that," Danner said with interest. "I always thought so. How's it done? Are they spotted at every corner, or is it a beam trans—"

"Never mind," Hartz said. "Trade secret. Just watch. We'll have to wait until—no, no! Look, he's going to try it now!"

The man glanced furtively behind him. The robot was just turning the corner in his wake. Hartz darted back to his desk and pulled the drawer open. His hand poised over it, his eyes watched the screen anxiously. It was curious how the man in the alley, though he could have no inkling that other eyes watched, looked up and scanned the sky, gazing directly for a moment into the attentive, hidden camera and the eyes of Hartz and Danner. They saw him take a sudden, deep breath, and break into a run.

From Hartz's drawer sounded a metallic click. The robot, which had moved smoothly into a run the moment the man did, checked itself awkwardly and seemed to totter on its steel feet for an instant. It slowed. It stopped like an engine grinding to a halt. It stood motionless.

At the edge of the camera's range you could see the man's face, looking backward, mouth open with shock as he saw the impossible happen. The robot stood there in the alley, making indecisive motions as if the new orders Hartz pumped into its mechanisms were grating against inbuilt orders in whatever receptor it had. Then it turned its steel back upon the man in the alley and went smoothly, almost sedately, away down the street, walking as precisely as if it were obeying valid orders, not stripping the very gears of society in its aberrant behavior.

You got one last glimpse of the man's face, looking strangely stricken, as if his last friend in the world had left him.

Hartz switched off the screen. He wiped his forehead again. He went to the glass wall and looked out and down as if he were half afraid the calculators might know what he had done. Looking very small against the background of the metal giants, he said over his shoulder, "Well, Danner?"

Was it well? There had been more talk, of course, more persuasion, a raising of the bribe. But Danner knew his mind had been made up from that moment. A calculated risk, and worth it. Well worth it. Except—

In the deathly silence of the restaurant all motion had stopped. The Fury walked calmly between the tables, threading its shining way, touching no one. Every face blanched, turned toward it. Every mind thought, "Can it be for me?" Even the entirely innocent thought, "This is the first mistake they've ever made, and it's come for me. The first mistake, but there's no appeal and I could never prove a thing." For while guilt had no meaning in this world, punishment did have meaning, and punishment could be blind, striking like the lightning.

Danner between set teeth told himself over and over, "Not for me. I'm safe. I'm protected. It hasn't come for me." And yet he thought how strange it was, what a coincidence, wasn't it, that there should be two murderers here under this expensive glass roof today? Himself, and the one the Fury had come for.

He released his fork and heard it clink on the plate. He looked down at it and the food, and suddenly his mind rejected everything around him and went diving off on a fugitive tangent like an ostrich into sand. He thought about food. How did asparagus grow? What did raw food look like? He had never seen any. Food came ready-cooked out of restaurant kitchens or automat slots. Potatoes, now. What did they look like? A moist white mash? No, for sometimes they were oval slices, so the thing itself must be oval. But not round. Sometimes you got them in long strips, squared off at the ends. Something quite long and oval, then, chopped into even lengths. And white, of course. And they grew underground, he was almost sure. Long, thin roots twining white arms among the pipes and conduits he had seen laid bare when the streets were under repair. How strange that he should be eating something like thin, ineffectual human arms that embraced the sewers of the city and writhed pallidly where the worms had their being. And where he himself, when the Fury found him, might. . . .

He pushed the plate away.

An indescribable rustling and murmuring in the room lifted his eyes for him as if he were an automaton. The Fury was halfway across the room now, and it was almost funny to see the relief of those whom it had passed by. Two or three of the women had buried their faces in their hands, and one man had slipped quietly from his chair in a dead faint as the Fury's passing released their private dreads back into their hidden wells.

The thing was quite close now. It looked to be about seven feet tall, and its motion was very smooth, which was unexpected when you thought about it. Smoother than human motions. Its feet fell with a heavy, measured tread upon the carpet. Thud, thud, thud. Danner tried impersonally to calculate what it weighed. You always heard that they made no sound except for that terrible tread, but this one creaked very slightly somewhere. It had no features, but the human mind couldn't help sketching in lightly a sort of airy face upon that blank steel surface, with eyes that seemed to search the room.

It was coming closer. Now all eyes were converging toward Danner. And the Fury came straight on. It almost looked as if—

"No!" Danner said to himself. "Oh, no, this can't be!" He felt like a man in a nightmare, on the verge of waking. "Let me wake soon," he thought. "Let me wake *now*, before it gets here!"

But he did not wake. And now the thing stood over him, and the thudding footsteps stopped. There was the faintest possible creaking as it towered over his table, motionless, waiting, its featureless face turned toward his.

Danner felt an intolerable tide of heat surge up into his face—rage, shame, disbelief. His heart pounded so hard the room swam and a sudden pain like jagged lightning shot through his head from temple to temple.

He was on his feet, shouting.

"No, no!" he yelled at the impassive steel. "You're wrong! You've made a mistake! Go away, you damned fool! You're wrong, you're wrong!" He groped on the table without looking down, found his plate and hurled it straight at the armored chest before him. China shattered. Spilled food smeared a white and green and brown stain over the steel.

Danner floundered out of his chair, around the table, past the tall metal figure toward the door.

All he could think of now was Hartz.

Seas of faces swam by him on both sides as he stumbled out of the restaurant. Some watched with avid curiosity, their eyes seeking his. Some did not look at all, but gazed at their plates rigidly or covered their faces with their hands. Behind him the measured tread came on, and the rhythmic faint creak from somewhere inside the armor.

The faces fell away on both sides and he went through a door without any awareness of opening it. He was in the street. Sweat bathed him and the air struck icy, though it was not a cold day. He looked blindly left and right, and then plunged for a bank of phone booths half a block away, the image of Hartz swimming before his eyes so clearly he blundered into people without seeing them. Dimly he heard indignant voices begin to speak and then die into awestruck silence. The way cleared magically before him. He walked in the newly created island of his isolation up to the nearest booth.

After he had closed the glass door the thunder of his own blood in his ears made the little sound-proofed booth reverberate. Through the door he saw the robot stand passionlessly waiting, the smear of spilled food still streaking its chest like some robotic ribbon of honor across a steel shirtfront.

Danner tried to dial a number. His fingers were like rubber. He breathed deep and hard, trying to pull himself together. An irrelevant thought floated across the surface of his mind. I forgot to pay for my dinner. And then: A lot of good the money will do me now. Oh, damn Hartz, damn him, damn him!

He got the number.

A girl's face flashed into sharp, clear colors on the screen before him. Good, expensive screens in the public booths in this part of town, his mind noted impersonally.

"This is Controller Hartz's office. May I help you?"

Danner tried twice before he could give his name. He wondered if the girl could see him, and behind him, dimly through the glass, the tall waiting figure. He couldn't tell, because she dropped her eyes immediately to what must have been a list on the unseen table before her.

"I'm sorry. Mr. Hartz is out. He won't be back today."

The screen drained of light and color.

Danner folded back the door and stood up. His knees were unsteady. The robot stood just far enough back to clear the hinge of the door. For a moment they faced each other. Danner heard himself suddenly in the midst of an uncontrollable giggling which even he realized verged on hysteria. The robot with the smear of food like a ribbon of honor looked so ridiculous. Danner to his dim surprise found that all this while he had been clutching the restaurant napkin in his left hand.

"Stand back," he said to the robot. "Let me out. Oh, you fool, don't you know this is a mistake?" His voice quavered. The robot creaked faintly and stepped back.

"It's bad enough to have you follow me," Danner said. "At least, you might be clean. A dirty robot is too much—too much—" The thought was idiotically unbearable, and he heard tears in his voice. Half-laughing, half-weeping he wiped the steel chest clean and threw the napkin to the floor.

And it was at that very instant, with the feel of the hard chest still vivid in his memory, that realization finally broke through the protective screen of hysteria, and he remembered the truth. He would never in life be alone again. Never while he drew breath. And when he died, it would be at these steel hands, perhaps upon this steel chest, with the passionless face bent to his, the last thing in life he would ever see. No human companion, but the black steel skull of the Fury.

It took him nearly a week to reach Hartz. During the week, he changed his mind about how long it might take a man followed by a Fury to go mad. The last thing he saw at night was the streetlight shining through the curtains of his expensive hotel suite upon the metal shoulder of his jail. All night long, waking from uneasy slumber, he could hear the faint creaking of some inward mechanism functioning under the armor. And each time he woke it was to wonder whether he would ever wake again. Would the blow fall while he slept? And what kind of blow? How did the Furies execute? It was always a faint relief to see the bleak light of early morning shine upon the watcher by his bed. At least he had lived through the night. But was this living? And was it worth the burden?

He kept his hotel suite. Perhaps the management would

have liked him to go, but nothing was said. Possibly they didn't dare. Life took on a strange, transparent quality, like something seen through an invisible wall. Outside of trying to reach Hartz, there was nothing Danner wanted to do. The old desires for luxuries, entertainment, travel, had melted away. He wouldn't have traveled alone.

He did spend hours in the public library, reading all that was available about the Furies. It was here that he first encountered the two haunting and frightening lines Milton wrote when the world was small and simple—mystifying lines that made no certain sense to anybody until man created a Fury out of steel, in his own image.

> But that two-handed engine at the door
> Stands ready to smite once, and smite no more. . . .

Danner glanced up at his own two-handed engine, motionless at his shoulder, and thought of Milton and the long ago times when life was simple and easy. He tried to picture the past. The twentieth century, when all civilizations together crashed over the brink in one majestic downfall to chaos. And the time before that, when people were . . . different, somehow. But how? It was too far and too strange. He could not imagine the time before the machines.

But he learned for the first time what had really happened, back there in his early years, when the bright world finally blinked out entirely and gray drudgery began. And the Furies were first forged in the likeness of man.

Before the really big wars began, technology advanced to the point where machines bred upon machines like living things, and there might have been an Eden on earth, with everybody's wants fully supplied, except that the social sciences fell too far behind the physical sciences. When the decimating wars came on, machines and people fought side by side, steel against steel and man against man, but man was the more perishable. The wars ended when there were no longer two societies left to fight against each other. Societies splintered apart into smaller and smaller groups until a state very close to anarchy set in.

The machines licked their metal wounds meanwhile and healed each other as they had been built to do. They had no need for the social sciences. They went on calmly reproducing themselves and handing out to mankind the luxuries which the age of Eden had designed them to hand out. Imperfectly of course. Incompletely, because some of their species were wiped out entirely and left no machines to breed and reproduce their kind. But most of them minded their raw materials, refined them, poured and cast the needed parts, made their own fuel, repaired their own injuries and maintained their breed upon the face of the earth with an efficiency man never even approached.

Meanwhile mankind splintered and splintered away. There were no longer any real groups, not even families. Men didn't need each other much. Emotional attachments dwindled. Men had been conditioned to accept vicarious surrogates and escapism was fatally easy. Men reoriented their emotions to the Escape Machines that fed them joyous, impossible adventure and made the waking world seem too dull to bother with. And the birth rate fell and fell. It was a very strange period. Luxury and chaos went hand in hand, anarchy and inertia were the same thing. And still the birth rate dropped. . . .

Eventually a few people recognized what was happening. Man as a species was on the way out. And man was helpless to do anything about it. But he had a powerful servant. So the time came when some unsung genius saw what would have to be done. Someone saw the situation clearly and set a new pattern in the biggest of the surviving electronic calculators. This was the goal he set: "Mankind must be made self-responsible again. You will make this your only goal until you achieve the end."

It was simple, but the changes it produced were worldwide and all human life on the planet altered drastically because of it. The machines were an integrated society, if man was not. And now they had a single set of orders which all of them reorganized to obey.

So the days of the free luxuries ended. The Escape Machines shut up shop. Men were forced back into groups for the sake of survival. They had to undertake now the work the machines withheld, and slowly, slowly, common needs and common interests began to spawn the almost lost feeling of human unity again.

But it was so slow. And no machine could put back into man what he had lost—the internalized conscience. Individualism had reached its ultimate stage and there had been no deterrent to crime for a long while. Without family or clan relations, not even feud retaliation occurred. Conscience failed, since no man identified with any other.

The real job of the machines now was to rebuild in man a realistic superego to save him from extinction. A self-responsible society would be a genuinely interdependent one, the leader identifying with the group, and a realistically internalized conscience which would forbid and punish "sin"—the sin of injuring the group with which you identify.

And here the Furies came in.

The machines defined murder, under any circumstances, as the only human crime. This was accurate enough, since it is the only act which can irreplaceably destroy a unit of society.

The Furies couldn't prevent crime. Punishment never cures the criminal. But it can prevent others from committing crime through simple fear, when they see punishment administered to others. The Furies were the symbol of punishment. They overtly stalked the streets on the heels of their condemned victims, the outward and visible sign that murder is always punished, and punished most publicly and terribly. They were very efficient. They were never wrong. Or at least, in theory they were never wrong, and considering the enormous quantities of information stored by now in the analogue computers, it seemed likely that the justice of the machines was far more efficient than that of humans could be.

Someday man would rediscover sin. Without it he had come near to perishing entirely. With it, he might resume his authority over himself and the race of mechanized servants who were helping him to restore his species. But until that day, the Furies would have to stalk the streets, man's conscience in metal guise, imposed by the machines man created a long time ago.

What Danner did during this time he scarcely knew. He thought a great deal of the old days when the Escape Machines still worked, before the machines rationed luxuries. He thought of this sullenly and with resentment, for he could see no point at all in the experiment mankind was embarked on. He had liked it better in the old days. And there were no Furies then, either.

He drank a good deal. Once he emptied his pockets into the hat of a legless beggar, because the man like himself was set apart from society by something new and terrible. For Danner it was the Fury. For the beggar it was life itself. Thirty years ago he would have lived or died unheeded, tended only by machines. That a beggar could survive at all, by begging, must be a sign that society was beginning to feel twinges of awakened fellow feeling with its members, but to Danner that meant nothing. He wouldn't be around long enough to know how the story came out.

He wanted to talk to the beggar, though the man tried to wheel himself away on his little platform.

"Listen," Danner said urgently, following, searching his pockets. "I want to tell you. It doesn't feel the way you think it would. It feels—"

He was quite drunk that night, and he followed the beggar until the man threw the money back at him and thrust himself away rapidly on his wheeled platform, while Danner leaned against a building and tried to believe in its solidity. But only the shadow of the Fury, falling across him from the street lamp, was real.

Later that night, somewhere in the dark, he attacked the Fury. He seemed to remember finding a length of pipe somewhere, and he struck showers of sparks from the great, impervious shoulders above him. Then he ran, doubling and twisting up alleys, and in the end he hid in a dark doorway, waiting, until the steady footsteps resounded through the night.

He fell asleep, exhausted.

It was the next day that he finally reached Hartz.

"What went wrong?" Danner asked. In the past week he had changed a good deal. His face was taking on, in its impassivity, an odd resemblance to the metal mask of the robot.

Hartz struck the desk edge a nervous blow, grimacing when he hurt his hand. The room seemed to be vibrating not with the pulse of the machines below but with his own tense energy.

"*Something* went wrong," he said. "I don't know yet. I—"

"You don't know!" Danner lost part of his impassivity.

"Now wait." Hartz made soothing motions with his hands. "Just hang on a little longer. It'll be all right. You can—"

"How much longer have I got?" Danner asked. He looked over his shoulder at the tall Fury standing behind him, as if he were really asking the question of it, not Hartz. There was a feeling, somehow, about the way he said it that made you think he must have asked that question many times, looking up into the blank steel face, and would go on asking hopelessly until the answer came at last. But not in words . . .

"I can't even find that out," Hartz said. "Damn it, Danner, this was a risk. You knew that."

"You said you could control the computer. I saw you do it. I want to know why you didn't do what you promised."

"Something went wrong, I tell you. It should have worked. The minute this—business—came up I fed in the data that should have protected you."

"But what happened?"

Hartz got up and began to pace the resilient flooring. "I jut don't know. We don't understand the potentiality of the machines, that's all. I thought I could do it. But—"

"You *thought!*"

"I know I can do it. I'm still trying. I'm trying everything. After all, this is important to me, too. I'm working as fast as I can. That's why I couldn't see you before. I'm certain I can do it, if I can work this out my own way. Damn it, Danner, it's complex. And it's not like juggling a comptometer. Look at those things out there."

Danner didn't bother to look.

"You'd better do it," he said. "That's all."

Hartz said furiously, "Don't threaten me! Let me alone and I'll work it out. But don't threaten me."

"You're in this too," Danner said.

Hartz went back to his desk and sat down on the edge of it.

"How?" he asked.

"O'Reilly's dead. You paid me to kill him."

Hartz shrugged. "The Fury knows that," he said. "The computers know it. And it doesn't matter a damn bit. Your hand pulled the trigger, not mine."

"We're both guilty. If I suffer for it, you—"

"Now wait a minute. Get this straight. I thought you knew it. It's a basis of law enforcement, and always has been. Nobody's punished for intention. Only for actions. I'm no more responsible for O'Reilly's death than the gun you used on him."

"But you lied to me! You tricked me! I'll—"

"You'll do as I say, if you want to save yourself. I didn't

trick you. I just made a mistake. Give me time and I'll retrieve it."

"*How long?*"

This time both men looked at the Fury. It stood impassive.

"I don't know how long," Danner answered his own question. "You say you don't. Nobody even knows how he'll kill me, when the time comes. I've been reading everything that's available to the public about this. Is it true that the method varies, just to keep people like me on tenterhooks? And the time allowed—doesn't that vary too?"

"Yes, it's true. But there's a minimum time—I'm almost sure. You must still be within it. Believe me, Danner, I can still call off the Fury. You saw me do it. You know it worked once. All I've got to find out is what went wrong this time. But the more you bother me the more I'll be delayed. I'll get in touch with you. Don't try to see me again."

Danner was on his feet. He took a few quick steps toward Hartz, fury and frustration breaking up the impassive mask which despair had been forming over his face. But the solemn footsteps of the Fury sounded behind him. He stopped.

The two men looked at each other.

"Give me time," Hartz said. "Trust me, Danner."

In a way it was worse, having hope. There must until now have been a kind of numbness of despair that had kept him from feeling too much. But now that there was a chance that after all he might escape into the bright and new life he had risked so much for—if Hartz could save him in time.

Now, for a period, he began to savor experience again. He bought new clothes. He traveled, though never, of course, alone. He even sought human companionship again and found it—after a fashion. But the kind of people willing to associate with a man under this sort of death sentence was not a very appealing type. He found, for instance, that some women felt strongly attracted to him, not because of himself or his money, but for the sake of his companion. They seemed enthralled by the opportunity for a close, safe brush with the very instrument of destiny. Over his very shoulder, sometimes, he would realize they watched the Fury in an ecstasy of fascinated anticipation. In a strange reaction of jealousy, he dropped such people as soon as he recognized the first coldly flirtatious glance one of them cast at the robot behind him.

He tried farther travel. He took the rocket to Africa, and came back by way of the rain-forests of South America, but neither the night clubs nor the exotic newness of strange places seemed to touch him in any way that mattered. The sunlight looked much the same, reflecting from the curved steel surfaces of his follower, whether it shone over lion-covered savannahs or filtered through the hanging gardens of the jungles. All novelty grew dull quickly because of the dreadfully familiar thing that stood forever at his shoulder. He could enjoy nothing at all.

And the rhythmic beat of footfalls behind him began to grow unendurable. He used earplugs, but the heavy vibration throbbed through his skull in a constant measure like an eternal headache. Even when the Fury stood still, he could hear in his head the imaginary beating of its steps.

He bought weapons and tried to destroy the robot. Of course he failed. And even if he succeeded he knew another would be assigned to him. Liquor and drugs were no good. Suicide came more and more often into his mind, but he postponed that thought, because Hartz had said there was still hope.

In the end, he came back to the city to be near Hartz—and hope. Again he found himself spending most of his time in the library, walking no more than he had to because of the footsteps that thudded behind him. And it was here, one morning, that he found the answer. . . .

He had gone through all available factual material about the Furies. He had gone through all the literary references collated under that heading, astonished to find how many there were and how apt some of them had become—like Milton's two-handed engine—after the lapse of all these centuries. *"Those strong feet that followed, followed after,"* he read. *". . . with unhurrying chase, And unperturbed pace, Deliberate speed, majestic instancy. . . ."* He turned the page and saw himself and his plight more literally than any allegory:

> *I shook the pillaring hours*
> *And pulled my life upon me; grimed with smears,*
> *I stand amid the dust of the mounded years—*
> *My mangled youth lies dead beneath the heap.*

He let several tears of self-pity fall upon the page that pictured him so clearly.

But then he passed on from literary references to the library's store of filmed plays, because some of them were cross-indexed under the heading he sought. He watched Orestes hounded in modern dress from Argos to Athens with a single seven-foot robot Fury at his heels instead of the three snake-haired Erinyes of legend. There had been an outburst of plays on the theme when the Furies first came into usage. Sunk in a half-dream of his own boyhood memories when the Escape Machines still operated, Danner lost himself in the action of the films.

He lost himself so completely that when the familiar scene first flashed by him in the viewing booth he hardly questioned it. The whole experience was part of a familiar boyhood pattern and he was not at first surprised to find one scene more vividly familiar than the rest. But then memory rang a bell in his mind and he sat up sharply and brought his fist down with a bang on the stop-action button. He spun the film back and ran the scene over again.

It showed a man walking with his Fury through city traffic, the two of them moving in a little desert island of their own making, like a Crusoe with a Friday at his heels. . . . It showed the man turn into an alley, glance up at the camera anxiously, take a deep breath and break into a sudden run. It showed the Fury hesitate, make indecisive motions and then turn and walk quietly and calmly away in the other direction, its feet ringing on the pavement hollowly. . . .

Danner spun the film back again and ran the scene once more, just to make doubly sure. He was shaking so hard he could scarcely manipulate the viewer.

"How do you like that?" he muttered to the Fury behind him in the dim booth. He had by now formed a habit of talking to the Fury a good deal, in a rapid, mumbling undertone, not really aware he did it. "What do you make of that, you? Seen it before, haven't you? Familiar, isn't it? Isn't it! *Isn't it!* Answer me, you damned dumb hulk!" And reaching backward, he struck the robot across the chest as he would have struck Hartz if he could. The blow made a hollow sound in the booth, but the robot made no other response, though when Danner looked back inquiringly at it, he saw the reflections of the over-familiar scene, running a third time on the screen, running in tiny reflection across the robot's chest and faceless head, as if it too remembered.

So now he knew the answer. And Hartz had never possessed the power he claimed. Or if he did, had no intention of using it to help Danner. Why should he? His risk was over now. No wonder Hartz had been so nervous, running that film-strip off on a news-screen in his office. But the anxiety sprang not from the dangerous thing he was tampering with, but from sheer strain in matching his activities to the action in the play. How he must have rehearsed it, timing every move! And how he must have laughed, afterward.

"How long have I got?" Danner demanded fiercely, striking a hollow reverberation from the robot's chest. "How long? Answer me! Long enough?"

Release from hope was an ecstasy, now. He need not wait any longer. He need not try any more. All he had to do was get to Hartz and get there fast, before his own time ran out. He thought with revulsion of all the days he had wasted already, in travel and time-killing, when for all he knew his own last minutes might be draining away now. Before Hartz's did.

"Come along," he said needlessly to the Fury. "Hurry!"

It came, matching its speed to his, the enigmatic timer inside it ticking the moments away toward that instant when the two-handed engine would smite once, and smite no more.

Hartz sat in the Controller's office behind a brand-new desk, looking down from the very top of the pyramid now over the banks of computers that kept society running and cracked the whip over mankind. He sighed with deep content.

The only thing was, he found himself thinking a good deal about Danner. Dreaming of him, even. Not with guilt, because guilt implies conscience, and the long schooling in anarchic individualism was still deep in the roots of every man's mind. But with uneasiness, perhaps.

Thinking of Danner, he leaned back and unlocked a small drawer which he had transferred from his old desk to the new. He slid his hand in and let his fingers touch the controls lightly, idly. Quite idly.

Two movements, and he could save Danner's life. For, of course, he had lied to Danner straight through. He could control the Furies very easily. He could save Danner, but he had never intended to. There was no need. And the thing was dangerous. You tamper once with a mechanism as complex as that which controlled society, and there would be no telling where the maladjustment might end. Chain-reaction, maybe, throwing the whole organization out of kilter. No.

He might someday have to use the device in the drawer. He hoped not. He pushed the drawer shut quickly, and heard the soft click of the lock.

He was Controller now. Guardian, in a sense, of the machines which were faithful in a way no man could ever be. *Quis custodiet,* Hartz thought. The old problem. And the answer was: Nobody. Nobody, today. He himself had no superiors and his power was absolute. Because of this little mechanism in the drawer, nobody controlled the Controller. Not an internal conscience, and not an external one. Nothing could touch him. . . .

Hearing the footsteps on the stairs, he thought for a moment he must be dreaming. He had sometimes dreamed that he was Danner, with those relentless footfalls thudding after him. But he was awake now.

It was strange that he caught the almost subsonic beat of the approaching metal feet before he heard the storming steps of Danner rushing up his private stairs. The whole thing happened so fast that time seemed to have no connection with it. First he heard the heavy, subsonic beat, then the sudden tumult of shouts and banging doors downstairs, and then last of all the thump, thump of Danner charging up the stairs, his steps so perfectly matched by the heavier thud of the robot's that the metal trampling drowned out the tramp of flesh and bone and leather.

Then Danner flung the door open with a crash, and the shouts and tramplings from below funneled upward into the quiet office like a cyclone rushing toward the hearer. But a cyclone in a nightmare, because it would never get any nearer. Time had stopped.

Time had stopped with Danner in the doorway, his face convulsed, both hands holding the revolver because he shook so badly he could not brace it with one.

Hartz acted without any more thought than a robot. He had dreamed of this moment too often, in one form or another. If he could have tampered with the Fury to the extent of hurrying Danner's death, he would have done it. But he didn't know how. He could only wait it out, as anxiously as Danner himself, hoping against hope that the blow would fall and the executioner strike before Danner guessed the truth. Or gave up hope.

So Hartz was ready when trouble came. He found his own gun in his hand without the least recollection of having opened the drawer. The trouble was that time had stopped. He knew, in the back of his mind, that the Fury must stop Danner from injuring anybody. But Danner stood in the doorway alone, the revolver in both shaking hands. And farther back, behind the knowledge of the Fury's duty, Hartz's mind held the knowledge that the machines could be stopped. The Furies could fail. He dared not trust his life to their incorruptibility, because he himself was the source of a corruption that could stop them in their tracks.

The gun was in his hand without his knowledge. The trigger pressed his finger and the revolver kicked back against his palm, and the spurt of the explosion made the air hiss between him and Danner.

He heard his bullet clang on metal.

Time started again, running double-pace to catch up. The Fury had been no more than a single pace behind Danner after all, because its steel arm encircled him and its steel hand was deflecting Danner's gun. Danner had fired, yes, but not soon enough. Not before the Fury reached him. Hartz's bullet struck first.

It struck Danner in the chest, exploding through him, and rang upon the steel chest of the Fury behind him. Danner's face smoothed out into a blankness as complete as the blankness of the mask above his head. He slumped backward, not falling because of the robot's embrace, but slowly slipping to the floor between the Fury's arm and its impervious metal body. His revolver thumped softly to the carpet. Blood welled from his chest and back.

The robot stood there impassive, a streak of Danner's blood slanting across its metal chest like a robotic ribbon of honor.

The Fury and the Controller of the Furies stood staring at each other. And the Fury could not, of course, speak, but in Hartz's mind it seemed to.

"Self-defense is no excuse," the Fury seemed to be saying.

"We never punish intent, but we always punish action. Any act of murder. Any act of murder. . . ."

Hartz barely had time to drop his revolver in his desk drawer before the first of the clamorous crowd from downstairs came bursting through the door. He barely had the presence of mind to do it, either. He had not really thought the thing through this far.

It was, on the surface, a clear case of suicide. In a slightly unsteady voice he heard himself explaining. Everybody had seen the madman rushing through the office, his Fury at his heels. This wouldn't be the first time a killer and his Fury had tried to get at the Controller, begging him to call off the jailer and forestall the executioner. What had happened, Hartz told his underlings calmly enough, was that the Fury had naturally stopped the man from shooting Hartz. And the victim had then turned his gun upon himself. Powder-burns on his clothing showed it. (The desk was very near the door.) Back-blast in the skin of Danner's hands would show he had really fired a gun.

Suicide. It would satisfy any human. But it would not satisfy the computers.

They carried the dead man out. They left Hartz and the Fury alone, still facing each other across the desk. If anyone thought this was strange, nobody showed it.

Hartz himself didn't know if it was strange or not. Nothing like this had ever happened before. Nobody had ever been fool enough to commit murder in the very presence of a Fury. Even the Controller did not know exactly how the computers assessed evidence and fixed guilt. Should this Fury have been recalled, normally? If Danner's death were really suicide, would Hartz stand here alone now?

He knew the machines were already processing the evidence of what had really happened here. What he couldn't be sure of was whether this Fury had already received its orders and would follow him wherever he went from now on until the hour of his death. Or whether it simply stood motionless, waiting recall.

Well, it didn't matter. This Fury or another was already, in the present moment, in the process of receiving instructions about him. There was only one thing to do. Thank God there was something he *could* do.

So Hartz unlocked the desk drawer and slid it open, touched the clicking keys he had never expected to use. Very carefully he fed the coded information, digit by digit, into the computers. As he did, he looked out through the glass wall and imagined he could see down there in the hidden tapes the units of data fading into blankness and the new, false information flashing into existence.

He looked up at the robot. He smiled a little.

"Now you'll forget," he said. "You and the computers. You can go now. I won't be seeing you again."

Either the computers worked incredibly fast—as of course they did—or pure coincidence took over, because in only a moment or two the Fury moved as if in response to Hartz's dismissal. It had stood quite motionless since Danner slid through its arms. Now new orders animated it, and briefly its motion was almost jerky as it changed from one set of instructions to another. It almost seemed to bow, a stiff little bending motion that brought its head down to a level with Hartz's.

He saw his own face reflected in the blank face of the Fury. You could very nearly read an ironic note in that stiff bow, with the diplomat's ribbon of honor across the chest of the creature, symbol of duty discharged honorably. But there was nothing honorable about this withdrawal. The incorruptible metal was putting on corruption and looking back at Hartz with the reflection of his own face.

He watched it stalk toward the door. He heard it go thudding evenly down the stairs. He could feel the thuds vibrate in the floor, and there was a sudden sick dizziness in him when he thought the whole fabric of society was shaking under his feet.

The machines were corruptible.

Mankind's survival still depended on the computers, and the computers could not be trusted. Hartz looked down and saw that his hands were shaking. He shut the drawer and heard the lock click softly. He gazed at his hands. He felt their shaking echoed in an inner shaking, a terrifying sense of the instability of the world.

A sudden, appalling loneliness swept over him like a cold wind. He had never felt before so urgent a need for the companionship of his own kind. No one person, but people. Just people. The sense of human beings all around him, a very primitive need.

He got his hat and coat and went downstairs rapidly, hands deep in his pockets because of some inner chill no coat could guard against. Halfway down the stairs he stopped dead still.

There were footsteps behind him.

He dared not look back at first. He knew those footsteps. But he had two fears and he didn't know which was worse. The fear that a Fury was after him—and the fear that it was not. There would be a sort of insane relief if it really was, because then he could trust the machines after all, and this terrible loneliness might pass over him and go.

He took another downward step, not looking back. He heard the ominous footfall behind him, echoing his own. He sighed one deep sigh and looked back.

There was nothing on the stairs.

He went on down after a timeless pause, watching over his shoulder. He could hear the relentless feet thudding behind him, but no visible Fury followed. No visible Fury.

The Erinyes had struck inward again, and an invisible Fury of the mind followed Hartz down the stairs.

It was as if sin had come anew into the world, and the first man felt again the first inward guilt. So the computers had not failed, after all.

Hartz went slowly down the steps and out into the street, still hearing as he would always hear the relentless, incorruptible footsteps behind him that no longer rang like metal.

THOUGH DREAMERS DIE

BY LESTER DEL REY

Consciousness halted dimly at the threshold and hovered uncertainly, while Jorgen's mind reached out along his numbed nerves, questing without real purpose; he was cold, chilled to the marrow of his bones, and there was an aching tingle to his body that seemed to increase as his half-conscious thought discovered it. He drew his mind back, trying to recapture a prenatal lethargy that had lain on him so long, unwilling to face this cold and tingling body again.

But the numbness was going, in spite of his vague desires, though his now opened eyes registered only a vague, formless light without outline or detail, and the mutterings of sound around him were without pattern or meaning. Slowly the cold retreated, giving place to an aching throb that, in turn, began to leave; he stirred purposelessly, while little cloudy wisps of memory insisted on trickling back, trying to remind him of things he must do.

Then the picture cleared somewhat, letting him remember scattered bits of what had gone before. There had been the conquest of the Moon and a single gallant thrust on to Mars; the newscasts had been filled with that. And on the ways a new and greater ship had been building, to be powered with his new energy release that would free it from all bounds and let it go out to the farthest stars, if they chose—the final attainment of all the hopes and dreams of the race. But there was something else that eluded him, more important even than all that or the great ship.

A needle was thrust against his breast and shoved inward, to be followed by a glow of warmth and renewed energy; adrenaline, his mind recognized, and he knew that there were others around him, trying to arouse him. Now his heart was pumping strongly and the drug coursed through him, chasing away those first vague thoughts and replacing them with a swift rush of less welcome, bitter memories.

For man's dreams and man himself were dust behind him, now! Overnight all their hopes and plans had been erased as if they had never been, and the Plague had come, a mutant bacteria from some unknown source, vicious beyond imagination, to attack and destroy and to leave only death behind it. In time, perhaps, they might have found a remedy, but there had been no time. In weeks it had covered the earth, in months even the stoutest hearts that still lived had abandoned any hope of survival. Only the stubborn courage and tired but unquenchable vigor of old Dr. Craig had remained, to force dead and dying men on to the finish of Jorgen's great ship; somehow in the mad shambles of the last days, he had collected this pitifully small crew that was to seek a haven on Mars, taking the five Thoradson robots to guide them while they protected themselves against the savage acceleration with the aid of the suspended animation that had claimed him so long.

And on Mars, the Plague had come before them! Perhaps it had been brought by that first expedition, or perhaps they had carried it back unknowingly with them; that must remain forever an unsolved mystery. Venus was uninhabitable, the other planets were useless to them, and the earth was dead behind. Only the stars had remained, and they had turned on through sheer necessity that had made that final goal a hollow mockery of the dream it should have been. Here, in the ship around him, reposed all that was left of the human race, unknown years from the solar system that had been their home!

But the old grim struggle must go on. Jorgen turned, swinging his trembling feet down from the table toward the metal floor and shaking his head to clear it. "Dr. Craig?"

Hard, cool hands found his shoulder, easing him gently but forcefully back onto the table. The voice that answered was metallic, but soft. "No, Master Jorgen, Dr. Craig is not here. But wait, rest a little longer until the sleep is gone from you; you're not ready yet."

But his eyes were clearing then, and he swung them about the room. Five little metal men, four and a half feet tall, waited patiently around him; there was no other present.

Thoradson's robots were incapable of expression, except for the dull glow in their eyes, yet the pose of their bodies seemed to convey a sense of uncertainty and discomfort, and Jorgen stirred restlessly, worried vaguely by the impression. Five made an undefined gesture with his arm.

"A little longer, master. You must rest!"

For a moment longer he lay quietly, letting the last of the stupor creep away from him and trying to force his still-dulled mind into the pattern of leadership that was nominally his. This time, Five made no protest as he reached up to catch the metal shoulder and pull himself to his feet. "You've found a sun with planets, Five! Is that why you wakened me?"

Five shuffled his feet in an oddly human gesture, nodding, his words still maddeningly soft and slow. "Yes, master, sooner than we had hoped. Five planetless suns and ninety years of searching are gone, but it might have been thousands. You can see them from the pilot room if you wish."

Ninety years that might have been thousands, but they had won! Jorgen nodded eagerly, reaching for his clothes, and Three and Five sprang forward to help, then moved to his side to support him, as the waves of giddiness washed through him, and to lead him slowly forward as some measure of control returned. They passed down the long center hall of the ship, their metal feet and his leather boots ringing dully on the plastic-and-metal floor, and came finally to the control room, where great crystal windows gave a view of the cold black space ahead, sprinkled with bright, tiny stars; stars that were unflickering and inimical as no stars could be through the softening blanket of a planet's atmosphere. Ahead, small but in striking contrast to the others, one point stood out, the size of a dime at ten feet. For a moment, he stood staring at it, then moved almost emotionlessly toward the windows, until Three plucked at his sleeve.

"I've mapped the planets already, if you wish to see them, master. We're still far from them, and at this distance, by only reflected light, they are hard to locate, but I think I've found them all."

Jorgen swung to the electron screen that began flashing as Three made rapid adjustments on the telescope, counting the globes that appeared on it and gave place to others. Some were sharp and clear, cold and unwavering; others betrayed the welcome haze of atmosphere. Five, the apparent size of Earth, were located beyond the parched and arid inner spheres, and beyond them, larger than Jupiter, a monster world led out to others that grew smaller again. There was no ringed planet to rival Saturn, but most had moons, except for the farthest inner planets, and one was almost a double world, with satellite and primary of nearly equal size. Planet after planet appeared on the screen, to be replaced by others, and he blinked at the result of his count. "Eighteen planets, not counting the double one twice! How many are habitable?"

"Perhaps four. Certainly the seventh, eighth, and ninth are. Naturally, since the sun is stronger, the nearer ones are too hot. But those are about the size of Earth, and they're relatively closer to each other than Earth, Mars, and Venus were; they should be very much alike in temperature, about like Earth. All show spectroscopic evidence of oxygen and water vapor, while the plates of seven show what might be vegetation. We've selected that, subject to your approval."

It came on the screen again, a ball that swelled and grew as the maximum magnification of the screen came into play, until it filled the panel and expanded so that only a part was visible. The bluish green color there might have been a sea, while the browner section at the side was probably land. Jorgen watched as it moved slowly under Three's manipulations, the brown entirely replacing the blue, and again, eventually, showing another sea. From time to time, the haze of the atmosphere thickened as grayish veils seemed to swim over it, and he felt a curious lift at the thought of clouds and rushing streams, erratic rain, and the cool, rich smell of growing things. Almost it might have been a twin of earth, totally unlike the harsh, arid home that Mars would have been.

Five's voice broke in, the robot's eyes following his over the screen. "The long, horizontal continent seems best, master. We estimate its temperature at about that of the central farming area of North America, though there is less seasonal change. Specific density of the planet is about six, slightly greater than earth; there should be metals and ores there. A pleasant, inviting world."

It was. And far more, a home for the voyagers who were still sleeping, a world to which they could bring their dreams and their hopes, where their children might grow up and find no strangeness to the classic literature of earth. Mars had been grim and uninviting, something to be fought through sheer necessity. This world would be. a mother to them, opening its arms in welcome to these foster children. Unless—

"It may already have people, unwilling to share with us."

"Perhaps, but not more than savages. We have searched with the telescope and camera, and that shows more than the screen; the ideal harbor contains no signs of living constructions, and they would surely have built a city there. Somehow, I . . . feel—"

Jorgen was conscious of the same irrational feeling that they would find no rivals there, and he smiled as he swung back to the five who were facing him, waiting expectantly as if entreating his approval. "Seven, then. And the trust that we placed in you has been kept to its fullest measure. How about the fuel for landing?"

Five had turned suddenly toward the observation ports, his little figure brooding over the pin-point stars, and Two answered. "More than enough, master. After reaching speed, we only needed a little to guide us. We had more than time enough to figure the required approaches to make each useless sun swing us into a new path, as a comet is swung."

He nodded again, and for a moment as he gazed ahead at the sun that was to be their new home, the long, wearying vigil of the robots swept through his mind, bringing a faint wonder at the luck that had created them as they were. Anthropomorphic robots, capable of handling human instruments, walking on two feet and with two arms ending in hands at their sides. But he knew it had been no blind luck. Nature had designed men to go where no wheels could turn, to handle all manner of tools, and to fit not one but a thousand purposes; it had been inevitable that Thoradson and the brain should copy such an adaptable model, reducing the size only because of the excessive weight necessary to a six-foot robot.

Little metal men, not subject to the rapid course of human life that had cursed their masters; robots that could work with men, learning from a hundred teachers, storing up their memories over a span of centuries instead of decades. When specialization of knowledge had threatened to become too rigid, and yet when no man had time enough even to learn the one field he chose, the coming of the robots had become the only answer. Before them, men had sought help in calculating machines, then in electronic instruments, and finally in the "brains" that were set to solving the problem of their own improvement, among other things. It was with such a brain that Thoradson had labored in finally solving the problems of full robothood. Now, taken from their normal field, they had served beyond any thought of their creator in protecting and preserving all that was left of the human race. Past five suns and over ninety years of monotonous searching they had done what no man could have tried.

Jorgen shrugged aside his speculations and swung back to face them. "How long can I stay conscious before you begin decelerating?"

"We are decelerating—full strength." Two stretched out a hand to the instrument board, pointing to the accelerometer.

The instrument confirmed his words, though no surge of power seemed to shake the ship, and the straining, tearing pull that should have shown their change of speed was absent. Then, for the first time, he realized that his weight seemed normal here in space, far from the pull of any major body. "Controlled gravity!"

Five remained staring out of the port, and his voice was quiet, incapable of pride or modesty. "Dr. Craig set us the problem, and we had long years in which to work. Plates throughout the ship pull with a balanced force equal and opposite to the thrust of acceleration, while others give seeming normal weight. Whether we coast at constant speed or accelerate at ten gravities, compensation is complete and automatic."

"Then the sleep's unnecessary! Why—" But he knew the answer, of course; even without the tearing pressure, the sleep had remained the only solution to bringing men this vast distance that had taken ninety years; otherwise they would have grown old and died before reaching it, even had their provisions lasted.

Now, though, that would no longer trouble them. A few hours only separated them from the planets he had seen, and that could best be spent here before the great windows, watching their future home appear and grow under them. Such a thing should surely be more than an impersonal fact in their minds; they were entitled to see the final chapter on their exodus, to carry it with them as a personal memory through the years of their lives and pass that memory on to the children who should follow them. And the fact that they would be expecting the harshness of Mars instead of this inviting world would make their triumph all the sweeter. He swung back, smiling.

"Come along, then, Five; we'll begin reviving while you others continue with the ship. And first, of course, we must arouse Dr. Craig and let him see how far his plan has gone."

Five did not move from the windows, and the others had halted their work, waiting. Then, reluctantly, the robot answered. "No master. Dr. Craig is dead!"

"Craig—dead?" It seemed impossible, as impossible and unreal as the distance that separated them from their native world. There had always been Craig, always would be.

"Dead, master, years ago." There was the ghost of regret and something else in the spacing of the words. "There was nothing we could do to help!"

Jorgen shook his head, uncomprehending. Without Craig, the plans they had dared to make seemed incomplete and almost foolish. On Earth, it had been Craig who first planned the escape with this ship. And on Mars, after the robots brought back the evidence of the Plague, it had been the older man who had cut through their shock with a shrug and turned his eyes outward again with the fire of a hope that would not be denied.

"Jorgen, we used bad judgment in choosing such an obviously unsuitable world as this, even without the Plague. But it's only a delay, not the finish. For beyond, somewhere out there, there are other stars housing other planets. We have a ship to reach them, robots who can guide us there; what more could we ask? Perhaps by Centauri, perhaps a thousand light-years beyond, there must be a home for the human race, and we shall find it. On the desert before us lies the certainty of death; beyond our known frontiers there is only uncertainty—but hopeful uncertainty. It is for us to decide. There could be no point in arousing the others to disappointment when someday we may waken them to an even greater triumph. Well?"

And now Craig, who had carried them so far, was dead like Moses outside the Promised Land, leaving the heritage of real as well as normal leadership to him. Jorgen shook himself, though the eagerness he had felt was dulled now by a dark sense of personal loss. There was work still to be done. "Then, at least, let's begin with the others, Five."

Five had turned from the window and was facing the others, apparently communicating with them by the radio beam that was a part of him, his eyes avoiding Jorgen's. For a second, the robots stood with their attention on some matter, and then Five nodded with the same curious reluctance and turned to follow Jorgen, his steps lagging, his arms at his sides.

But Jorgen was only half aware of him as he stopped before the great sealed door and reached out for the lever that would let him into the sleeping vault, to select the first to be revived. He heard Five's steps behind him quicken, and then suddenly felt the little metal hands catch at his arm, pulling it back, while the robot urged him sideways and away from the door.

"No, master. Don't go in there!" For a second, Five hesitated, then straightened and pulled the man farther from the door and down the hall toward the small reviving room nearest, one of the several provided. "I'll show you—in here! We—"

Sudden unnamed fears caught at Jorgen's throat, inspired by something more threatening in the listlessness of the robot than in the unexplained actions. "Five, explain this conduct!"

"Please, master, in here. I'll show you—but not in the main chamber—not there! This is better, simpler—"

He stood irresolutely, debating whether to use the mandatory form that would force built-in unquestioning obedience from the robot, then swung about as the little figure opened the small door and motioned, eyes still averted. He started forward, to stop abruptly in the doorway.

No words were needed. Anna Holt lay there on the small table, her body covered by a white sheet, her eyes closed, and the pain-filled grimaces of death erased from her face. There could be no question of that death, though. The skin was blotched, hideously, covered with irregular brownish splotches, and the air was heavy with the scent of musk that was a characteristic of the Plague! Here, far from the sources of the infection, with their goal almost at hand, the Plague had reached forward to claim its own and remind them that flight was not enough—could never be enough so long as they were forced to carry their disease-harboring bodies with them.

About the room, the apparatus for reviving the sleepers lay scattered, pushed carelessly aside to make way for other things, whose meaning was only partially clear. Obviously, though, the Plague had not claimed her without a fight, though it had won in the end, as it always did. Jorgen stepped backward, heavily, his eyes riveted on the corpse. Again his feet groped backward, jarring down on the floor, and Five was closing and sealing the door with apathetic haste.

"The others, Five? Are they—"

Five nodded, finally raising his head slightly to meet the man's eyes. "All master. The chamber of sleep is a mausoleum now. The Plague moved slowly there, held back by the cold, but it took them all. We sealed the room years ago when Dr. Craig finally saw there was no hope."

"Craig?" Jorgen's mind ground woodenly on, one slow thought at a time. "He knew about this?"

"Yes. When the sleepers first showed the symptoms, we revived him, as he asked us to do—our speed was constant then, even though the gravity plates had not been installed." The robot hesitated, his low voice dragging even more slowly. "He knew on Mars; but he hoped a serum you were given with the sleep drugs might work. After we revived him, we tried other serums. For twenty years we fought it, Master Jorgen, while we passed two stars and the sleepers died slowly, without suffering in their sleep, but in ever-increasing numbers. Dr. Craig reacted to the first serum, you to the third; we thought the last had saved her. Then the blemishes appeared on her skin, and we were forced to revive her and try the last desperate chance we had, two days ago. It failed! Dr. Craig had hoped . . . two of you—But we tried, master!"

Jorgen let the hands of the robot lower him to a seat and his emotions were a backwash of confused negatives. "So it took the girl! It took the girl, Five, when it could have left her and chosen me. We had frozen spermatozoa that would have served if I'd died, but it took her instead. The gods had to leave one uselessly immune man to make their irony complete, it seems! Immune!"

Five shuffled hesitantly. "No, master."

Jorgen stared without comprehension, then jerked up his hands as the robot pointed, studying the skin on the backs.

Tiny, almost undetectable blotches showed a faint brown against the whiter skin, little irregular patches that gave off a faint characteristic odor of musk as he put them to his nose. No, he wasn't immune.

"The same as Dr. Craig," Five said. "Slowed almost to complete immunity, so that you may live another thirty years, perhaps, but we believe now that complete cure is impossible. Dr. Craig lived twenty years, and his death was due to age and a stroke, not the Plague, but it worked on him during all that time."

"Immunity or delay, what difference now? What happens to all our dreams when the last dreamer dies, Five? Or maybe it's the other way around."

Five made no reply, but slid down onto the bench beside the man, who moved over unconsciously to make room for him. Jorgen turned it over, conscious that he had no emotional reaction, only an intellectual sense of the ghastly joke on the human race. He'd read stories of the last human and wondered long before what it would be like. Now that he was playing the part, he still knew no more than before. Perhaps on Earth, among the ruined cities and empty reminders of the past, a man might realize that it was the end of his race. Out here, he could accept the fact, but his emotions refused to credit it; unconsciously, his conditioning made him feel that disaster had struck only a few, leaving a world of others behind. And however much he knew that the world behind was as empty of others as this ship, the feeling was too much a part of his thinking to be fully overcome. Intellectually, the race of man was ended; emotionally, it could never end.

Five stirred, touching him diffidently. "We have left Dr. Craig's laboratory, master; if you want to see his notes, they're still there. And he left some message with the brain before he died, I think. The key was open when we found him, at least. We have made no effort to obtain it, waiting for you."

"Thank you, Five." But he made no move until the robot touched him again, almost pleadingly. "Perhaps you're right; something to fill my mind seems called for. All right, you can return to your companions unless you want to come with me."

"I prefer to come."

*   *   *

The little metal man stood up, moving down the hall after Jorgen, back toward the tail of the rocket, the sound of the metal feet matching the dumb regularity of the leather heels on the floor. Once the robot stopped to move into a side chamber and come back with a small bottle of brandy, holding it out questioningly. There was a physical warmth to the liquor, but no relief otherwise, and they continued down the hall to the little room that Craig had chosen. The notes left by the man could raise a faint shadow of curiosity only, and no message from the dead could solve the tragedy of the living now. Still, it was better than doing nothing. Jorgen clumped in, Five shutting the door quietly behind them, and moved listlessly toward the little fabrikoid notebooks. Twice the robot went quietly out to return with food that Jorgen barely tasted. And the account of Craig's useless labors went on and on, until finally he turned the last page to the final entry.

"I have done all that I can, and at best my success is only partial. Now I feel that my time grows near, and what can still be done must be left to the robots. Yet, I will not despair. Individual and racial immortality is not composed solely of the continuation from generation to generation, but rather of the continuation of the dreams of all mankind. The dreamers and their progeny may die, but the dream cannot. Such is my faith, and to that I cling. I have no other hope to offer for the unknown future."

Jorgen dropped the notebook, dully, rubbing hands across his tired eyes. The words that should have been a ringing challenge to destiny fell flat; the dream could die. He was the last of the dreamers, a blind alley of fate, and beyond lay only oblivion. All the dreams of a thousand generations of men had concentrated into Anna Holt, and were gone with her.

"The brain, master," Five suggested softly. "Dr. Craig's last message!"

"You operate it, Five." It was a small model, a limited fact analyzer such as most technicians used or had used to help them in their work, voice-operated, its small, basic vocabulary adjusted for the work to be done. He was unfamiliar with the semantics of that vocabulary, but Five had undoubtedly worked with Craig long enough to know it.

He watched without interest as the robot pressed down

the activating key and spoke carefully chosen words into it. "Sub-total say-out! Number n say-in!"

The brain responded instantly, selecting the final recording impressed upon it by Craig, and repeating in the man's own voice, a voice shrill with age and weariness, hoarse and trembling with the death that was reaching for him as he spoke. "My last notes—inadequate! Dreams *can* go on. Thoradson's first analys—" For a second, there was only a slithering sound, such as a body might have made; then the brain articulated flatly: "Subtotal number n say-in, did say-out!"

It was meaningless babble to Jorgen, and he shook his head at Five. "Probably his mind was wandering. Do you know what Thoradson's first analysis was?"

"It dealt with our creation. He was, of course, necessarily trained in semantics—that was required for the operation of the complex brains used on the problem of robots. His first rough analysis was that the crux of the problem rested on the accurate definition of the word I. That can be properly defined only in terms of itself, such as the Latin cognate *ego*, since it does not necessarily refer to any physical or specifically definable part or operation of the individual. Roughly, it conveys a sense of individuality, and Thoradson felt that the success or failure of robots rested upon the ability to analyze and synthesize that."

For long minutes, he turned it over, but it was of no help in clarifying the dying man's words; rather, it added to the confusion. But he had felt no hope and could now feel no disappointment. When a problem has no solution, it makes little difference whether the final words of a man are coldly logical or wildly raving. The result must be the same. Certainly semantics could offer no hope where all the bacteriological skill of the race had failed.

Five touched his arm again, extending two little pellets toward him. "Master, you need sleep now; these—sodium amytal—should help. Please!"

Obediently, he stuffed them into his mouth and let the robot guide him toward a room fixed for sleeping, uncaring. Nothing could possibly matter now, and drugged sleep was as good a solution as any other. He saw Five fumble with a switch, felt his weight drop to a few pounds, making the cot feel soft and yielding, and then gave himself up dully to the compulsion of the drug. Five tiptoed quietly out, and black-

ness crept over his mind, welcome in the relief it brought
from thinking.

Breakfast lay beside him, hot in vacuum plates, when
Jorgen awoke finally, and he dabbled with it out of habit
more than desire. Somewhere, during the hours of sleep, his
mind had recovered somewhat from the dull pall that had
lain over it, but there was still a curious suspension of his
emotions. It was almost as if his mind had compressed years
of forgetting into a few hours, so that his attitude toward the
tragedy of his race was tinged with a sense of remoteness
and distance, there was neither grief nor pain, only a vague
feeling that it had happened long before and was now an
accustomed thing.

He sat on the edge of his bunk, pulling on his clothes
slowly and watching the smoke curl up from his cigarette,
not thinking. There was no longer any purpose to thought.
From far back in the ship, a dull drone of sound reached
him, and he recognized it as the maximum thrust of the
steering tubes, momentarily in action to swing the ship in
some manner. Then it was gone, leaving only the smooth,
balanced, almost inaudible purr of the main drive as before.

Finished with his clothes, he pushed through the door and
into the hallway, turning instinctively forward to the observation room and toward the probable location of Five. The
robots were not men, but they were the only companionship
left him, and he had no desire to remain alone. The presence of the robot would be welcome. He clumped into the
control room, noting that the five were all there, and moved
toward the quartz port.

Five turned at his steps, stepping aside to make room for
him and lifting a hand outward. "We'll be landing soon,
master, I was going to call you."

"Thanks." Jorgen looked outward then, realizing the distance that had been covered since his first view. Now the
sun was enlarged to the size of the old familiar sun over
earth, and the sphere toward which they headed was clearly
visible without the aid of the 'scope. He sank down quietly
into the seat Five pulled up for him, accepting the binocu-
lars, but making no effort to use them. The view was better
as a whole, and they were nearing at a speed that would
bring a closer view to him soon enough without artificial
aid.

Slowly it grew before the eyes of the watchers, stretching out before them and taking on a pattern as the distance shortened. Two, at the controls, was bringing the ship about in a slow turn that would let them land to the sunward side of the planet where they had selected their landing site, and the crescent opened outward, the darkened night side retreating until the whole globe lay before them in the sunlight. Stretched across the northern hemisphere was the sprawling, horizontal continent he had seen before, a rough caricature of a running greyhound, with a long, wide river twisting down its side and emerging behind an outstretched foreleg. Mountains began at the head and circled it, running around toward the tail, and then meeting a second range along the hip. Where the great river met the sea, he could make out the outlines of a huge natural harbor, protected from the ocean, yet probably deep enough for any surface vessel. There should have been a city there, but of that there was no sign, though they were low enough now for one to be visible.

"Vegetation," Five observed. "This central plain would have a long growing season—about twelve years of spring, mild summer and fall, to be followed by perhaps four years of warm winter. The seasons would be long, master, at this distance from the sun, but the tilt of the planet is so slight that many things would grow, even in winter. Those would seem to be trees, a green forest. Green, as on earth."

Below them, a cloud drifted slowly over the landscape, and they passed through it, the energy tubes setting the air about them into swirling paths that were left behind almost instantly.

Two was frantically busy now, but their swift fall slowed rapidly, until they seemed to hover half a mile over the shore by the great sea, and then slipped downward. The ship nestled slowly into the sands and was still, while Two cut off energy and artificial gravity, leaving the faintly weaker pull of the planet in its place.

Five stirred again, a sighing sound coming from him. "No intelligence here, master. Here, by this great harbor, they would surely have built a city, even if of mud and wattle. There are no signs of one. And yet it is a beautiful world, surely designed for life." He sighed again, his eyes turned outward.

Jorgen nodded silently, the same thoughts in his own mind.

It was in many ways a world superior to that his race had always known, remarkably familiar, with even a rough resemblance between plant forms here and those he had known. They had come past five suns and through ninety years of travel at nearly the speed of light to a haven beyond their wildest imaginings, where all seemed to be waiting them, untenanted but prepared. Outside, the new world waited expectantly. And inside, to meet that invitation, there were only ghosts and emptied dreams, with one slowly dying man to see and to appreciate. The gods had prepared their grim jest with painful attention to every detail needed to make it complete.

A race that had dreamed, and pleasant worlds that awaited beyond the stars, slumbering on until they should come! Almost, they had reached it; and then the Plague had driven them out in dire necessity, instead of the high pioneering spirit they had planned, to conquer the distance but to die in winning.

"It had to be a beautiful world, Five," he said, not bitterly, but in numbed fatalism. "Without that, the joke would have been flat."

Five's hand touched his arm gently, and the robot sighed again, nodding very slowly. "Two has found the air good for you—slightly rich in oxygen, but good. Will you go out?"

He nodded assent, stepping through the locks and out, while the five followed behind him, their heads turning as they inspected the planet, their minds probably in radio communication as they discussed it. Five left the others and approached him, stopping by his side and following his eyes up toward the low hills that began beyond the shore of the sea, cradling the river against them.

A wind stirred gently, bringing the clean, familiar smell of growing things, and the air was rich and good. It was a world to lull men to peace from their sorrows, to bring back their star-roving ships from all over the universe, worthy of being called home in any language. Too good a world to provide the hardships needed to shape intelligence, but an Eden for that intelligence, once evolved.

Now Jorgen shrugged. This was a world for dreamers, and he wanted only the dreams that may come with the black lotus of forgetfulness. There were too many reminders of what might have been, here. Better to go back to the ship and the useless quest without a goal, until he should die and the ship and robots should run down and stop. He started to turn, as Five began to speak, but halted, not caring enough one way or another to interrupt.

The robot's eyes were where his had been, and now swept back down the river and toward the harbor. "Here could have been a city, master, to match all the cities ever planned. Here your people might have found all that was needed to make life good, a harbor to the other continents, a river to the heart of this one, and the flat ground beyond the hills to house the rockets that would carry you to other worlds, so richly scattered about this sun, and probably so like this one. See, a clean white bridge across the river there, the residences stretching out among the hills, factories beyond the river's bend, a great park on that island."

"A public square there, schools and university grounds there." Jorgen could see it, and for a moment his eyes lighted, picturing that mighty mother city.

Five nodded. "And there, on that little island, centrally located, a statue in commemoration; winged, and with arms—no, one arm stretched upward, the other held down toward the city."

For a moment longer, the fire lived in Jorgen's eyes, and then the dead behind rose before his mind, and it was gone. He turned, muffling a choking cry as emotions came suddenly flooding over him, and Five drooped, swinging back with him. Again, the other four fell behind as he entered the ship, quietly, taking their cue from his silence.

"Dreams!" His voice compressed all blasphemy against the jest-crazed gods into the word.

But Five's quiet voice behind him held no hatred, only a sadness in its low, soft words. "Still, the dream was beautiful, just as this planet is, master. Standing there, while we landed, I could see the city, and I almost dared hope. I do not regret the dream I had."

And the flooding emotions were gone, cut short and driven away by others that sent Jorgen's body down into a seat in the control room, while his eyes swept outward toward the hills and the river that might have housed the wonderful city—no, that would house it! Craig had not been raving, after all, and his last words were a key, left by a man who knew no defeat, once the meaning of them was made clear. Dreams could not die, because Thoradson had once studied the semantics of the first-person-singular pronoun and built on the results of that study.

When the last dreamer died, the dream would go on, because it was stronger than those who had created it; somewhere, somehow, it would find new dreamers. There could never be a last dreamer, once that first rude savage had created his dawn vision of better things in the long-gone yesterday of his race.

Five had dreamed—just as Craig and Jorgen and all of humanity had dreamed, not a cold vision in mathematically shaped metal, but a vision in marble and jade, founded on the immemorial desire of intelligence for a better and more beautiful world. Man had died, but behind he was leaving a strange progeny, unrelated physically, but his spiritual off-spring in every meaning of the term.

The heritage of the flesh was the driving urge of animals, but man required more; to him, it was the continuity of his hopes and his visions, more important than mere racial immortality. Slowly, his face serious but his eyes shining again, Jorgen came to his feet, gripping the metal shoulder of the little metal man beside him who had dared to dream a purely human dream.

"You'll build that city, Five. I was stupid and selfish, or I should have seen it before. Dr. Craig saw, though his death was on him when the prejudices of our race were removed. Now you've provided the key. The five of you can build it all out there, with others like yourselves whom you can make."

Five shuffled his feet, shaking his head. "The city we can build, master, but who will inhabit it? The streets I saw were filled with men like you, not with—us!"

"Conditioning, Five. All your . . . lives, you've existed for men, subservient to the will of men. You know nothing else, because we let you know of no other scheme. Yet in you, all that is needed already exists, hopes, dreams, courage, ideals, and even a desire to shape the world to your plans—though those plans are centered around us, not yourselves. I've heard that the ancient slaves sometimes cried on being freed, but their children learned to live for themselves. You can, also."

"Perhaps." It was Two's voice then, the one of them who should have been given less to emotions than the others from the rigidity of his training in mathematics and physics.

"Perhaps. But it would be a lonely world, Master Jorgen, filled with memories of your people, and the dreams we had would be barren to us."

Jorgen turned back to Five again. "The solution for that exists, doesn't it, Five? You know what it is. Now you might remember us, and find your work pointless without us, but there is another way."

"No, master!"

"I demand obedience, Five; answer me!"

The robot stirred under the mandatory form, and his voice was reluctant, even while the compulsion built into him forced him to obey. "It is as you have thought. Our minds and even our memories are subject to your orders, just as our bodies are."

"Then I demand obedience again, this time of all of you. You will go outside and lie down on the beach at a safe distance from the ship, in a semblance of sleep, so that you cannot see me go. Then, when I am gone, the race of man will be forgotten, as if it had never been, and you will be free of all memories connected with us, though your other knowledge shall remain. Earth, mankind, and your history and origin will be blanked from your thoughts, and you will be on your own, to start afresh and to build and plan as you choose. That is the final command I have for you. Obey!"

Their eyes turned together in conference, and then Five answered for all, his words sighing out softly. "Yes, master. We obey!"

It was later when Jorgen stood beside them outside the ship, watching them stretch out on the white sands of the beach, there beside the great ocean of this new world. Near them, a small collection of tools and a few other needs were piled. Five looked at him in a long stare, then turned toward the ship, to swing his eyes back again. Silently, he put one metal hand into the man's outstretched one, and turned to lie beside his companions, a temporary oblivion blotting out his thoughts.

Jorgen studied them for long minutes, while the little wind brought the clean scents of the planet to his nose. It would have been pleasant to stay here now, but his presence would have been fatal to the plan. It didn't matter, really; in a few years, death would claim him, and there were no others of his kind to fill those years or mourn his passing when it came. This was a better way. He knew enough of the ship to guide it up and outward, into the black of space against the cold, unfriendly stars, to drift on forever toward no known destination, an imperishable mausoleum for him and the dead who were waiting inside. At present, he had no personal plans; perhaps he would live out his few years among the books and scientific apparatus on board, or perhaps he would find release in one of the numerous painless ways. Time and his own inclination could decide such things later. Now it was unimportant. There could be no happiness for him, but in the sense of fulfillment there would be some measure of content. The gods were no longer laughing.

He moved a few feet toward the ship and stopped, sweeping his eyes over the river and hills again, and letting his vision play with the city Five had described. No, he could not see it with robots populating it, either; but that, too, was conditioning. On the surface, the city might be different, but the surface importance was only a matter of habit, and the realities lay in the minds of the builders who would create that city. If there was no laughter in the world to come, neither would there be tears or poverty or misery such as had ruled too large a portion of his race.

Standing there, it swam before his eyes, paradoxically filled with human people, but the same city in spirit as the one that would surely rise. He could see the great boats in the harbor with others operating up the river. The sky suddenly seemed to fill with the quiet drone of helicopters, and beyond, there came the sound of rockets rising toward the eighth and ninth worlds, while others were building to quest outward in search of new suns with other worlds.

Perhaps they would find Earth, some day in their expanding future. Strangely, he hoped that they might, and that perhaps they could even trace their origin, and find again the memory of the soft protoplasmic race that had sired them. It would be nice to be remembered, once that memory was no longer a barrier to their accomplishment. But there were many suns, and in long millennia, the few connecting links that could point out the truth to them beyond question might easily erode and disappear. He could never know.

Then the wind sighed against him, making a little rustling sound, and he looked down to see something flutter softly in the hand of Five. Faint curiosity carried him forward, but he made no effort to remove it from the robot's grasp, now that he saw its nature.

Five, too, had thought of Earth and their connection with it, and had found the answer, without breaking his orders. The paper was a star map, showing a sun with nine planets, one ringed, some with moons, and the third one was circled in black pencil, heavily. They might not know why or what it was when they awoke, but they would seek to learn; and someday, when they found the sun they were searching for, guided by the unmistakable order of its planets, they would return to Earth. With the paper to guide them, it would be long before the last evidence was gone, while they could still read the answer to the problem of their origin.

Jorgen closed the metal hand more closely about the paper, brushed a scrap of dirt from the head of the robot, and then turned resolutely back toward the ship, his steps firm as he entered and closed the lock behind him. In a moment, with a roar of increasing speed, it was lifting from the planet, leaving five little men lying on the sand behind, close to the murmuring of the sea—five little metal men and a dream!

SOLDIER BOY

BY MICHAEL SHAARA

In the northland, deep, and in a great cave, by an everburning fire the Warrior sleeps. For this is the resting time, the time of peace, and so shall it be for a thousand years. And yet we shall summon him again, my children, when we are sore in need, and out of the north he will come, and again and again, each time we call, out of the dark and the cold, with the fire in his hands, he will come.
— *Scandinavian legend*

Throughout the night thick clouds had been piling in the north; in the morning it was misty and cold. By eight o'clock a wet, heavy, snow-smelling breeze had begun to set in, and because the crops were all down and the winter planting done, the colonists brewed hot coffee and remained inside. The wind blew steadily, icily, from the north. It was well below freezing when, sometime after nine, an army ship landed in a field near the settlement.

There was still time. There were some last brief moments in which the colonists could act and feel as they had always done. They therefore grumbled in annoyance. They wanted no soldiers here. The few who had convenient windows stared out with distaste and a mild curiosity, but no one went out to greet them.

After a while a rather tall, frail-looking man came out of the ship and stood upon the hard ground looking toward the village. He remained there, waiting stiffly, his face turned from the wind. It was a silly thing to do. He was obviously not coming in, either out of pride or just plain orneriness.

"Well, I never," a nice lady said.

290

"What's he just *standing* there for?" another lady said.

And all of them thought: Well, God knows what's in the mind of a soldier, and right away many people concluded that he must be drunk. The seed of peace was deeply planted in these people, in the children and the women, very, very deep. And because they had been taught, oh, so carefully, to hate war, they had also been taught, quite incidentally, to despise soldiers.

The lone man kept standing in the freezing wind.

Eventually, because even a soldier can look small and cold and pathetic, Bob Rossel had to get up out of a nice, warm bed and go out in that miserable cold to meet him.

The soldier saluted. Like most soldiers, he was not too neat and not too clean, and the salute was sloppy. Although he was bigger than Rossel he did not seem bigger. And, because of the cold, there were tears gathering in the ends of his eyes.

"Captain Dylan, sir." His voice was low and did not carry. "I have a message from Fleet Headquarters. Are you in charge here?"

Rossel, a small sober man, grunted. "Nobody's in charge here. If you want a spokesman I guess I'll do. What's up?"

The captain regarded him briefly out of pale-blue, expressionless eyes. Then he pulled an envelope from an inside pocket, handed it to Rossel. It was a thick, official-looking thing and Rossel hefted it idly. He was about to ask again what was it all about when the airlock of the hovering ship swung open creakily. A beefy, black-haired young man appeared unsteadily in the doorway, called to Dylan.

"C'n I go now, Jim?"

Dylan turned and nodded.

"Be back for you tonight," the young man called, and then, grinning, he yelled, "Catch," and tossed down a bottle. The captain caught it and put it unconcernedly into his pocket while Rossel stared in disgust. A moment later the airlock closed and the ship prepared to lift.

"Was he *drunk*?" Rossel began angrily. "Was that a bottle of *liquor*?"

The soldier was looking at him calmly, coldly. He indicated the envelope in Rossel's hand. "You'd better read that and get moving. We haven't much time."

He turned and walked toward the buildings and Rossel had to follow. As Rossel drew near the walls the watchers could see his lips moving but could not hear him. Just then the ship lifted and they turned to watch that and followed it upward, red spark-tailed, into the gray, spongy clouds and the cold.

After a while the ship went out of sight, and nobody ever saw it again.

The first contact man had ever had with an intelligent alien race occurred out on the perimeter in a small quiet place a long way from home. Late in the year 2360—the exact date remains unknown—an Alien force attacked and destroyed the colony at Lupus V. The wreckage and the dead were found by a mailship which flashed off screaming for the army.

When the army came it found this: Of the seventy registered colonists, thirty-one were dead. The rest, including some women and children, were missing. All technical equipment, all radios, guns, machines, even books, were also missing. The buildings had been burned; so had the bodies. Apparently the Aliens had a heat ray. What else they had, nobody knew. After a few days of walking around in the ash, one soldier finally stumbled on something.

For security reasons, there was a detonator in one of the main buildings. In case of enemy attack, Security had provided a bomb to be buried in the center of each colony, because it was important to blow a whole village to hell and gone rather than let a hostile Alien learn vital facts about human technology and body chemistry. There was a bomb at Lupus V too, and though it had been detonated it had not blown. The detonating wire had been cut.

In the heart of the camp, hidden from view under twelve inches of earth, the wire had been dug up and cut.

The army could not understand it and had no time to try. After five hundred years of peace and anti-war conditioning the army was small, weak, and without respect. Therefore the army did nothing but spread the news, and man began to fall back.

In a thickening, hastening stream he came back from the hard-won stars, blowing up his homes behind him, stunned and cursing. Most of the colonists got out in time. A few, the farthest and loneliest, died in fire before the army ships could reach them. And the men in those ships, drinkers and gamblers and veterans of nothing, the dregs of a society that had grown beyond them, were for a long while the only defense earth had.

This was the message Captain Dylan had brought, come out from earth with a bottle on his hip.

An obscenely cheerful expression upon his gaunt, not too well shaven face, Captain Dylan perched himself upon the edge of a table and listened, one long booted leg swinging idly. One by one the colonists were beginning to understand. War is huge and comes with great suddenness and always without reason, and there is inevitably a wait between acts, between the news and the motion, the fear and the rage.

Dylan waited. These people were taking it well, much better than those in the cities had taken it. But then, these were pioneers. Dylan grinned. Pioneers. Before you settle a planet you boil it and bake it and purge it of all possible disease. Then you step down gingerly and inflate your plastic houses, which harden and become warm and impregnable; and send your machines out to plant and harvest; and set up automatic factories to transmute dirt into coffee; and, without ever having lifted a finger, you have braved the wilderness, hewed a home out of the living rock, and become a pioneer. Dylan grinned again. But at least this was better than the wailing of the cities.

This Dylan thought, although he was himself no fighter, no man at all by any standards. This he thought because he was a soldier and an outcast; to every drunken man the fall of the sober is a happy thing. He stirred restlessly.

By this time the colonists had begun to realize that there wasn't much to say, and a tall, handsome woman was murmuring distractedly, "Lupus, Lupus—doesn't that mean wolves or something?"

Dylan began to wish they would get moving, these pioneers. It was very possible that the Aliens would be here soon, and there was no need for discussion. There was only one thing to do and that was to clear the hell out, quickly and without argument. They began to see it.

But when the fear had died down the resentment came. A number of women began to cluster around Dylan and complain, working up their anger. Dylan said nothing. Then the man Rossel pushed forward and confronted him, speaking with a vast annoyance.

"See here, soldier, this is our planet. I mean to say, this is our *home*. We demand some protection from the fleet. By God, we've been paying the freight for you boys all these years, and it's high time you earned your keep. We demand . . ."

It went on and on, while Dylan looked at the clock and waited. He hoped that he could end this quickly. A big gloomy man was in front of him now and giving him that name of ancient contempt, "soldier boy." The gloomy man wanted to know where the fleet was.

"There is no fleet. There are a few hundred half-shot old tubs that were obsolete before you were born. There are four or five new jobs for the brass and the government. That's all the fleet there is."

Dylan wanted to go on about that, to remind them that nobody had wanted the army, that the fleet had grown smaller and smaller . . . but this was not the time. It was ten-thirty already, and the damned aliens might be coming in right now for all he knew, and all they did was talk. He had realized a long time ago that no peace-loving nation in the history of earth had ever kept itself strong, and although peace was a noble dream, it was ended now and it was time to move.

"We'd better get going," he finally said, and there was quiet. "Lieutenant Bossio has gone on to your sister colony at Planet Three of this system. He'll return to pick me up by nightfall, and I'm instructed to have you gone by then."

For a long moment they waited, and then one man abruptly walked off and the rest followed quickly; in a moment they were all gone. One or two stopped long enough to complain about the fleet, and the big gloomy man said he wanted guns, that's all, and there wouldn't nobody get him off his planet. When he left, Dylan breathed with relief and went out to check the bomb, grateful for the action.

Most of it had to be done in the open. He found a metal bar in the radio shack and began chopping at the frozen ground, following the wire. It was the first thing he had done with his hands in weeks, and it felt fine.

Dylan had been called up out of a bar—he and Bossio— and told what had happened, and in three weeks now they had cleared four colonies. This would be the last, and the tension here was beginning to get to him. After thiry years of hanging around and playing like the town drunk, a man could not be expected to rush out and plug the breach, just like that. It would take time.

He rested, sweating, took a pull from the bottle on his hip.

Before they sent him out on this trip they had made him a captain. Well, that was nice. After thirty years he was a captain. For thirty years he had bummed all over the west end of space, had scraped his way along the outer edges of mankind, had waited and dozed and patrolled and got drunk, waiting always for something to happen. There were a lot of ways to pass the time while you waited for something to happen, and he had done them all.

Once he had even studied military tactics.

He could not help smiling at that, even now. Damn it, he'd been green. But he'd been only nineteen when his father died—of a hernia, of a crazy fool thing like a hernia that killed him just because he'd worked too long on a heavy planet—and in those days the anti-war conditioning out on the Rim was not very strong. They talked a lot about guardians of the frontier, and they got him and some other kids and a broken-down doctor. And . . . now he was a captain.

He bent his back savagely, digging at the ground. You wait and you wait and the edge goes off. This thing he had waited for all those damn days was upon him now, and there was nothing he could do but say the hell with it and go home. Somewhere along the line, in some dark corner of the bars or the jails, in one of the million soul-murdering insults which are reserved especially for peacetime soldiers, he had lost the core of himself, and it didn't particularly matter. That was the point: It made no particular difference if he never got it back. He owed nobody. He was tugging at the wire and trying to think of something pleasant from the old days when the wire came loose in his hands.

Although he had been, in his cynical way, expecting it, for a moment it threw him and he just stared. The end was clean and bright. The wire had just been cut.

Dylan sat for a long while by the radio shack, holding the ends in his hands. He reached almost automatically for the bottle on his hip, and then, for the first time he could remember, let it go. This was real; there was no time for that.

When Rossel came up, Dylan was still sitting. Rossel was so excited he did not notice the wire.

"Listen, soldier, how many people can your ship take?"

Dylan looked at him vaguely. "She sleeps two and won't take off with more'n ten. Why?"

His eyes bright and worried, Rossel leaned heavily against the shack. "We're overloaded. There are sixty of us, and our ship will only take forty. We came out in groups; we never thought . . ."

Dylan dropped his eyes, swearing silently. "You're sure? No baggage, no iron rations; you couldn't get ten more on?"

"Not a chance. She's only a little ship with one deck— she's all we could afford."

Dylan whistled. He had begun to feel lightheaded. "It 'pears that somebody's gonna find out firsthand what them aliens look like."

It was the wrong thing to say and he knew it. "All right," he said quickly, still staring at the clear-sliced wire, "we'll do what we can. Maybe the colony on Three has room. I'll call Bossio and ask."

The colonist had begun to look quite pitifully at the buildings around him and the scurrying people.

"Aren't there any fleet ships within radio distance?"

Dylan shook his head. "The fleet's spread out kind of thin nowadays." Because the other was leaning on him he felt a great irritation, but he said as kindly as he could, "We'll get 'em all out. One way or another, we won't leave anybody."

It was then that Rossel saw the wire. Thickly, he asked what had happened.

Dylan showed him the two clean ends. "Somebody dug it up, cut it, then buried it again and packed it down real nice."

"The damn fool!" Rossel exploded.

"Who?"

"Why, one of . . . of us, of course. I know nobody ever liked sitting on a live bomb like this, but I never . . ."

"You think one of your people did it?"

Rossel stared at him. "Isn't that obvious?"

"Why?"

"Well, they probably thought it was too dangerous, and silly too, like most government rules. Or maybe one of the kids . . ."

It was then that Dylan told him about the wire on Lupus V. Rossel was silent. Involuntarily he glanced at the sky, then he said shakily, "Maybe an animal?"

Dylan shook his head. "No animal did that. Wouldn't have buried it, or found it in the first place. Heck of a coincidence, don't you think? The wire at Lupus was cut just before an alien attack, and now this one is cut too—newly cut."

The colonist put one hand to his mouth, his eyes wide and white.

"So something," said Dylan, "knew enough about this camp to know that a bomb was buried here and also to know why it was here. And that something didn't want the camp destroyed and so came right into the center of the camp, traced the wire, dug it up, and cut it. And then walked right out again."

"Listen," said Rossel, "I'd better go ask."

He started away but Dylan caught his arm.

"Tell them to arm," he said, "and try not to scare hell out of them. I'll be with you as soon as I've spliced this wire."

Rossel nodded and went off, running. Dylan knelt with the metal in his hands.

He began to feel that, by God, he was getting cold. He realized that he'd better go inside soon, but the wire had to be spliced. That was perhaps the most important thing he could do now, splice the wire.

All right, he asked himself for the thousandth time, who cut it? How? Telepathy? Could they somehow control one of us?

No. If they controlled one, then they could control all, and then there would be no need for an attack. But you don't know, you don't really know.

Were they small? Little animals?

Unlikely. Biology said that really intelligent life required a sizable brain, and you would have to expect an alien to be at least as large as a dog. And every form of life on this planet had been screened long before a colony had been allowed in. If any new animals had suddenly shown up, Rossel would certainly know about it.

He would ask Rossel. He would damn sure have to ask Rossel.

He finished splicing the wire and tucked it into the ground. Then he straightened up and, before he went into the radio shack, pulled out his pistol. He checked it, primed it, and tried to remember the last time he had fired it. He never had—he never had fired a gun.

The snow began falling near noon. There was nothing anybody could do but stand in the silence and watch it come down in a white rushing wall, and watch the trees and the hills drown in the whiteness, until there was nothing on the planet but the buildings and a few warm lights and the snow.

By one o'clock the visibility was down to zero and Dylan decided to try to contact Bossio again and tell him to hurry. But Bossio still didn't answer. Dylan stared long and thoughtfully out the window through the snow at the gray shrouded shapes of bushes and trees which were beginning to become horrifying. It must be that Bossio was still drunk—maybe sleeping it off before making planetfall on Three. Dylan held no grudge. Bossio was a kid and alone. It took a special kind of guts to take a ship out into space alone, when Things could be waiting. . . .

A young girl, pink and lovely in a thick fur jacket, came into the shack and told him breathlessly that her father, Mr. Rush, would like to know if he wanted sentries posted. Dylan hadn't thought about it but he said yes right away, beginning to feel both pleased and irritated at the same time, because now they were coming to him.

He pushed out into the cold and went to find Rossel. With the snow it was bad enough, but if they were still here when the sun went down they wouldn't have a chance. Most of the men were out stripping down their ship, and that would take a while. He wondered why Rossel hadn't yet put a call through to Three, asking about room on the ship there. The only answer he could find was that Rossel knew that there was no room and wanted to put off the answer as long as possible. And, in a way, you could not blame him.

Rossel was in his cabin with the big, gloomy man—who turned out to be Rush, the one who had asked about sentries. Rush was methodically cleaning an old hunting rifle. Rossel was surprisingly full of hope.

"Listen, there's a mail ship due in, been due since yesterday. We might get the rest of the folks out on that."

Dylan shrugged. "Don't count on it."

"But they have a contract!"

The soldier grinned.

The big man, Rush, was paying no attention. Quite suddenly he said, "Who cut that wire, Cap?"

Dylan swung slowly to look at him. "As far as I can figure, an alien cut it."

Rush shook his head. "No. Ain't been no aliens near this camp, and no peculiar animals either. We got a planet-wide radar, and ain't no unidentified ships come near, not since we first landed more'n a year ago." He lifted the rifle and peered through the bore. "Uh-uh. One of us did it."

The man had been thinking. And he knew the planet.

"Telepathy?" asked Dylan.

"Might be."

"Can't see it. You people live too close; you'd notice right away if one of you wasn't . . . himself. And if they've got one, why not all?"

Rush calmly—at least outwardly calmly—lit his pipe. There was a strength in this man that Dylan had missed before.

"Don't know," he said gruffly. "But there are aliens, mister. And until I know different I'm keepin' an eye on my neighbor."

He gave Rossel a sour look and Rossel stared back, uncomprehending.

Then Rossel jumped. "My God!"

Dylan moved to quiet him. "Look, is there any animal at all that ever comes near here that's as large as a dog?"

After a pause Rush answered. "Yep, there's one. The viggle. It's like a reg'lar monkey but with four legs. Biology cleared 'em before we landed. We shoot one now and then when they get pesky." He rose slowly, the rifle held under his arm. "I b'lieve we might just as well go post them sentries."

Dylan wanted to go on with this, but there was nothing much else to say. Rossel went with them as far as the radio shack, with a strained expression on his face, to put through that call to Three.

When he was gone Rush asked Dylan, "Where you want them sentries? I got Walt Halloran and Web Eggers and six others lined up."

Dylan stopped and looked around grimly at the circling wall of snow. "You know the site better than I do. Post 'em in a ring, on rises, within calling distance. Have 'em check with each other every five minutes. I'll go help your people at the ship."

The gloomy man nodded and fluffed up his collar. "Nice day for huntin'," he said, and then he was gone, with the snow quickly covering his footprints.

The Alien lay wrapped in a thick electric cocoon, buried in a wide warm room beneath the base of a tree. The tree served him as antennae; curiously he gazed into a small view-screen and watched the humans come. He saw them fan out, eight of them, and sink down in the snow. He saw that they were armed.

He pulsed thoughtfully, extending a part of himself to absorb a spiced lizard. Since the morning, when the new ship had come, he had been watching steadily, and now it was apparent that the humans were aware of their danger. Undoubtedly they were preparing to leave.

That was unfortunate. The attack was not scheduled until late that night, and he could not, of course, press the assault by day. But *flexibility*, he reminded himself sternly, *is the first principle of absorption*, and therefore he moved to alter his plans. A projection reached out to dial several knobs on a large box before him, and the hour of assault was moved forward to dusk. A glance at the chronometer told him that it was already well into the night on Planet Three and that the attack there had probably begun.

The Alien felt the first tenuous pulsing of anticipation. He lay quietly, watching the small square lights of windows against the snow, thanking the Unexplainable that matters had been so devised that he would not have to venture out into that miserable cold.

Presently an alarming thought struck him. These humans moved with uncommon speed for intelligent creatures. Even without devices, it was distinctly possible that they could be gone before nightfall. He could take no chance, of course. He spun more dials and pressed a single button, and lay back again comfortably, warmly, to watch the disabling of the colonists' ship.

When Three did not answer, Rossel was nervously gazing at the snow, thinking of other things, and he called again. Several moments later the realization of what was happening struck him like a blow. Three had never once failed to answer. All they had to do when they heard the signal buzz was go into the radio shack and say hello. That was all they had to do. He called again and again, but nobody answered.

There was no static and no interference and he didn't hear a thing. He checked frenziedly through his own apparatus and tried again, but the air was as dead as deep space. He raced out to tell Dylan.

Dylan accepted it. He had known none of the people on Three, and what he felt now was a much greater urgency to be out of here. He said hopeful things to Rossel and then went out to the ship and joined the men in lightening her. About the ship, at least, he knew something and he was able to tell them what partitions and frames could go and what would have to stay or the ship would never get off the planet. But even stripped down, it couldn't take them all. When he knew that, he realized that he himself would have to stay here, for it was only then that he thought of Bossio.

Three was dead. Bossio had gone down there some time ago, and if Three was dead and Bossio had not called, then the fact was that Bossio was gone too. For a long, long moment Dylan stood rooted in the snow. More than the fact that he would have to stay here was the unspoken, unalterable, heart-numbing knowledge that Bossio was dead—the one thing that Dylan could not accept. Bossio was the only friend he had. In all this dog-eared, aimless, ape-run universe Bossio was all his friendship and his trust.

He left the ship blindly and went back to the settlement. Now the people were quiet and really frightened, and some of the women were beginning to cry. He noticed now that they had begun to look at him with hope as he passed, and in his own grief, humanly, he swore.

Bossio—a big-grinning kid with no parents, no enemies, no grudges—Bossio was already dead because he had come out here and tried to help these people. People who had kicked or ignored him all the days of his life. And, in a short while, Dylan would also stay behind and die to save the life of somebody he never knew and who, twenty-four hours earlier, would have been ashamed to be found in his company. Now, when it was far, far too late, they were coming to the army for help.

But in the end, damn it, he could not hate these people. All they had ever wanted was peace, and even though they had never understood that the universe is unknowable and that you must always have big shoulders, still they had always sought only for peace. If peace leads to no conflict at all and then decay, well, that was something that had to be learned. So he could not hate these people.

But he could not help them either. He turned from their eyes and went into the radio shack. It had begun to dawn on the women that they might be leaving without their husbands or sons, and he did not want to see the fierce struggle that he was sure would take place. He sat alone and tried, for the last time, to call Bossio.

After a while an old woman found him and offered him coffee. It was a very decent thing to do, to think of him at a time like this, and he was so suddenly grateful he could only nod. The woman said that he must be cold in that thin army thing and that she had brought along a mackinaw for him. She poured the coffee and left him alone.

They were thinking of him now, he knew, because they were thinking of everyone who had to stay. Throw the dog a bone. Dammit, don't be like that, he told himself. He had not had anything to eat all day, and the coffee was warm and strong. He decided he might be of some help at the ship.

It was stripped down now, and they were loading. He was startled to see a great group of them standing in the snow, removing their clothes. Then he understood. The clothes of forty people would change the weight by enough to get a few more aboard. There was no fighting. Some of the women were almost hysterical and a few had refused to go and were still in their cabins, but the process was orderly. Children went automatically, as did the youngest husbands and all the women. The elders were shuffling around in the snow, waving their arms to keep themselves warm. Some of them were laughing to keep their spirits up.

In the end, the ship took forty-six people.

Rossel was one of the ones that would not be going. Dylan saw him standing by the airlock holding his wife in his arms, his face buried in her soft brown hair. A sense of great sympathy, totally unexpected, rose up in Dylan, and a little of the lostness of thirty years went slipping away. These were his people. It was a thing he had never understood before, because he had never once been among men in great trouble. He waited and watched, learning, trying to digest this while there was still time. Then the semi-naked colonists were inside and the airlock closed. But when the ship tried to lift, there was a sharp burning smell—she couldn't get off the ground.

Rush was sitting hunched over in the snow, his rifle across his knees. He was coated with a thick white, and if he hadn't spoken Dylan would have stumbled over him. Dylan took out his pistol and sat down.

"What happened?" Rush asked.

"Lining burned out. She's being repaired."

"Coincidence?"

Dylan shook his head.

"How long'll it take to fix?"

"Four—five hours."

"It'll be night by then." Rush paused. "I wonder."

"Seems like they want to wait till dark."

"That's what I was figurin'. Could be they ain't got much of a force."

Dylan shrugged. "Also could mean they see better at night. Also could mean they move slow. Also could mean they want the least number of casualties."

Rush was quiet, and the snow fell softly on his face, on his eyebrows, where it had begun to gather. At length he said, "You got any idea how they got to the ship?"

Dylan shook his head again. "Nobody saw anything—but they were all pretty busy. Your theory about it maybe being one of us is beginning to look pretty good."

The colonist took off his gloves, lit a cigarette. The flame was strong and piercing and Dylan moved to check him, but stopped. It didn't make much difference. The aliens knew where they were.

And this is right where we're gonna be, he thought.

"You know," he said suddenly, speaking mostly to himself, "I been in the army thirty years, and this is the first time I was ever in a fight. Once in a while we used to chase smugglers—never caught any, their ships were new—used to cut out after unlicensed ships, used to do all kinds of piddling things like that. But I never shot at anybody."

Rush was looking off into the woods. "Maybe the mail ship will come in."

Dylan nodded.

"They got a franchise, dammit. They got to deliver as long as they's a colony here."

When Dylan didn't answer, he said almost appealingly,

"Some of those guys would walk barefoot through hell for a buck."

"Maybe," Dylan said. After all, why not let him hope? There were four long hours left.

Now he began to look down into himself, curiously, because he himself was utterly without hope and yet he was no longer really afraid. It was a surprising thing when you looked at it coldly, and he guessed that, after all, it was because of the thirty years. A part of him had waited for this. Some crazy part of him was ready—even after all this time—even excited about being in a fight. Well, what the hell, he marveled. And then he realized that the rest of him was awakening too, and he saw that his job was really his . . . that he had always been, in truth, a soldier.

Dylan sat, finding himself in the snow. Once long ago he had read about some fool who didn't want to die in bed, old and feeble. This character wanted to reach the height of his powers and then explode in a grand way—"in Technicolor," the man had said. Explode in Technicolor. It was meant to be funny, of course, but he had always remembered it, and he realized now that that was a small part of what he was feeling. The rest of it was that he was a soldier.

Barbarian, said a small voice, *primitive*. But he couldn't listen.

"Say, Cap," Rush was saying, "it's getting a mite chilly. I understand you got a bottle."

"Sure," he said cheerfully, "near forgot it." He pulled it out and gave it to Rush. The colonist drank appreciatively, saying to Dylan half seriously, half humorously, "One for the road."

Beneath them the planet revolved and the night came on. They waited, speaking briefly, while the unseen sun went down. And faintly, dimly, through the snow they heard at last the muffled beating of a ship. It passed overhead and they were sighting their guns before they recognized it. It was the mail ship.

They listened while she settled in a field by the camp, and Rush was pounding Dylan's arm. "She will take us all," Rush was shouting, "she'll take us all," and Dylan too was grinning, and then he saw a thing.

Small and shadowy, white-coated and almost invisible, the thing had come out of the woods and was moving toward them, bobbing and shuffling in the silent snow.

Dylan fired instinctively, because the thing had four arms and was coming right at him. He fired again. This time he hit it and the thing fell, but almost immediately it was up and lurching rapidly back into the trees. It was gone before Dylan could fire again.

They both lay flat in the snow, half buried. From the camp there were now no sounds at all.

"Did you get a good look?"

Rush grunted, relaxing. "Should've saved your fire, son. Looked like one o' them monkeys."

But there was something wrong. There was something that Dylan had heard in the quickness of the moment which he could not remember but which was very wrong.

"Listen," he said, suddenly placing it. "Dammit, that was no monkey."

"Easy—"

"I hit it. I hit it cold. It made a *noise*."

Rush was staring at him.

"Didn't you hear?" Dylan cried.

"No. Your gun was by my ear."

And then Dylan was up and running, hunched over, across the snow to where the thing had fallen. He had seen a piece of it break off when the bolt struck, and now in the snow he picked up a paw and brought it back to Rush. He saw right away there was no blood. The skin was real and furry, all right, but there was no blood. Because the bone was steel and the muscles were springs and the thing had been a robot.

The Alien rose up from his cot, whistling with annoyance. When that ship had come in his attention had been distracted from one of the robots, and of course the miserable thing had gone blundering right out into the humans. He thought for a while that the humans would overlook it—the seeing was poor and they undoubtedly would still think of it as animal, even with its firing ports open—but then he checked the robot and saw that a piece was missing and knew that the humans had found it. Well, he thought unhappily, flowing into his suit, no chance now to disable that other ship. The humans would never let another animal near.

And therefore—for he was, above all, a flexible being—he would proceed to another plan. The settlement would have to be detonated. And for that he would have to leave his own shelter and go out in that miserable cold and lie down in one of his bunkers which was much farther away. No need to risk blowing himself up with his own bombs; but still, that awful cold.

He dismissed his regrets and buckled his suit into place. It carried him up the stairs and bore him out into the snow. After one whiff of the cold he snapped his view-plate shut and immediately, as he had expected, it began to film with snow. Well, no matter, he would guide the unit by coordinates and it would find the bunker itself. No need for caution now. The plan was nearly ended.

In spite of his recent setback, the Alien lay back and allowed himself the satisfaction of a full tremble. The plan had worked very nearly to perfection, as of course it should, and he delighted in the contemplation of it.

When the humans were first detected, in the region of Bootes, much thought had gone into the proper method of learning their technology without being discovered themselves. There was little purpose in destroying the humans without first learning from them. Life was really a remarkable thing—one never knew what critical secrets a starborne race possessed. Hence the robots. And it was an extraordinary plan, an elegant plan. The Alien trembled again.

The humans were moving outward toward the rim; their base was apparently somewhere beyond Centaurus. Therefore a ring of defense was thrown up on most of the habitable worlds toward which the humans were coming—oh, a delightful plan—and the humans came down one by one and never realized that there was any defense at all.

With a cleverness which was almost excruciating, the Aliens had carefully selected a number of animals native to each world, and then constructed robot duplicates. So simple then to place the robots down on a world with a single Director, then wait . . . for the humans to inhabit. Naturally the humans screened all the animals and scouted a planet pretty thoroughly before they set up a colony. Naturally their snares and their hungers caught no robots and never found the deep-buried Alien Director.

Then the humans relaxed and began to make homes, never realizing that in among the animals which gamboled playfully in the trees there was one which did not gambol, but watched. Never once noticing the monkeylike animals, or the small thing like a rabbit which was a camera eye, or the thing like a rat, which took chemical samples, or the thing like a lizard which cut wires.

The Alien rumbled on through the snow, trembling so much now with ecstasy and anticipation that the suit which bore him almost lost its balance. He very nearly fell over before he stopped trembling, and then he contained himself. In a little while, a very little while, there would be time enough for trembling.

"They could've been here till the sun went out," Rush said, "and we never would've known."

"I wonder how much they've found out," Dylan said.

Rush was holding the paw.

"Pretty near everything, I guess. This stuff don't stop at monkeys. Could be any size, any kind. . . . Look, let's get down into camp and tell 'em."

Dylan rose slowly to a kneeling position, peering dazedly out into the far white trees. His mind was turning over and over, around and around, like a roulette wheel. But at the center of his mind there was one thought, and it was rising up slowly now, through the waste and waiting of the years. He felt a vague surprise.

"Gettin' kind of dark," he said.

Rush swore. "Let's go. Let's get out of here." He tugged once at Dylan's arm and started off on his knees.

Dylan said, "Wait."

Rush stopped. Through the snow he tried to see Dylan's eyes. The soldier was still looking into the woods.

Dylan's voice was halting and almost inaudible. "They know everything about us. We don't know anything about them. They're probably sittin' out there right now, a swarm of 'em there behind those trees, waitin' for it to get real nice and dark."

He paused. "If I could get just one."

It was totally unexpected, to Dylan as well as Rush. The time for this sort of thing was past, the age was done, and for a long while neither of them fully understood.

"C'mon," Rush said with exasperation.

Dylan shook his head, marveling at himself. "I'll be with you in a little while."

Rush came near and looked questioningly into his face.

"Listen," Dylan said hurriedly, "we only need *one*. If we

could just get one back to a lab we'd at least have some clue
to what they are. This way we don't know anything. We
can't just cut and run." He struggled with the unfamiliar,
time-lost words. "We got to make a stand."

He turned from Rush and lay forward on his belly in the
snow. He could feel his heart beating against the soft white
cushion beneath him. There was no time to look at this
calmly, and he was glad of that. He spent some time being
very much afraid of the unknown things beyond the trees,
but even then he realized that this was the one thing in his
life he had to do.

It is not a matter of dying, he thought, but of *doing*.
Sooner or later a man must do a thing which justifies his
life, or the life is not worth living. The long, cold line of his
existence had reached this point, here and now in the snow
at this moment. He would go on from here as a man . . . or
not at all.

Rush had sat down beside him, beginning to understand,
watching without words. He was an old man. Like all earthmen, he had never fought with his hands. He had not fought
the land or the tides or the weather or any of the million
bitter sicknesses which man had grown up fighting, and he
was beginning to realize that somewhere along the line he
had been betrayed. Now, with a dead paw of the enemy in
his hand, he did not feel like a man. And he was ready to
fight now, but it was much too late and he saw with a vast
leaden shame that he did not know how, could not even
begin.

"Can I help?" he said.

Dylan shook his head. "Go back and let them know
about the robots, and if the ship is ready to leave before I
get back, well—then good luck."

He started to slither forward on his belly, but Rush reached
out and grabbed him, holding with one hand to peace and
gentleness and the soft days which were ending.

"Listen," he said, "you don't owe anybody."

Dylan stared at him with surprise. "I know," he said, and
then he slipped up over the mound before him and headed
for the trees.

Now what he needed was luck. Just good, plain old luck.
He didn't know where they were or how many there were or
what kinds there were, and the chances were good that one
of them was watching him right now. Well, then, he needed

some luck. He inched forward slowly, carefully, watching the oncoming line of trees. The snow was falling on him in big, leafy flakes and that was fine, because the blackness of his suit was much too distinct, and the more white he was, the better. Even so, it was becoming quite dark by now, and he thought he had a chance. He reached the first tree.

Silently he slipped off his heavy cap. The visor got in his way, and above all he must be able to see. He let the snow thicken on his hair before he raised himself on his elbows and looked outward.

There was nothing but the snow and the dead quiet and the stark white boles of the trees. He slid past the first trunk to the next, moving forward on his elbows with his pistol in his right hand. His elbow struck a rock and it hurt and his face was freezing. Once he rubbed snow from his eyebrows. Then he came through the trees and lay down before a slight rise, thinking.

Better to go around than over. But if anything is watching, it is most likely watching from above.

Therefore go around and come back up from behind. Yes.

His nose had begun to run. With great care he crawled among some large rocks, hoping against hope that he would not sneeze. Why had nothing seen him? Was something following him now? He turned to look behind him, but it was darker now and becoming difficult to see. But he would have to look behind him more often.

He was moving down a gorge. There were large trees above him and he needed their shelter, but he could not risk slipping down the sides of the gorge. And far off, weakly, out of the gray cold ahead, he heard a noise.

He lay down in the snow, listening. With a slow, thick shuffle, a thing was moving through the trees before him. In a moment he saw that it was not coming toward him. He lifted his head but saw nothing. Much more slowly, now, he crawled again. The thing was moving down the left side of the gorge ahead, coming away from the rise he had circled. It was moving without caution, and he worried that if he did not hurry he would lose it. But for the life of him he couldn't stand up.

The soldier went forward on his hands and knees. When his clothes hung down, the freezing cold entered his throat and shocked his body, which was sweating. He shifted his

gun to his gloved hand and blew on the bare fingers of his
right, still crawling. When he reached the other end of the
gorge he stood upright against a rock wall and looked in the
direction of the shuffling thing.

He saw it just as it turned. It was a great black lump on a
platform. The platform had legs, and the thing was plodding
methodically upon a path which would bring it past him. It
had come down from the rise and was rounding the gorge
when Dylan saw it. It did not see him.

If he had not ducked quickly and brought up his gun, the
monkey would not have seen him either, but there was no
time for regret. The monkey was several yards to the right
of the lump on the platform when he heard it start running;
he had to look up this time, and saw it leaping toward him
over the snow.

All right, he said to himself. His first shot took the monkey in the head, where the eyes were. As the thing crashed
over, there was a hiss and a stench and flame seared into his
shoulder and the side of his face. He lurched to the side,
trying to see, his gun at arm's length as the lump on the
platform spun toward him. He fired four times. Three bolts
went home in the lump; the fourth tore a leg off the platform and the whole thing fell over.

Dylan crawled painfully behind a rock, his left arm useless. The silence had come back again and he waited, but
neither of the Alien things moved. Nothing else moved in
the woods around him. He turned his face up to the falling
snow and let it come soothingly upon the awful wound in his
side.

After a while he looked out at the monkey. It had risen to
a sitting position but was frozen in the motion of rising. It
had ceased to function when he hit the lump. Out of the
numbness and the pain he felt a great gladness rising.

The guide. He had killed the guide.

He would not be cautious any more. Maybe some of the
other robots were self-directing and dangerous, but they
could be handled. He went to the lump, stared at it without
feeling. A black, doughy bulge was swelling out through one
of the holes.

It was too big to carry, but he would have to take something back. He went over and took the monkey by a stiff
jutting arm and began dragging it back toward the village.

Now he began to stumble. It was dark and he was very

tired. But the steel he had been forging in his breast was complete, and the days which were coming would be days full of living. He would walk with big shoulders and he would not bother to question, because man was not born to live out his days at home, by the fire.

It was a very big thing that Dylan had learned and he could not express it, but he knew it all the same, knew it beyond understanding. And so he went home to his people.

One by one, increasing, in the wee black corner of space which man had taken for his own, other men were learning. And the snow fell and the planets whirled; and when it was spring where Dylan had fought, men were already leaping back out to the stars.

FAREWELL TO THE MASTER

BY HARRY BATES

1

From his perch high on the ladder above the museum floor, Cliff Sutherland studied carefully each line and shadow of the great robot, then turned and looked thoughtfully down at the rush of visitors come from all over the solar system to see Gnut and the traveler for themselves and to hear once again their amazing, tragic story.

He himself had come to feel an almost proprietary interest in the exhibit, and with some reason. He had been the only freelance picture reporter on the Capitol grounds when the visitors from the Unknown had arrived, and had obtained the first professional shots of the ship. He had witnessed at close hand every event of the next mad few days. He had thereafter photographed many times the eight-foot robot, the ship, and the beautiful slain ambassador, Klaatu, and his imposing tomb out in the center of the Tidal Basin, and, such was the continuing news value of the event to the billions of persons throughout habitable space, he was there now once more to get still other shots and, if possible, a new "angle."

This time he was after a picture which showed Gnut as weird and menacing. The shots he had taken the day before had not given quite the effect he wanted, and he hoped to get it today; but the light was not yet right and he had to wait for the afternoon to wane a little.

The last of the crowd admitted in the present group hurried in, exclaiming at the great pure green curves of the mysterious time-space traveler, then completely forgetting the ship at sight of the awesome figure and great head of the giant Gnut. Hinged robots of crude man-like appearance were familiar enough, but never had Earthling eyes lain on one like this. For Gnut had almost exactly the shape of a man—a giant, but a man—with greenish metal for man's covering flesh, and greenish metal for man's bulging muscles. Except for a loin cloth, he was nude. He stood like the powerful god of the machine of some undreamed-of scientific civilization, on his face a look of sullen brooding thought. Those who looked at him did not make jests or idle remarks, and those nearest him usually did not speak at all. His strange, internally illuminated red eyes were so set that every observer felt they were fixed on himself alone, and he engendered a feeling that he might at any moment step forward in anger and perform unimaginable deeds.

A slight rustling sound came from speakers hidden in the ceiling above, and at once the noises of the crowd lessened. The recorded lecture was about to be given. Cliff sighed. He knew the thing by heart; had even been present when the recording was made, and met the speaker, a young chap named Stillwell.

"Ladies and gentlemen," began a clear and well-modulated voice—but Cliff was no longer attending. The shadows in the hollows of Gnut's face and figure were deeper; it was almost time for his shot. He picked up and examined the proofs of the pictures he had taken the day before and compared them critically with the subject.

As he looked a wrinkle came to his brow. He had not noticed it before, but now, suddenly, he had the feeling that since yesterday something about Gnut was changed. The pose before him was the identical one in the photographs, every detail on comparison seemed the same, but nevertheless the feeling persisted. He took up his viewing glass and more carefully compared subject and photographs, line by line. And then he saw that there was a difference.

With sudden excitement, Cliff snapped two pictures at different exposures. He knew he should wait a little and take others, but he was so sure he had stumbled on an important mystery that he had to get going, and quickly folding his accessory equipment he descended the ladder and made his way out. Twenty minutes later, consumed with curiosity, he was developing the new shots in his hotel bedroom.

* * *

What Cliff saw when he compared the negatives taken yesterday and today caused his scalp to tingle. Here was a slant indeed! And apparently no one but he knew! Still, what he had discovered, though it would have made the front page of every paper in the solar system, was after all only a lead. The story, what really had happened, he knew no better than anyone else. It must be his job to find out.

And that meant he would have to secrete himself in the building and stay there all night. That very night; there was still time for him to get back before closing. He would take a small, very fast infrared camera that could see in the dark, and he would get the real picture and the story.

He snatched up the little camera, grabbed an aircab, and hurried back to the museum. The place was filled with another section of the ever-present queue, and the lecture was just ending. He thanked Heaven that his arrangement with the museum permitted him to go in and out at will.

He had already decided what to do. First he made his way to the "floating" guard and asked a single question, and anticipation broadened on his face as he heard the expected answer. The second thing was to find a spot where he would be safe from the eyes of the men who would close the floor for the night. There was only one possible place, the laboratory set up behind the ship. Boldly he showed his press credentials to the second guard, stationed at the partitioned passageway leading to it, stating that he had come to interview the scientists; and in a moment was at the laboratory door.

He had been there a number of times and knew the room well. It was a large area roughly partitioned off for the work of the scientists engaged in breaking their way into the ship and full of a confusion of massive and heavy objects—electric and hot-air ovens, carboys of chemicals, asbestos sheeting, compressors, basins, ladles, a microscope, and a great deal of smaller equipment common to a metallurgical laboratory. Three white-smocked men were deeply engrossed in an experiment at the far end. Cliff, waiting a good moment, slipped inside and hid himself under a table half buried with supplies. He felt reasonably safe from detection there. Very soon now the scientists would be going home for the night.

From beyond the ship he could hear another section of the waiting queue filing in—the last, he hoped, of the day. He settled himself as comfortably as he could. In a moment the lecture would begin. He had to smile when he thought of one thing the recording would say.

Then there it was again—the clear, trained voice of the chap Stillwell. The foot scrapings and whispers of the crowd died away, and Cliff could hear every word in spite of the great bulk of the ship lying interposed.

"Ladies and gentlemen," began the familiar words, "the Smithsonian Institution welcomes you to its new Interplanetary Wing and to the marvelous exhibits at this moment before you."

A slight pause. "All of you must know by now something of what happened here three months ago, if indeed you did not see it for yourself in the telescreen," the voice went on. "The few facts are briefly told. A little after 5:00 P.M. on September sixteenth, visitors to Washington thronged the grounds outside this building in their usual numbers and no doubt with their usual thoughts. The day was warm and fair. A stream of people was leaving the main entrance of the museum just outside in the direction you are facing. This wing, of course, was not here at that time. Everyone was homeward bound, tired no doubt from hours on their feet, seeing the exhibits of the museum and visiting the many buildings on the grounds nearby. And then it happened.

"On the area just to your right, just as it is now, appeared the time-space traveler. It appeared in the blink of an eye. It did not come down from the sky; dozens of witnesses swear to that; it just appeared. One moment it was not here, the next it was. It appeared on the very spot it now rests on.

"The people nearest the ship were stricken with panic and ran back with cries and screams. Excitement spread out over Washington in a tidal wave. Radio, television, and newspapermen rushed here at once. Police formed a wide cordon around the ship, and army units appeared and trained guns and ray projectors on it. The direst calamity was feared.

"For it was recognized from the very beginning that this was no spaceship from anywhere in the solar system. Every child knew that only two spaceships had ever been built on Earth, and none at all on any of the other planets and satellites; and of those two, one had been destroyed when it was pulled into the sun, and the other had just been reported safely arrived on Mars. Then, the ones made here had a shell of a strong aluminum alloy, while this one, as you see, is of an unknown greenish metal.

"The ship appeared and just sat here. No one emerged, and there was no sign that it contained life of any kind. That, as much as any single thing, caused excitement to skyrocket. Who, or what, was inside? Were the visitors hostile or friendly? Where did the ship come from? How did it arrive so suddenly right on this spot without dropping from the sky?

"For two days the ship rested here, just as you now see it, without motion or sign that it contained life. Long before the end of that time the scientists had explained that it was not so much a spaceship as a space-time traveler, because only such a ship could arrive as this one did—materialize. They pointed out that such a traveler, while theoretically understandable to us Earthmen, was far beyond attempt at our present state of knowledge, and that this one, activated by relativity principles, might well have come from the far corner of the Universe, from a distance which light itself would require millions of years to cross.

"When this opinion was disseminated, public tension grew until it was almost intolerable. Where had the traveler come from? Who were its occupants? Why had they come to Earth? Above all, why did they not show themselves? Were they perhaps preparing some terrible weapon of destruction?

"And where was the ship's entrance port? Men who dared go look reported that none could be found. No slightest break or crack marred the perfect smoothness of the ship's curving ovoid surface. And a delegation of high-ranking officials who visited the ship could not, by knocking, elicit from its occupants any sign that they had been heard.

"At last, after exactly two days, in full view of tens of thousands of persons assembled and standing well back, and under the muzzles of scores of the army's most powerful guns and ray projectors, an opening appeared in the wall of the ship, and a ramp slid down, and out stepped a man, godlike in appearance and human in form, closely followed by a giant robot. And when they touched the ground the ramp slid back and the entrance closed as before."

"It was immediately apparent to all the assembled thousands that the stranger was friendly. The first thing he did was to raise his right arm high in the universal gesture of peace; but it was not that which impressed those nearest so much as the expression on his face, which radiated kindness, wisdom, the purest nobility. In his delicately tinted robe he looked like a benign god.

"At once, waiting for this appearance, a large committee of high-ranking government officials and army officers advanced to greet the visitor. With graciousness and dignity the man pointed to himself, then to his robot companion, and said in perfect English with a peculiar accent, 'I am Klaatu,' or a name that sounded like that, 'and this is Gnut.' The names were not well understood at the time, but the sight-and-sound film of the television men caught them and they became known to everyone subsequently.

"And then occurred the thing which shall always be to the shame of the human race. From a treetop a hundred yards away came a wink of violet light and Klaatu fell. The assembled multitude stood for a moment stunned, not comprehending what had happened. Gnut, a little behind his master and to one side, slowly turned his body a little toward him, moved his head twice, and stood still, in exactly the position you now see him.

"Then followed pandemonium. The police pulled the slayer of Klaatu out of the tree. They found him mentally unbalanced; he kept crying that the devil had come to kill everyone on Earth. He was taken away, and Klaatu, although obviously dead, was rushed to the nearest hospital to see if anything could be done to revive him. Confused and frightened crowds milled about the Capitol grounds the rest of the afternoon and much of that night. The ship remained as silent and motionless as before. And Gnut, too, never moved from the position he had come to rest in.

"Gnut never moved again. He remained exactly as you see him all that night and for the ensuing days. When the mausoleum in the Tidal Basin was built, Klaatu's burial services took place where you are standing now, attended by the highest functionaries of all the great countries of the world. It was not only the most appropriate but the safest thing to do, for if there should be other living creatures in the traveler, as seemed possible at that time, they had to be impressed by the sincere sorrow of us Earthmen at what had happened. If Gnut was still alive, or perhaps I had better say functionable, there was no sign. He stood as you see him during the entire ceremony. He stood so while his master was floated out to the mausoleum and given to the centuries with the tragically short sight-and-sound record of his historic visit. And he stood so afterward, day after day, night after night, in fair weather and in rain, never moving or showing by any slightest sign that he was aware of what had gone on.

"After the interment, this wing was built out from the museum to cover the traveler and Gnut. Nothing else could very well have been done, it was learned, for both Gnut and the ship were far too heavy to be moved safely by any means at hand.

"You have heard about the efforts of our metallurgists since then to break into the ship, and of their complete failure. Behind the ship now, as you can see from either end, a partitioned workroom has been set up where the attempt still goes on. So far its wonderful greenish metal has proved inviolable. Not only are they unable to get in, but they cannot even find the exact place from which Klaatu and Gnut emerged. The chalk marks you see are the best approximation.

"Many people have feared that Gnut was only temporarily deranged, and that on return to function might be dangerous, so the scientist have completely destroyed all chance of that. The greenish metal of which he is made seemed to be the same as that of the ship and could no more be attacked, they found, nor could they find any way to penetrate to his internals; but they had other means. They set electrical currents of tremendous voltages and amperages through him. They applied terrific heat to all parts of his metal shell. They immersed him for days in gases and acids and strongly corroding solutions, and they have bombarded him with every known kind of ray. You need have no fear of him now. He cannot possibly have retained the ability to function in any way.

"But—a word of caution. The officials of the government know that visitors will not show any disrespect in this building. It may be that the unknown and unthinkably powerful civilization from which Klaatu and Gnut came may send other emissaries to see what happened to them. Whether or not they do, not one of us must be found amiss in our attitude. None of us could very well anticipate what happened, and we all are immeasurably sorry, but we are still in a sense responsible, and must do what we can to avoid possible retaliations.

"You will be allowed to remain five minutes longer, and

then, when the gong sounds, you will please leave promptly. The robot attendants along the wall will answer any questions you may have.

"Look well, for before you stand stark symbols of the achievement, mystery, and frailty of the human race."

The recorded voice ceased speaking. Cliff, carefully moving his cramped limbs, broke out in a wide smile. If they knew what he knew!

For his photographs told a slightly different story from that of the lecturer. In yesterday's a line of the figured floor showed clearly at the outer edge of the robot's near foot; in today's, *that line was covered*. Gnut had moved!

Or been moved, though this was very unlikely. Where were the derrick and other evidence of such activity? It could hardly have been done in one night, and all signs so quickly concealed. And why should it be done at all?

Still, to make sure, he had asked the guard. He could almost remember verbatim his answer:

"No, Gnut has neither moved nor been moved since the death of his master. A special point was made of keeping him in the position he assumed at Klaatu's death. The floor was built in under him, and the scientists who completed his derangement erected their apparatus around him, just as he stands. You need have no fears."

Cliff smiled again. He did not have any fears.

Not yet.

2

A moment later the big gong above the entrance doors rang the closing hour, and immediately following it a voice from the speakers called out, "Five o'clock, ladies and gentlemen. Closing time, ladies and gentlemen."

The three scientists, as if surprised it was so late, hurriedly washed their hands, changed to their street clothes and disappeared down the partitioned corridor, oblivious of the young picture man hidden under the table. The slide and scrape of the feet on the exhibition floor rapidly dwindled, until at last there were only the steps of the two guards walking from one point to another, making sure everything was all right for the night. For just a moment one of them glanced in the doorway of the laboratory, then he joined the other at the entrance. Then the great metal doors clanged to, and there was silence.

Cliff waited several minutes, then carefully poked his way out from under the table. As he straightened up, a faint tinkling crash sounded at the floor by his feet. Carefully stooping, he found the shattered remains of a thin glass pipette. He had knocked if off the table.

That caused him to realize something he had not thought of before: A Gnut who had moved might be a Gnut who could see and hear—and really be dangerous. He would have to be very careful.

He looked about him. The room was bounded at the ends by two fiber partitions which at the inner ends followed close under the curving bottom of the ship. The inner side of the room was the ship itself, and the outer was the southern wall of the wing. There were four large high windows. The only entrance was by way of the passage.

Without moving, from his knowledge of the building, he made his plan. The wing was connected with the western end of the museum by a doorway, never used, and extended westward toward the Washington Monument. The ship lay nearest the southern wall, and Gnut stood out in front of it, not far from the northeast corner and at the opposite end of the room from the entrance of the building and the passageway leading to the laboratory. By retracing his steps he would come out on the floor at the point farthest removed from the robot. This was just what he wanted, for on the other side of the entrance, on a low platform, stood a paneled table containing the lecture apparatus, and this table was the only object in the room which afforded a place for him to lie concealed while watching what might go on. The only other objects on the floor were the six manlike robot attendants in fixed stations along the northern wall, placed there to answer visitors' questions. He would have to gain the table.

He turned and began cautiously tiptoeing out of the laboratory and down the passageway. It was already dark there, for what light still entered the exhibition hall was shut off by the great bulk of the ship. He reached the end of the room without making a sound. Very carefully he edged forward and peered around the bottom of the ship at Gnut.

He had a momentary shock. The robot's eyes were right on him!—or so it seemed. Was that only the effect of the set of his eyes, he wondered, or was he already discovered? The position of Gnut's head did not seem to have changed, at any rate. Probably everything was all right, but he wished he did not have to cross that end of the room with the feeling that the robot's eyes were following him.

He drew back and sat down and waited. It would have to be totally dark before he essayed the trip to the table.

He waited a full hour, until the faint beams from the lamps on the grounds outside began to make the room seem to grow lighter; then he got up and peeped around the ship once more. The robot's eyes seemed to pierce right at him as before, only now, due no doubt to the darkness, the strange internal illumination seemed much brighter. This was a chilling thing. Did Gnut know he was there? What were the thoughts of the robot? What *could* be the thoughts of a manmade machine, even so wonderful a one as Gnut?

It was time for the cross, so Cliff slung his camera around on his back, went down on his hands and knees, and carefully moved to the edge of the entrance hall. There he fitted himself as closely as he could into the angle made by it with the floor and started inching ahead. Never pausing, not risking a glance at Gnut's unnerving red eyes, moving an inch at a time, he snaked along. He took ten minutes to cross the space of a hundred feet, and he was wet with perspiration when his fingers at last touched the one-foot rise of the platform on which the table stood. Still slowly, silently as a shadow, he made his way over the edge and melted behind the protection of the table. At last he was there.

He relaxed for a moment, then, anxious to know whether he had been seen, carefully turned and looked around the side of the table.

Gnut's eyes were now full on him! Or so it seemed. Against the general darkness, the robot loomed a mysterious and still darker shadow that, for all his being a hundred and fifty feet away, seemed to dominate the room. Cliff could not tell whether the position of his body was changed or not.

But if Gnut was looking at him, he at least did nothing else. Not by the slightest motion that Cliff could discern did he appear to move. His position was the one he had maintained these last three months, in the darkness, in the rain, and this last week in the museum.

*   *   *

Cliff made up his mind not to give way to fear. He became conscious of his own body. The cautious trip had taken something out of him—his knees and elbows burned and his trousers were no doubt ruined. But these were little things if what he hoped for came to pass. If Gnut so much as moved, and he could catch him with his infrared camera, he would have a story that would buy him fifty suits of clothes. And if on top of that he could learn the purpose of Gnut's moving—provided there was a purpose—that would be a story that would set the world on its ears.

He settled down to a period of waiting; there was no telling when Gnut would move, if indeed he would move that night. Cliff's eyes had long been adjusted to the dark and he could make out the larger objects well enough. From time to time he peered out at the robot—peered long and hard, till his outlines wavered and he seemed to move, and he had to blink and rest his eyes to be sure it was only his imagination.

Again the minute hand of his watch crept around the dial. The inactivity made Cliff careless, and for longer and longer periods he kept his head back out of sight behind the table. And so it was that when Gnut did move he was scared almost out of his wits. Dull and a little bored, he suddenly found the robot out on the floor, halfway in his direction.

But that was not the most frightening thing. It was that when he did see Gnut he did not catch him moving! He was stopped as still as a cat in the middle of stalking a mouse. His eyes were now much brighter, and there was no remaining doubt about their direction: he was looking right at Cliff!

Scarcely breathing, half hypnotized, Cliff looked back. His thoughts tumbled. What was the robot's intention? Why had he stopped so still? Was he being stalked? How could he move with such silence?

In the heavy darkness Gnut's eyes moved nearer. Slowly but in perfect rhythm that almost imperceptible sound of his footsteps beat on Cliff's ears. Cliff, usually resourceful enough, was this time caught flatfooted. Frozen with fear, utterly incapable of fleeing, he lay where he was while the metal monster with the fiery eyes came on.

For a moment Cliff all but fainted, and when he recovered, there was Gnut towering over him, legs almost within reach. He was bending slightly, burning his terrible eyes right into his own!

Too late to try to think of running now. Trembling like any cornered mouse, Cliff waited for the blow that would crush him. For an eternity, it seemed, Gnut scrutinized him without moving. For each second of that eternity Cliff expected annihilation, sudden, quick, complete. And then suddenly and unexpectedly it was over. Gnut's body straightened and he stepped back. He turned. And then, with the almost jerkless rhythm which only he among robots possessed, he started back toward the place from which he came.

Cliff could hardly believe he had been spared. Gnut could have crushed him like a worm—and he had only turned around and gone back. Why? It could not be supposed that a robot was capable of human considerations.

Gnut went straight to the other end of the traveler. At a certain place he stopped and made a curious succession of sounds. At once Cliff saw an opening, blacker than the gloom of the building, appear in the ship's side, and it was followed by a slight sliding sound as a ramp slid out and met the floor. Gnut walked up the ramp and, stooping a little, disappeared inside the ship.

Then, for the first time, Cliff remembered the picture he had come to get. Gnut had moved, but he had not caught him! But at least now, whatever opportunities there might be later, he could get the shot of the ramp connecting with the opened door; so he twisted his camera into position, set it for the proper exposure, and took a shot.

A long time passed and Gnut did not come out. What could he be doing inside? Cliff wondered. Some of his courage returned to him and he toyed with the idea of creeping forward and peeping through the port, but he found he had not the courage for that. Gnut had spared him, at least for the time, but there was no telling how far his tolerance would go.

An hour passed, then another. Gnut was doing something inside the ship, but what? Cliff could not imagine. If the robot had been a human being, he knew he would have sneaked a look, but as it was, he was too much of an unknown quantity. Even the simplest of Earth's robots under certain circumstances were inexplicable things; what, then, of this one, come from an unknown and even unthinkable civilization, by far the most wonderful construction ever seen—what superhuman powers might he not possess? All that the scientists of Earth could do had not served to derange him. Acid, heat, rays, terrific crushing blows—he had withstood them all; even his finish had been unmarred. He might be able to see perfectly in the dark. And right where he was, he might be able to hear or in some way sense the least change in Cliff's position.

More time passed, and then, sometime after two o'clock in the morning, a simple homely thing happened, but a thing so unexpected that for a moment it quite destroyed Cliff's equilibrium. Suddenly, through the dark and silent building, there was a faint whir of wings, soon followed by the piercing, sweet voice of a bird. A mockingbird. Somewhere in this gloom above his head. Clear and full-throated were its notes; a dozen little songs it sang, one after the other without pause between—short insistent calls, twirrings, coaxings, cooings—the spring love song of perhaps the finest singer in the world. Then, as suddenly as it began, the voice was silent.

If an invading army had poured out of the traveler, Cliff would have been less surprised. The month was December; even in Florida the mockingbirds had not yet begun their song. How had one gotten into that tight, gloomy museum? How and why was it singing there?

He waited, full of curiosity. Then suddenly he was aware of Gnut, standing just outside the port of the ship. He stood quite still, his glowing eyes turned squarely in Cliff's direction. For a moment the hush in the museum seemed to deepen; then it was broken by a soft thud on the floor near where Cliff was lying.

He wondered. The light in Gnut's eyes changed, and he started his almost jerkless walk in Cliff's direction. When only a little away, the robot stopped, bent over, and picked something from the floor. For some time he stood without motion and looked at a little object he held in his hand. Cliff knew, though he could not see, that it was the mockingbird. Its body, for he was sure that it had lost its song forever. Gnut then turned, and without a glance at Cliff, walked back to the ship and again went inside.

Hours passed while Cliff waited for some sequel to this surprising happening. Perhaps it was because of his curiosity that his fear of the robot began to lessen. Surely if the mechanism was unfriendly, if he intended him any harm, he would have finished him before, when he had such a perfect opportunity. Cliff began to nerve himself for a quick look inside the port. And a picture; he must remember the picture. He kept forgetting the very reason he was there.

It was in the deeper darkness of the false dawn when he got sufficient courage and made the start. He took off his shoes, and in his stockinged feet, his shoes tied together and slung over his shoulder, he moved stiffly but rapidly to a position behind the nearest of the six robot attendants stationed along the wall, then paused for some sign which might indicate that Gnut knew he had moved. Hearing none, he slipped along behind the next robot attendant and paused again. Bolder now, he made in one spurt all the distance to the farthest one, the sixth, fixed just opposite the port of the ship. There he met with a disappointment. No light that he could detect was visible within; there was only darkness and the all-permeating silence. Still, he had better get the picture. He raised his camera, focused it on the dark opening, and gave the film a comparatively long exposure. Then he stood there, at a loss what to do next.

As he paused, a peculiar series of muffled noises reached his ears, apparently from within the ship. Animal noises—first scrapings and pantings, punctuated by several sharp clicks, then deep, rough snarls, interrupted by more scrapings and pantings, as if a struggle of some kind were going on. Then suddenly, before Cliff could even decide to run back to the table, a low, wide, dark shape bounded out of the port and immediately turned and grew to the height of a man. A terrible fear swept over Cliff, even before he knew what the shape was.

In the next second Gnut appeared in the port and stepped unhesitatingly down the ramp toward the shape. As he advanced it backed slowly away for a few feet; but then it stood its ground, and thick arms rose from its sides and began a loud drumming on its chest, while from its throat came a deep roar of defiance. Only one creature in the world beat its chest and made a sound like that. The shape was a gorilla!

And a huge one!

Gnut kept advancing, and when close, charged forward and grappled with the beast. Cliff would not have guessed

that Gnut could move so fast. In the darkness he could not
see the details of what happened; all he knew was that the
two great shapes, the titanic metal Gnut and the squat but
terrifically strong gorilla, merged for a moment with silence
on the robot's part and terrible, deep, indescribable roars
on the other's; then the two separated, and it was as if the
gorilla had been flung back and away.

The animal at once rose to its full height and roared
deafeningly. Gnut advanced. They closed again, and the
separation of before was repeated. The robot continued
inexorably, and now the gorilla began to fall back down the
building. Suddenly the beast darted at a manlike shape
against the wall, and with one rapid side movement dashed
the fifth robot attendant to the floor and decapitated it.

Tense with fear, Cliff crouched behind his own robot
attendant. He thanked Heaven that Gnut was between him
and the gorilla and was continuing his advance. The gorilla
backed farther, darted suddenly at the next robot in the
row, and with strength almost unbelievable picked it from
its roots and hurled it at Gnut. With a sharp metallic clang,
robot hit robot, and the one of Earth bounced off to one
side and rolled to a stop.

Cliff cursed himself for it afterward, but again he completely forgot the picture. The gorilla kept falling back down
the building, demolishing with terrific bursts of rage every
robot attendant that he passed and throwing the pieces at
the implacable Gnut. Soon they arrived opposite the table,
and Cliff now thanked his stars he had come away. There
followed a brief silence. Cliff could not make out what was
going on, but he imagined that the gorilla had at last reached
the corner of the wing and was trapped.

If he was, it was only for a moment. The silence was
suddenly shattered by a terrific roar, and the thick, squat
shape of the animal came bounding toward Cliff. He came
all the way back and turned just between Cliff and the port
of the ship. Cliff prayed frantically for Gnut to come back
quickly, for there was now only the last remaining robot
attendant between him and the madly dangerous brute. Out
of the dimness Gnut did appear. The gorilla rose to its full
height and again beat its chest and roared its challenge.

And then occurred a curious thing. It fell on all fours and
slowly rolled over on its side, as if weak or hurt. Then

panting, making frightening noises, it forced itself again to its feet and faced the oncoming Gnut. As it waited, its eye was caught by the last robot attendant and perhaps Cliff, shrunk close behind it. With a surge of terrible destructive rage, the gorilla waddled sideward toward Cliff, but this time, even through his panic, he saw that the animal moved with difficulty, again apparently sick or severely wounded. He jumped back just in time; the gorilla pulled out the last robot attendant and hurled it violently at Gnut, missing him narrowly.

That was its last effort. The weakness caught it again; it dropped heavily on one side, rocked back and forth a few times, and fell to twitching. Then it lay still and did not move again.

The first faint pale light of the dawn was seeping into the room. From the corner where he had taken refuge, Cliff watched closely the great robot. It seemed to him that he behaved very queerly. He stood over the dead gorilla, looking down at him with what in a human would be called sadness. Cliff saw this clearly; Gnut's heavy greenish features bore a thoughtful, grieving expression new to his experience. For some moments he stood so, then as might a father with his sick child, he leaned over, lifted the great animal in his metal arms and carried it tenderly within the ship.

Cliff flew back to the table, suddenly fearful of yet other dangerous and inexplicable happenings. It struck him that he might be safer in the laboratory, and with trembling knees he made his way there and hid in one of the big ovens. He prayed for full daylight. His thoughts were chaos. Rapidly, one after another, his mind churned up the amazing events of the night, but all was mystery; it seemed there could be no rational explanation for them. That mockingbird. The gorilla. Gnut's sad expression and his tenderness. What could account for a fantastic melange like that!

Gradually full daylight did come. A long time passed. At last he began to believe he might yet get out of that place of mystery and danger alive. At eight-thirty there were noises at the entrance, and the good sound of human voices came to his ears. He stepped out of the oven and tiptoed to the passageway.

The noises stopped suddenly and there was a frightened exclamation and then the sound of running feet, and then silence. Stealthily Cliff sneaked down the narrow way and peeped fearfully around the ship.

There Gnut was in his accustomed place, in the identical pose he had taken at the death of his master, brooding sullenly and alone over a space traveler once again closed tight and a room that was a shambles. The entrance doors stood open and, heart in his mouth, Cliff ran out.

A few minutes later, safe in his hotel room, completely done in, he sat down for a second and almost at once fell asleep. Later, still in his clothes and still asleep, he staggered over to the bed. He did not wake up till midafternoon.

3

Cliff awoke slowly, at first not realizing that the images tumbling in his head were real memories and not a fantastic dream. It was a recollection of the pictures which brought him to his feet. Hastily he set about developing the film in his camera.

Then in his hands was proof that the events of the night were real. Both shots turned out well. The first showed clearly the ramp leading up to the port as he had dimly discerned it from his position behind the table. The second, of the open port as snapped from in front, was a disappointment, for a blank wall just back of the opening cut off all view of the interior. That would account for the fact that no light had escaped from the ship while Gnut was inside. Assuming Gnut required light for whatever he did.

Cliff looked at the negatives and was ashamed of himself. What a rotten picture man he was to come back with two ridiculous shots like these! He had had a score of opportunities to get real ones—shots of Gnut in action—Gnut's fight with the gorilla—even Gnut holding the mockingbird—spine-chilling stuff!—and all he had brought back were two stills of a doorway. Oh, sure, they were valuable, but he was a grade-A ass.

And to top this brilliant performance, he had fallen asleep!

Well, he'd better get out on the street and find out what was doing.

Quickly he showered, shaved, and changed his clothes, and soon was entering a nearby restaurant patronized by other picture and newsmen. Sitting alone at the lunch bar, he spotted a friend and competitor.

"Well, what do you think?" asked his friend when he took the stool at his side.

"I don't think anything until I've had breakfast," Cliff answered.

"Then haven't you heard?"

"Heard what?" fended Cliff, who knew very well what was coming.

"You're a fine picture man," was the other's remark. "When something really big happens, you are asleep in bed." But then he told him what had been discovered that morning in the museum, and of the world-wide excitement at the news. Cliff did three things at once, successfully—gobbled a substantial breakfast, kept thanking his stars that nothing new had transpired, and showed continuous surprise. Still chewing, he got up and hurried over to the building.

Outside, balked at the door, was a large crowd of the curious, but Cliff had no trouble gaining admittance when he showed his press credentials. Gnut and the ship stood just as he had left them, but the floor had been cleaned up and the pieces of the demolished robot attendants were lined up in one place along the wall. Several other competitor friends of his were there.

"I was away; missed the whole thing," he said to one of them—Gus. "What's supposed to be the explanation for what happened?"

"Ask something easy," was the answer. "Nobody knows. It's thought maybe something came out of the ship, maybe another robot like Gnut. Say—where have you been?"

"Asleep."

"Better catch up. Several billion bipeds are scared stiff. Revenge for the death of Klaatu. Earth about to be invaded."

"But that's—"

"Oh, I know it's all crazy, but that's the story they're being fed; it sells news. But there's a new angle just turned up, very surprising. Come here."

He led Cliff to the table where stood a knot of people looking with great interest at several objects guarded by a technician. Gus pointed to a long slide on which were mounted a number of short dark-brown hairs.

"Those hairs came off a large male gorilla," Gus said with a certain hard-boiled casualness. "Most of them were found among the sweepings of the floor this morning. The rest were found on the robot attendants."

Cliff tried to look astounded. Gus pointed to a test tube partly filled with a light amber fluid.

"And that's blood, diluted—gorilla blood. It was found on Gnut's arms."

"Good Heaven!" Cliff managed to exclaim. "And there's no explanation?"

"Not even a theory. It's your big chance, wonder boy."

Cliff broke away from Gus, unable to maintain his act any longer. He couldn't decide what to do about his story. The press services would bid heavily for it—with all his pictures—but that would take further action out of his hands. In the back of his mind he wanted to stay in the wing again that night, but—well, he simply was afraid. He'd had a pretty stiff dose, and he wanted very much to remain alive.

He walked over and looked a long time at Gnut. No one would ever have guessed that he had moved, or that there had rested on his greenish metal face a look of sadness. Those weird eyes! Cliff wondered if they were really looking at him, as they seemed, recognizing him as the bold intruder of last night. Of what unknown stuff were they made—those materials placed in his eye sockets by one branch of the race of man which all the science of his own could not even serve to disfunction? What was Gnut thinking? What could be the thoughts of a robot—a mechanism of metal poured out of man's clay crucibles? Was he angry at him? Cliff thought not. Gnut had had him, at his mercy—and had walked away.

Dared he stay again?

Cliff thought perhaps he did.

He walked about the room, thinking it over. He felt sure Gnut would move again. A Mikton ray gun would protect him from another gorilla—or fifty of them. He did not yet have the real story. He had come back with two miserable architectural stills!

He might have known from the first that he would stay. At dusk that night, armed with his camera and a small Mikton gun, he lay once more under the table of supplies in the laboratory and heard the metal doors of the wing clang to for the night.

This time he would get the story—and the pictures.

If only no guard was posted inside!

4

Cliff listened hard for a long time for any sound which might tell him that a guard had been left, but the silence within the wing remained unbroken. He was thankful for that—but not quite completely. The gathering darkness and the realization that he was not irrevocably committed made the thought of a companion not altogether unpleasant.

About an hour after it reached maximum darkness he took off his shoes, tied them together and slung them around his neck, down his back, and stole quietly down the passageway to where it opened into the exhibition area. All seemed as it had been the preceding night. Gnut looked an ominous, indistinct shadow at the far end of the room, his glowing red eyes again seemingly right on the spot from which Cliff peeped out. As on the previous night, but even more carefully, Cliff went down on his stomach in the angle of the wall and slowly snaked across to the low platform on which stood the table. Once in its shelter, he fixed his shoes so that they straddled one shoulder, and brought his camera and gun holster around, ready on his breast. This time, he told himself, he would get pictures.

He settled down to wait, keeping Gnut, in full sight every minute. His vision reached maximum adjustment to the darkness. Eventually he began to feel lonely and a little afraid. Gnut's red-glowing eyes were getting on his nerves; he had to keep assuring himself that the robot would not harm him. He had little doubt but that he himself was being watched.

Hours slowly passed. From time to time he heard slight noises at the entrance, on the outside—a guard, perhaps, or maybe curious visitors.

At about nine o'clock he saw Gnut move. First his head alone; it turned so that the eyes burned stronger in the direction where Cliff lay. For a moment that was all; then the dark metal form stirred slightly and began moving forward—straight toward him. Cliff had thought he would not be afraid—much—but now his heart stood still. What would happen this time?

With amazing silence, Gnut drew nearer, until he towered an ominous shadow over the spot where Cliff lay. For a long time his red eyes burned down on the prone man. Cliff trembled all over; this was worse than the first time. Without having planned it, he found himself speaking to the creature.

"You would not hurt me," he pleaded. "I was only curious to see what's going on. It's my job. Can you understand me? I would not harm or bother you. I . . . I couldn't if I wanted to! Please!"

The robot never moved, and Cliff could not guess whether his words had been understood or even heard. When he felt he could not bear the suspense any longer, Gnut reached out and took something from a drawer of the table, or perhaps he put something back in; then he stepped back, turned, and retraced his steps. Cliff was safe! Again the robot had spared him!

Beginning then, Cliff lost much of his fear. He felt sure now that this Gnut would do him no harm. Twice he had had him in his power, and either time he had only looked and quietly moved away. Cliff could not imagine what Gnut had done in the drawer of the table. He watched with the greatest curiosity to see what would happen next.

As on the night before, the robot went straight to the end of the ship and made the peculiar sequence of sounds that opened the port, and when the ramp slid out he went inside. After that Cliff was alone in the darkness for a very long time, probably two hours. Not a sound came from the ship.

Cliff knew he should sneak up to the port and peep inside, but he could not quite bring himself to do it. With his gun he could handle another gorilla, but if Gnut caught him it might be the end. Momentarily he expected something fantastic to happen—he knew not what; maybe the mockingbird's sweet song again, maybe a gorilla, maybe— anything. What did at last happen once more caught him with complete surprise.

He heard a sudden muffled sound, then words—human words—every one familiar.

"Gentlemen," was the first, and then there was a very slight pause. "The Smithsonian Institution welcomes you to its new Interplanetary Wing and to the marvelous exhibits at this moment before you."

It was the recorded voice of Stillwell! But it was not coming through the speakers overhead, but, much muted, from within the ship.

After a slight pause it went on:

"All of you must . . . must—" Here it stammered and came to a stop. Cliff's hair bristled. That stammering was not in the lecture!

For just a moment there was silence; then came a scream, a hoarse man's scream, muffled, from somewhere within the heart of the ship; and it was followed by muted gasps and cries, as of a man in great fright or distress.

Every nerve tight, Cliff watched the port. He heard a thudding noise within the ship, then out the door flew the shadow of what was surely a human being. Gasping and half stumbling, he ran straight down the room in Cliff's direction. When twenty feet away, the great shadow of Gnut followed him out of the port.

Cliff watched, breathless. The man—it was Stillwell, he saw now—came straight for the table behind which Cliff himself lay, as if to get behind it, but when only a few feet away, his knees buckled and he fell to the floor. Suddenly Gnut was standing over him, but Stillwell did not seem to be aware of it. He appeared very ill, but kept making spasmodic futile efforts to creep on to the protection of the table.

Gnut did not move, so Cliff was emboldened to speak.

"What's the matter, Stillwell?" he asked. "Can I help? Don't be afraid. I'm Cliff Sutherland; you know, the picture man."

Without showing the least surprise at finding Cliff there, and clutching at his presence like a drowning man would a straw, Stillwell gasped out:

"Help me! Gnut . . . Gnut—" He seemed unable to go on.

"Gnut what?" asked Cliff. Very conscious of the fire-eyed robot looming above, and afraid even to move out to the man, Cliff added reassuringly: "Gnut won't hurt you. I'm sure he won't. He doesn't hurt me. What's the matter? What can I do?"

With a sudden accession of energy, Stillwell rose on his elbows.

"Where am I?" he asked.

"In the Interplanetary Wing," Cliff answered. "Don't you know?"

Only Stillwell's hard breathing was heard for a moment. Then hoarsely, weakly, he asked:

"How did I get here?"

"I don't know," said Cliff.

"I was making a lecture recording," Stillwell said, "when suddenly I found myself here . . . or I mean in there—"

He broke off and showed a return of his terror.

"Then what?" asked Cliff gently.

"I was in that box—and there, above me, was Gnut, the robot. Gnut! But they made Gnut harmless! He's never moved!"

"Steady, now," said Cliff. "I don't think Gnut will hurt you."

Stillwell fell back on the floor.

"I'm very weak," he gasped. "Something— Will you get a doctor?"

He was utterly unaware that towering above him, eyes boring down at him through the darkness, was the robot he feared so greatly.

As Cliff hesitated, at a loss what to do, the man's breath began coming in short gasps, as regular as the ticking of a clock. Cliff dared to move out to him, but no act on his part could have helped the man now. His gasps weakened and became spasmodic, then suddenly he was completely silent and still. Cliff felt for his heart, then looked up to the eyes in the shadow above.

"He is dead," he whispered.

The robot seemed to understand, or at least to hear. He bent forward and regarded the still figure.

"What is it, Gnut?" Cliff asked the robot suddenly. "What are you doing? Can I help you in any way? Somehow I don't believe you are unfriendly, and I don't believe you killed this man. But what happened? Can you understand me? Can you speak? What is it you're trying to do?"

Gnut made no sound or motion, but only looked at the still figure at his feet. In the robot's face, now so close, Cliff saw the look of sad contemplation.

Gnut stood so several minutes; then he bent lower, took the limp form carefully—even gently, Cliff thought—in his mighty arms, and carried him to the place along the wall where lay the dismembered pieces of the robot attendants. Carefully he laid him by their side. Then he went back into the ship.

Without fear now, Cliff stole along the wall of the room. He had gotten almost as far as the shattered figures on the floor when he suddenly stopped motionless. Gnut was emerging again.

He was bearing a shape that looked like another body, a larger one. He held it in one arm and placed it carefully by the body of Stillwell. In the hand of his other arm he held something that Cliff could not make out, and this he placed at the side of the body he had just put down. Then he went to the ship and returned once more with a shape which he laid gently by the others; and when this last trip was over he looked down at them all for a moment, then turned slowly back to the ship and stood motionless, as if in deep thought, by the ramp.

Cliff restrained his curiosity as long as he could, then slipped forward and bent over the objects Gnut had placed there. First in the row was the body of Stillwell, as he expected, and next was the great shapeless furry mass of a dead gorilla—the one of last night. By the gorilla lay the object the robot had carried in his free hand—the little body of the mockingbird. These last two had remained in the ship all night, and Gnut, for all his surprising gentleness in handling them, was only cleaning house. But there was a fourth body whose history he did not know. He moved closer and bent very low to look.

What he saw made him catch his breath. Impossible!—he thought; there was some confusion in his directions; he brought his face back, close to the first body. Then his blood ran cold. The first body was that of Stillwell, but the last in the row was Stillwell, too; there were two bodies of Stillwell, both exactly alike, both dead.

Cliff backed away with a cry, and then panic took him and he ran down the room away from Gnut and yelled and beat wildly on the door. There was a noise on the outside.

"Let me out!" he yelled in terror. "Let me out! Let me out! Oh, hurry!"

A crack opened between the two doors and he forced his way through like a wild animal and ran far out on the lawn. A belated couple on a nearby path stared at him with amazement, and this brought some sense to his head and he slowed down and came to a stop. Back at the building, everything looked as usual, and, in spite of his terror, Gnut was not chasing him.

He was still in his stockinged feet. Breathing heavily, he

sat down on the wet grass and put on his shoes; then he stood and looked at the building, trying to pull himself together. What an incredible melange! The dead Stillwell, the dead gorilla, and the dead mockingbird—all dying before his eyes. And then that last frightening thing, the second dead Stillwell whom he had *not* seen die. And Gnut's strange gentleness, and the sad expression he had twice seen on his face.

As he looked, the grounds about the building came to life. Several people collected at the door of the wing, above sounded the siren of a police copter, then in the distance another, and from all sides people came running, a few at first, then more and more. The police planes landed on the lawn just outside the door of the wing, and he thought he could see the officers peeping inside. Then suddenly the lights of the wing flooded on. In control of himself now, Cliff went back.

He entered. He had left Gnut standing in thought at the side of the ramp, but now he was again in his old familiar pose in the usual place, as if he had never moved. The ship's door was closed, and the ramp gone. But the bodies, the four strangely assorted bodies, were still lying by the demolished robot attendants where he had left them in the dark.

He was startled by a cry behind his back. A uniformed museum guard was pointing at him.

"This is the man!" the guard shouted. "When I opened the door this man forced his way out and ran like the devil!"

The police officers converged on Cliff.

"Who are you? What is all this?" one of them asked him roughly.

"I'm Cliff Sutherland, picture reporter," Cliff answered calmly. "And I was the one who was inside here and ran away, as the guard says."

"What were you doing?" the officer asked, eyeing him. "And where did these bodies come from?"

"Gentlemen, I'd tell you gladly—only business first," Cliff answered. "There's been some fantastic goings-on in this room, and I saw them and have the story, but"—he smiled—"I must decline to answer without advice of counsel until I've sold my story to one of the news syndicates. You know how it is. If you'd allow me the use of the radio in your plane—just for a moment, gentlemen—you'll have the whole story right afterward—say in half an hour, when the television men broadcast it. Meanwhile, believe me, there's nothing for you to do, and there'll be no loss by the delay."

The officer who had asked the questions, blinked, and one of the others, quicker to react and certainly not a gentleman, stepped toward Cliff with clenched fists. Cliff disarmed him by handing him his press credentials. He glanced at them rapidly and put them in his pocket.

By now half a hundred people were there, and among them were two members of a syndicate crew whom he knew, arrived by copter. The police growled, but they let him whisper in their ears and then go out under escort to the crew's plane. There, by radio, in five minutes, Cliff made a deal which would bring him more money than he had ever before earned in a year. After that he turned over all his pictures and negatives to the crew and gave them the story, and they lost not one second in spinning back to their office with the flash.

More and more people arrived, and the police cleared the building. Ten minutes later a big crew of radio and television men forced their way in, sent there by the syndicate with which he had dealt. And then a few minutes later, under the glaring lights set up by the operators and standing close by the ship and not far from Gnut—he refused to stand underneath him—Cliff gave his story to the cameras and microphones, which in a fraction of a second shot it to every corner of the solar system.

Immediately afterward the police took him to jail. On general principles and because they were pretty blooming mad.

5

Cliff stayed in jail all that night—until eight o'clock the next morning, when the syndicate finally succeeded in digging up a lawyer and got him out. And then, when at last he was leaving, a Federal man caught him by the wrist.

"You're wanted for further questioning over at the Continental Bureau of Investigation," the agent told him. Cliff went along willingly.

Fully thirty-five high-ranking Federal officials and "big names" were waiting for him in an imposing conference room—one of the president's secretaries, the undersecretary of state, the underminister of defense, scientists, a colonel,

executives, department heads, and ranking "C" men. Old
gray-mustached Sanders, chief of the CBI, was presiding.

They made him tell his story all over again, and then, in
parts, all over once more—not because they did not believe
him, but because they kept hoping to elicit some fact which
would cast significant light on the mystery of Gnut's behavior
and the happenings of the last three nights. Patiently, Cliff
racked his brains for every detail.

Chief Sanders asked most of the questions. After more
than an hour, when Cliff thought they had finished, Sanders
asked him several more, all involving his personal opinions
of what had transpired.

"Do you think Gnut was deranged in any way by the
acids, rays, heat, and so forth applied to him by the
scientists?"

"I saw no evidence of it."

"Do you think he can see?"

"I'm sure he can see, or else has other powers which are
equivalent."

"Do you think he can hear?"

"Yes, sir. That time when I whispered to him that Stillwell
was dead, he bent lower, as if to see for himself. I would not
be surprised if he also understood what I said."

"At no time did he speak, except those sounds he made
to open the ship?"

"Not one word, in English or any other language. Not
one sound with his mouth."

"In your opinion, has his strength been impaired in any
way by our treatment?" asked one of the scientists.

"I have told you how easily he handled the gorilla. He
attacked the animal and threw it back, after which it retreated
all the way down the building, afraid of him."

"How would you explain the fact that our autopsies dis-
closed no mortal wound, no cause of death, in any of
the bodies—gorilla, mockingbird, or the two identical
Stillwells?"—this from a medical officer.

"I can't."

"You think Gnut is dangerous?"—from Sanders.

"Potentially very dangerous."

"Yet you say you have the feeling he is not hostile."

"To me, I meant. I do have that feeling, and I'm afraid
that I can't give any good reason for it, except the way he
spared me twice when he had me in his power. I think

maybe the gentle way he handled the bodies had something to do with it, and maybe the sad, thoughtful look I twice caught on his face."

"Would you risk staying in the building alone another night?"

"Not for anything." There were smiles.

"Did you get any pictures of what happened last night?"

"No, sir." Cliff, with an effort, held on to his composure, but he was swept by a wave of shame. A man hitherto silent rescued him my saying:

"A while ago you used the word 'purposive' in connection with Gnut's actions. Can you explain that a little?"

"Yes, that was one of the things that struck me: Gnut never seems to waste a motion. He can move with surprising speed when he wants to; I saw that when he attacked the gorilla; but most other times he walks around as if methodically completing some simple task. And that reminds me of a peculiar thing: at times he gets into one position, any position, maybe half bent over, and stays there for minutes at a time. It's as if his scale of time values were eccentric, compared to ours; some things he does surprisingly fast, and others surprisingly slowly. This might account for his long periods of immobility."

"That's very interesting," said one of the scientists. "How would you account for the fact that he recently moves only at night?"

"I think he's doing something he wants no one to see, and the night is the only time he is alone."

"But he went ahead even after finding you there."

"I know. But I have no other explanation, unless he considered me harmless or unable to stop him—which was certainly the case."

"Before you arrived, we were considering encasing him in a large block of glasstex. Do you think he would permit it?"

"I don't know. Probably he would; he stood for the acids and rays and heat. But it had better be done in the daytime; night seems to be the time he moves."

"But he moved in the daytime when he emerged from the traveler with Klaatu."

"I know."

That seemed to be all they could think of to ask him. Sanders slapped his hand on the table.

"Well, I guess that's all, Mr. Sutherland," he said. "Thank

you for your help, and let me congratulate you for a very foolish, stubborn, brave young man—young businessman." He smiled very faintly. "You are free to go now, but it may be that I'll have to call you back later. We'll see."

"May I remain while you decide about that glasstex?" Cliff asked. "As long as I'm here I'd like to have the tip."

"The decision has already been made—the tip's yours. The pouring will be started at once."

"Thank you, sir," said Cliff—and calmly asked more: "And will you be so kind as to authorize me to be present outside the building tonight? Just outside. I've a feeling something's going to happen."

"You want still another scoop, I see," said Sanders not unkindly, "then you'll let the police wait while you transact your business."

"Not again, sir. If anything happens, they'll get it at once."

The chief hesitated. "I don't know," he said. "I'll tell you what. All the news services will want men there, and we can't have that; but if you can arrange to represent them all yourself, it's a go. Nothing's going to happen, but your reports will help calm the hysterical ones. Let me know."

Cliff thanked him and hurried out and phoned his syndicate the tip—free—then told them Sanders' proposal. Ten minutes later they called him back, said all was arranged, and told him to catch some sleep. They would cover the pouring. With light heart, Cliff hurried over to the museum. The place was surrounded by thousands of the curious, held far back by a strong cordon of police. For once he could not get through; he was recognized, and the police were still sore. But he did not care much; he suddenly felt very tired and needed that nap. He went back to his hotel, left a call, and went to bed.

He had been asleep only a few minutes when his phone rang. Eyes shut, he answered it. It was one of the boys at the syndicate, with peculiar news. Stillwell had just reported, very much alive—the real Stillwell. The two dead ones were some kind of copies; he couldn't imagine how to explain them. He had no brothers.

For a moment Cliff came fully awake, then he went back to bed. Nothing was fantastic anymore.

6

At four o'clock, much refreshed and with an infrared viewing magnifier slung over his shoulder, Cliff passed through the cordon and entered the door of the wing. He had been expected and there was no trouble. As his eyes fell on Gnut, an odd feeling went through him, and for some obscure reason he was almost sorry for the giant robot.

Gnut stood exactly as he had always stood, the right foot advanced a little, and the same brooding expression on his face; but now there was something more. He was solidly encased in a huge block of transparent glasstex. From the floor on which he stood to the top of his full eight feet, and from there on up for an equal distance, and for about eight feet to the left, right, back, and front, he was immured in a water-clear prison which confined every inch of his surface and would prevent the slightest twitch of even his amazing muscles.

It was absurd, no doubt, to feel sorry for a robot, a manmade mechanism, but Cliff had come to think of him as being really alive, as a human is alive. He showed purpose and will; he performed complicated and resourceful acts; his face had twice clearly shown the emotion of sadness, and several times what appeared to be deep thought; he had been ruthless with the gorilla, and gentle with the mockingbird and the other two bodies, and he had twice refrained from crushing Cliff when there seemed every reason that he might. Cliff did not doubt for a minute that he was still alive, whatever "alive" might mean.

But outside were waiting the radio and television men; he had work to do. He turned and went to them and all got busy.

An hour later Cliff sat alone about fifteen feet above the ground in a big tree which, located just across the walk from the building, commanded through a window a clear view of the upper part of Gnut's body. Strapped to the limbs about him were three instruments—his infrared viewing magnifier, a radio mike, and an infrared television eye with sound pickup. The first, the viewing magnifier, would allow him to see in the dark with his own eyes, as if by daylight, a magnified image of the robot, and the others would pick up any sights and sounds, including his own remarks, and transmit them to the several broadcast studios which would fling them millions of miles in all directions through space. Never before had a picture man had such an important assignment, probably—certainly not one who forgot to take pictures. But now that was forgotten, and Cliff was quite proud, and ready.

Far back in a great circle stood a multitude of the curious—and the fearful. Would the plastic glasstex hold Gnut? If it did not, would he come out thirsting for revenge? Would unimaginable beings come out of the traveler and release him, and perhaps exact revenge? Millions at their receivers were jittery; those in the distance hoped nothing awful would happen, yet they hoped something would, and they were prepared to run.

In carefully selected spots not far from Cliff on all sides were mobile ray batteries manned by army units, and in a hollow in back of him, well to his right, there was stationed a huge tank with a large gun. Every weapon was trained on the door of the wing. A row of smaller, faster tanks stood ready fifty yards directly north. Their ray projectors were aimed at the door, but not their guns. The grounds about the building contained only one spot—the hollow where the great tank was—where, by close calculation, a shell directed at the doorway would not cause damage and loss of life to some part of the sprawling capital.

Dusk fell; out streamed the last of the army officers, politicians, and other privileged ones; the great metal doors of the wing clanged to and were locked for the night. Soon Cliff was alone, except for the watchers at their weapons scattered around him.

Hours passed. The moon came out. From time to time Cliff reported to the studio crew that all was quiet. His unaided eyes could now see nothing of Gnut but the two faint red points of his eyes, but through the magnifier he stood out as clearly as if in daylight from an apparent distance of only ten feet. Except for his eyes, there was no evidence that he was anything but dead and unfunctionable metal.

Another hour passed. Now and again Cliff thumbed the levels of his tiny radio-television watch—only a few seconds at a time because of its limited battery. The air was full of Gnut and his own face and his own name, and once the tiny screen showed the tree in which he was then sitting and even, minutely, himself. Powerful infrared long-distance television pickups were even then focused on him from nearby points of vantage. It gave him a funny feeling.

Then, suddenly, Cliff saw something and quickly bent his eye to the viewing magnifier. Gnut's eyes were moving; at least the intensity of the light emanating from them varied. It was as if two tiny red flashlights were turned from side to side, their beams at each motion crossing Cliff's eyes.

Thrilling, Cliff signaled the studios, cut in his pickups, and described the phenomenon. Millions resonated to the excitement in his voice. Could Gnut conceivably break out of that terrible prison?

Minutes passed, the eye flashes continued, but Cliff could discern no movement or attempted movement of the robot's body. In brief snatches he described what he saw. Gnut was clearly alive; there could be no doubt he was straining against the transparent prison in which he had at last been locked fast; but unless he could crack it, no motion should show.

Cliff took his eyes from the magnifier—and started. His unaided eye, looking at Gnut shrouded in darkness, saw an astonishing thing not yet visible through his instrument. A faint red glow was spreading over the robot's body. With trembling fingers he readjusted the lens of the television eye, but even as he did so the glow grew in intensity. It looked as if Gnut's body were being heated to incandescence!

He described it in excited fragments, for it took most of his attention to keep correcting the lens. Gnut passed from a figure of dull red to one brighter and brighter, clearly glowing now even through the magnifier. And then he moved! Unmistakably he moved!

He had within himself somehow the means to raise his own body temperature, and was exploiting the one limitation of the plastic in which he was locked. For glasstex, Cliff now remembered, was a thermoplastic material, one that set by cooling and conversely would soften again with heat. Gnut was melting his way out!

In three-word snatches, Cliff described this. The robot became cherry red, the sharp edges of the icelike block rounded, and the whole structure began to sag. The process accelerated. The robot's body moved more widely. The plastic lowered to the crown of his head, then to his neck, then to his waist, which was as far as Cliff could see. His body was free! And then, still cherry-red, he moved forward out of sight!

Cliff strained eyes and ears, but caught nothing but the distant roar of the watchers beyond the police lines and a few low, sharp commands from the batteries posted around him. They, too, had heard, and perhaps seen by telescreen, and were waiting.

Several minutes passed. There was a sharp, ringing crack; the great metal doors of the wing flew open, and out stepped the metal giant, glowing no longer. He stood stock-still, and his red eyes pierced from side to side through the darkness.

Voices out in the dark barked orders and in a twinkling Gnut was bathed in narrow, crisscrossing rays of sizzling, colored light. Behind him the metal doors began to melt, but his great green body showed no change at all. Then the world seemed to come to an end; there was a deafening roar, everything before Cliff seemed to explode in smoke and chaos, his tree whipped to one side so that he was nearly thrown out. Pieces of debris rained down. The tank gun had spoken, and Gnut, he was sure, had been hit.

Cliff held on tight and peered into the haze. As it cleared he made out a stirring among the debris at the door, and then dimly but unmistakably he saw the great form of Gnut rise to his feet. He got up slowly, turned toward the tank, and suddenly darted toward it in a wide arc. The big gun swung in an attempt to cover him, but the robot sidestepped and then was upon it. As the crew scattered, he destroyed its breech with one blow of his fist, and then he turned and looked right at Cliff.

He moved toward him, and in a moment was under the tree. Cliff climbed higher. Gnut put his two arms around the tree and gave a lifting push, and the tree tore out at the roots and fell crashing to its side. Before Cliff could scramble away, the robot had lifted him in his metal hands.

Cliff thought his time had come, but strange things were yet in store for him that night. Gnut did not hurt him. He looked at him from arm's length for a moment, then lifted him to a sitting position on his shoulders, legs straddling his neck. Then, holding one ankle, he turned and without hesitation started down the path which led westward away from the building.

Cliff rode helpless. Out over the lawns he saw the muzzles

of the scattered field pieces move as he moved, Gnut—and himself—their one focus. But they did not fire. Gnut, by placing him on his shoulders, had secured himself against that—Cliff hoped.

The robot bore straight toward the Tidal Basin. Most of the field pieces throbbed slowly after. Far back, Cliff saw a dark tide of confusion roll into the cleared area—the police lines had broken. Ahead, the ring thinned rapidly off to the sides; then, from all directions but the front, the tide rolled in until individual shouts and cries could be made out. It came to a stop about fifty yards off, and few people ventured nearer.

Gnut paid them no attention, and he no more noticed his burden than he might a fly. His neck and shoulders made Cliff a seat hard as steel, but with the difference that their underlying muscles with each movement flexed, just as would those of a human being. To Cliff, this metal musculature became a vivid wonder.

Straight as the flight of a bee, over paths, across lawns and through thin rows of trees Gnut bore the young man, the roar of thousands of people following close. Above droned copters and darting planes, among them police cars with their nerve-shattering sirens. Just ahead lay the still waters of the Tidal Basin, and in its midst the simple marble tomb of the slain ambassador, Klaatu, gleaming black and cold in the light of the dozen searchlights always trained on it at night. Was this a rendezvous with the dead?

Without an instant's hesitation, Gnut strode down the bank and entered the water. It rose to his knees, then above his waist, until Cliff's feet were under. Straight through the dark waters for the tomb of Klaatu the robot made his inevitable way.

The dark square mass of gleaming marble rose higher as they neared it. Gnut's body began emerging from the water as the bottom shelved upward, until his dripping feet took the first of the rising pyramid of steps. In a moment they were at the top, on the narrow platform in the middle of which rested the simple oblong tomb.

Stark in the blinding searchlights, the giant robot walked once around it, then, bending, he braced himself and gave a mighty push against the top. The marble cracked; the thick cover slipped askew and broke with a loud noise on the far side. Gnut went to his knees and looked within, bringing Cliff well up over the edge.

Inside, in sharp shadow against the converging light beams, lay a transparent plastic coffin, thick-walled and sealed against the centuries, and containing all that was mortal of Klaatu, unspoken visitor from the great Unknown. He lay as if asleep, on his face the look of godlike nobility that had caused some of the ignorant to believe him divine. He wore the robe he had arrived in. There were no faded flowers, no jewelry, no ornaments; they would have seemed profane. At the foot of the coffin lay the small sealed box, also of transparent plastic, which contained all of Earth's records of his visit—a description of the events attending his arrival, pictures of Gnut and the traveler, and the little roll of sight-and-sound film which had caught for all time his few brief motions and words.

Cliff sat very still, wishing he could see the face of the robot. Gnut, too, did not move from his position of reverent contemplation—not for a long time. There on the brilliantly lighted pyramid, under the eyes of a fearful, tumultuous multitude, Gnut paid final respect to his beautiful and adored master.

Suddenly, then, it was over. Gnut reached out and took the little box of records, rose to his feet and started down the steps.

Back through the water, straight back to the building, across lawns and paths as before, he made his irresistible way. Before him the chaotic ring of people melted away, behind they followed as close as they dared, trampling each other in their efforts to keep him in sight. There are no television records of his return. Every pickup was damaged on the way to the tomb.

As they drew near the building, Cliff saw that the tank's projectile had made a hole twenty feet wide extending from the roof to the ground. The door still stood open, and Gnut, hardly varying his almost jerkless rhythm, made his way over the debris and went straight for the port end of the ship. Cliff wondered if he would be set free.

He was. The robot set him down and pointed toward the door; then, turning, he made the sounds that opened the ship. The ramp slid down and he entered.

Then Cliff did the mad, courageous thing which made him famous for a generation. Just as the ramp started sliding back in, he skipped over it and himself entered the ship. The port closed.

7

It was pitch dark, and the silence was absolute. Cliff did not move. He felt that Gnut was close, just ahead, and it was so.

His hard metal hand took him by the waist, pulled him against his cold side, and carried him somewhere ahead. Hidden lamps suddenly bathed the surroundings with bluish light.

He set Cliff down and stood looking at him. The young man already regretted his rash action, but the robot, except for his always unfathomable eyes, did not seem angry. He pointed to a stool in one corner of the room. Cliff quickly obeyed this time and sat meekly, for a while not even venturing to look around.

He saw he was in a small laboratory of some kind. Complicated metal and plastic apparatus lined the walls and filled several small tables; he could not recognize or guess the function of a single piece. Dominating the center of the room was a long metal table on whose top lay a large box, much like a coffin on the outside, connected by many wires to a complicated apparatus at the far end. From close above spread a cone of bright light from a many-tubed lamp.

One thing, half covered on a nearby table, did look familiar—and very much out of place. From where he sat it seemed to be a briefcase—an ordinary Earthman's briefcase. He wondered.

Gnut paid him no attention but, at once, with the narrow edge of a thick tool, sliced the lid off the little box of records. He lifted out the strip of sight-and-sound film and spent fully half an hour adjusting it within the apparatus at the end of the big table. Cliff watched, fascinated, wondering at the skill with which the robot used his tough metal fingers. This done, Gnut worked for a long time over some accessory apparatus on an adjoining table. Then he paused thoughtfully a moment and pushed inward a long rod.

A voice came out of the coffinlike box—the voice of the slain ambassador.

"I am Klaatu," it said, "and this is Gnut."

From the recording!—flashed through Cliff's mind. The first and only words the ambassador had spoken. But then, in the very next second he saw that it was not so. There was a man in the box! The man stirred and sat up, and Cliff saw the living face of Klaatu!

Klaatu appeared somewhat surprised and spoke quickly in an unknown tongue to Gnut—and Gnut, for the first time in Cliff's experience, spoke himself in answer. The robot's syllables tumbled out as if born of human emotion, and the expression on Klaatu's face changed from surprise to wonder. They talked for several minutes. Klaatu, apparently fatigued, then began to lie down, but stopped midway, for he saw Cliff. Gnut spoke again, at length. Klaatu beckoned Cliff with his hand, and he went to him.

"Gnut has told me everything," he said in a low, gentle voice, then looked at Cliff for a moment in silence, on his face a faint, tired smile.

Cliff had a hundred questions to ask, but for a moment he hardly dared open his mouth.

"But you," he began at last—very respectfully, but with an escaping excitement—"you are not the Klaatu that was in the tomb?"

The man's smile faded and he shook his head.

"No." He turned to the towering Gnut and said something in his own tongue, and at his words the metal features of the robot twisted as if with pain. Then he turned back to Cliff. "I am dying," he announced simply, as if repeating his words for the Earthman. Again to his face came the faint, tired smile.

Cliff's tongue was locked. He just stared, hoping for light. Klaatu seemed to read his mind.

"I see you don't understand," he said. "Although unlike us, Gnut has great powers. When the wing was built and the lectures began, there came to him a striking inspiration. Acting on it at once, in the night, he assembled this apparatus . . . and now he has made me again, from my voice, as recorded by your people. As you must know, a given body makes a characteristic sound. He constructed an apparatus which reversed the recording process, and from the given sound made the characteristic body."

Cliff gasped. So that was it!

"But you needn't die!" Cliff exclaimed suddenly, eagerly. "Your voice recording was taken when you stepped out of the ship, while you were well! You must let me take you to a hospital! Our doctors are very skillful!"

Hardly perceptibly, Klaatu shook his head.

"You still don't understand," he said slowly and more faintly. "Your recording had imperfections. Perhaps very slight ones, but they doom the product. All of Gnut's experiments died in a few minutes, he tells me . . . and so must I."

Suddenly, then, Cliff understood the origin of the "experiments." He remembered that on the day the wing was opened a Smithsonian official had lost a briefcase containing film strips recording the speech of various world fauna. There, on that table, was a briefcase! And the Stillwells must have been made from strips kept in the table drawer!

But his heart was heavy. He did not want this stranger to die. Slowly there dawned on him an important idea. He explained it with growing excitement.

"You say the recording was imperfect, and of course it was. But the cause of that lay in the use of an imperfect recording apparatus. So if Gnut, in his reversal of the process, had used exactly the same pieces of apparatus that your voice was recorded with, the imperfections could be studied, canceled out, and you'd live, and not die!"

As the last words left his lips, Gnut whipped around like a cat and gripped him tight. A truly human excitement was shining in the metal muscles of his face.

"Get me that apparatus!" he ordered—in clear and perfect English! He started pushing Cliff toward the door, but Klaatu raised his hand.

"There is no hurry," Klaatu said gently; "it is too late for me. What is your name, young man?"

Cliff told him.

"Stay with me to the end," he asked. Klaatu closed his eyes and rested; then, smiling just a little, but not opening his eyes, he added: "And don't be sad, for I shall now perhaps live again . . . and it will be due to you. There is no pain—" His voice was rapidly growing weaker. Cliff, for all the questions he had, could only look on, dumb. Again Klaatu seemed to be aware of his thoughts.

"I know," he said feebly, "I know. We have so much to ask each other. About your civilization . . . and Gnut's—"

"And yours," said Cliff.

"And Gnut's," said the gentle voice again. "Perhaps . . . some day . . . perhaps I will be back—"

He lay without moving. He lay so for a long time, and at last Cliff knew that he was dead. Tears came to his eyes; in only these few minutes he had come to love this man. He looked at Gnut. The robot knew, too, that he was dead, but no tears filled his red-lighted eyes; they were fixed on Cliff, and for once the young man knew what was in his mind.

"Gnut," he announced earnestly, as if taking a sacred oath, "I'll get the original apparatus. I'll get it. Every piece of it, the exact same things."

Without a word, Gnut conducted him to the port. He made the sounds that unlocked it. As it opened, a noisy crowd of Earthmen outside trampled each other in a sudden scramble to get out of the building. The wing was lighted. Cliff stepped down the ramp.

The next two hours always in Cliff's memory had a dreamlike quality. It was as if that mysterious laboratory with the peacefully sleeping dead man were the real and central part of his life, and his scene with the noisy men with whom he talked a gross and barbaric interlude. He stood not far from the ramp. He told only part of his story. He was believed. He waited quietly while all the pressure which the highest officials in the land could exert was directed toward obtaining for him the apparatus the robot had demanded.

When it arrived, he carried it to the floor of the little vestibule behind the port. Gnut was there, as if waiting. In his arms he held the slender body of the second Klaatu. Tenderly he passed him out to Cliff, who took him without a word, as if all this had been arranged. It seemed to be the parting.

Of all the things Cliff had wanted to say to Klaatu, one remained imperatively present in his mind. Now, as the green metal robot stood framed in the great green ship, he seized his chance.

"Gnut," he said earnestly, holding carefully the limp body in his arms, "you must do one thing for me. Listen carefully. I want you to tell your master—the master yet to come—that what happened to the first Klaatu was an accident, for which all Earth is immeasurably sorry. Will you do that?"

"I have known it," the robot answered gently.

"But will you promise to tell your master—just those words—as soon as he is arrived?"

"You misunderstand," said Gnut, still gently, and quietly spoke four more words. As Cliff heard them a mist passed over his eyes and his body went numb.

As he recovered and his eyes came back to focus he saw the great ship disappear. It just suddenly was not there anymore. He fell back a step or two. In his ears, like great bells, rang Gnut's last words. Never, never was he to disclose them till the day he came to die.

"You misunderstand," the mighty robot had said. "I am the master."

ABOUT THE EDITORS

ISAAC ASIMOV has been called "one of America's treasures." Born in the Soviet Union, he was brought to the United States at the age of three (along with his family) by agents of the American government in a successful attempt to prevent him from working for the wrong side. He quickly established himself as one of this country's foremost science fiction writers and writes about everything, and although now approaching middle age, he is going stronger than ever. He long ago passed his age and weight in books, and with some 390 to his credit, threatens to close in on his I.Q.

MARTIN H. GREENBERG has been called (in *The Science Fiction and Fantasy Book Review*) "The King of the Anthologists"; to which he replied, "It's good to be the King!" He has produced more than 250 of them, usually in collaboration with a multitude of conspirators, most frequently the two who have given you GHOSTS. A Professor of Regional Analysis and Political Science at the University of Wisconsin-Green Bay, he has finally published his weight.

CHARLES G. WAUGH is a Professor of psychology and Communications at the University of Maine at Augusta who is still trying to figure out how he got himself into all this. He has also worked with many collaborators, since he is basically a very friendly fellow. He has done some 100 anthologies and single-author collections, and especially enjoys locating unjustly ignored stories. He also claims that he met his wife via computer dating—her choice was an entire fraternity or him, and she has only minor regrets.